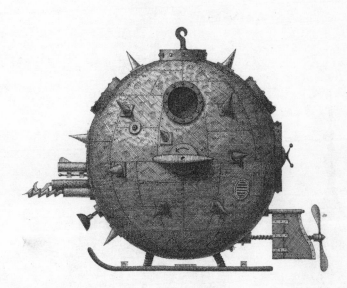

VLAM

THE HOUSE OF THRONES

MW 2007

THE HOUSE OF MYSTERIES

THE HOUSE OF SPIRITS

Londoner Mike Wilks is an award-winning artist and bestselling author of *The Ultimate Alphabet, The Ultimate Noah's Ark* and *Mirrorscape*. His paintings, which have been described as 'meticulous and eye-bending', can be found in public and private collections in Europe and the USA. The Mirrorscape books transport the reader into Mike's compelling inner world.

www.mike-wilks.com
www.mirrorscape.co.uk

Other books by Mike Wilks

Pile – Petals from St. Klaed's Computer
(With Brian Aldiss)

In Granny's Garden
(With Sarah Harrison)

The Weather Works

The Ultimate Alphabet

The Annotated Ultimate Alphabet

The BBC Drawing Course

The Ultimate Noah's Ark

The Ultimate Spot-The-Difference Book
(Metamorphosis)

Mirrorscape

Mirrorshade

MIKE WILKS

MirrorStorm

EGMONT

For Penny

EGMONT
We bring stories to life

Mirrorstorm first published in Great Britain 2009
by Egmont UK Limited
239 Kensington High Street, London W8 6SA

ISBN 978 1 4052 3746 8

1 3 5 7 9 10 8 6 4 2

A CIP catalogue record for this title is available from the British Library

Typeset by Avon DataSet Ltd, Bidford on Avon
Printed and bound in Great Britain by the CPI Group

Contents

Prologue   ix

THE FIRST STORM

Chapter 1. The Hall of Awakenings   3

Chapter 2. The Maven's Library   18

Chapter 3. The Evening Book-Run   29

Chapter 4. The Leviathan   44

Chapter 5. The Hold   68

Chapter 6. Rat Power   84

THE SECOND STORM

Chapter 7. The Paper Belfry   105

Chapter 8. Beauty & the Beast   127

Chapter 9. Sparkfall   147

Chapter 10. View Halloo   164

Chapter 11. The Chrysalis Tower   176

Chapter 12. King M-morpho   190

Chapter 13. Mirrorblood   203

THE THIRD STORM

Chapter 14. The Wedding   215

Chapter 15. Dust   235

Chapter 16. The Merry-Go-Anywhere-You-Want-To   241

Chapter 17. Anywhere   254

Chapter 18. The Hyper-Clot   270

Chapter 19. Pilfer by Name, Pilfer by Nature   287

THE MIRRORSTORM

Chapter 20. The Hollow World   307

Chapter 21. Cogito the Lucubrator   325

Chapter 22. The Demon-Finder-General   341

Chapter 23. Nowhere   363

Chapter 24. The Cloud Sculptor   384

Chapter 25. Schmooze, Schmooze   406

Chapter 26. Cumulus   424

Chapter 27. The Return to Vlam   441

Chapter 28. The Filigree Suit   450

Chapter 29. Grootscape   467

Chapter 30. The Brass Monkeys   482

Chapter 31. Smoke and Mirrors   498

Chapter 32. The Serpent   519

Epilogue   538

Glossary of Terms   546

Sneak Preview of Chapter One of *Mirrorshade*   555

Acknowledgements   559

Prologue

A fierce, scalping wind blew across a featureless wasteland devoid of any tree or blade of grass. Funnelled through hollow, wind-blasted rocks, it howled an eerie drone. The sky, the same leaden colour as the stone-strewn ground, seemed low enough to touch.

Across this desolation moved a line of three, squat figures with the unmistakable, wide-legged gait of gnomes. They were swathed in heavy cloaks against the chill blast and had cowls pulled low over their deep crimson faces. Large, open-topped baskets were strapped to their hunched backs. Each carried a glowing crystal rod in one hand, a beam of light shining from the end and crisscrossing the way before them. Their glittering black eyes moved as regularly as pendulums, following the beams as they searched back and forth over the barren ground. From time to time one of the group would stoop, pick up a rock and split it with his small hammer. Most of the shattered rocks were thrown aside with a curse but, occasionally, one revealed a shining crystal within and was tossed over the finder's shoulder into his basket with an ugly cackle of delight. Onward the trio moved, stopping neither to eat nor drink although they were aware that night would never fall in that weird, twilit land.

The ground began to rise and, against every rule of nature, a thick clinging mist started to seep from the rocks beneath their feet, rendering everything indistinct. The gnomes moved closer together but their search for the stone-gripped treasure did not slacken. Then their leader halted and called to his companions. They picked their way up the slope and peered down at his find. It was a tall skeleton, white against the grey rocks. Then, on the headwind, came the sound of voices and the smell of cooking. The gnomes knew this smell. It was the odour of roasting human flesh.

Cautiously now, crystal rods dimmed, they continued up the slope, their mineralogy for the moment forgotten. Ahead of them glowed a fire haloed by the mist into a red-orange blur. Three indistinct figures were silhouetted against the dancing flames:

two adults and, possibly, a child who blew inter-mittently on a musical instrument. To one side stood a makeshift tent made from mismatched articles of clothing stretched between upright stones and the bloody remains of another butchered carcass. The strange Mirrorscape wind that was powerful enough to sculpt rocks but permitted mist to form blew the group's words apart so that their sound reached the gnomes' ears in brittle, fractured shards.

'. . . return to the Seven Kingdoms and take back . . .'

'. . . he may be Blenk's youngest apprentice but . . .'

'. . . just to see him die slowly . . .'

'. . . and his meddling friends . . .'

'. . . if only we had an ally . . .'

'. . . someone who's hungry for power and untold riches . . .'

'. . . to help us lure them into a trap . . .'

'. . . plant a traitor in their midst . . .'

'. . . lead them to us once we have . . .'

'. . . but what hope is there of ever finding . . .'

'. . . not while we're marooned here . . .'

The head gnome had heard little but he had heard the words dearest to a gnome's black heart. He exchanged a meaningful look with his companions who nodded back. He climbed through the mist towards the fire.

'If there's riches involved, I have the answer to your dilemma.'

The First Storm

The Hall of Awakenings

It was the creaking that was so unnerving. When Mel had first climbed into the large wicker basket the noise had not bothered him. In fact, he had not noticed it, such was his excitement. But that was at ground level. As he was hauled higher and higher up the towering facade of the House of Spirits the sound of the creaking became ever more insistent. Now, at several hundred feet above the dwindling rooftops, the noise became impossible to ignore. Suddenly Mel realised it was not just the basket; it was the rope itself that was creaking. Creaking with the strain as if it was about to break! He reached up and grasped it firmly in his small hands. It felt fat and substantial, as taut as a bowstring, as thick as his wrist. *It couldn't possibly break. Could it? I don't weigh much and the basket even less.* Then he realised something else. The hempen rope was not only bearing the weight of him and the basket but also its own weight. He tried to calculate how long the rope might be. *Hundreds and hundreds of feet. A fat rope that long must weigh – ever such a lot!*

Halfway up he passed a stone counterweight attached to the other end of the rope as it descended. More weight! *Calm down, Mel*, he heard the voice of his mentor, Fa Theum, say inside his head, *get a grip on yourself. You're thirteen years old; too old for this nonsense.* He took a deep breath and ran a hand through his blond hair as his own inner voice joined in reassuring him. *The basket's been used to lift blocks of masonry up to the works, hasn't it? I weigh nothing compared to them.* It worked for a moment. But his relief was short-lived as he realised yet another thing. *The rope must be worn out and knackered by now. It's not going to last forever. It's going to break.*

Then a pigeon soared by, close to the basket. Silent. Graceful. Effortless. Mel followed it with his eager, blue eyes and his fear receded as he took in the stunning view over the city of Vlam. As the basket spun on its rope Mel was treated to a slowly revolving panorama. In a magical moment he saw everything afresh.

Seeing the city for the first time, a stranger might have supposed that it was built upon three steep hills, each surmounted by an immense palace that reached skywards like a monumental stalagmite. In fact, Mel knew what few others did; that the hills on which these ancient structures stood were composed of the very buildings themselves. For, as generation had succeeded countless generation, each had added to the original structures as their wealth and self-importance grew. First, they spread outwards and then, when they could spread no more, upwards. As each addition was completed, the older apartments, and their contents, were abandoned and the most recent inhabited and furnished anew. The core of each of the Great Houses consisted of nothing but vacant galleries and chambers, as hollow as an abandoned termitarium, empty and forgotten.

After a great many years the original structures had become impossible to discern due to the countless arcades, domes, turrets, spires, towers and minarets that encrusted the outer parts. These were laced together with such a collection of passerelles, bridges and flying buttresses and sprinkled with such a profusion of tracery, gargoyles and folderols that they seemed like insanely tall wedding cakes that had been iced by a demented confectioner. The towering and precarious structures loomed over the rest of the bustling city. By night, with their windows lit, they appeared as columns of stars and by day as great, dark gnomons that slowly cast their shadows, hour by hour, over the surrounding districts.

At Mel's back, in the eastern precincts, stood the Maven's palace, the House of Spirits, the golden diaglyph crowning its topmost pinnacle. In the west of the city, beneath the purple royal banner, was King Spen's House of Thrones, while to the north, the coloured banners of the five Mysteries – secretive guilds representing crafts governing each of the five senses – fluttered from the lofty towers of the House of Mysteries. The rest of Vlam occupied what space it could as it tumbled down the hills beneath the three Great Houses only to be checked by the high city walls.

Mel took in the River Farn dividing Vlam into unequal halves. Its course looked like a steep-sided canyon as it carved its way through the city, exposing ever older strata of buildings as it cut deeper. From his vantage point he could clearly see the city's seven bridges in the early autumn sunshine. Swirling patterns of people and carriages could be seen crossing them like ants scurrying to and from their nests, while underneath the dark shapes of wherries and lighters were busy plying their trade on the silver water. Jittering highlights flecked the river, the brightest notes in the composition. The masts and rigging of many craft and riverside cranes were silhouetted starkly against it.

Mel was startled as the basket slowly revolved and he briefly came face to face with a hideous gargoyle, its stony expression pockmarked with pale lichen. The revolution completed itself and he was staring into the sky once more. *That strange-looking cloud's still there. It reminds me of something, I'm sure it does. It almost looks like . . .* Mel stared harder. *A great city. I can see towers and battlements and . . .* He stared harder still. *What are those swirling lines underneath it? I've seen castles in the air before but never one as clear as that. And those lines could almost be . . .*

Suddenly, the basket reached the end of its upwards journey with a sudden jolt, cutting his thought off before he could complete it.

'Here you go, lad. Mind your footing as you step out.'

A powerfully built mason took hold of Mel's arm

and guided him on to the covered wooden platform that jutted out from the side of the building like a temporary balcony. On the platform was a treadmill that worked the hoist that had raised Mel from the city below. Inside the wheel were two more masons, stripped to the waist and glistening with sweat from the long pull. The fact that all three men had brightly coloured skin – one red, one blue, the other green – did not surprise Mel at all. He recognised them as recently freed prisoners of the Fifth Mystery who had earned their vivid hues from a cruel spell in the mines on the island of Kig where they, like thousands of others, had hewn pigment from the chromatic rocks.

'You'll be for the new hall, I guess. Your friends are back there,' said the red mason, jerking his thumb over his shoulder.

'Is it still there, mate?' called one of the men in the treadmill.

'Aye, that it is,' answered the red man, glancing skywards. 'Skegging odd, if you ask me. I've never seen a cloud that stayed put before. It's been there for days. Hasn't budged an inch in spite of the breeze. Just keeps getting bigger. It ain't right.' Then, looking down at Mel, 'Come on, lad. Jump to it. We've got work to do, even if you haven't.'

With a last glance up at the cloud, Mel smiled his thanks to the masons and threaded his way through the piles of building materials to the rear of the platform and through the open window that served as a temporary doorway into the House of Spirits. Standing waiting for him were Ludo and Wren, his best friends and fellow apprentices. All three wore the deep blue velvet doublets, white silk shirts and tight-fitting hose that made up the livery of their master, Ambrosius Blenk, the greatest artist in the Seven Kingdoms.

'Come on, slowcoach, there's still a way to go yet,' said Wren as she led the trio down a corridor.

'You haven't crushed the drawing, have you, Mel?' said Ludo. 'We've sweated blood over that.'

'It's fine. *See.*' Mel waved the large rolled drawing, squeezing it slightly to pop out the kink caused by his too-firm grip during the ascent. 'Anyway, I was the one who was up half the night finishing it.'

'You lost the cut,' said Ludo.

'I still think those cards of yours are marked. Whenever we cut for anything you never lose. It's always Wren or me.'

'Stop bickering, you two. Save your breath – you're going to need it,' said Wren. 'Look.'

They stood in the entrance to the incomplete Hall of Awakenings, craning their necks to take in the ordered forest of scaffolding that filled the space right up to the lofty ceiling. A small army of masons in their leather aprons were scampering over it and up and down the scores of ladders that threaded their way through the poles and planking that formed the many platforms. Several more treadmill hoists were also in evidence, lifting bundles of timber and blocks of dressed stone. The hall was filled with the echoing sounds of wood being sawed, nails being hammered and stone being chipped.

'Shall we ask if we can go up in one of the hoists?' said Wren.

'No, let's use the ladders,' said Mel. 'One trip in a hoist's enough for today.'

'What's the matter? Scared?' said Ludo.

'Who, me?'

'Stop it, you two.'

By the time they had climbed to the top Mel wished they had taken a hoist. 'Nobody told me that ladders wobble so much.'

'It's not the wobbling so much as all that climbing.' Wren rubbed her aching thighs. 'And it's so dusty in here.' She shook her long, auburn locks, making a tiny snowstorm of fine stone dust. 'Where's Ludo?'

'I'm here.' Ludo's dark-haired head emerged through the scaffolding and his hazel eyes widened. '*Scrot!* I didn't realise it would be so big.' He reached the top of the ladder and stepped on to the planking that formed the temporary floor of what seemed an enormous low-ceilinged space. The vaulting arched overhead, giving the impression they had entered a vast cavern – an effect reinforced by the dozens of candles and oil lamps that lit the scene with puddles of yellow light. The three friends stood there, suddenly realising the scale of their master's latest commission to decorate the ceiling of the Hall of Awakenings. 'It's going to take us *ages*,' said Ludo.

'Not really,' said Wren. 'This high up there won't need to be as much detail as there would if it was a painting on canvas.'

Mel looked down through the ladder hole at the receding platforms and increasingly smaller workmen. 'Wren's right. Any fine detail will be lost when seen from down there.'

Ludo looked down and abruptly took a step backwards. '*Whoah!* We are high up, aren't we?'

'What's the matter, Ludo? Scared?'

'Don't start that again.' Wren walked towards the far corner of the platform. 'Unroll the cartoon, Mel.'

Mel held his end of the working drawing as Wren unrolled it against the arched niche they had been allotted in one corner of the master's grand, overall design, most of which was already marked out in bold, simple lines. Huge sleeping figures, human, monster and everything in between, populated a mythical landscape over which the sun was rising. The far side of the composition was to be in darkness and, as the dawn stole across the scene, the shadows receded, the daylight increased and the figures awoke. The friends' small contribution depicted a three-headed monster. Each of them had designed one of the heads; one sleeping, one stirring and the other fully awake. After much argument they had decided on a common body.

'You've made it too small, Ludo. It doesn't fit.' Wren shook her head.

'It's not my fault. The architects must have made a mistake with the scale.'

'It couldn't have been you that made the mistake, by any chance?' said Mel.

'Let's not start blaming each other,' said Wren. 'The point is the drawing's too small. Bex won't be best pleased.' Mel and Ludo knew she was right. The new head apprentice was better than Groot, the cruel and bullying former incumbent, but was a stickler for accuracy.

'We can't mess this up,' said Mel. 'The master only gave this niche to us because we rescued him from the Mirrorscape.'

'The question is, what're we going to do about it?' asked Wren.

'If we just put a bit more space between the

monster's heads and stretch out the body, it won't show,' said Mel.

'But that's even more work for us,' complained Ludo. 'Today's supposed to be our day off.'

'We wouldn't have to work today if we'd agreed about the creature sooner,' said Mel.

'It's got to be done before the real work starts tomorrow,' said Wren.

'Nag, nag, nag,' said Ludo.

'She's right, Ludo. But we can't all work on it at once,' said Mel. 'We'll only get in each other's way.'

'Why don't we cut for it? Loser stays behind and reworks the drawing.' Ludo pulled a pack of cards from inside his doublet.

'Not with your dodgy cards,' said Mel. 'We all know who'll win. Look, I don't mind resizing it. I'll meet you back at the mansion later.'

'Are you sure?' said Wren.

'He said so, didn't he?' said Ludo. 'Let's go. It'll be supper time soon.'

Before Mel had time to change his mind, his friends had disappeared down the ladder.

After he had painstakingly altered the drawing and transferred it to the fresh plaster of the niche, Mel tidied away his materials. As he gathered his courage and prepared to make the long descent to the floor of the now deserted hall, his unfinished thought about the mysterious cloud completed itself and elbowed its way into the front of his mind. *It's a mirrormark! The swirling lines underneath the cloud city look just like the first few strokes of a mirrormark! There's no way a mirrormark could have got there by chance.*

About halfway down the scaffolding he heard a peal of bells calling the Fas to their evening prayers, followed closely and nearer by another and then another. *Squit, vespers. I didn't realise it was that late. That's why there're no masons about.* He hurried on down. As he reached the last platform, no higher than the upstairs storey of a house, he heard approaching footsteps. They halted beneath his platform and two female voices began talking quietly. He looked down. Just visible between the gaps in the planking stood two figures, one very large and the other small. They wore long, grey robes with deep cowls pulled forward, hiding their faces.

'It's quiet; we can talk here, Tunk.'

'How goes our Great Project, Mudge?'

'Now that the first obstacle is locked away in the House's dungeon it goes well, sister.'

'And work in the Paper Belfry?'

'That also proceeds well. Since our allies in the world beyond joined us with their skills and cunning the sisterhood's great plan has at last become reality. We have been ignored for too long. Soon the people will realise our true worth. Work proceeds apace. The alignment of the crystals will be perfected within the next few days. I'm sure you've seen the first results.'

'So has everyone else in Vlam.'

'So what? They're blind fools, every last one of them. They wouldn't know what they were looking at. Soon the sign will be complete and the wound into the world beyond can open. The first storm will begin.'

'And then?'

'We will create a storm over each of the Great Houses. Three storms to engender the final storm and then the great wound between the worlds will fester and ooze demons. Our mistress can have all the demons she desires. The city will be overrun with them. There will be more demons in the streets of Vlam than fleas on a dog's back. Our allies can join us and together we'll vanquish the demon invaders and save the city. The people will be so grateful. They'll give us all we desire.'

'Soon the realm will topple. All of Nem will be ours!'

The Maven's Library

Mel suddenly felt very cold. He listened to the sound of footsteps as they receded into the distance. After what seemed an age he let out the breath he had been unconsciously holding. He cautiously moved to the edge of the platform and peered over. No one; he was quite alone. He descended the final ladder and stood on the floor. He was not sure if the faint trembling in his legs was from the long climb or from what he had just overheard.

The world beyond? I bet that's the Mirrorscape! And the 'sign' must be the mirrormark. That means they know the secret. Demons in the streets of Vlam! Mel shuddered. *I must get back to the mansion and tell the others.*

Mel made his way through the deserted House of Spirits to the grand staircase that spiralled its way down through much of the vast building. As he raced down the stairs he passed the tall open doors to the Maven's library. It was a cavernous room that seemed to be built of leather-bound books from the floor to the towering ceiling. Down the centre was a long table bathed in the dappled rainbow light of a tall stained-glass window. Lying open on it were several large volumes. The temptation was too great. He went in and flicked through the first one he came to.

Scree-scrick, scree-scrick. 'Melkin Womper, what are you up to?' An elderly priest wheeled himself in a squeaky wheelchair from one of the side galleries.

'You only call me by my full name when I'm being foolish or I've done something wrong.'

'And have you?'

'Who me?' said Mel with feigned innocence and a broad smile. 'How are you, Fa? I thought you might be at vespers with all the other Fas.'

'Old cripples like me are consigned to the library. No one notices if we're not at our devotions. Besides, there's too much work to be done here. You wouldn't believe how many books are missing. And what are you doing here? Not come just to ask after my health.'

'Oh, I was working late. The master's given me and Ludo and Wren a bit of his ceiling in the Hall of Awakenings to work on. All on our own. What we've done is a three-headed . . . Sorry. I've told you this before, haven't I?'

'No more than a couple of dozen times.' The old man smiled.

'I was on my way back to the mansion when I saw the library door open. But now I need to get back to the mansion so that . . . so that I don't miss my supper.'

'The Mel I know was never so concerned with his stomach. It's all right; you don't have to tell me what you're up to. It's probably best I don't know anyway. If you'll just lend me a hand for a moment, I'll show you the way out.' *Scree-scrick.* Fa Theum wheeled himself to one of the tables and opened a large, leather-bound book with iron hinges.

'That's the House of Spirits!'

'Well spotted,' said the Fa as he smoothed out the illustrated pages of the tome. 'Look here.' He turned the thick, creamy leaves until he was at the beginning. 'This is how the House looked nearly a thousand years ago.' The hand-drawn illustration showed a stunted version of the building, its profile like a squat triangle. 'The pictures show the building at intervals of about eighty or a hundred years.' As the pages were turned the House of Spirits seemed to grow. 'And this last picture is as it was in my great-grandfather's time. There ought to be another after this but it's been torn out. If I ever catch who's responsible . . . Very soon there will need to be an addition to feature the new Hall of Awakenings and the parts that have been added in my lifetime.'

Mel leaned closer. 'Where's the Paper Belfry?'

'The *Paper* Belfry? I've never heard of that. Let's see.' The Fa turned to the index at the rear of the book. 'There is no Paper Belfry. This list is up to date even if the illustrations aren't. Where did you hear of that?'

'One of the masons mentioned it. I must have misheard. Fa, are there any women Fas?'

'Ters, Mel. They're called Ter This or Ter That. A few. Why do you ask? Your masons again? Don't pay attention to anything you learn from them. All they know about is building, drinking and swearing.'

'What do they do, the Ters?'

'Nothing much, nowadays. Long ago the then Maven got it into his head that women could sniff out devils and demons. He founded a sisterhood, here in the House of Spirits, and appointed some mad woman to lead them. I believe her name was Morgana. She would have been better off in an asylum. I'm afraid that many people were tortured and burnt before everyone realised that there were no such things as demons . . .'

Oh yes there are.

'. . . But that was all a long, long time ago. There're still a few hereditary Ters – they come down through the female line, you know – but they're just for ceremonial purposes. There's talk of disbanding the sisterhood altogether.'

'Do they wear brown robes, like yours? Or black, like the other Fas?'

'You're all questions today, Mel.'

'Sorry.'

'No, don't apologise. You only learn through asking questions. The Fas Minor wear the brown habit and the Fas Major wear black.'

'Why the different colours?'

'We all used to be the same order but over the years

differences in doctrine has meant that we split. I'm sorry to say that there is little in common between the two orders today. *We* believe in helping the needy, while the Fas Major – well, they believe in other things. Some suspect that the Fas Major wish to disband the Fas Minor and become the sole order.' The old priest's brow creased. 'But you don't need to know about the political intrigues within the House of Spirits. Where was I? Oh yes, colours. The Hierarchs wear red –'

'Just like the Fifth Mystery,' blurted Mel.

The old man unconsciously cradled his right hand. The nails had grown back but his fingers were permanently stiff, a constant reminder of his torture by the Fifth Mystery.

'Sorry, Fa. I didn't . . . you know.'

Fa Theum smiled weakly. 'No matter, no matter. As for the Ters, they wear grey habits if my memory serves me correctly. They always keep their cowls up when they are outside the order's apartments. They have their own peculiar tonsure – not like the Fas' shaved spot at all. They keep very much to themselves; they're rarely seen about the House. There has been some upheaval in the upper echelons of the House lately but I don't believe the sisterhood will be with us for very much longer. Why are you so interested in the workings of the House of Spirits all of a sudden?'

'Just curious, that's all.'

Fa Theum looked hard at his protégé. 'I recognise that look. Whatever you're up to, promise me you'll be careful. Now come here and hold this page flat while I paste in this strip to repair it. It's difficult with only one hand. Then I'll point the way home for you.'

'How many books are missing?'

'I don't know, Ludo. Fa Theum didn't say. I didn't like to ask any more questions. I could tell he was getting suspicious.'

Mel, Ludo and Wren were inside the works of the great clock that adorned the front of Ambrosius Blenk's mansion. Wren's father had built it and it had become their secret clubhouse. All around them, lit by the diffused light entering through the huge, glass clock face, the machinery ticked, tocked, whirred and danced.

Wren stopped adjusting one of the automated

figures that paraded across the clock face each time the hour struck. 'So this Ter said that the first obstacle was out of the way. What kind of obstacle?'

'It's got to be a person,' said Mel. 'That's what you usually lock in a dungeon.'

'All right. But what about the rest?' asked Ludo.

'I still think that funny cloud's got a mirrormark,' said Mel. 'Or at least the start of one.'

'Don't talk daft,' said Ludo. 'Mirrormarks are made on pictures. You can't make them on the sky. Clouds aren't paint.'

'What do *you* think it looks like then?' asked Mel.

'A cloud,' said Ludo. 'All clouds look like clouds.'

'Not all clouds,' said Wren. 'I've seen castles and animals. I bet you have too.'

'Yeah. But they're not *real* pictures,' said Ludo. 'They just look a bit like them.'

'So does something in a painting,' said Mel. 'They're just paint stains but you believe they're something else.'

'But that's different. Paint stays where the artist puts it. Clouds blow about all over the place. Wherever the wind blows.' Ludo looked sceptical.

'That one doesn't,' said Wren.

'You really think that the Ters can paint a mirrormark with cloud?' said Ludo. 'For starters, they don't know what it looks like. And even if they could, there's nothing on this "other side" of theirs for demons to come from. There's only sky.'

'There's only canvas and air on the other side of a painting,' said Mel. 'And we all know the Mirrorscape's there. Anyway, clouds make storms. You've got to admit that.'

'It doesn't look like a storm cloud to me,' said Ludo. 'Let alone this "wound into the world beyond". So who are these mysterious "allies" then? Raindrops?'

'What's this "world beyond" if it's not the Mirrorscape?' asked Mel.

'I don't know. Perhaps it's what the Ters call the afterlife,' ventured Wren.

'An afterlife where there are demons?'

'Might be,' said Ludo. 'It depends how bad you've been.'

'We should ask the master,' suggested Wren. 'He'd know.'

'Ask him what?' said Mel. 'We don't know anything except what I overheard. He'd say I misheard them or something. Then he'd ask what we were doing in the Hall on our day off. We'd have to admit that we were late with our drawing. You know how strict he is when it comes to work.'

'We could consult the cards.' Ludo shuffled his pack.

'Not those cards again,' said Mel with a weary sigh. 'They won't tell us anything.'

'Sure they will. They can tell your fortune – I've seen it done. Why not where this wound thing is?'

'You have to be a fortune teller to do that,' said Mel. 'Where did you get them from anyway?'

'He took them from Groot's locker. Before Bex cleared it out,' said Wren.

'Then they're *definitely* crooked if they belonged to that drunk bully,' said Mel.

'Yeah, but he's gone,' said Ludo. 'Him and Adolfus Spute and their henchmen.'

'Do you think they're still locked inside that painting deep under Vlam?' said Wren.

'Got to be,' said Mel. 'The mirrormark that opened

the picture is no longer there. There's no *way* they could escape. It's impossible.'

The friends exchanged nervous smiles.

Wren came and sat down on the floor with the boys. 'Look, why don't we look into this Paper Belfry? I bet if we can find that, we will learn a lot more about all this.'

'Supposing there is one,' said Ludo.

'Well, we're all going to be working in the House of Spirits for a while. I bet someone there knows,' said Ludo.

'Yeah,' said Mel. 'But we've got to be really careful. I've got a horrible feeling that if the Ters hear about this *we'll* be headed for the dungeon. Or worse.'

The Evening Book-Run

By the end of the next day the friends knew no more. Ambrosius Blenk's entire studio had decamped from his rambling mansion to the Hall of Awakenings to work on the giant ceiling painting. As the youngest apprentices they had been kept busy fetching, carrying and generally tidying up after the master and the older boys.

'Come on, you youngsters,' chivvied Bex. 'Henk needs some more colours and one of you mop up that spilt oil before someone takes a nose-dive off the scaffolding.'

'He's an old slave-driver, that one,' complained Ludo in a low voice.

'Would you rather have Groot back in charge?' said Wren.

'Bex's all right,' said Mel. 'He's strict but he's fair. Groot was just plain evil.'

'But at this rate we'll never get to start on our niche,' said Ludo.

'I'll ask him if we can stay late and work on it when it's quiet,' said Mel.

'Mel, Ludo, Wren. Use your hands, not your tongues,' called Bex as he worked.

Later, when Mel was sent below to retrieve a dropped paintbrush, he asked a mason if he knew about the Paper Belfry.

'Are you having a laugh, son? There ain't no such thing. Skegging belfries are made out of skegging stone. Stands to reason. What do you think would happen to a paper belfry the first time it skegging rained?'

Ludo's idea of a subtle approach to the master was no more enlightening.

'Cleef, fetch me a pencil, will you, please?'

'Yes, Master. There's one here on this *paper*.'

'Come on, come on. Any one will do.'

'So this one on the *paper's*, OK?' said Ludo hopefully. 'Pencils and *paper* go together like . . . like bells and *belfries*, don't they?'

'Yes, yes. Give it here. Thank you.'

'Now there's an idea, Master; a *paper belfry*.'

'Paper bells won't work, Cleef,' said Ambrosius

Blenk distractedly as he drew. 'No resonance. Best you could manage would be a dull crinkle. Bronze is best for bells. Disturbs the bats though. The bats in the belfries. They're mammals, you know, just like us. Aerial mammals as opposed to terrestrial mammals or aquatic mammals like seals.' Ambrosius Blenk twirled his long beard with the fingers of one hand as he sketched a fat seal in the margin of his working drawing. 'Aerial, aquatic,' he said to himself. 'I wonder . . .' His piercing blue eyes sparkled as he added a pair of bat's wings and then a pair of human legs with a few, deft lines. 'Not bad, not bad. Needs something else . . .' He made the feet webbed and then drew a set of antlers with flames at the tip of the tines, turning the creation into a living candelabrum. 'Mmmm. More light, I need more light. Fetch me some more candles, Cleef. I can't see what I'm doing here.' He sketched a night sky behind the flying seal. 'Stars, constellations, planets, maybe if . . .' The master looked up. 'Well, Cleef? What are you standing about for? Haven't you got work to do?'

From pencils to outer space in ten seconds flat. How does he do it? Ludo walked away, shaking his head.

31

When a young, novice Fa in his beige robes climbed the scaffolding to look at the nascent ceiling Wren had tried to pump him for information.

'Well, seeing as you ask, my child, I do know about the bells. It's one of the many things we have to memorise in the seminary. Each day they're rung seven times, you know.' The novice folded his hands in front of him as he settled into his subject.

Oh, no. Why did I have to pick a bell-swot? Wren tuned out for a while as he recited everything he knew about bells in excruciating detail. Her attention snapped back in when she heard a certain word.

'. . . belfries from which the peals are rung. I'm sure I can name them all. There's the Granite Belfry, the South Belfry, the Hierarch's Belfry, the Marble Belfry, the Mizzen Belfry – there's an interesting story attached to that one. Way back in the year . . .'

More than twenty minutes later, Wren, practically weeping from boredom, politely thanked the Fa for his 'fascinating explanation' and returned to her duties. The Paper Belfry was conspicuous by its absence.

*

'Very well,' said Bex as Mel and his friends were tidying up at the end of the day, 'you can stay on for another few hours and work on your niche. Mind you all get back to the mansion before lock-up though. Help yourself to today's leftovers. You're going to miss supper.'

The friends worked on their creation for an hour or more as they discussed what they had not found out about the Paper Belfry between mouthfuls of cheese, ham and slightly stale bread they had taken from the buffet that had been set up on the working platform. When the vespers bells sounded they made their way down off the scaffolding.

'We won't be able to use the hoist this late,' said Wren.

'I know the way out,' said Mel. 'Follow me.'

When they reached a landing on the grand staircase they heard echoing footsteps coming towards them. Ludo peered down the spiral. 'Hide, quick! There're some grey-robes coming.'

From behind a fat pillar they watched as two hooded figures, one very large, the other slight, ascended from the direction of the library, each carrying an armful of books.

'I think it's *them*,' said Mel softly. 'Mudge and Tunk. The two I overheard.'

'Come on, you two,' whispered Wren. 'Let's see where they're going.'

The friends shadowed the Ters until they left the staircase, walked a short distance down a corridor and rapped on a large door with an obviously coded series of knocks.

'Quick, in here.' Wren flattened herself in a doorway and the two boys joined her. There was a muffled crash.

Ludo peeped out. 'The small one's dropped her books. Now the big one's helping her pick them up.' They heard the door close.

'She missed one,' said Mel.

'I'll fetch it,' said Wren. 'Stay here.' She retrieved the outsized book from behind a tall ornamental urn and a loose page slipped out, landing at Mel's feet. Mel scooped it up and the friends hurried along and stopped when they felt they were far enough away.

'It's just a collection of old speeches,' said Wren, leafing through the book. 'And pretty boring ones too. What's on the bookmark, Mel?'

'It's the House of Spirits,' said Mel, unfolding the illustration. 'The page that was missing from the book Fa Theum showed me.'

'But why did she have it?' asked Wren.

'A souvenir, maybe,' suggested Ludo.

Mel shook his head. 'She didn't strike me as the sentimental type. Maybe she didn't want anyone else to see it. Look, we should return these to the library.'

'Sure, but not now,' said Ludo. 'We have to be back at the mansion before lock-up.'

The next morning the friends left the mansion even earlier than usual. They planned to return the book and to get in an extra hour's painting on their niche before the day's work started. As they made their way up the narrow, winding streets towards the House of Spirits the sun was rising, washing the stones of Vlam with soft, golden light, glinting off burnished copper domes and turning window panes into daytime stars.

'Skegging hills; we're knackered before we even reach the House of scrotting Spirits.'

'Your language, Ludo. You've been spending too much time with the masons,' said Wren.

'What's up with you? You're very tetchy this morning,' said Ludo.

'Am I? Sorry. It's just that I had a bad night. The thunder woke me up and I couldn't get back to sleep.'

'There's no way that's a thunder cloud.' Ludo glanced up at the strangely shaped cloud in the otherwise clear sky.

'I heard it too,' said Mel. 'But it couldn't have been made by that. Thunder clouds are big and black and anvil-shaped. Ludo's right about one thing, though, it's uphill all the way.' He nodded towards their towering destination as it came into view, framed by the end of the narrow street. 'You know, I bet that illustration was drawn from somewhere near here.' He slipped the torn page from inside the volume of speeches, where he had placed it for safekeeping. 'Yeah, look.'

'Pretty poor observation,' said Ludo dismissively as

he looked over Mel's shoulder. 'Whoever drew it didn't get it right. Look, there's construction on the north face that doesn't match.' He pointed to it on the page.

'That's the Hall of Awakenings,' said Mel. 'This drawing was made before that was begun.'

'Not that. *That.*' Ludo jabbed his finger harder at a point immediately above.

'What is it?' Mel held the drawing up for better comparison. There was another construction visible on the building that was not in the illustration. 'Some kind of turret? Or maybe a . . .'

They all said it at once. 'Belfry!'

'You were quick,' said Ludo as Mel joined them to work on the niche. 'Did you tell Fa Theum where we found the book?'

'No. I thought we ought to find out more about all this before we tell anyone else. But he did say there were more books missing since yesterday.'

'Why are they taking all these books?' said Wren. 'It doesn't make any sense.'

'Search me. He says there's even more books

missing than he first thought, many of them very valuable.'

'What type of books?' asked Wren. 'If we knew the subject it might give us a clue why the Ters are stealing them.'

'All different subjects,' said Mel. 'Collections of speeches like the one we found, herbals, atlases, charters – even old ledgers of accounts. There's only one thing I can see that links them together.'

'And what's that?' said Ludo.

'They're all big,' said Wren. 'But why would anyone want just big books?'

'Are you staying again or coming back to the mansion with us?' called Bex as he and the other apprentices prepared to leave for the day.

'We're going to stay on for a bit. Work some more on our niche,' said Mel. 'If that's OK with you.'

Bex nodded. 'All right. But make sure you tidy up after you.'

'Are they gone?' asked Ludo after a while.

'Yes,' said Wren, peering over the edge of the

scaffolding. 'Now, from the illustration the mysterious belfry must be just above where we are. I bet it's this Paper Belfry. How do we get there?'

'The grand staircase?' suggested Ludo.

'That'd be my guess,' said Mel.

They ended up outside the same door the two Ters had disappeared through the previous evening.

'We must be right above the Hall of Awakenings,' said Mel. 'This door is probably the only way to get to the belfry.'

'What now?' said Ludo. 'Do we make the old rat-tat-tat?'

'It was in a kind of code and I can't remember it,' said Wren. 'Besides, we hardly look like Ters. We'd never be let in.'

'Maybe there's another way in. If we could –'

'Quick, someone's coming!' Wren led them behind one of the large urns that flanked the doorway.

'Looks like the evening book-run,' whispered Ludo. They held their breath as the footsteps grew louder.

'Are we there yet, Tunk? I can't see where I'm going,' said the small Ter.

'Serves you right for trying to carry so many.'

'The more we carry the fewer trips we'll have to make.'

'Suit yourself. Arm-ache or leg-ache, it all amounts to the same thing; a right pain in the –'

'Tunk!'

Ter Tunk made the secret knock. She made it again after it had gone unanswered and then a third time. She muttered something under her breath and then there was a jingle of keys on a chain as she unlocked the door, followed by a series of thumps as books fell to the floor.

'Not again, Mudge. No, no, leave them there. Don't close the door. There's no one about, they're all at vespers. Help me take these upstairs first and we'll come down for those in a moment.'

'Yes, Tunk. I'm coming.'

The footsteps faded inside.

'Quick,' whispered Mel. 'We may not get another chance.'

After a moment's hesitation, Wren and then Ludo followed him through the door.

The friends found themselves in a dark, vaulted

hallway with many arched doors opening off it. On the walls between the doors hung large paintings and tapestries, difficult to see clearly in the dim light. Directly ahead of them was a wide, branching staircase also lined with pictures. The hallway continued on either side.

There came the sound of footsteps descending the stairs.

Mel looked around and then motioned to Wren and Ludo to follow him down the darkened hallway. He tried a door: locked. So was the second. Just then, a door at the far end of the hallway opened and bright light flooded out.

'Who's there?' said a tall, elegant woman as she stood silhouetted against the light. Her long shadow spilled down the hallway like an oil slick. She looked straight at Mel.

Mel's heart skipped a beat. 'Quick, link arms,' he hissed. As his friends threaded their arms through his he made the complicated gesture of the mirrormark in the air to unlock one of the paintings. The three friends vanished.

'It's only Tunk and me, mistress,' said Ter Mudge as she reached the foot of the stairs. She tried to see the darkened face of the tall woman to gauge her mood but it was unreadable against the bright light.

'Did you hear something? Children's voices?'

'No, mistress.'

'Fool! You've left the door open. I can feel the draught.'

'It was only for a moment, mistress. While we took the latest batch of books upstairs.'

'Mudge, you imbecile! We can't afford any slip-ups now we're this close.'

'No, mistress. Sorry, mistress,' said Ter Mudge as she retrieved the dropped books and closed the door.

Then there came a ghastly snuffling noise and a hideous, half-human shape slunk from behind the woman. It half-walked, half-crawled along the hallway and crouched in front of a painting. It sniffed loudly and scratched at the surface of the canvas with its horny, curved nails. Its dark, malformed outline was haloed by the light behind it. Then it put back its spiky head and howled a terrible howl.

'Something's amiss,' said the woman. 'The Morg scents demons!'

The Leviathan

'She was looking straight at us. She *must* have seen us,' said Wren. 'We only just got away in time. Where are we?'

'Safe; that's where,' said Ludo.

'For now.' Mel looked around. The three of them were standing in a landscape made entirely of crafted wood. Beneath their feet was caulked, wooden planking and low hills formed from the same material rose up all around them. They could smell the distinctive salty tang of the sea mixed with tar. The ground (if that's what it was) seemed unsteady as if it was moving very slowly. They were quite alone.

'Well,' said Wren. 'I didn't think we'd be back in the Mirrorscape quite so soon.'

By tracing the hidden mirrormark in the air in front of the canvas Mel had unlocked the surface and they been drawn inside the weird world that existed beyond the picture plane. Whatever the artist imagined and painted became real. The mirrormarked pictures all joined up to form the Mirrorscape. As unpredictable as it was beautiful, it was a land where the normal laws of common sense no longer existed. The last time the friends had been in the Mirrorscape they had barely escaped with their lives.

'Come on. Let's try and find out where we are.' Mel led the way up the nearest hill. When they reached the top they could see that the planked, wooden landscape extended all around them. The windswept hill they stood on was one of many that receded into the distance and in the valleys between them they could see small villages nestling. There were black rivers meandering along the valleys and dark smudges of forests. Way off in the distance, both immediately in front and behind, they could make out towering buildings as big as small cities. At regular intervals between these two huge edifices rose four colossal columns that disappeared into the low clouds that scudded above their heads. All around them they could see a coastline.

'We're on an island,' said Wren. 'But a pretty strange one.'

'I'm not so sure,' said Ludo. 'Islands aren't made from planks and they don't move about like this. I think we're on a galleon.'

'A *galleon*?' said Wren.

'Well, definitely some kind of big ship.'

'If it's a ship, where're the crew?'

'I think Ludo's right,' said Mel. 'Remember the Mirrorscape isn't like the real world; anything's possible. Look, those ginormous buildings at each end are the whatsits . . .'

'Forecastle and quarterdeck,' said Ludo smugly.

'. . . Did you just swallow a dictionary or something? The four columns are the masts and what looks like the coastline's just the edge of the vessel.'

'But it's *huge*,' said Wren. 'Ships aren't this big. It'd take ages to walk from one end to the other.'

'Then we'd better get a move on. There's no point staying here. You remember how time works in the Mirrorscape. We could wait here for a week and only a moment will have passed back in the real world. The Ters will still be waiting for us. If we're ever going to get back to Nem, we need to find another way out.'

Mel glanced behind them at the wall of mist that rose up sheer from the deck and disappeared into the clouds. He knew that it was the surface of the painting they had entered and that it was only visible when seen from head on. 'So, which way?'

'Let's head for the quarterdeck. We'll probably find some figments up there,' said Ludo, referring to the inhabitants of the Mirrorscape. 'That's where a ship is steered from – normally.'

'There's nothing normal about this ship,' said Wren as they set off.

After a while they came to one of the villages. All of the dwellings were made from upturned boats with crude holes cut into them as doors and windows. Smoke drifted in lazy spirals from improvised chimney-pots secured with scruffy rigging. One of the boat-buildings had a nameplate attached to its bow.

Mel tilted his head to read the upside-down lettering. 'Le-vi-ath-an.' He stood up straight. 'There's no one around. It's totally deserted.'

'It's a bit spooky.' Wren hugged herself and looked about.

'Spooky or not,' said Ludo, 'this place looks like an inn. Let's see if we can get something to eat. I don't know about you two but I'm starving.' He pushed open a wonky door cobbled together from pieces of driftwood and entered.

It was dark inside and Mel reached into his doublet and pulled out his most precious possession. It was a quill pen made from an angel's feather that glowed with its own inner light. 'I'll open a shutter.'

Once opened, they could see a long bar made from rough planks set on top of upright casks. Several more casks rested on top, supported between chocks. From one of them ale was pouring out of a wooden spigot into an overflowing tankard. The walls were decorated with oars, fishing nets and all kinds of nautical objects; a stuffed swordfish, a shark's jaw, a brass porthole, various pieces of carved sea-ivory and naive paintings of vessels. There were coils of rope for seats.

'Well, someone's been here recently,' observed Wren. 'The fire's still lit.'

'And I can smell cooking.' Ludo lifted the lid on a large pot that hung simmering over the fire. 'Mmmm.'

'Look,' said Mel, 'there're half-drunk pots of ale. Whoever was here must have left in a hurry.' He tucked his feather away.

'What's that noise?' said Ludo, replacing the pot lid.

'It came from outside.' Wren went to the door and opened it wide.

'Ahoy, my lovely!'

'*Figments*,' said Mel.

Wren was confronted by about a dozen figments. They all wore striped sailor's shirts and their powerful, tattooed arms protruded from the sleeves. Baggy sailcloth trousers hovered at half-mast above shoes with silver buckles. But by far the strangest thing about them was that they all had dog's heads. The leader – like his men, an unidentifiable mongrel – slapped his cudgel into the open palm of his hand and clunked towards them on his peg leg. 'Well, well, well. Three more. Not as fast on their feet as the rest of the village. That improves our quota.' The dog-men surged into the inn.

'Who're you?' asked Ludo.

'That's the wrong question, matey,' said the leader. 'The right question's "what are you?"'

'OK, then, what are you?'

'We're the press gang, that's what we are.'

'What's a press gang?' said Wren.

'A press gang, my lovely, has the power to seize and impress anyone it chooses to sail a ship,' said the leader. 'Whether they like it or not. Make their hands fast and put 'em with the other one.'

'But you can't do that,' protested Mel as he was grabbed. 'That's kidnapping.'

'Let me go,' cried Wren.

'We're only passing through,' added Ludo. 'We're no sailors.'

The leader laughed. 'You are now.'

The friends struggled as their hands were tied and they were dragged outside. Standing dejectedly between two more dog-men was another figment. Unlike his captors he was more or less human and without his towering, extravagantly coiffed and very fluffy wig would have been only slightly taller than Ludo, the tallest of the three friends. As it was, he was half as tall again. He was dressed in knee-britches and an elaborate, golden frock coat covered with florid embroidery that ran down the front, along the hem and exploded in a firework display of fancy needlework all over the back. Long lace sleeves emerged from his enormous, turned-back cuffs and a frilly jabot rested on his scarlet waistcoat. On his delicate hands were several large, jewelled rings. He stood in an almost balletic pose, his finely shod feet pointing at a precise angle. His white, powdered face wore a look of the utmost distain. He turned to the leader. 'Look, whatever your name is, I shouldn't be here. I'm on an important mission. If you don't let me go this instant –'

'Pipe down, Wiggy,' said the leader. 'That's what they all say. All you've done is complain. There'll be more than enough to moan about once yer sworn in. Now get in line, all o' yer.'

'You heard the boatswain,' snapped one of the gang.

Mel, Wren, Ludo and the foppish figment were marched away from the village, occasionally urged on by the boatswain's sharp tongue and even sharper strokes from the knotted rope-ends that the press gang wielded. As they marched, pieces of the fop's wig drifted apart until it seemed like there were lots of pieces following along in close formation. Whatever it was made from, it was not hair.

'Oh, the ignominy of it all,' complained the fop to no one in particular. 'To be herded along like cattle by these . . . these *clichés*.'

'What're you talking about?' asked Mel.

The fop raised an eyebrow and looked down his nose at Mel, which meant that he had to tilt his head backwards. As he did this small clumps of his wig drifted away. Slowly they drifted back and rejoined it. Suddenly, Mel realised. *His wig's made from clouds!*

'Were you addressing me?'

'Yes,' said Mel. 'Please tell us what you mean?'

The fop turned his haughty stare on Ludo and then Wren. He sighed and relaxed and his supercilious expression became more friendly. 'I suppose we're all in the same boat. *Oh, no!* Now even I'm doing it.' He rolled his eyes.

'Doing what?' asked Wren.

'Can't you see? It's all so obvious.'

The friends stared back blankly.

'We're all trapped inside a bad work of art. In a

minute someone's going to shout "avast there" or something equally predictable.'

'Avast there!' snapped the boatswain. 'Belay those tongues, yer lubbers!'

'*See.*'

'Are you saying that you know what's going to happen?' asked Wren quietly.

'No, of course not. It's just that this dreadful painting we unfortunately find ourselves in was clearly made by someone with a feeble imagination. My dear, we're in a bad joke.'

'Do you know what he's talking about?' Ludo asked the others.

'Not a clue,' said Mel.

Wren shrugged and shook her head.

'You'll see,' said the fop, 'you'll see.' He walked on ahead.

'Something's really wrong here,' said Mel. 'If this is such a bad painting, then how come it's got a mirrormark?'

'That's right,' said Wren. 'Only masterpieces are supposed to have a mirrormark.'

'This one's got one, sure enough,' said Mel. 'Otherwise we wouldn't be in this mess.'

'Someone must have drawn one on this picture,' said Ludo, tugging at his bound hands.

'But *who*?' said Mel.

'And why?' added Wren. 'Do you think it was so that the Ters could get into the Mirrorscape?'

'Or maybe it's to let someone out,' said Mel.

After a long time marching up the wooden hills and down the wooden dales of the ship the press gang and their prisoners arrived outside the towering structure at the stern of the Leviathan. The boatswain pushed open a doorway as large as the city gates of Vlam and the captives were herded in after him. Inside, the structure was either unfinished or partially in ruins as most of it was missing, with just the vast skeleton of the building open to the elements.

'How much would you say is missing, my dears?' asked the fop. 'About seventy-five per cent? Still don't get it?'

The friends looked bewildered and shook their heads.

The party trudged up wide stairs until the

boatswain signalled them to stop outside a cabin door. He turned to the press gang. 'Right, mates, I'll get this lot entered into the ship's books and whistle you up some grog.' He pushed the captives into the cabin and blew the boatswain's whistle that hung from a lanyard around his neck. There was no sound that Mel and his friends could hear but the dog-headed figments evidently did and rushed off with a wild stamping of feet shouting, 'Grog, grog, grog.' It sounded strangely like barking.

'What's this?' said the fop in mock surprise. 'Why, it's the *bridge*.'

The cabin had no rear bulkhead and vaulting out into the skeletal void of the unfinished structure and ending in mid-air was a bridge – the kind used to cross rivers or chasms. In front of the bridge was a table with a blue-uniformed figure asleep on it, his head resting on folded arms resplendent with curlicues of gold braid. A brace of flintlock pistols lay alongside him.

'Stow it, Wiggy. Step lively now,' ordered the boatswain as he marched them up to the table and untied their hands. 'Officer present. Stand to attention.' He blew his silent whistle again.

The figure at the table stirred and raised a bleary head – this time a pedigree spaniel – belched and slumped back again. He began to snore.

'Don't tell me,' said the fop wearily, 'a drunken sailor. Sea-dogs, quarterdeck, bridge. It's all too, too literal.'

'*Now* I get it,' said Wren. 'The entire picture's a great big pun.'

'Belay that lip! The ship's company's below complement. The Leviathan's crew's aloft, trimming the sails. They'll be down in a week or two. Until then all I've got is that rabble of a press gang and you four to make everything shipshape and sail the ship.' The boatswain kicked the sleeping officer's chair with his peg leg. 'New hands to be signed on, if you please, sir.'

The lieutenant snored louder.

'Never mind, I'll enter yer m'self.' The boatswain laid his cudgel on the table and pried a large ledger from beneath the sleeping officer, dipped a quill in a pot of ink and held it out. 'First volunteer sign yer name. *Or else.*'

'Or else what? You'll make us walk the plank?' said the fop.

'How did you know that, Wiggy?' said the boatswain, astonished.

'You're such a cliché.'

'Who're yer calling names?'

'Oh stop it, you two,' said Wren. 'No one's going to be signing anything.'

'Oh, they all say that – until they see the plank. Then I bet yer will, my lovely. I bet yer will.'

'How much?' said Ludo.

'What?'

'You said "I bet you will". How much?'

'You're getting out of yer depth, matey.'

'I bet you my signature against . . . against that whistle of yours that I can cut a higher card than you can.' Ludo took out his pack of cards.

'Like a lamb to the slaughter,' said the boatswain, rubbing his hands. 'I was playing cards before yer was even a twinkle in yer daddy's eye. All right. There! Ten of porcupines.'

Ludo winked at his friends. 'Queen of ravens.'

The boatswain reluctantly unslung his whistle and handed it to Ludo. 'Tell you what; best of three. My whistle against this trinket here.' He pulled what looked like a watch on a chain from his pocket.

'That's mine, you knave,' said the fop. His wig darkened and lightning flashed somewhere deep inside it.

'*Was* yours, Wiggy. Pressed person's baubles are the boatswain's perks. Always have been, always will be.'

Three cards were cut and the boatswain lost each time. He passed over the watch.

'Double or quits,' suggested Ludo. 'Our freedom against your whistle and trinket.'

'*My* trinket,' corrected the fop.

'Yer can't keep being that lucky. OK, matey, yer on.' The boatswain rubbed his sweaty palm on his trousers. 'Queen of starfish. Ha! Beat that!'

'King of salamanders! Come on, let's go. We've wasted enough time already.' Ludo pocketed his winnings.

'I've never seen luck like that, never in all my years at sea. All right, matey, yer's won fair and square. But can I ask a favour before yer go?' The boatswain turned his mournful dog's eyes on Ludo. 'Can I just say goodbye to my whistle. We've been together now for a long time.'

'I don't know . . .'

'*Please.*'

'Don't do it, Ludo,' said Mel. 'It's a trick.'

'It's no trick, matey. Honest.' The boatswain widened his big, doggy eyes.

Ludo melted. 'I don't suppose it can do any harm. Here.' He handed the boatswain back his whistle.

'Thanks, matey.' He stroked the gleaming instrument lovingly. 'Just one last toot.' He blew a silent blast before handing it back to Ludo with a tear in his eye. 'Goodbye. Yer know the way out.'

'The sooner we're out of here the better,' said the fop. 'I've important business to attend to and I've been badly delayed by this tomfoolery. If I can just trouble you for the return of my – can you hear something?'

'It sounds like running feet,' said Wren as she opened the cabin door.

'Grog, grog, grog.' The press gang were surging up the stairs towards them.

'I knew we couldn't trust him,' said Mel. 'He called them with the whistle.'

'Yer got to get up early to outwit the boatswain. OK, matey, yer all re-pressed!' He reached for his cudgel.

'I think not, scoundrel,' said the fop, grabbing and cocking the pistols. He slammed the door with his foot and Mel turned the key. 'Leave that knobbler where it is.'

There was a fearful pounding on the door.

'I've spent too long in this dreadful painting,' said the fop. 'I'm going back the way I came to continue my quest.'

'You're on a quest?' said Mel.

'Certainly I am. I'm looking for –' The fop stopped and looked intently at the friends. 'Perhaps our meeting isn't an accident. You'd better come with me. Here,' he handed a pistol to Mel. 'Keep him covered. There's some equipment that I need in my drawers.'

'You keep equipment in your *drawers*?' said Mel.

'Certainly I do.'

'Uncomfortable,' said Ludo. 'Now what?'

The fop turned his back on everyone, fiddled with his clothing and when he turned back was holding a large coil of rope with a grappling hook attached.

'Those must be some drawers,' said Ludo, eyeing the fop with curiosity.

'Indeed they are.' The fop swung the hook around and around and cast it over a beam of the exposed superstructure above the cabin. He gave it a good tug to make sure it was secure. 'I can't say it's been fun.' He kicked the end of the rope over the void, tucked his pistol into one of the large pockets of his frock coat and disappeared, hand over hand, down the rope. 'Are you coming or not?'

There was the sound of wood shattering as the door was battered with something heavy.

'Heave-ho, me hearties,' shouted the boatswain.

'Well, what're we waiting for?' said Ludo as he followed the fop.

'You next, Wren,' said Mel.

'What about you?'

'Don't worry about me. I'm just going to slow this one up.' Mel took careful aim and pulled the trigger. There was a deafening report and the boatswain toppled over.

'Mel! You've killed him!' screamed Wren.

The smoke from the pistol cleared and the boatswain lay slumped on the floor, his peg leg shattered.

Mel winked at his friend.

Wren disappeared down the rope, followed closely by Mel. Above them, they heard the door finally shatter and the noise of the press gang as they piled into the cabin.

'After them, yer scurvy lubbers,' roared the boatswain. 'Don't let them get away.'

'Step away from the rope, my dears,' said the fop as Mel reached the bottom. He was holding a blazing tinder box which he touched to the rope. The flame crept rapidly upwards. 'That'll hold them for a while but they'll be able to lay their hands on another rope soon enough. Follow me.'

They ran along a murky, low-ceilinged space

littered with old coils of rope, loose blocks and tackle, empty casks and discarded bolts of sailcloth. It was lit at infrequent intervals by dim, overhead lamps that cast yellow pools of light on the deck. Suddenly, the fop stopped and the friends cannoned into him. He lit his tinder box again.

'Look!' exclaimed Mel as he stared into the black void just inches from where they'd stopped. 'We've run out of deck.'

'That's the hold,' said the fop. 'The cargo's down there and our way out's among it.' He kicked a loose block lying on the floor into the blackness. No one heard it hit the bottom. 'Let me show you what I've got in my drawers.'

'Did he say what I thought he did?' whispered Ludo.

'Yes, he did,' said Wren, averting her eyes.

'No, it's all right. Look,' said Mel.

They watched, fascinated, as the fop opened his coat and then his waistcoat to reveal four drawers set into his chest, each with gilded handles. He tugged the topmost one and it slid out. 'Aha! This will serve.' He reached in and pulled out a number of bamboo rods that were much longer than could possibly fit into the space of his chest. He laid them on the floor. 'Now, if you'll be so kind as to help me assemble these – just match the numbered ends – we'll see about getting into the hold.'

'What are they?' said Ludo, fitting together a couple of the rods.

'It looks like some kind of flying machine,' said Wren as the structure began to take shape.

By the time the rods were assembled and some spare sailcloth stretched over them the friends saw a large, skeletal bird held together with lots of complicated pulleys and ropes. There was room in a long cockpit behind the bird's head for all four of them. The fop wedged a lantern in the contraption's beak.

'Are we supposed to get in there?' said Mel. He felt an intoxicating mixture of fear and elation. From the look in his friends' faces, they felt the same. 'Can that thing actually *fly?*'

Behind them they could hear the pounding feet of the press gang running towards them and their strange barking voices.

'Time we were off.' The fop stepped into the machine. 'Get in, my dears, one behind the other. Thread your arms through these ropes.' As they stood up they found they were wearing the contraption suspended from their shoulders with their legs poking through the bottom in place of an undercarriage. The fop was in front, followed by Mel, Wren and Ludo. 'Here we go. All together now – left, right, left, right, left, right – faster, faster – *jump!*'

'*Aaaaahhhh!*' The friends screamed as they launched themselves out into the blackness above the hold. For a sickening moment they fell, leaving their stomachs high over their heads before the wings began to beat and their descent was checked. They glided into the darkness, accompanied by the slow *thwap, thwap* of the beating wings. The fop in the pilot's seat pulled on the ropes and they banked left, then right as he accustomed himself to the controls. His cloudy wig held together surprisingly well, considering their airspeed.

'Where did you learn to fly this thing?' shouted Ludo from the back.

'Learn? This is my maiden flight, my dears. How difficult can it be?' The flying machine did a barrel-roll. 'Whoops.' The contraption righted itself. His wig rejoined him as it completed the roll slightly after its wearer. 'That's better. I'm beginning to get the hang of this. Shall we try it again?'

'Noooo!' shouted the friends in unison.

The fop looked back over his elegant, embroidered shoulder. 'Heads down. Evasive action!' He banked the machine sharply as a swarm of rockets trailing bright sparks whooshed by and disappeared into pinpoints of light ahead of them before exploding in showers of colour like a luminous flowerbed; geranium red, heliotrope blue, daffodil yellow. By their light the gargantuan hold of the Leviathan and the weird subterranean landscape was momentarily revealed. 'They're trying to bring us down with signal rockets.' Slowly, the hole made by a rocket that had passed clean through his wig resealed itself.

Mel tapped the fop on the shoulder and pointed. One of the rockets had hit the starboard wing and set it alight.

'Oh dear.' The fop manoeuvred the flying machine violently into a dive, using the airflow to extinguish the fire. 'That seems to have done the trick.' He levelled out and glanced at the damaged wing. 'For now, anyway.'

They flew on through the darkness but, little by little, they lost altitude. The beam of their lantern picked out huge stalactites made from planked wood as they sped on and the fop successfully piloted the contraption through arches and around monumental columns as they wove through the bowels of the ship.

'Hey, this is really good fun,' shouted Mel as he began to enjoy the experience.

'You call this *fun?*' said Wren.

'Fun, as in gargling with frogspawn?' added Ludo.

Suddenly, there came an ominous tearing sound. As one, all four heads snapped round and saw the charred cloth of the wing ripped away by the slipstream.

'That's torn it,' said Ludo.

'Hold on!' shouted the fop. 'We're going down.'

The Hold

Dreadful images of burning birds falling from the sky filled the friends' minds as the rushing air tore at their hair and clothing. They desperately scanned the blackness below, searching for somewhere to land as the lame craft flapped lower and lower.

'Everyone brace themselves,' called the fop.

Seconds later, the craft skimmed over a bare island and belly-flopped into the freezing, stinking water beyond. A huge bow wave was thrown up, drenching everyone and extinguishing the lantern with a hiss. In the blackness the lightweight craft floated on the stagnant water.

'There was an island of some sort back there,' said the fop. 'Paddle around with your legs and we'll try and beach ourselves.'

'I feel like a duck,' complained Wren.

Ludo spat a stream of bilge water from his mouth. 'Quack, quack.'

Eventually, numb with cold, they felt the bottom

shelving beneath their feet and they stumbled up on to the island. They wriggled out of the harness and stepped from the machine. In the darkness there was a *click-click-click* sound.

'Blast! My tinder box is soaked,' said the fop. 'If only we had some light.'

'Here, this might help.' Mel withdrew his quill from inside his doublet. It cast a warm golden glow.

'An *angel's* feather.' The astonishment was evident in the fop's voice. 'Where did you get it?'

'It was . . . left to me. By some friends I made in the Mirrorscape.'

'It *is* you.' The fop turned to Ludo. 'May I impose upon you for the return of my property?'

'You mean your watch? Sure.' Ludo blushed and handed it over. 'I meant to give it back to you, but we've been kind of busy.' He smiled sheepishly.

Immediately the fop touched the watch it began chiming. The tune was happy and jaunty. He flipped open the cover and consulted it by the light of the feather. He laughed out loud. 'I've come all this way and never imagined that I would reach my goal in the filthy bilges of this hulk.' He looked at the perplexed expression on the friends' faces. 'I think I owe you an explanation. But first – some warm blankets and something to eat.'

'Oh, yes please,' smiled Wren through chattering teeth.

The fop opened his frock coat and red waistcoat and tugged vainly at his drawers. 'Oh dear. The water's swollen them. They're stuck fast. Food and warmth will have to wait until they dry out but my story can't.'

The smiles faded as everyone slumped cross-legged on the planked island. Four bedraggled, shivering faces were lit by the glow of the feather. They looked like disembodied heads floating in the darkness as the fop began his tale. He was in a worse state than the others. A storm had formed inside his wig and rain was running down his face, leaving streaks in the white powder.

'My dears, my name is Cassetti. Forgive me for not introducing myself before but, as you pointed out, we've been rather occupied since we first met. Among other things, I'm ambassador-at-large to Nephonia.'

'Where?' asked Wren.

'Nephonia, otherwise known as the Cloud Kingdoms. There are four principal Kingdoms – Cumulus, Cirrus, Nimbus and Stratus. I myself am a Cumulan.'

'We have clouds in our world, too,' said Mel.

'I know, my dear. Your clouds and mine are one and the same.'

'But you're from the Mirrorscape. Are you saying that our clouds are part of the Mirrorscape as well?' Ludo, like his friends, looked confused.

'In a way, they are. How can I explain this?' Cassetti paused. 'Do you know what an iceberg is?'

'Of course,' said Wren. 'They have them floating in the sea off the north coast of Borealis in winter.'

'Then you'll know that while a part of an iceberg is above the sea and visible, by far the largest part of it is below the waters.'

The friends nodded.

'So it is with Nephonia. The lesser part visible from your world is just the base – the foundations, if you like – of mine.'

'Like a footprint?' ventured Mel.

71

Cassetti nodded. 'Exactly. Clouds are one of the few places where your world and the Mirrorscape touch.'

'But the Mirrorscape's to do with pictures,' reasoned Ludo.

Cassetti raised an eyebrow. 'And you've never seen the pictures in clouds?'

'You mean they're not accidental,' said Mel. 'You know, made by the wind.'

'Goodness me, no. Clouds take a lot of work to get them looking as they do. It's a part of my job. You see, before I was appointed ambassador, I was a cloud-sculptor.'

'So Nephonia's a kind of picture, then,' said Wren. 'Does that mean you can travel between the worlds through the clouds?'

'It's not quite that simple,' said Cassetti. 'Normally, the way between the worlds is sealed – and for very good reasons – but recently the Cumulan surveyors noticed something unusual. In the lowest levels of the city a strange cloud had formed. It had an odd knot-like shape.'

'It's a mirrormark,' said Mel, instantly grasping the

connection, 'or at least the start of one. The cloud you mean is over Vlam, where we come from.'

'Don't you *dare* say "I told you so",' said Ludo.

Cassetti nodded as if he was confirming something to himself. 'So, the city mounted an investigation and sent a team down to investigate. But as soon as they approached this shape they were gripped by strong currents drawing them towards it. They only just managed to free themselves and return to report their findings. It was evident that if something was not done – and done soon – then the whole of Cumulus risked being drawn to this irregularity and thence to we knew not where.'

'That's what mirrormarks do,' said Mel. 'They keep the worlds apart, but if they're opened then things are sucked through.'

Cassetti smiled. 'It *is* you! I *knew* it!' He raised his watch to his lips and kissed it. 'It's never wrong. So I've found you at last – the friend of angels and his friends. The very people that understand how this mirrormark works.' The rain in his wig ceased.

'*Us?*' said Mel.

'Certainly. My . . . my navigational aid was leading me to a wall of mist on the Leviathan's deck when I was apprehended by that evil press gang. It suggested that you were beyond.'

'Well, we were,' said Ludo.

'That's how we got on board the ship,' said Wren.

'It never lies,' said Cassetti. 'You're going to save the Cloud Kingdoms.'

'We are? But how?' asked Wren.

'I can't tell you.'

'But where do we start?' said Ludo.

'I can't tell you.'

'You're asking us to help you save your precious Cloud Kingdoms but you won't even offer us any help?' said Mel.

'I didn't say that. I said "I can't *tell* you." However,' said Cassetti, pre-empting Mel's interruption, 'I can give you this.' He handed Mel his watch.

'What use is this?'

'I can't –'

'Tell you,' finished Ludo. 'Great! You won't tell us how, you won't tell us why and you won't tell us where. But, hey, here's a watch. Why don't you time yourselves guessing?'

'It's not a watch.'

'What is it then?' said Mel.

'*I can't tell you*,' said Ludo and Wren.

'Just so,' said Cassetti, smiling. 'The device will only function if you work out for yourself what it is and how to use it. I will tell you this, though: I believe it is the most valuable thing you will ever own.'

That grabbed their attention. Wren and Ludo gathered around and studied it with Mel. The finely tooled silver case had a crystal window at its centre, revealing a large, facetted ruby beneath. Mel flipped it open. Inside it certainly looked and felt like a watch but the dial suggested it was something different. On its circular face were three smaller, round dials arranged like a triangle with minute, arcane symbols on them where the numerals would normally be. The bottom two dials each had a single hand. The one on the left swung wildly about first one way and then another with no apparent purpose. Its neighbour hovered twitching at what, on a watch, would be nine o'clock. The dial above was more like a conventional watch face except the hands were moving backwards. Right in the centre, where the hands would be attached on a conventional timepiece, was the large ruby.

'I think some water must have got into it,' said Mel. 'It doesn't seem to be working properly.'

Cassetti smiled again. 'Oh, it's working all right.'

'We heard the whatsit chime,' said Ludo.

'That's right. Why . . .?' Wren did not bother finishing the question.

'Do you suppose it's some kind of compass?' said Mel. 'You said it was a navigational aid. At least it might help us get out of here.'

'Talking of getting out of here,' shivered Ludo, 'you don't happen to have a boat tucked away in your drawers, do you?'

'I have indeed. A small but adequate dinghy. I wouldn't have embarked on such a quest unless I was properly equipped. But until we can dry out a bit there's no hope of extracting it. Sorry.' Cassetti shrugged.

'So we're stuck,' said Wren, 'in more ways than one.

We need something to help us dry out. Then we can concentrate on working out what that watch-thing really is. What've we got between us? Turn out your pockets.'

Apart from the watch (or whatever it was), two waterlogged pistols and the boatswain's whistle that Ludo had won, there was only Mel's feather.

'Not a very inspiring collection, is it?' said Mel. 'We're probably going to die of boredom before we dry out.'

'I nearly forgot these.' Ludo pulled a pack of very soggy cards from inside his doublet. 'Let's have a round of cards. It'll cheer us up.' He saw the looks on his friends' faces. 'All right, no betting.' He attempted to shuffle them. 'They're too wet to play a game. Why don't we just cut? Highest card gets the first blanket out of Cassetti's drawers.' But as Ludo attempted to cut the deck they all stuck together.

'I know.' Ludo peeled off each card and laid them face down in rows. 'Just pick a card. Highest wins. Who's first?'

'Two of salamanders,' said Wren, turning her choice.

'Bad luck, my dear. Five of starfish.'

'Prince of ravens! Beat that, Mel.'

As Mel reached towards his chosen card the watch-thing sounded a sad chime. 'That's odd.' He withdrew his hand and the chiming ceased. He reached for another card and the same thing happened. Mel reached out towards a third card and the happy tune rang from the device. He looked up at Cassetti. His eyes were twinkling and a silver lining appeared around his wig. Mel picked up the card and turned it over. 'King of porcupines.' He looked at his friends in amazement.

Ludo scowled. 'That was a fluke. Let's go again. Me first. King of ravens. The only card that can beat that is the jester.'

Cassetti drew the seven of ravens and Wren the four of porcupines. As soon as Mel reached for the cards the sad chimes tinkled. He passed his open hand over the rows of cards until the jaunty chime sounded. He flipped the card. 'The jester!'

'You're cheating,' said Ludo.

'Look who's talking,' said Wren.

'I'm *not* cheating,' insisted Mel. 'It's the watch-thing. It seems to know where the winning cards are.' Mel opened it. The dials looked as they had before. 'Everyone put your cards back and pick another.' There were two fives and, inevitably, a queen for Ludo. Mel passed his hand over the cards again as he watched the dials. The one with the backwards clock ticked quickly towards twelve o'clock. The lower left dial pointed to the right hand side of the cards and the remaining dial flipped between six and twelve o'clock. Each time it registered six, it chimed sadly and at twelve, brightly. Mel moved his hand to the right. When it chimed the happy chime, Mel flipped the card. 'King of ravens!' Mel was amazed. 'That means . . . That means . . .'

'Is it some kind of . . . of . . . fortune-teller?' said Ludo.

'No, not that,' said Mel.

'It's some kind of luck-guesser then,' said Wren.

'No, it's more than a guess; somehow it *knows*. It's more of a . . . *luck-compass!*' exclaimed Mel. He looked at Cassetti.

A ray of sunshine shone from Cassetti's wig.

'So what're you saying, Mel?' asked Wren. 'That the happy chime's for good luck and the sad one's for bad?'

'I think it's more sophisticated than that. Look, this dial here shows the direction or where luck is – just like a compass. This one like a backwards clock shows when the luck's going to happen and this other one the kind of luck. Twelve o'clock's for good luck, six o'clock's for bad and the bits in between are for the strength of the luck. You know; towards the bottom's increasingly bad and towards the top's increasingly good. To get the good luck chimes or the bad luck ones all the pointers have to agree.'

'Well done, Mel,' said Cassetti. 'When His Majesty the king of Cumulus gave it to me before I began my quest it took me several hours to figure out what it was. He told me it would lead me to Nephonia's saviours. Just remember to keep it wound up.'

'You know, we're never going to be poor again,' said Ludo. 'With this luck-compass we could –'

'I don't think it's meant for gambling, my dear,' said

Cassetti. 'That would be an ignoble use for such a wondrous object.'

'Oh? No, of course not.' Ludo looked disappointed.

'We have to use it to help Cassetti and the people of Nephonia,' said Mel.

'After we've used it to get off this stinking island.' Ludo sneezed.

'I most heartily agree,' said Cassetti.

'Why don't we search the island?' said Wren. 'Maybe we'll find some flotsam or jetsam or whatever it's called.'

The island was not very big and all they managed to find was a collection of dry driftwood from old casks and packing cases.

'What do you suppose these grooves are?' asked Ludo.

Wren examined the driftwood by the light of the feather. 'I'm not sure. Some kind of gouge marks?'

'They look more like teeth marks,' said Cassetti.

Ludo laughed nervously. 'Don't be silly. They're much too big for teeth marks.'

Everyone turned and scanned the darkness.

'Let's keep searching,' said Wren. 'Maybe we

missed something useful. If only it wasn't so dark.'

'I've got a better idea.' Mel flipped open the luck-compass. 'The pointer thing's pointing this way.'

'What's the strength hand say?' asked Ludo.

'It's about halfway. No, wait; it's moving up. Come on. Over here. Now it's near the top.'

'Ouch!' Wren tumbled over a small cask.

'Oh, it's just some more wood,' said Ludo. 'Let's take it anyway. We can burn it with the other driftwood when Cassetti's tinder box has dried out. *Offff!* It's heavy. It's full of something. Hang on, there's a bung here.' He prised open the stopper and sniffed it. 'It's rum. A tot of that will soon warm us up.'

'Better than that; it's inflammable,' said Wren. 'We can make a fire.'

'My dear, you're a genius,' said Cassetti.

'Hang on, though,' said Ludo. 'We still won't be able to light it until the tinder is dry.'

'Yes we can,' said Mel. 'We can use this.' He cocked and fired the empty flintlock pistol. There was a loud click and a bright spark.

In no time at all they had a roaring driftwood fire

going in the middle of the island. It smelled strongly of rum. Everyone stood around it, their clothes steaming.

'Ah, that's got it.' There was the scraping sound of one of Cassetti's drawers opening. 'How about some sausages?'

Soon the sausages were sizzling over the fire on driftwood skewers. Their delicious smell almost blocked out the stinking bilge water all around them.

'So where's this famous dinghy of yours then?' said Ludo, looking about.

'You couldn't take your eyes off the sausages,' said Mel. 'Cassetti's already assembled it. Look behind you.'

Just then the luck-compass began chiming from inside Mel's doublet where he had stashed it. It was the sad tune.

'Uh-oh. Look out there.' Ludo pointed out into the darkness. Staring at them were many pairs of huge, blood-red eyes. There came a loud squeaking sound. 'What're they?'

'Bilge-rats,' said Cassetti. Lightning flashed deep inside his wig. 'Giant, ravenous bilge-rats!'

Rat Power

'It must have been the fire that attracted them,' said Mel. 'Or the smell of the sausages.'

'Maybe it was the rum. Perhaps they're alcoholics; their eyes are bloodshot enough.' Ludo backed away and huddled closer to the others.

'It doesn't matter what attracted them,' said Wren. 'How do we *un*-attract them?'

'I don't think we'll be able to manage that, my dears. Now would be a good time to make use of my boat.' Cassetti was trying to act calm but the friends could tell he was as scared as they were.

'We're going to have to sail through them,' said Mel. 'They're all around us and they're getting closer.'

'Make some noise to scare them back a bit,' said Wren. 'We'll need room to launch the boat. *Yah-yah-yah-yah!*' She began to shout, picking up two pieces of driftwood and beating them together.

Mel did the same while Cassetti hurriedly loaded and primed the pistols with some gunpowder and balls from one of his drawers.

All the while, the sad chimes of the luck-compass continued.

The eyes continued to stare at them balefully, unperturbed by the rumpus.

Ludo began to beat the empty rum cask with one hand and brought out the boatswain's whistle with the other.

'Will that work? It doesn't make any sound,' said Wren as she beat her pieces of wood even harder.

'Those sea-dogs could hear it.' Ludo blew a silent blast. 'There! Look!'

There was a panicked squealing and splashing and the red eyes vanished.

'They *hate* it,' said Ludo triumphantly.

'The big question is, do they hate it more than they love the smell of sausages?' said Mel as the rats reappeared. He pulled a length of burning driftwood from the fire and waved it in front of him like a sword.

'I don't think they'll settle for sausages,' said Cassetti. 'Come on; time we were off. Help me launch the dinghy.'

Mel tried to still his trembling hand as he knelt in the bow, holding his driftwood torch aloft to light their way while Cassetti frantically pulled on the oars. Wren and Ludo sat at the stern, each clutching a pistol and looking over their shoulders across the black water at the diminishing island and its flickering fire. As they watched, the friends saw rats as big as dogs crawl from the bilge water and on to the island. They grabbed the cooking sausages in a shower of sparks and fought savagely with each other until the food was consumed. Then, one by one, the rats came down to the water's edge and stared after the dinghy. As if they had heard a starting gun, they all dived in and began swimming rapidly after it.

Mel licked his dry lips and struggled to gain control of his too-rapid breathing. He felt sick with fear. Ludo and Wren looked no better.

'Don't shoot until you see the reds of their eyes,' said Ludo with forced bravado.

'We've only got one shot each,' said Wren, 'and there're dozens of rats. I don't suppose you've got anything in your drawers that could help us?'

'I wish I had.' Cassetti rowed harder.

'Steer to the right,' said Mel. The chimes had ceased and he was consulting the luck-compass.

The dinghy swung around.

'No, the other right,' said Mel.

'Sorry,' said Cassetti. 'I'm sitting the wrong way round.'

'I think we need to keep going this way for about an hour.'

'An *hour!*' said Wren and Ludo.

'That's what this says,' said Mel.

Cassetti sighed. 'If our luck's that far away, we're going to need something else to tide us over.' His cloud-wig darkened.

Mel suddenly had an idea. 'Have you got a rope?' he asked Cassetti. 'Here, take this.' He passed his flaming torch to Wren.

'That I can do.' Cassetti stopped rowing and opened one of his drawers. He handed a large coil to Mel, who tied a noose in the end.

As he took up the oars again, Mel said, 'No. Stop rowing.'

'Mel! Have you gone mad?' cried Wren.

'You're all going to have to trust me on this one.'

'Well, if you're sure this is going to work,' said Cassetti.

The boat drifted to a standstill.

'I don't like this,' said Ludo. 'I hope you know what you're doing.'

There was an ominous splashing as the rats circled the dinghy, spiralling closer. Ludo and Wren, eyes wide with fear, cocked their pistols. Ludo raised the whistle to his lips with a shaky hand.

'No, Ludo. Don't blow the whistle.' Mel began to swing the lasso around over his head. 'Not yet.'

The rats circled ever closer. As they swam in and out of the light cast by the burning brand, they appeared even bigger, their eyes even redder, their teeth even longer. They were nearly up to the boat, their soaking fur and whiskers clearly visible. Their musky rat-smell was evident, despite the stink of the bilge water. Ludo and Wren fired their pistols, shooting two between the eyes but the others, undaunted, kept advancing. The friends shrank back inside the frail dinghy and as far from the gunwales as they could get. One of the rats lunged at the boat, its savage jaws snapping just inches from Cassetti's arm. The dinghy rocked violently, threatening to capsize as the creature splashed back into the water. Ahead of them, one of the rats raised its head for another attack and Mel cast his rope, ensnaring the giant rodent around the neck. The panicked creature thrashed about as it attempted to free itself. Mel quickly secured the free end of the rope to a cleat on the bow. 'Hold tight, everyone. Now, Ludo! Blow your whistle!'

Ludo realised at once what Mel was up to. He put the whistle to his lips and blew hard. The rats reacted to the silent blast as if they had been scalded and shot off away from the dinghy, squealing loudly. The remainder of the rope, which lay coiled at Mel's feet, rapidly unwound and snapped taut. The boat took off as if rocket-powered. Mel and Cassetti were thrown backwards on top of Wren and Ludo.

'Here, use the rudder.' Cassetti disentangled himself and lifted a rudder from the bottom of the boat. Ludo fitted it in place and he and Wren grabbed the tiller, handing the flaming torch back to Mel.

Mel held the torch up and saw the remainder of the pack swimming after them in the boat's wake. He picked his way around Cassetti and regained his position in the bow, flipping the luck-compass open with his other hand. 'Left a bit . . . a bit more . . . a bit more . . .That's it! Keep going this way and we'll be there in . . . five minutes at this speed.'

Ludo blew his whistle each time their pace slackened, keeping the rat swimming as fast as it would go. 'This is great. We've got a one rat-power motor.'

When the luck-compass indicated that they had come far enough, Mel cast off the rope and Cassetti took up the oars. Mel guided them towards a flight of wooden steps.

'I recognise where we are, my dears. Follow me. The picture that brought me here is this way.' Cassetti led the friends between huge crates and bales stacked as tall as houses. It was like walking through the narrow streets of Vlam. Eventually, at the end of a slim gangway stood a large canvas inside an opened packing crate. 'You obviously know how the gateways in the Mirrorscape work. Join hands.'

As they emerged they all felt the familiar pins and needles tingling that accompanied trips through a mirrormarked canvas. They blinked at the sudden bright light of the Arcadian landscape they found themselves standing in. The nauseating stench of the bilges was gone, replaced by fresh air and the sweet smell of grass. Everything was beautifully lit and perfectly composed, quite unlike the real world, where even the most idyllic landscape has its pockets of disorder. A herd of white deer with gilded antlers grazed on the nearby sward and rolling, forested hills rose up all around. Visible above the treetops were the fairytale pinnacles of a gleaming castle, its walls clothed in ivy. Everyone breathed a sigh of relief.

'The way back to Cumulus is through a picture in yonder castle,' said Cassetti. 'If we step out we should be there within the hour.' A rainbow had appeared in his wig.

'I'm sorry, but we can't come with you right now,' apologised Mel. 'We need to return to Vlam. Just for a while.'

'That's right,' said Ludo. 'We have to tell our master what the cloud really is. We have to warn him that it's dangerous.'

'And then we'll come and help you,' added Wren.

'What if this master of yours refuses to let you come back?' asked Cassetti.

'Then we'll come anyway,' said Ludo.

'That's a promise,' said Mel.

'Very well,' said Cassetti. 'This is where my quest ends and yours begins. I will return and report to the king that my mission was successful and that help is on the way. Goodbye, Mel. Goodbye, Wren. Goodbye, Ludo. We'll meet again soon.'

'Come on, you two,' said Mel, waving their new friend goodbye. 'I recognise this painting. It hangs in the House of Spirits. There must be a wall of mist around here somewhere.'

'We'll be back at the mansion within the hour,' said Wren.

'King of porcupines. Let me pick another. King of ravens! That's fourteen times in a row. By my giddy aunt, this device of yours is quite remarkable, Womper.'

It was evening and Mel, Ludo and Wren were standing in Ambrosius Blenk's private studio watching him pick cards from Ludo's pack. Ever since Mel had shown him the luck-compass he had been like a child with a new toy.

'About the mirrormark in the cloud over Vlam –'

'Ha! The jester!'

'What should we do, master?'

'Do? Why we could try making inkblots. With this kind of luck they would be bound to form recognisable shapes.'

'No, about the mirrormark. It's going to be getting bigger and bigger. Cassetti said Cumulus is being pulled down into it.'

Ambrosius Blenk stopped mixing ink and glanced up at Mel. 'A mirrormark, is it? What makes you so sure? When you've seen as many clouds as I have, Womper, you'll realise that they can adopt an amazing variety of forms.'

'But Cassetti said –'

The master waved his hand impatiently. 'All right,

supposing it is a mirrormark? What then?' He put down his paintbrush and turned to the friends. 'If there *is* a rift forming between the worlds then it's not something a bunch of children can fix, is it? No, your place is here, not gallivanting around in the Mirror-scape. You know what happened the last time you went there.'

'As I remember it, Mel rescued you from the High-Bailiff and the Fifth Mystery, got rid of that tyrant Lord Brool and changed everyone's life in Nem for the better.' Dirk Tot stood up, dwarfing everyone else in the studio.

Mel stared gratefully at Ambrosius Blenk's steward. He had become accustomed to the huge frame and horribly disfigured face that was so frightening to most people. The entire left-hand side looked as if it had melted.

'I also can't forget that without Mel, Ludo and Wren's intervention I would still be rotting in a dungeon in the House of Mysteries.' The giant placed his beautifully crafted artificial silver hand on Mel's shoulder.

The master picked up a larger brush and charged it to make an inkblot. 'And as for this conspiracy of the Ters, I'm sure my good friend the Maven would know about such an outrage. He would have stamped on it before now. I find it all unlikely.' He was trying to sound unconcerned but Mel could tell from his manner that he was as disturbed as he, Ludo and Wren were.

'Nephonia, eh?' continued Ambrosius Blenk. 'I've been there – once. Cumulus, I think it was. Or maybe Nimbus. Most disconcerting. The place keeps chopping and changing all the time. One moment you're in a palace, the next a hovel. Fascinating, mind you. Never a dull moment in Nimbulus. In fact, the Maven has some fine paintings of Nephonia by Midas Garf in his collection. Now *there's* an artist who could paint clouds. I met this Confetti of yours. He was one of Cumulus's most gifted cloud-sculptors. He could do amazing things with water vapour. He would take something that looked like an omelette and sculpt it into a dragon – and then back into a saucepan. All before you could say –'

'Master, I think this affair needs looking into,' interrupted Dirk Tot.

The master paused and looked up from his ink blots. 'Looking into? It most certainly does.' He stared at the friends. 'But not by these three. Their place is at work. Ceilings don't paint themselves, you know.'

'Perhaps if I were to ask Green and Blue to investigate?' suggested Dirk Tot.

'The former Rainbow Rebels? A splendid idea. Now that the unpleasantness with the Mysteries is over they're probably at a loose end. See to it at once, will you. If there is any trouble brewing they are more capable than these youngsters. An apprentice's place is with me in the Hall of Awakenings – *working*. Do we understand each other?'

'But, master, we promised Cassetti we'd go back.'

'The Mirrorscape is a dangerous place – or have you forgotten? What if something were to happen to you? No, you can't go. I need you all here. Art must come first – *always*. Without art there would be no Mirrorscape; don't forget that. I need everyone fresh for work. That's my final word. Now take your gizmo and go to supper. Work recommences first thing tomorrow.'

'But –' protested Mel.

'Now off with you.'

'I didn't think he wouldn't let us go,' said Ludo once they were outside.

'He thinks that if a bit of the Mirrorscape goes wrong that he can repair it with a few dabs of paint,' said Wren.

Mel shook his head. 'He won't be able to repair a wound between the worlds with a lick of paint. We all know what happens if the Mirrorscape gets mixed up with the real world. And demons are a lot worse than those colour-eating worms that we had to deal with last time.'

'*Shhhh.* Keep your voice down.' Wren gazed at the studio door. 'No one knows it was us.'

'We can't break our promise to Cassetti,' said Mel. 'He's counting on us.'

'All the master cares about is work,' said Ludo. 'Work, work, work. He's an old slave-driver.'

'That's a fine way to talk of your master.' Dirk Tot closed the door after him.

Ludo blushed. 'I'm sorry. I didn't mean to . . .'

'It's all right, Ludo. The master's very preoccupied with this commission. Artists sometimes get so tightly focused on details that they can lose sight of the bigger picture. Genius can be like that. But he's right about Green and Blue. If there *is* trouble brewing then they're the men for the job.'

'The master didn't actually say we *couldn't* go back into the Mirrorscape,' said Ludo.

'He didn't actually say we could, either.' Wren wrapped her blanket tighter around her.

'But what we do in our own time doesn't count,' said Ludo. 'Besides, how's he going to know?'

It was after three o'clock in the morning and Wren, Ludo and Mel had crept from their dormitories in their nightclothes to the semaphore tower that sat high atop Ambrosius Blenk's mansion. Their faces were lit from below by Mel's glowing quill. Through the tower's arched windows they could see the moonlit rooftops of Vlam all around and, jutting out over the tops of them, the dark, soaring silhouettes of the three Great Houses, studded here and there with lit windows. All of their attention was focused on the House of Spirits and the cloud above it.

'We promised Cassetti,' said Mel.

'He's counting on us to help. It's why he gave us the luck-compass. We can't let him down,' said Wren.

'It's cold. Let's all go back to bed,' said Ludo. 'We can discuss this in the morning.'

'Look; we know now that that cloud is leaking through from Nephonia. What we don't know is how or why. Even if Green and Blue are trying to find out more we could help them. What time did you hear that thunder last night?'

'I don't know, Mel. Very late,' said Wren.

'It's no longer very late,' said Ludo, yawning. 'It's now officially very early.'

'Don't, Ludo, you're making us all yawn,' said Wren, stifling one of her own.

'Yaaahhh.'

'That's not even a real yawn,' said Mel, trying not to laugh as he fought back a yawn of his own. 'We ought to –'

Then it happened. The hands on the luck-compass

that Mel was holding shifted downwards. For an instant, the world was turned a stark blue-white by the flash of a lightning bolt. The harsh, black shadows of the friends were painted around the inside of the tower. An instant later there was a deafening clap of thunder.

Wren blinked her green eyes rapidly. 'I saw it. I was looking right at it. The lightning hit the Paper Belfry.'

'Look,' said Mel.

'Now I can't see a thing.' Wren rubbed her eyes. 'What is it?'

'The swirling shape under the cloud's completed itself,' said Mel. 'It *is* a mirrormark!'

'Now there're things falling out of it,' said Ludo.

'What things? Demons?'

'No. Cloud-things,' said Mel. 'There're horses and boots and trees . . .'

'. . . And whales and pineapples and anvils,' continued Ludo. 'But they're all drifting away before they reach the ground.'

'It'd be beautiful if we didn't know what it really was,' said Wren as her eyesight returned to normal.

There came a second flash and then a third. This

time they came from a cloudless part of the sky.

'How can that happen? I've never seen lightning come from a clear sky before,' said Ludo as the thunder died away.

'It wasn't coming from the sky,' said Mel. 'It was coming from the Paper Belfry. The lightning was shooting up *into* the sky. The Ters are opening a second hole.'

Then, carried on the wind, came the echo of a chilling, inhuman howl. It was a sound that made the hair at the backs of their heads stand up. It chilled their blood.

'What was *that?*'

The Second Storm

The Paper Belfry

Inevitably, they overslept. As Mel, Ludo and Wren raced bleary-eyed towards the House of Spirits through streets choked with people, every window had a face in it. The entire population of Vlam seemed to be standing around transfixed by the never-ending cascade of shapes that fell from the spinning cloud hovering above the House of Spirits.

'Never in all my life . . .' said an elderly burger.

'Never in anyone's life,' said his companion. 'It's some kind of omen if you ask me.'

'An omen? I can see a camel but I can't spot an omen.' A passer-by scratched her head. 'What's one look like anyway?'

'I can't see.' A small girl tugged at her mother's skirts until she was lifted to see over the heads of the crowd. 'Mummy, Mummy, I can see a castle and a seahorse and, and, and – a tree.'

'Mummy, Mummy,' mimicked Ludo. 'I can see ghouls and demons and, and, and – they're ripping peoples' faces off.'

'*Shhh!* Shut up.' Wren dug her friend in the ribs with her elbow. 'It's not funny.'

By the time they arrived at the Hall of Awakenings and climbed up to the platform, the master and all of the other apprentices were already hard at work.

'And what time do you call this?' said Bex, shaking his head. 'Work starts at eight sharp.' Then, in a lower voice so that the other apprentices couldn't hear, 'Look, it's not fair on the others if you don't pull your weight. At least try and be on time from now on, OK?'

'Sorry, Bex,' said Mel.

'Yeah, sorry,' added Ludo.

At the end of a long day, the three weary friends slumped down in front of their niche and watched as everyone left the platform.

'I've been thinking,' said Wren. 'The lightning we saw was coming from somewhere here, in the House of Spirits. I bet it's causing the cloud-things. Maybe we'll find the answer to Cassetti's mystery in this Paper Belfry.'

'It's worth a try,' said Ludo. 'The master's been keeping his beady eyes on us all day. It might be easier than getting back into the Mirrorscape. I think he knows we're going to try and help Cassetti.'

'We won't be able to get in to the Ters' apartments by the front door again,' said Mel. 'That was just a fluke.'

'We could try and retrace our steps,' said Wren. 'You know, and come out of the painting in the hallway.'

'The rats, the flying machine, the boatswain, the press gang? My dears, I don't think so,' said Ludo, imitating Cassetti. Then, in his own voice, 'Anyway, we promised the master we wouldn't go back into the Mirrorscape. Well, *kind* of.'

'That only leaves us one other way,' said Mel. 'We'll have to go in through the window.'

'Get real, will you,' said Ludo. 'We're hundreds of feet up in the air.'

'If you can think of another way, then tell me.'

'What about . . . about . . . Oh, *scrot!*' said Ludo.

'"Scrot" about sums it up,' said Wren. 'Mel's right. I don't like the idea but I can't think of another way.'

It proved easier than any of them expected – at least to begin with. They found an unlocked door that led them out on to an open-air terrace. One side looked out over the city and the other had a sheer wall many storeys high. Above it they could see the underside of the slowly rotating mirrormark cloud. They followed the terrace and then climbed several flights of stairs until they stood before a door in a turret.

'It's locked.' Mel tried putting his shoulder to the sturdy door but it would not budge. 'It seemed too good to be true.' He went to the terrace wall and leaned out.

'You weren't thinking of . . . No, of course you weren't.' Ludo laughed nervously. 'What now?'

'Try the luck-compass,' suggested Wren. 'You never know.'

Mel flipped it open.

'Well?' said Ludo. 'What's it say?'

Mel crossed back to the wall.

'Oh, no,' said Ludo. 'Mel, tell me it's not . . .'

'Yes it is. There's a ledge down there. It runs all the way around the turret.'

'Hang on,' said Wren. 'I didn't hear it chime.'

'It didn't,' said Mel. 'The luck-hand's at about three o'clock – but the other hand's definitely pointing this way.'

'*Three o'clock!* That means there's only a fifty-fifty chance.' Ludo shook his head.

'Fifty-fifty's all we've got,' said Mel. 'Maybe it'll get better as we go along.'

'And maybe it'll get worse,' said Ludo.

Mel eased out over the parapet and let himself down. 'The ledge is wider than it looks and there're sculpted bosses we can use as handholds. Come on if you're coming. It'll be all right as long as you don't look down,' he said, sounding braver than he felt.

Reluctantly, Wren and Ludo joined him. All three stood on the narrow ledge, facing the wall with their arms outstretched like a string of cut-out paper dolls. They edged their way around the bulge of the turret as the wind tugged at their clothing. Then, the luck-compass slung around Mel's neck began chiming. It was the sad chime. Mel reached his hand up for another handhold and a pigeon shot from a hidden cranny with a noisy flapping of wings. He tottered and overbalanced and began to fall backwards.

'Got you!' Ludo grabbed his doublet with the hand that was not gripping a sculpted boss. For an instant both boys tottered on the ledge before Ludo managed to pull them both back.

'Thanks. That was close.' Mel's stomach resumed its former place and his heart beat less wildly. He found his handhold again and edged further round the ledge. 'Ah!'

Ludo watched, aghast, as Mel jumped from the ledge. '*Mel!*'

'It's all right. There's a roof here.'

Tentatively, Ludo looked down and then jumped the short distance to land beside his friend. Wren jumped down after them. The roof stretched up before them like some kind of sloping, leaden sports field. Rising from the city-side edge on their left was a row of slender, intricately carved spires and springing from them, high over their heads, were flying buttresses thrusting against a soaring wall to their right. In the centre of the wall was a huge, circular stained glass window. Apart from the friends it was the only patch of colour on the grey roofscape.

Mel led Wren and Ludo as they crawled up the roof slope to a ledge at the base of the wall. 'Here, Ludo, give me a leg up.' He stepped into the stirrup formed by Ludo's cupped hands and stood up. He was just tall enough to peer over the base of the window.

'What can you see?' asked Wren.

'Not a lot. The stained glass is very thick. It looks like some sort of hall but everything's distorted.' Mel stepped down. 'We'll have to get up to that little row of windows just under the roof.'

Ludo craned his neck to look up. He looked back at Mel and followed his gaze to the spires and then up and across the flying buttresses. 'Oh, no. You're not thinking . . .'

'It won't be that bad,' said Mel. 'Look, the spires are covered with tracery and carving. There're lots of handholds. Then we can use a flying buttress like a bridge.'

'Let's do it now; before our courage fails us,' said Wren.

Ludo gulped. 'What about if you haven't got any courage to begin with?'

The friends slid down the slope of the roof to the spires and then began to climb over writhing monsters frozen in stone, thrusting their booted feet into gaping mouths and grasping tails and horns as they hauled themselves upwards. When he reached the flying buttress at the top, Mel straddled it as if it were a horse. Very slowly he stood up. Then, arms outstretched like a tightrope walker, he carefully walked up the incline towards the windows. The surface was covered with pigeon droppings and halfway across he almost slipped.

'Careful!' called Ludo.

'Thanks for reminding me.' Mel went even slower until he reached the wall. 'It's all right as long as you . . .'

'. . . Don't look down,' said Wren as she and Ludo followed him. 'Yeah, we *know*.'

They knelt side by side on the narrow ledge underneath the windows. All around them hideous stone gargoyles gaped, open-mouthed, at the city far below. Ludo made a gargoyle face and Wren giggled as much with relief as at Ludo's hopeless attempt. Mel pushed at a window and it opened inwards. He consulted the luck-compass, made a fifty-fifty rocking gesture with his hand and crawled in.

The friends dropped down on to a narrow walkway that ran the length of a hall. Although not as grand as the Hall of Awakenings, it was still a sickeningly long way down to the patterned, mosaic floor. The foreshortened shapes of several Ters could be seen below. The walkway supported a row of flagstaffs that jutted out horizontally. Hanging from them were banners with vivid heraldic devices. Just above their heads were the intricately carved beams of the ceiling and, suspended in the centre, three huge, iron candelabra that looked like dead spiders lying on their backs, legs in the air.

Ludo rapped on the wall. 'This doesn't feel like paper.'

'I don't think we've climbed high enough yet,' said Wren quietly. 'It must be somewhere up there.' She waved her hand towards the beams.

'There's a door at the end of the walkway. Come on.' Mel led them along the gallery, stepping over the flagstaffs. 'Keep down. We mustn't be seen.'

'Thanks for reminding me,' said Ludo.

They pushed open the door to find a tight spiral staircase. When they got to the top there was another open doorway. They could hear women's voices. Mel put his finger to his lips, consulted the luck-compass and motioned his friends forward.

They emerged on to a small minstrel's gallery set high up on a wall covered with ornate, moss-covered statuary.

'That's funny,' whispered Mel. 'Moss growing inside a building.'

Wren put her finger to her lips and pointed below them.

The gallery overlooked a strange, windowless chamber lit by the flickering light of many free-standing candelabra.

'Look at all that scaffolding,' whispered Wren.

'If that's scaffolding,' said Mel, 'it was put up by a madman.'

Wooden beams and poles of all different lengths and thicknesses were lashed together at crazy angles in an improvised, haphazard pattern. It looked like a giant bundle of sticks that had been dropped and frozen in mid-fall. It seemed to be holding the walls and ceiling in place.

'That's odd,' said Ludo. 'I thought I saw the walls move.'

'Me too,' said Mel. 'They seem very flimsy.'

On the floor beneath the scaffolding about a dozen grey-robed Ters were busy. Some were tearing pages from stacks of books and piling them up. Behind them was a heap of empty, discarded covers. Others were taking bundles of torn pages and mounting ladders to stick them to the wall with large brushes and buckets of paste. The resulting wallpaper was as crazy as the scaffolding, with pages of script juxtaposed with upside-down illustrations next to sideways sheets of musical notation alongside wonky pages of maps.

In the centre of the chamber was what looked like a giant sculpture. Three elaborately carved and highly polished brass snakes intertwined with each other in a triple spiral to form a long, twisted tube shape. Nestling within them were many large, egg-shaped coloured crystals. A weird collection of planet-like spheres projected above it, and spaced around it were a battery of concave mirrors mounted on gimbals that allowed them to be twisted in all directions. At the end near the snakes' tails were a number of pivoted lenses in front of a large, shallow cage and some kind of furnace with a glass reservoir on top. Running from the cage were gutters with sluices at intervals that led to large, shallow bowls set into a mosaic floor in the shape of a palette. Two seats with levers and wheels were mounted either side of the sculpture. At the rear of the chamber, almost directly under the gallery, was a large capstan. From above it looked like a spindly starfish.

'I didn't realise there were so many Ters,' said Mel. 'And look. They've all got that funny hairstyle Fa Theum mentioned. It's all combed over their right ears.'

'So now what do we do?' whispered Ludo.

'There's another door back here,' said Wren.

They left the gallery by the second door and descended another narrow staircase that ended in a closed door. Mel tried it but it was locked. 'Dead end.'

'Well, we've found the Paper Belfry,' said Wren, 'and where the stolen books ended up. But why should they be papering the walls with pages torn from books? It must be the most expensive wallpaper in history.'

'Maybe they're using them for insulation?' said Ludo.

Mel shrugged. 'I should imagine that's the last thing they were thinking of. And whoever heard of a belfry without any bells? Come on, we can think about all this later. Let's go back. It'll be getting dark soon. I don't fancy trying to climb back down in the dark.'

'Oh, no,' said Ludo, dismayed. 'I was counting on finding another way out.'

'Well, maybe there is,' said Mel as he led them back up the spiral staircase.

Suddenly, the luck-compass slung around Mel's neck began its sad chiming.

They stopped and exchanged worried glances. Mel quickly muffled the chiming with his doublet until it ceased. Then, as quietly as possible they continued. As they neared the top they could hear two female voices. They sounded close. Mel edged further up and peered around the final twist of the spiral. Standing on the gallery and staring down at the activity below were the two Ters they had seen carrying the stolen books. They now had their cowls thrown back and Mel could see that the big Ter had spiky, brown hair brushed to one side. She wore spectacles with iron frames and lenses as thick as the bottom of a bottle. Behind them her eyes were magnified enormously. Above the glasses hovered a single eyebrow. Her long arms gave her an ape-like appearance. She looked very strong. The small Ter had very pale skin like old parchment and wispy grey hair. Her shiny skull was visible through it and her skeletal hands were like talons.

'What a shambles, Mudge,' said the big Ter.

'It doesn't matter how untidy it is, Tunk. As long as the Serpent is hidden from view until it's completed its task. The second storm is brewing. It will be ready soon.'

'More than pretty cloud-shapes next time, eh?'

'Oh, much more if our friends in the Mirrorscape have their coordinates right.'

'I hear those fools in the city have been –'

'You there! Yes, you Ter Dern,' shouted the grey-haired Ter. 'More paper to your right. I can see daylight through the wall. The illusion must be kept intact. The last thing we want is masons up here seeking to repair the non-existent stonework.'

'I can deal with nosy parkers, Mudge.'

'I've no doubt of that, Tunk.'

'I'd break their legs and then their arms. Then, I'd suck their eyes out and –'

'Calm down, Tunk, calm down. No one's going to come sniffing around here. You won't need to go breaking anyone. Not while there's the Morg.'

'The mistress cares more for the Morg than she does for us. We're her friends, not him.'

'Stop that! You must keep that jealousy of yours under control. The mistress loves us all – in her own way – and the Morg's necessary for the work to come. Soon there'll be a new Morg. Meanwhile, we're here to ensure there's no slacking. There's to be a test firing of the Serpent just as soon as it's dark and it's been fed. It's a risk firing it so early but one of our allies wants to see that it's working properly now the crystals have been re-aligned. If it works there'll be a storm to remember later. It could even open the second wound. We've amassed quite a larder for the Serpent. Enough to keep it fed until all three wounds are open.'

'What are they up to?' whispered Wren.

Mel shook his head.

Ludo shrugged.

The friends were forced to wait in agonising silence for an hour or more without fidgeting or even breathing too loudly as the two Ters remained on the gallery, directing their sisters below. Eventually, the friends heard the two women leave by the other door. They crept back up to the gallery.

'Now what?' said Ludo, easing his stiff legs. 'It'll be dark outside by now. It looks like we're stuck here for the night.'

'I've a feeling that we're about to find out what that serpent-thing is for,' said Mel. 'Look.'

All of the decorating materials had been tidied away and now the Ters were busy around the Serpent. Two of them were feeding the empty book bindings into the open jaws of the furnace, while another two were filling the reservoir with an amber liquid from large carboys. When this was complete, one put a match to the book covers and closed the doors. Her companion began to work a pump attached to the side. Bubbles appeared in the reservoir and the furnace began to roar.

As the friends continued to observe the goings-on below them, a painting was carried into the Paper Belfry. It depicted a magnificent sunset, the sky streaked with deep purple, fire-red and gold. Beneath this was a strange and beautiful orchard. The leaves of each tree were alive with fire like brightly glowing embers. They seemed to threaten the splendour of the sky with their fiery magnificence. In the background rose a seven-tiered mountain with waterfalls cascading down its flanks like silver curtains. Two Ters lifted the large canvas and secured it upright in the shallow cage and closed the doors. Even from their high angle the friends could see the luminous quality of the picture.

'That looks like –' gasped Mel.

'It is,' said Ludo. 'It's one of the master's paintings. He sold it to the Maven last year. It's one of a set on the same theme.'

'It's a masterpiece,' whispered Wren. 'What're they going to do with it?'

Ter Mudge and Ter Tunk appeared in the room and mounted the Serpent, taking the seats at either side. The roaring of the furnace grew louder. One by one the candles were extinguished. The only light in the room was that leaking from the furnace door and diffused through the bubbling reservoir. There were some shouted orders and a number of Ters moved to the capstan and took up their positions on the arms. On a command they began to march round, turning it. There was the creaking sound of ropes stretching and then the squealing of pulleys moving and a low rumbling. Slowly, the flimsy walls and ceiling of the chamber began to move like the stage scenery they were. Little by little, the city came into view as the entire Paper Belfry was hauled aside, leaving only the Serpent in place. Streetlights twinkled far below and the tall, spangled forms of the House of Mysteries and House of Thrones appeared.

Mel, Ludo and Wren looked at each other in the dim light leaking up from below and then back at the choreographed movements of the Ters. The capstan stopped and the walls became stationary. It was clear that the entire Paper Belfry had been constructed against the outer wall of the House of Spirits. That explained the moss.

The murmur of voices ceased abruptly as a tall, cowled figure emerged on to the darkness of what was now an open-air platform. She was leading some kind of large, lumpen animal on a leash. At her side was a small cloaked figure no taller than a child. He had his cloak drawn around him and his cowl pulled forward, hiding his face.

'Very well, sisters. Continue.' The tall woman had a refined, melodious voice. 'We must be quick.'

Ter Tunk and Ter Mudge began turning wheels and pulling levers at the side of the Serpent. The furnace door swung open and a shaft of searing bright light pierced the darkness. More wheels were turned and the pivoted lenses swung down, intensifying the beam even more. The spheres above began to rotate in a complicated celestial dance. Levers were pulled and the gimballed mirrors intercepted the beam and focused it back on to the caged painting. For a moment nothing happened and then the surface began to smoke. Minute adjustments were made to the mirrors and the canvas began to bubble and blister. Then, to the friends' horror, it began to melt. Starting with the reds and oranges and progressing to the greens and blues, the image began to dissolve. As slow as poured treacle, months and months of Ambrosius Blenk's masterly brushwork melted in glutinous streaks down the canvas like fat, coloured slugs. As the streaks reached the bottom of the picture the molten paint was channelled into the gutters where it flowed along like rainbow lava. As one colour passed, sluices were closed, directing the next hue into another channel, gradually reducing the masterpiece to its component parts and filling the bowls of the mosaic palette with liquid colour.

After a while there was just a blank canvas standing naked in the cage. But still the light scorched on. Then the mirrormark that the master had first applied to the canvas began to glow white on white. On a shouted command the mirrors and lenses were rotated to new positions and the white-hot mirrormark flowed off the canvas into the remaining channel. As it reached a crucible in the centre of the palette another lens was lowered, focusing the pure white light on to a prism within the Serpent. The separated rainbow beams of light each hit a similarly coloured crystal. They began to glow. One after the other they lit up and a low hum mounted in intensity until a loud detonation filled the air. A jitterbug streak of lightning exploded from the mouth of the Serpent, turning everything into stark monochrome for an instant. As the thunder died away a hideous howl echoed from below. Up in the sky the friends saw that a cloud had begun to take shape.

At the sound of a handclap the Paper Belfry was hauled back into place and the candles relit. Everything was silent. The small figure said something to the tall woman in a gravelly voice. He sounded pleased.

Then, up in the minstrel's gallery and audible to everyone, Mel's luck-compass began to chime its sad tune.

'Uh, oh,' said Ludo softly. 'Now we're in it.'

There was the dreadful howl again.

'The Morg scents demons!' called the beautiful voice. 'The mirror. Up there.' A Ter grabbed one of the gimballed mirrors and twisted it. The beam of white light swept round, picking out the minstrel's gallery and on it, like actors frozen in a spotlight, stood

Mel, Wren and Ludo, their shadows black and huge behind them on the wall.

Beauty and the Beast

In the second before the sweeping beam dazzled him Mel just had time to see the woman who had spoken and her creature: beauty and the beast.

Beauty was the most beautiful woman Mel had ever seen. The grey robe she wore seemed to enhance her figure where it served to disguise those of the other Ters. She was tall and slim and stood upright with the grace and poise of a dancer. She had a straight nose, a flawless pale complexion and lustrous black hair framed by the drape of her cowl. She seemed a portrait of perfection. She raised her head to look at Mel, and as she did so the colour of her eyes changed from blue to green to lavender.

The beast was hideous in every respect. Squat. Misshapen. Filthy. Any humanity he might once have had lay hidden beneath his deformed appearance. He was naked apart from a dirty loincloth and every muscle stood out as clearly as an anatomical diagram. His pale body was covered in hundreds of red scars, each in the shape of some arcane symbol. As he crouched on the floor it was as if his misshapen spine was trying to burst through his flesh. He was crowned with an unruly mane of matted red hair that grew down his neck and ended in a point halfway down his back. Long, broken teeth protruded from his mouth at eccentric angles and spittle glistened on his stubbly chin. His amber eyes were cunning, mean and pitiless.

Beauty reached down with her long, elegant fingers and unfastened his leash. 'Morg. *Seek.*'

'Mel! *Come on!*' Mel was snapped from his trance by Wren's urgent shout and the beast's terrifying howl.

The Morg leapt from the floor up into the scaffolding with one prodigious bound. He swung though the maze of poles with the agility of an ape until he landed on the minstrel's gallery. He lowered his snout to the floor and scented which door his quarry had left by. With another howl, he set off in pursuit on all fours.

The friends made it to the walkway above the hall and hurdled the flagstaffs until they reached the window they had entered by. Mel slammed it shut after them. In the night the flying buttress they had climbed up was indistinct. It seemed to vault out into nothing.

'We can't go back that way,' said Wren. 'It'd be suicide.'

'This way then. There's just enough light coming from inside to see where we're going.' Mel led them along the narrow ledge that ran in front of the row of windows. They followed it around the apse-like curve of the hall. Behind them they heard the smashing of glass and the dreadful howl again.

The Morg squatted on the ledge, sniffing for his prey. He picked up two trails. One led along the ledge and another over the flying buttress. He chose the second. By the time he reached the far end he scented that the trail was old and retraced his path. When he regained the window ledge he loped off at speed after the friends.

The ledge ran out where the hall abutted the bulk of the House of Spirits. To Mel's right stood a row of seven giant statues of former Mavens protruding in high-relief from the wall above the Hall of Awakenings. Underneath them was a long, long drop to the rooftops below. He tried not to look.

Ludo came to a halt behind him. 'Quick, Mel. The whatsit,' he panted.

Mel flipped open the luck-compass and tilted it to read it by the light behind him. The ruby seemed to wink at him as it caught the light. The direction-hand pointed out over the statues. The strength-hand was rising. 'Ten o'clock. Good enough. It says this way.'

'Are you *sure?*' asked Ludo.

'Cassetti said it's never wrong. We have to trust it. We don't have any other choice – unless you want to go back that way.'

'*That* way? No way!' said Ludo.

Mel went first. If the statues had been closer together it would have been like using their heads as stepping-stones. As it was they were more like leaping-stones. The night wind was blowing harder now in strong eddies around the towering building and each time he landed he had to wave his arms to maintain his balance. His legs were wobbly and the Maven's heads slippery. He felt sick with fear. When he reached the fourth Maven he paused and looked behind him.

Ludo had made it to the third figure's head. 'Don't stop.'

'Where's Wren?'

Ludo turned. 'Wren? *Wren!*'

Wren stood cowering on the ledge, her back pressed to the wall. Crouching in front of her was the Morg. The creature moved towards her.

Mel shouted, 'Wren, this way. *Jump!*'

She edged sideways and tried to leap to the first statue but her foot slipped. Her other leg buckled beneath her and she toppled off the ledge, arms flailing.

'*No!*' screamed Mel.

As quick as lightning, the Morg reached out and grabbed Wren's wrist. She hung there swaying, looking up into his feral, amber eyes, smelling his rank breath. Slowly and effortlessly, he pulled her up until she was standing on the ledge once more. He cocked his head to one side like a dog and looked at her more closely. He moved forward and sniffed and then put out his callused hand and stroked her leg. Drool hung like a spider's thread from his chin. Wren tried to back away even more but was already flat against the wall. Then the Morg reached out and picked her up and, with surprising gentleness, lifted her across to the first statue.

'Did you see that?' said Ludo. 'He's *helping* her.'

Mel was as astonished as his friend. 'I saw it but I still don't believe it.'

'Quickly, Wren. This way,' shouted Ludo.

When the three of them reached the relative safety of another ledge at the end of the row of statues they looked back. The Morg was sitting still staring at them, the light of the hall behind him. He made no sign of following them.

'Scrot, that was close,' said Ludo. 'What do you make of that Morg-thing helping you like that?'

'It was horrible. It stank. And it *touched* me.' Wren shuddered and began to wipe her wrist against her doublet. 'I can't bear to even look at it.' She turned away.

Keeping one eye on the ghastly creature, Mel consulted the luck-compass. 'This seems to say we're safe.' He looked back at the Morg. He knew that it could easily leap over the statues if it chose, but it just sat there staring at Wren.

'*Please*, can we get out of here?' pleaded Wren. '*Now*.'

*

Later that night, in a spacious but otherwise austerely furnished chamber deep in the House of Spirits, sat the beautiful woman in the grey robe. The Morg lay at her feet. There was a knock on the door.

'Come.'

The door opened. 'Mistress?'

'Ter Mudge. Come in. Have you brought him?'

'Yes, mistress.' The small Ter entered, followed by the bulky figure of Ter Tunk. She held a young boy of no more than seven or eight years old, who struggled in her vice-like grasp. Plainly terrified, he was dirty and dressed only in a grubby loincloth. He was emaciated and his red hair was matted against his skull. All down one arm and across his shoulders were the raw scabs of recently inflicted wounds, shaped like arcane letters or symbols.

'Bring him here.'

Ter Tunk dragged the frightened child in front of her mistress and forced him to his knees. The Morg looked up listlessly, sniffed in the boy's direction and then lay his head back down on his crossed arms.

The beautiful woman reached out and touched the boy's face. He winced and tried to turn away but Ter Tunk's strong hands grabbed his hair and wrenched him back as he was forced to endure the touch of those long, delicate fingers. She held his chin and lifted his face. 'What is your name?' Her voice was soft and gentle.

The boy whimpered, his glance flitting between the beautiful woman and the Morg.

'Answer the mistress,' said Ter Tunk as she pulled his hair.

'Je . . . Jenk.'

'*Wrong answer!*' screamed the beautiful woman with the shriek of a harpy as she struck him hard across the face. Then, in her soft voice, 'What is your name?'

'Jenk.'

'*Wrong answer!*' Another blow, even harder.

'What is your –'

'Tell me what you want me to say. Just tell me and I'll say it,' gasped Jenk.

Another painful slap. 'You must tell me yourself. Now, what is your name?'

The boy exploded into tears. 'I don't know. I don't *know!*' He struggled to free himself from Ter Tunk's merciless grip.

'He's not ready,' said the beautiful woman. 'Time for another lesson. Ter Mudge!'

'Yes, mistress.' The small Ter opened a large book on an ornate lectern. 'Bring him here.'

Ter Tunk dragged the struggling boy over to her companion and again forced him to his knees. Ter Mudge took up an implement that looked like a cross between a pen and some exotic surgical instrument, its nib a long, tapering blade. 'Where were we?' She turned the pages of the book. 'Ah, yes.' She raised the instrument. 'This is the sixty-sixth letter of your name.' The boy swooned as she lowered the tool. 'Hold him up, Tunk. How can I be expected to write if he's like that?'

'He's fainted, Mudge.' Ter Tunk let the limp body fall to the floor.

The beautiful woman clapped her hands. 'Enough! This is hopeless. How can I be expected to make another Morg if all you bring me are insipid weaklings?'

'But, mistress –'

'How dare you interrupt me!' shouted the beautiful woman. 'Have you forgotten your vows?'

'No, mistress.' Ter Mudge bowed her head. Ter Tunk did the same.

'That's better. If you remember your vows then you'll know why we must have a demon-sniffer.'

'Ter Morgana, the founder of our order, ordained that the sisterhood should always have a demon-sniffer. A creature that could seek out any demons that threatened us.' Ter Mudge recited the creed in a monotone.

'Go on.'

'She set out the ritual for creating Morgs. The red hair is to honour her fiery locks and his true name must be spelled out on his body in blood.'

'And remind me of just why that is.'

'So that Ter Morgana is forever here with us in spirit, mistress.'

'Bless her memory,' said the beautiful woman.

'Bless her memory,' echoed the two Ters.

The Morg looked up from his resting place. For a moment a flicker of intelligence crossed his face as if he was remembering words from a language he had not heard since childhood. It soon passed and he lowered his head again.

'But, mistress, it's getting harder and harder to snatch boys from the streets. And there are so few left that have the red hair. To find this one we had to –'

'Enough, I said! Hold your tongue. I won't listen to your feeble excuses. Twelve you've brought me and each has failed. This Morg grows old. If he were still human, he'd be a man. His power wanes. Soon he will become impossible to control. We must replace him – but not with weaklings like this boy here. Take him away.'

'But, mistress, we haven't –'

'Did you hear me? I said take him away. I have no more use for such a puny child. The seven hundred and seventy-seven letters of the Morg's ritual name are to educate him. They are to make him strong. To bend him to my will. To make him *mine*. If he can't stand the first sixty-six letters –'

'Sixty-five, mistress. Mudge only wrote sixty-five.'

'How *dare* you!' screamed the beautiful woman. 'How dare you correct me!' For a moment her face was a mask of fury.

Ter Tunk backed away from Jenk and cowered, raising her arms to protect herself. She cast a terrified glance at the Morg. 'Mistress, I'm sorry. I'm truly sorry. I didn't mean to . . .'

'Enough! Enough, I said. Take him away. I have no more use for him.'

'But where to, mistress?' said Ter Mudge.

'Where to? Where do you usually dispose of such waste? The eels in the Farn must be growing fat on your mistakes. And, while you're doing that, think about where you're going to find me another child. A boy worthy to be made into a Morg. Now, get out!'

The beautiful woman was in a foul mood until later that night when the Serpent was fired six times from the Paper Belfry. As the last peal of thunder drifted away over the sleeping city the second cloud was almost whole, the mirrormark almost complete. 'It will be finished tomorrow night for certain.' She reached down and jerked the leash attached to the creature at her feet. He gripped a pigeon in his horny hands, its head hanging limp and lifeless.

'No howling tonight? What's the matter, Morg? And off your food? Are you pining for something? Is it because those wretched children escaped you? Or something else? Tell me, Morg?'

The Morg looked up at his mistress and then away again. He lay down.

The beautiful woman was lost in her own thoughts. 'Tomorrow, Morg. Tomorrow will see the second wound complete. Soon there will be demons for you to hunt; lots of demons. That will improve your spirits.'

'*Us?* The Maven wants to see us?' asked Mel in disbelief. 'But *why?*'

As soon as Mel, Ludo and Wren had arrived on the platform at the top of the hoist the next morning they were met by a black-robed Fa Major.

'Yours is not to question. Yours is to obey. Now, smarten yourselves up and follow me.'

'But our master. We need to tell him . . .'

'He will be told. Now hurry up.'

Mel tucked the chain of the luck-compass hanging around his neck securely inside his doublet and buttoned it up. Ludo brushed dust from his sleeves and Wren ran her fingers through her hair in an attempt to tidy it. As soon as they stepped in through the makeshift doorway four more black Fas fell into step with them as they were marched along the corridor.

'What do you think the Maven wants?' asked Ludo in a whisper. 'Do you suppose it's about last night? As soon as they saw the Blenk livery they would've known who we are.'

'Quiet!' barked the Fa in charge.

They were marched along twisting corridors and up and down sweeping staircases until they had lost all sense of direction. Eventually, the black-robed Fa Major signalled them to halt in a splendid antechamber before a huge set of carved doors.

'I am Fa Craw. You are first to meet Fa Odum, the Maven's personal secretary. When you are shown into his presence you will bow and wait. You will only approach when you are bidden to do so. You will only speak when spoken to. At all times you will address him as "serenity". You will on no account ask a direct question. Now, wait here.' Fa Craw entered and closed the door behind him. The four Fas remained behind, glowering at the friends.

'You will grovel and scrape. You will lick my boots. On no account will you ask what the skeg is going on,' said Ludo.

Mel and Wren suppressed giggles.

One of the Fas touched Ludo on the shoulder. When Ludo looked up the man put his finger to his lips and then drew it across his throat. Ludo swallowed with an audible gulp and tried to force a smile to show his friends he wasn't scared. It didn't work.

After a few minutes the door opened and Fa Craw beckoned them inside. They entered a magnificent suite of rooms with doors opening on to other rooms that receded in front of them. The first room seemed to be made entirely of burnished bronze. Flamboyant furniture was reflected in honey-coloured marble and stood in front of walls swagged with bronze-coloured moiré silk. Even the bronze-framed paintings that graced the walls were painted in tones of orange and brown. At the far end of the long room double doors stood open on to another room furnished in equally lavish style in tones of silver. Beyond that, through a third set of doors, was a golden room.

Three more crow-like Fas Major stood around a huge gilded desk in the farthest room. Seated at the desk was a small, grey-haired priest dressed in the scarlet robes of a Hierarch. A jewel-encrusted diaglyph hung around his neck on a gold chain. Fa Craw strode ahead and took up position alongside the desk. As the friends and their guards approached, Fa Odum stood and beckoned them forward with a ring-encrusted hand. As they had been instructed, the friends bowed.

Fa Odum walked around the desk and folded his hands in front of him. He smiled at the friends. It was a smile full of warmth. 'How good of you to come so swiftly. I'm sorry if the Fas alarmed you. They can seem a mite intimidating. So you are assisting Ambrosius Blenk with the ceiling painting in the Hall of Awakenings?'

Mel glanced at Fa Craw, who nodded. 'Yes, serenity.'

'And a splendid job you're making of it. Such finesse, such artistry. You must be very proud. Tell me, have you breakfasted yet? When I was your age I was always hungry.' He gestured towards a long sideboard where gold-covered dishes were arranged.

Ludo was about to accept, but Fa Craw caught his eye and shook his head. 'Thank you, serenity, but we're not hungry.'

'And you, young lady. Ambrosius told me he had a female apprentice but he didn't tell me she was quite so pretty.'

Wren blushed. 'Thank you, serenity.'

'I'm sorry. I didn't mean to embarrass you. It's true, though.'

One of his aides handed Fa Odum a sheet of paper. 'It's Melkin, Ludolf and Wren, isn't it? Do you mind if I call you by your first names? I won't keep you from your work long. I expect you're wondering why I asked you here. It's just that there seems to have been a lot of the Maven's treasures going missing lately. My old friend Fa Theum has informed me that a lot of valuable books have gone astray from the library and now I learn that at least one of the Maven's precious paintings can't be found. A beautiful work by your master. It's causing everyone here a great deal of anguish. Ambrosius has spoken to me of how observant and resourceful you three are and the Maven has asked me if you might be prepared to help us get to the bottom of this. You will be working here in the House of Spirits until the ceiling is complete and we were wondering – hoping – that you might keep your eyes and ears open. See if you can find out anything about these worrisome crimes; anything at all. The Maven – indeed all of us – would be very grateful. You can come here and see me any time. Just tell Fa Craw. Any time at all, day or night.'

Mel looked at Wren and Ludo. Could they trust Fa Odum? His smile reminded Mel of Fa Theum.

'Go on, Mel,' said Ludo.

'Yes, tell him,' said Wren.

'Don't say that you've already found something out? Ambrosius was right. You really are remarkable young people.'

'Please, serenity, we do know something about this; well, quite a bit actually.'

Fa Odum listened patiently as Mel related everything they knew about the Paper Belfry, the brass Serpent and the thieving Ters.

'My, my. Such perceptive minds. You really do know a lot. If the three of you weren't already apprenticed to Ambrosius, why we might have positions for you all here in the Maven's service.'

'To be honest, it's a relief to tell someone,' confessed Mel.

'You have been carrying a great burden between you. But you're not alone any more. Now we know, we can help. But first I think you need to tell all this to someone else. Someone very important. If you can bear to repeat it all, that is?'

Mel looked at his friends and they both nodded.

Fa Odum turned to his aides. 'Would you tell our esteemed visitor we're ready, please?'

Mel straightened his garments and smoothed down his hair. They were about to meet the Maven. He heard the sound of the door opening behind him.

The friends turned and the room seemed to turn several degrees colder. They stared in disbelief. It was not the Maven.

Fa Odum said, 'I don't believe you've been formally introduced to Ter Selen, the Demon-Finder-General.'

145

Standing in the doorway was the tall, elegant figure of the beautiful woman. Straining against the leash she held was the Morg.

Sparkfall

Mel's heart seemed to stop. For a moment he thought there must have been some terrible mistake. But only for a moment. He looked at his friends as the awful realisation hit them all like a fist. Ludo was the first to speak.

'You lied to us! We trusted you and you lied to us. You and the Ters are all in this together!'

'Opening a hole between the worlds and letting the demons in,' said Mel. 'So that it looks like they're saving Nem. That way the Ters won't be disbanded and everyone will think they're all heroes. That'll make the Maven as powerful as the Mysteries used to be.'

'He's clever, this one,' said Ter Selen as she struggled to hold back the Morg. He was straining at his leash to get at the friends. Wren was trembling and the colour had drained from her face. She clung to Ludo's sleeve and tried to hide behind him as the Morg's amber eyes seemed to bore into her like glowing needles. Ter Selen allowed herself to be dragged forward by the creature. He moved on his knuckles like an ape, his face contorted by the strangling collar. Ter Mudge and Ter Tunk followed them into the room. 'Where is this boy? Bring him to me.' She yanked the Morg's leash hard, bringing him to a halt. He made a painful coughing sound and sat down on his haunches, his whole body quivering with tension.

Ter Tunk grabbed Mel by the arm and hauled him before her mistress. He struggled but she was too strong. Ter Selen reached out her hand and sought Mel's face.

Mel looked up into her beautiful, multicoloured eyes as they cycled through their spectrum. Her perfect face held him spellbound. At that moment he was prepared to do anything she asked him to. All he wanted to do was to please her. The spell broke the instant she touched him. *She's blind.* Her fingers were ice-cold. 'Leave me alone!'

'Spirited, too. What colour is his hair?'

'Fair, mistress,' said Ter Mudge.

'What a pity. He has the makings of a fine Morg.'

'*What!*' exclaimed Ludo.

'I hear the other boy.'

'Brown hair, mistress.'

Ter Selen was quiet for a moment. 'What is it, Morg?' She allowed the Morg to lead her towards Wren. Mute with fear, Wren looked around frantically for a way out as Ter Selen's hand reached out and touched her face. It moved to grasp her long hair. 'The *girl?* Morg, can it be?'

The Morg crouched, looking up at Wren. She did not dare move. She stood transfixed by the ugly creature's alien stare and Ter Selen's probing fingers. Then the creature uttered a strange, plaintive cry.

Ter Selen laughed out loud.

'Mistress?' said Ter Mudge, confused. 'What's the matter?'

'The matter? Nothing's the matter. Can't you see?'

'See what?'

'The Morg. He's been off his food. He's been pining since yesterday. It's so obvious now. I do believe the Morg's in love! Tell me; what colour is her hair?'

'*Her* hair? Why, it's auburn.'

'Ha! It's perfect. This is the answer.'

'The answer? The answer to what, mistress? She's a girl.'

'You stupid, short-sighted woman. The answer to making a Morg. No more snatching children from the street. Ter Morgana's time-consuming ritual for making Morgs is at an end. The Morg is going to be *married*. She's young – in time there'll be plenty of babies. There're sure to be boys. It will be so much easier to train them from infants. We'll have a whole family of Morgs.' Ter Selen laughed her beautiful laugh.

'You can't!' shouted Mel.

Wren looked stricken. 'Mel! Ludo!' The Morg stroked her leg. She recoiled but the powerful creature grabbed her ankle and held her fast. He raised his slobbering face to Wren's and smiled his broken-toothed travesty of a smile. The remains of feathers and rotting meat were lodged between his teeth. His breath was as rank as a sewer.

'Quiet, child. Ter Mudge, take her.'

'What about the two boys, mistress?'

'They know too much. As soon as it's dark you can have them fed to the eels like the others.'

As Mel and Ludo were hauled past the Fas and out of the door the last they saw of Wren was the Morg stroking her. Silver streaks of his saliva stood out on the ultramarine sleeve of her doublet. Mel mouthed the words, 'We'll save you.' He did not know how.

The boys were taken even deeper into the House of Spirits and eventually flung into a bare, dingy storeroom. The only light came from a fanlight above the door. They heard the key turned in the lock.

Ludo rushed to the door and tugged frantically at the handle. 'We've got to get out of here. Wren's going to be . . . *Scrot!* Scrot, scrot, scrot, scrot, scrot!'

'That's not going to do any good.'

'We've got to do *something*. And where was your precious whatsit when we needed it? Why didn't it warn us?'

'I don't know.' Mel unbuttoned his doublet and fished it out. He flipped it open and tilted it to catch the light. 'The strength hand's on eleven o'clock and . . .' He shook it and then held it to his ear. 'It's stopped.'

'Please don't tell me you forgot to keep it wound up.'

Mel wound it and it began its sad chiming.

'Great! *Now* it tells us. Last night, when we didn't need it, it chimed and now . . . *Ahhhh!*' Ludo kicked the door in frustration.

'Feel better now?'

'The amazing memory-man. He can't even remember to wind his whatsit,' scoffed Ludo. 'Stop acting so cool. We've got to get out of here and help Wren.'

'Don't you think I know that? But we're never going to kick that door down. If we're going to get out of here we're going to have to use our heads. That, and be lucky.'

'You're the one with the luck. Cassetti should have given the whatsit to me. I'm the eldest. I've been an apprentice longer than you. If it wasn't for my cards, you wouldn't have worked out what it is. If I had it we wouldn't be here now and Wren wouldn't be . . . It's not skegging fair.'

'Ludo . . .'

'What? Ludo, quit being such a pain?'

'Nothing.'

They were silent for a time. Then the anger drained

from Ludo and he said, 'Sorry, Mel. I . . .' He sighed.

'It's OK. I know just how you feel.' He patted Ludo on the shoulder and stood up. 'How are we going to get out of here?'

'What's the whatsit say?'

Mel flipped the luck-compass open again. 'Not too good.'

'That's it then.'

'No, Ludo. We've got out of tighter spots than this before. And we didn't have a luck-compass then. It was worse than this that time in the Mine of Inspiration. Let's use our eyes. What's that? There on the wall.'

'Just some graffiti.' Ludo went closer to the rust-coloured scrawls. 'Some boys' names. Marco, Pieter, Brin, Herg, Jenk. Looks like they're written in . . . You don't want to know.'

'What about the fanlight?'

'No good. It's barred.'

Mel sat down on the bare floor. 'We're going to have to wait until one of the Ters comes back. Maybe we can surprise her.'

'What? Overpower a great ape like that?'

'Let's just wait and see what happens when she comes back.'

They waited on the hard floor throughout the long day. Eventually, the fanlight dimmed and then went dark. The boys' spirits sank with the sun. They must have dozed because they were both awoken in the darkness by a noise in the corridor beyond the door. The fanlight brightened. They heard footsteps and a key being turned in the lock. The door opened and silhouetted against the light from the corridor stood two men. They were swathed in black and wore broad-brimmed hats. Black scarves were wound around their faces like masks. One of them carried two rolled rugs and a lantern.

The boys backed up until they were stopped by the far wall. Mel noticed that his hands were trembling. He looked vainly around the bare room for some kind of weapon. 'Sorry, Ludo,' he croaked. 'Sorry for getting you into this mess.'

'That's OK, Mel.' There was a catch in Ludo's voice as well. 'It's my fault too.'

The second man turned to someone out of sight

beyond the doorway and said, 'You won't want to see this, Ter. It's a nasty business.' He withdrew a knotted garrotte from inside his clothing.

The men entered the storeroom and closed the door after them, setting the rugs and the lantern on the floor. The man with the garrotte advanced. He was tall and powerful and towered over the boys. He put a finger to his lips and with his other hand pulled down his scarf to reveal his face. It was bright green.

'Green?' said Mel. His surprise was rapidly replaced by relief. '*Green!*'

'Quiet, Mel.'

'Who's that with you?' asked Ludo.

'It's me.' The other man pulled down his mask to reveal a blue face.

'Blue. What are you two doing here?' Mel could hardly believe it.

'Dirk Tot sent us to keep an eye on this place,' said Green. 'After you told him and the master your suspicions he asked if we'd help. We've been posing as masons. Blue, here, who's . . . let's just say he's led a more chequered life than mine, noticed Spiky and

Dreck – a couple of the worst villains you could ever hope to meet. They were the very last people anyone would ever expect to see in the House of Spirits. So we waylaid them and they told us they'd been disposing of boys for the Ters.' Everyone present understood what 'disposing of' meant.

'They told you? Just like that?' said Ludo.

'Blue can be very persuasive – as I'm sure you remember. So we changed places with them and found you here. But where's Wren?'

'We don't know,' said Mel.

'The Ters are going to make her marry this Morgthing of theirs,' said Ludo.

'They can't do that,' said Blue.

'Yes they can,' said Mel. 'They've got Fa Odum and the Fas Major on their side and everything. We've got to save her.'

'Yes. But first things first,' said Green. 'We need to get you two out of here.'

Blue unrolled the rugs. 'OK, you two, in here.' Mel and Ludo lay down and allowed themselves to be rolled up inside. 'Right, lads. Keep absolutely still and don't make a sound. Go as limp as you can. Remember, you're both dead.'

Mel almost choked on the musty, dusty smell as he felt himself hoisted on to one of the men's shoulders and then joggled along as they made their way out of the storeroom. Afterwards, they descended a great many stairs until he felt the night air and was flung on to a cart and wheeled away. A short while later they stopped.

'It's all quiet here,' said Green as he and Blue unrolled the rugs. 'Well done, lads.'

Mel sat up stiffly and glanced at Ludo as he emerged from his cocoon. They were in a stable lit by a single lantern hanging from an overhead beam. At the edge of the pool of light it cast were two figures bound and gagged on the straw-strewn floor. The marks of Blue's 'persuasion' were clearly etched on their battered faces.

'Spiky and Dreck?' asked Ludo.

Blue smiled. 'Don't you worry your head about those two scrots.'

'Come on, we've got to rescue Wren,' said Mel.

'Not so fast,' said Green. 'First of all, you can't plan a wedding overnight – and they're not going to harm the bride, are they? It won't be pleasant for her but Wren's safe for a while. Blue and I are going back to the House of Spirits. See if we can find out where she's being held.'

'And you two are going into hiding,' said Blue.

'We can't! Not while Wren's –'

'Look; you're both dead. You've got to keep out of sight . . .' Green held up his hands to silence the boys' objections. 'Just for a while. You leave rescuing Wren to Blue and me. All right?'

'But –' said Mel.

'There're no "buts" about it,' said Green. 'Dirk Tot's orders. OK?'

'I suppose so,' said Mel reluctantly.

'OK,' said Ludo with a shrug.

Green opened the stable door. 'As quietly as you can, lads, follow me.'

They made their way through the deserted streets, keeping to the shadows and avoiding streetlamps.

'I know somewhere that will suit just fine. Tonight

you'll be sleeping in a prince's bed. You'll be as snug as two bugs in a rug.' Green laughed.

'Not more skegging rugs,' said Ludo.

'Rugs I can handle,' said Mel. 'But I wish you hadn't mentioned *bugs*.'

Just then, high above their heads, lightning flashed. Then three times more. The second cloud had taken the form of a forest, the crowns of its trees in ordered rows. On its underside a mirrormark began to spin.

Then it began to snow sparks.

'It's the master's painting,' gasped Mel. 'It's painted in the sky.'

They ducked into a doorway as the sparks drifted down and started to settle on the city's rooftops and cobblestones. Gingerly, Mel reached out his hand. The bright spark-flakes lay in his palm without burning or melting. Soon the streets were ankle-deep in glowing drifts, turning them into rivers of light.

'Hey, we could make spark-balls.' Ludo gathered a handful of the glowing flakes. 'What's this?' In amongst the spark-flakes was a single radiant chrysalis. It was as big as an olive and as light as a feather. As they looked closer they could see a dark shape writhing inside. The shape twisted and they saw a tiny demonic face before it rotated away again. Ludo dropped it quickly. There were more floating down along with the sparks. Perhaps one in ten thousand contained a demon embryo, but in the steady sparkfall that amounted to a great many.

'I don't like this,' said Mel.

'Like it or not, there're too many to do anything about,' said Green. 'You two need to get hidden – and quickly. As soon as the citizens see this lot the streets will be packed. Nobody will be going anywhere. Who can resist a firework display?'

They hurried away, spark-flakes settling on their shoulders and in their hair like miniature fairy lights.

In less than an hour, Mel and Ludo found themselves in an ornate and crumbling bedchamber deep inside the abandoned core of the House of Thrones. It was lit by a spark-ball they had brought from outside.

'Who do you think owned this room?' said Mel.

'Probably some long-dead prince,' said Ludo. 'To look at the decoration he must have loved hunting.'

The bedchamber had an outdoorsy theme. The great bed had its four gilded bedposts shaped like tree trunks, and golden branches intertwined overhead to form the canopy. The glowing spark-ball cast their crisscross shadows on to a ceiling painted with billowing clouds. The mouldy carpet had fallen leaves woven into it and several big landscape paintings decorated the walls.

'I'm going to clear away some of these cobwebs on the bed,' said Mel. 'You check for spiders.'

'Why me?' Ludo went ahead and checked anyway. 'It's quite comfortable,' said Ludo as he bounced up and down on the bed. 'Even if it's a bit damp and smells too much like those rugs.'

'What's in the sack Green left us?'

'There's bread and cheese – and there are some apples.'

'Anything to drink?'

'There's a flask of water,' said Ludo as he sorted through the sack.

The boys were ravenous after their day-long imprisonment and ate their fill.

As soon as they were satisfied Mel got up from the bed and examined one of the paintings. It depicted a dark forest. But his mind wandered. 'I wonder what Wren's doing now?' He felt the luck-compass vibrate slightly where it lay against his chest. He withdrew it and flipped it open. The direction hand pointed towards the painting. 'Hey, look at this, Ludo. I just thought of Wren and the luck-compass vibrated. It's pointing at this painting.'

'Try thinking of Cassetti and Nephonia.'

'There, it's done it again. It's swung round the other way.' Mel showed his friend.

'Try thinking of something else. The master and the mansion. You're right, it changes direction depending on what you're thinking.'

'Where's Wren?' said Mel. They watched as the direction hand swung back to point at the painting. 'It must mean that if we go in there it'll lead us to Wren.'

'We promised the master we wouldn't go into the

Mirrorscape and we promised Green that we'd wait
here until he came back for us.'

'Yes,' agreed Mel, 'we did. Dirk Tot's orders.'

'So?' Ludo nodded at the canvas.

'A promise is a promise.'

'Yeah; it is, isn't it.'

'And we couldn't break our word.'

'Absolutely not.'

'Do you suppose it's got a mirrormark?'

'Only one way to find out.'

Mel picked up the spark-ball and Ludo the sack.
They linked arms and Mel traced the mirrormark.

View Halloo

The forest was not as dark as it appeared from outside the canvas. Thick, leaf-laden branches arched overhead, blocking out any daylight, but the whole forest seemed to be imbued with its own inner light. It was impossible to tell exactly where it was coming from. Underfoot, the forest floor was carpeted with dark, soft grass peppered with tiny purple and blue flowers. Echoing birdsong filled the air and, somewhere out of sight, a fast stream flowed. Apart from the crepuscular light it seemed almost normal.

'I guess we won't be needing this.' Ludo took the spark-ball from Mel and threw it. It left a meteor-bright trail before silently exploding against a tree trunk in a shower of sparks. 'Bull's-eye!'

Mel consulted the luck-compass. 'Looking good,' he said. 'This way.' They set off into the forest.

After they had gone a short distance, Ludo asked, 'How do you suppose the whatsit works? I mean, how does it know what we're after? We might *think* it's directing us towards luck that will save Wren but it could be pointing us towards luck that will save Nephonia all the time.'

'Well, it worked back in the room. It hasn't led us to Nephonia.'

'But do you think we can trust Cassetti? What if he's primed the whatsit to always point to his, you know, Nephonia's luck, rather than ours? And another thing. Why didn't the whatsit chime when Green and Blue came for us? Being rescued from the Ters murdering us is about the best luck you could have. It should have chimed the happy tune. It's as if –'

'Shhh! Did you hear that?' said Mel. It was a deep, melodic phrase that rose and fell in pitch. 'There it is again. It sounded like a hunting horn. *Look.*'

In the depths of the forest they saw a tiny group of lights move from right to left and then vanish. They heard the hunting horn again but fainter. Then silence.

'What was that?' asked Ludo.

'No idea. But according to the luck-compass we're headed that way.'

'Can we stop for a bit first? I'm feeling really tired,'

said Ludo as the exhaustion of two sleepless nights finally overtook him.

'Me too.' They sat down with their backs to a tree trunk. 'Just five minutes.'

'Yeah, just five minutes.'

Mel awoke with a start. Ludo was fast asleep at his side. 'Ludo.' He shook him. 'Ludo, wake up.' His voice had an echo.

Ludo sat up and rubbed his eyes. 'What?'

'We've been asleep.'

'Asleep? How long for?'

'I don't know. We're in the Mirrorscape, remember. That's funny. What would you say these trees are made of?'

'Custard? *Wood*, of course, stupid.' Ludo turned to look at the trunk. 'It's . . . it's made of stone. And it's carved with grooves to look like bark. There's even mortar between the blocks. They were made of normal tree-wood when we came in. And they were when we sat down. I'm sure they were.' Ludo looked up. 'It's . . . scrot!'

'Exactly,' said Mel.

The branches had changed into vaulting. There was a ceiling above them and the grass had become flagstones. Although there was still something of the forest in the way the irregular vaulting resembled branches, they now appeared to be in some vast crypt.

'How did it do that? The Mirrorscape's never done that before,' said Ludo.

'The forest couldn't have, you know, petrified?'

'That takes millions of years.'

'We *were* pretty tired.'

Mel and Ludo looked at each other. '*Nah.*' They shook their heads.

They looked back the way they had come and it appeared the same. In fact, it looked the same in every direction. Just a forest of equally sized, equally spaced columns that receded in geometric progression into the darkness. There was no more birdsong, just the echoing *plip plip* sound of water dripping on stone. 'What now?' said Ludo.

'The luck-compass still says this way.'

They got to their feet and set out once more. After

a moment, Ludo stopped. 'Mel, can you feel that? It feels like the ground's trembling.'

'Yeah, and it's getting stronger. Maybe it's an earthquake.'

Something fluttered across their path. Then came the sound of the hunting horn. It was very close.

'Quick, Ludo. Hide behind this column.'

A swarm of lights appeared in the darkness ahead. They were coming towards the boys – fast. Then the horn blew very loud and a shout was heard. 'View Halloo! View Halloo!' From out of the murk of the crypt thundered a strange hunt. The noise was deafening. Mel and Ludo were frightened and amazed and confused and delighted – all at the same time. Dozens of tiny, human-shaped figments wearing scarlet coats and wielding huge, fine-meshed nets attached to long poles were mounted on a bizarre assortment of beasts. There were giant scaly sloths running on their hind limbs, transparent jellyfish with ostrich legs, and huge half-crab, half-scorpion creatures that scuttled sideways with surprising speed. Most of the mounts were warty-skinned dinosaurs of all shapes, sizes and colours with lanterns slung around their necks or hanging from their horns. Alongside them flew an assortment of weird creatures – some like long-necked vultures and others that appeared to be more nest than bird – while weaving in and out of the stampeding feet darted dozens of small yelping creatures that seemed to be a cross between weasels and spiny lizards.

Leading this strange company was a tiny, scarlet-coated huntsman mounted on a peacock-hued elephant whose impossibly long trunk coiled round and round and ended in a trumpet-like bell. As it passed, it blew another of its melodic hunting calls. The hunt galloped by, crashing into the columns and shattering the flagstones as if they were sheets of thin ice. They passed Mel and Ludo and disappeared into the gloom of the crypt, leaving a cloud of stone dust behind them. The shout of 'View Halloo' and the notes of the horn grew fainter and then vanished.

'What the *skeg* was that?'

Mel shook his head. 'Let's get out of here in case they come back.'

'Hang on,' said Ludo. 'What's that on your sleeve?'

'It looks like a leaf.' But as Mel moved his hand to brush it away it unfolded to reveal itself as a very large and very strange butterfly. On each wing, as clear as the finest painted image, was a human eye. As Mel looked at them, they blinked. Then the eyes turned to regard Ludo.

Ludo looked closer.

It stared right back.

'So what is it?' asked Mel.

'No idea. How about you?'

Mel shrugged. 'Do you suppose that the hunt was after it? They had butterfly nets.'

The eyes blinked once.

'All those monsters after this little thing?'

The eyes blinked again; once and very deliberately.

'I think it's trying to tell us something,' said Mel. '*Are* you trying to tell us something?'

The eyes blinked once more.

'Is it one blink for "yes" and two for "no"?' asked Mel.

One blink.

'Are you a cucumber?' said Ludo.

Two blinks.

'Scrot,' said Ludo, 'a talking butterfly.'

'Talking?'

'You know what I mean. We should leave it here.'

'Leave it? With the hunt after it?'

The eyes were blinking rapidly.

'I think it wants to come with us,' said Mel. 'We'll take it along.'

The eyes blinked once.

'With that lot after it? I'm sure they didn't want to catch it so that they could tuck it up in bed and read it a bedtime story. If we take it with us it'll be like trying to swim in a pool of piranhas with a pork chop hung round our necks.'

'We can't leave it, Ludo. It'll be OK. Come on. The luck-compass says this way.'

'I'm sure we've passed this way before,' said Ludo after they had gone some distance into the forest of columns. 'It all looks the same.'

Mel glanced at the luck-compass. 'It's been pointing this direction all along. We must be getting somewhere.' The ruby looked unnaturally bright.

'My legs ache. Can't we sit down for a bit?'

'We'd better not. Look what happened the last time. We've got to get on and rescue Wren.'

'Yeah, you're right.' Ludo looked at the butterfly that rested on Mel's shoulder. 'How about you; do you know where we're going? Hey! It blinked "yes", Mel.'

'Really? Ask it some more.'

'OK, Blinky, where are we going?'

'No; it has to be something simple. Something it can answer yes or no.'

'Are we going to find Wren?'

'What'd it say?'

'Nothing. I think it's trying to stare me out.'

'It probably doesn't know who Wren is,' said Mel.

'Do you know who Wren is? It says "no". Well, she's our friend and she's been –' Ludo was interrupted by the luck-compass's sad chime. '*Uh-oh.* I told you we shouldn't have let Blinky hitch a ride. It's the piranhas back for their pork chop. Hide!'

The lights were heading their way. The hunting horn. The thundering of many, many feet. 'View

Halloo! View Halloo!' Suddenly, the hunt was upon them again.

The ground shook and huge clouds of dust were thrown up as the monstrous herd charged by, pulverising the flagstones. Several of the larger and less agile dinosaurs failed to turn as tightly as the others and collided with one of the columns. It crashed to the floor with a shudder. The noise of the pursuit died away.

'That was close,' said Mel, peering at the retreating hunt.

The boys got to their feet and dusted off their clothes. Just then there was a loud groan and the ceiling above the shattered column fell in with a crash. A huge cloud of dust rose up and bright light streamed down into the crypt.

'Where's Blinky going?' said Ludo as the dust settled.

'He's flying up into the light,' said Mel. 'Come on.'

The boys climbed over the fallen column and stood for a moment beneath the gaping hole, blinking at the brilliance above. The luck-compass chimed happily. With a glance at his friend, Mel clambered on to the pile of rubble and hauled himself upwards towards the light. Ludo grabbed the sack of provisions and followed.

'I won't! You can't make me!' shouted Wren.

'Oh, I think you'll find we can.' Ter Mudge bent and picked up the white garment from the floor where Wren had flung it. 'We can make you do anything we want. Tunk?'

The big Ter moved towards Wren.

'You won't get away with this. My father knows I'm here. He'll come looking for me.'

'Your father's away in Monder, installing one of his clocks for a rich client,' said Ter Mudge. 'We checked.'

'My master will know I'm missing by now. He'll go and see the Maven. They're friends.' Wren backed into the corner of the room.

'I don't think the Maven will be helping you, Miss Pretty-Pretty. Now, are you going to stand still for your fitting? No? Perhaps we should go and get the Morg to help. He'll make you stand still. Would you like that? We know how much you adore your fiancé.'

'We can't do that, Mudge. It's bad luck for the groom to see the wedding dress before the marriage.'

'Bad luck, Tunk? I think that's the least of Miss Pretty-Pretty's problems.'

Wren stared at the two Ters. What could she do? Mel and Ludo would rescue her. She was sure of it. Even if they were only two boys against the might of the Ters and their Fa allies, she knew they would find a way. She'd do as her captors asked. For now. She held out her hand.

'Ah, that's better. Now slip off your clothes like a good girl. You and the Morg are going to make an extraordinary couple. *Extraordinary*.'

The Chrysalis Tower

Mel and Ludo emerged on to the slopes of an island plumb dead centre of a large and perfectly circular lake. So still was the mirror-like surface that it might have been a bowl full of the ethereal blue sky and wispy, mare's-tail clouds captured in its reflection. The wooded island was conical and at its summit stood a pale building shaped like a tapering, spiral chrysalis. Far off at the edge of the lake was a forested shoreline so straight and uniform it could have been planted by an especially pernickety gardener. From out of the hole at their feet drifted the faint echo of the hunting horn. Then nothing.

'Listen,' said Mel.

'I can't hear anything.'

'Exactly. There's no wind; no birdsong; no insect noise. Just silence.'

The air was crystal clear and it seemed like they could see forever. They stood for a moment and drank in the sublime scene.

'The luck-compass is pointing to that building,' said Mel.

'That's where Blinky's headed as well, by the look of it,' said Ludo, watching the butterfly dance away from them in the still air.

They followed the butterfly up the hill towards the chrysalis tower. As they climbed, they passed huge, dew-flecked flowers in vivid colours that grew at the base of the trees. The air was very thin, like that at the top of a mountain, and they were both out of breath by the time they reached the building.

The walls of the tower were translucent, bathing the interior with an even, nacreous light. It was hollow and empty except for a bare tree that stood in the centre. Its branches formed a vaguely human outline like a roughly crosshatched silhouette. Suspended from a gnarled branch near the top was a single pupa case. The butterfly fluttered across and settled above it. Its eyes went from Mel to Ludo to the chrysalis.

'Are you trying to tell us something?' asked Mel.

One blink.

'Is it something about this chrysalis?'

One blink.

'Is it a friend of yours?' asked Ludo.

Two blinks.

'Family?'

One blink then two blinks.

'Yes *and* no. Either it is or it isn't,' said Mel.

It repeated its answer. Clearly one blink then two.

'Come on, Mel. We can't stand around here all day playing a guessing game with an insect. Think about Wren. What's the whatsit say?'

Mel asked the luck-compass, 'Which way to Wren?' The direction hand swung around. 'It's pointing to them. To the butterfly and the chrysalis.' He looked at them closely. 'If it is and isn't family, what is it?' Mel looked at the shape of the tree. 'Is it you? Like a *part* of you?'

One, very emphatic, blink.

'How the *skeg* can it be him . . . her . . . it? Blinky's here; the chrysalis is there. Two things; two different places. It doesn't make sense.'

'Since when has the Mirrorscape made sense?' said Mel.

'OK; have it your own way. The two things are one. Problem solved. Now let's get on and find Wren.'

The eyes blinked rapidly.

'I think that maybe it wants us to stay here. Until the chrysalis hatches,' said Mel.

One blink.

'I'm sorry but we can't,' said Mel.

'Our friend's in danger and we have to rescue her,' added Ludo. 'Oh, and then we've got a world or two to save.'

Mel looked at the luck-compass but it was still pointing unerringly at the butterfly and chrysalis. He shook it but the hands stayed the same. 'Scrot!'

'Why don't we take them with us? Maybe that'd do the trick.' Ludo leaned towards the butterfly. 'Can we take junior with us? Then it can hatch out somewhere else. Would that be all right?'

The eyes looked at Ludo, then Mel, then back again. Eventually they blinked once.

'Thank skeg for that.' Mel carefully detached the chrysalis from the branch and gently placed it inside his doublet. He consulted the luck-compass. 'That did the trick. It's pointing outside now.'

Mel and Ludo, with the butterfly fluttering along between them, left the building and descended the hill. The luck-compass led them to a weird speckled boat drawn up on the shore.

'Looks like some kind of broken eggshell,' said Ludo.

'Eggs are hard,' said Mel. 'This one feels kind of leathery.'

'Birds' eggs are hard,' said Ludo. 'But there're other kinds of eggs; soft ones.'

'Such as?'

'Such as turtle eggs. Or . . .' Ludo stopped.

'Or what?'

'Or crocodile eggs.'

'*Crocodile eggs!* Look at the *size* of it!'

'It was only a "such as".' Ludo kicked the craft. 'Anyway, it seems strong enough and it looks like the only way we're going to get off this island. Look, Blinky thinks so too.' The butterfly was already on board, which was enough to convince Mel.

The boys pushed the eggshell-boat down into the

water and hopped in. The odd vessel was like a large, broad canoe. It could have easily held four or five passengers and there was some tackle stowed in the bottom.

'Any oars down there?' said Ludo.

'Nope. But there's this.' Mel hauled a short mast upright. It was only about as tall as him. 'There's a hole for it here.' He stepped the mast and secured it with a cotter pin. 'Now all we need's a sail.'

'How about this?' Ludo held up one corner of some kind of leathery fabric attached to the tackle.

'It's a bit big and floppy for a sail, isn't it? And it's not as if we have much of a mast. *And* there's much too much rigging.'

'It can't be anything else. Look, it must attach like this.' Ludo hooked it to an eye at the top of the stubby mast. The sail lay limp in the bottom of the boat. The masses of rigging lay coiled on top. 'What we really need is some wind.'

There was none. Not a breath; not a whiff; not a puff.

'Mel, I think Blinky's trying to attract our attention.'

'Do you know what this is?' asked Mel.

One blink.

'He says "yes". Is it a sail?'

Two blinks.

'He says "no". Should we take it down?'

Two blinks.

'What should we do? Wait?'

One blink.

'He says "yes".'

So they waited. But no breeze sprung up.

'Mel? What about Wren? While we're sitting here like a lily on a pond with a blinking butterfly for company she's in really big trouble.'

'I know. But the luck-compass is pointing the way the boat's going.'

'But that's the point. We're not going anywhere.'

'Yes we are. The island's getting smaller and the shoreline's getting bigger. There must be a current carrying us along. Look.' Behind them there were the unmistakable ripples of a wake disturbing the mirrored surface of the water.

They drifted on in silence for a while.

'You know, you're right. We're moving faster.' Ludo

picked up a corner of the limp sail but dropped it again. 'I just wish we could hurry this tub along.'

'It seems quite fast to me. There's a gap in the trees. We're heading right for it.'

The nearer they got to it the faster the boat moved forward. Soon they could make out individual trees on either side of the gap and hear the rush of water along the boat's side.

'This is more like it,' said Ludo. 'What we need is some kind of rudder. We're going too much towards that gap. We need to steer for the bank.'

'There's nothing like that down here,' said Mel, rummaging through the tackle in the bottom of the boat.

'Hey, we're going really fast now,' shouted Ludo over the rush of water.

Mel pointed to his ears and shook his head. He shouted, 'It's too loud. I can't hear you.'

'What?' Ludo fell over as the speed of the craft increased dramatically. The rush of water grew louder. The eggshell boat fairly leapt across the lake towards the gap.

Mel looked down as he felt the luck-compass vibrating against his chest. He wished he could hear whether it was the sad or happy chime above the roar of the water. Faster and faster sped the boat towards the gap. Mel looked up and could see nothing beyond it. Just sky.

Then they reached the edge. The edge of an enormous waterfall.

Deep in the House of Spirits, Wren cowered in the corner of a cage that hung suspended from the ceiling in a room in the Ter's quarters. It was being rocked to and fro by the Morg as he reached his powerful, scarred arm through the bars to push his gift of a dead pigeon towards her. Then he dropped to the floor, only to leap back up at the other side of the cage. The game was tiring Wren out and the violent rocking making her feel sick. The mere thought of the Morg actually touching her made her flesh crawl.

'Morg, be still! I can sense his restlessness. How he longs for his bride.' Ter Selen turned in her chair. 'Mudge? Tell me how the embroidery's progressing?'

The small Ter stopped sewing and held up the wedding gown, admiring her blood-red needlework. It matched the scars on the Morg. 'Nearly one hundred letters, mistress. One sleeve is complete.'

'It's taking so long. Can't you sew any faster? You must see how eager the groom is for his bride.'

'Eager? Yes, mistress. Very eager. But the true name must be spelt correctly for Ter Morgana's ritual to be observed. It's important that the embroidery is as fine as my calligraphy.'

'As fast as you can, Mudge. Once the gown is complete the wedding can take place.'

'I can't understand it. He wouldn't see me. Fa Odum told me that the Maven was indisposed and not seeing anyone. Indisposed, I ask you.' Ambrosius Blenk paced up and down in his private studio. He was wearing a long, black robe embroidered with silver and a pointed, black skullcap that extended over his ears. 'What's *that* supposed to mean?' He stopped and turned to his steward. 'And these mirrormark-shaped clouds.' He shook his head. 'I'm beginning to think that Womper

185

and his friends were right. And those spark-flakes remind me of one of my paintings. But who's creating the clouds and why? Those youngsters picked a fine time to go missing.'

Dirk Tot asked, 'Do you suppose the Maven knows the whereabouts of Mel, Ludo and Wren?'

The master tugged his long beard. 'Those three are always getting into mischief. I warned them not to neglect their duties. And now my ceiling's behind schedule and they've decided to take off. Half of Vlam is out looking at those peculiar clouds. It's like a carnival out there. Did you know they've set up fairs beneath them? Cloud-shape fair and spark-fall fair. It's hard enough getting my other apprentices to work on time without such distractions.'

'I'm sure Mel and his friends wouldn't let something like that distract them. Perhaps it's got something to do with the power struggle that's going on in the House of Spirits?'

'That's no more than a rumour.'

'But a very strong one.'

'If there is some kind of upheaval within the

Fas then the Maven's got nothing to do with it, that's for sure. He's an old friend. He'd never be involved with something so . . . so vulgar. However, those around him are always scheming. But the Maven's above all those kinds of shenanigans. I'll stake my . . .' The master looked around his cluttered studio and then down at his hands. '. . . I'll stake my beard on it.'

'Green and Blue will find out what's afoot. As soon as we have a few facts at our fingertips we can confront the Maven. See what he's got to say.'

The master shook his head. 'If we can get past Fa Odum and that bunch of crows that always surround him lately. And where did they all come from, eh? One moment they were bit players in the House of Spirits and now they seem to be running the Maven's affairs for him. Maybe the rumour of a schism between the Fas is right. The priesthood is almost as bad as the Mysteries were in their heyday.'

'I'll go and see my people right now. See if they have any news.'

*

'Good news and bad news! What's that supposed to mean?'

Green exchanged glances with Blue and then looked back at Dirk Tot. Even though they were old comrades from the time of their battle against the Mysteries, the giant made him nervous – especially when he was angry. 'The good news is that we've found out what's happened to Mel, Ludo and Wren.'

'And?'

'And the bad news is that Mel and Ludo have vanished and . . .' Green hesitated. 'Wren's been kidnapped.'

'*Kidnapped?*'

'Yes.' Green told Dirk Tot everything he had learned from Mel and Ludo.

'And where are the boys now?'

'We had them but now we've lost them.'

'What exactly do you mean by "lost"?'

'It's almost certain that they've gone into the Mirrorscape,' said Green. 'They'll be trying to rescue Wren from that direction.'

'You have to admire their loyalty – and their

courage. Still, if that's where they've gone it'll be fruitless trying to follow them and bring them back. They're on their own. We'll just have to trust that they can look after themselves.' Dirk Tot turned and looked out of the window at the view over Vlam and its two strange clouds. 'So, do you know where Wren's being held?'

'We're working on it,' said Green.

'The House of Spirits is no different from anywhere else in Vlam,' said Blue. 'There are those who respond to threats and those who respond to gold. A little bit of each in the right place and we'll soon find out where Wren is.'

'All right. Do what must be done. But get the master's apprentices back safe and sound.'

King M-morpho

'You knew this was going to happen, didn't you?' bellowed Mel.

The butterfly blinked once just as the boat reached the lip of the waterfall. The world lurched as it upended over the edge. Below them, Mel saw a great cloud of mist and an arching rainbow. The boat and its passengers plummeted towards them.

Mel and Ludo's terrified cries were drowned out by the thundering roar of the water. Then the sail filled with air and billowed above their heads. It was not a sail. It was a parachute. The fabric looked to be something natural and translucent with red veins crisscrossing it.

The friends were thrust down into the bottom of the boat by the sudden deceleration. When they raised their heads and peered over the gunwales they were floating slowly down through the spray. So gentle was their descent that they only became aware that they had stopped falling when the damp, leathery canopy collapsed over them. Mel clambered out from one end and Ludo from the other. They looked like two boys lying in a giant bed with a thick and very wet blanket pulled up around their chins. They were borne along by the swift current and the thundering of the falling water diminished behind them.

They hardly had time to get their breath back before the craft tipped over the edge of another water-fall. Then another, and another, and another.

When, shaken but unharmed, they reached the bottom of a seventh waterfall they found themselves on a swiftly moving river that flowed across a flat plain.

Mel wriggled out from under the parachute. 'Ludo, look!' He stood up in the shell-boat and looked back.

'It's the master's painting,' gasped Ludo. 'The one the Ters melted with that snake-machine.'

Sure enough, behind them stood the tall, flat-topped mountain like a seven-tiered wedding cake. Falling from each of the tiers were the waterfalls they had navigated. As they left the mountain behind them the sun set. Before them they could see a corona in the sky like the reflected lights of an approaching city. After

191

a while the river slowed to a muddy trickle and the boat grounded.

Mel and Ludo climbed out and squelched to the shore.

'There's the glowing orchard,' said Ludo as they reached the top of the riverbank. 'It's just like it was in the master's painting.'

'And it's being sucked away!'

They stood at the edge of the incandescent orchard the master had painted. The trees lined the slopes of a wide, deep hollow several miles across. As they looked towards the centre of the bowl they could see that the trees were moving; slowly near the edges and faster the nearer they got to the middle, in a great, galaxy-like spiral. At the very centre they were rotating extremely rapidly and disappearing up into a black whirlwind funnel. It swayed to and fro as it spun. They followed it upwards with their eyes but its end became lost high above in the evening sky.

'What's Blinky got to say about this?' said Ludo. 'You're the official translator.'

'Are we still going the right way?' said Mel as he

gazed down at the butterfly resting on his sleeve.

'What's it say?'

'Nothing. Its eyes are closed. I think it's asleep.'

'Wakey-wakey!' shouted Ludo.

'Sh-shut up!'

'What?'

'I didn't say anything,' said Mel.

'Who did then?'

'We d-did. We said sh-shut up!'

'Oh, no,' said Ludo, 'not another one.'

Crawling out of Mel's doublet was a second butterfly. The markings on its wings were shaped like lips – half on each wing – as precise and vividly formed as the other one's eyes. They spoke. 'And another th-thing.'

'What?'

'Stop calling us B-blinky!'

'So what should we call you?' asked Mel.

'You can c-call us Your M-majesty!'

'You're a king?'

'We're King M-morpho.'

'King Morpho,' repeated Mel.

'No, c-cloth ears. King M-morpho!'

'That's what he said.'

'I think he means King M-morpho,' said Mel.

'*Yaaaah.*' The king yawned. The eyes on the first butterfly opened and it fluttered into the air. The second butterfly also took to the wing and the two fluttered before Mel and Ludo in closely synchronised formation, the eyes above the lips. 'We have s-summoned you here on royal b-business.'

'Is that the royal "we" or just the plain old plural "we"?' said Ludo.

'B-both.'

Ludo rolled his eyes. 'I think I liked him better when he could only blink.'

'What's this business, your majesty?' asked Mel.

'All in good t-time. F-first we need to assemble our c-court. Here we are n-now.'

Mel and Ludo looked around expectantly. All they could see were the trees laden with spark-blossom. But as they looked closer they saw that hanging from the branches were hundreds – thousands – tens of thousands of chrysalises. They were opening and more butterflies were emerging. Soon the air of the orchard was a teeming, multi-coloured blizzard of them. They all fluttered towards the king and assumed the form of a flickering figure around the eyes and lips of their ruler – some his bearded head, others his arms and legs and the rest his body all resplendent in his regalia. The figure was many times Mel's height and in constant motion. He could see right through it. It made an eerie sight in the spark-lit orchard.

'Now,' said King M-morpho to Mel and Ludo, 'I expect you're w-wondering why we s-summoned you here.'

'You summoned us?' said Mel.

'Certainly. Without our h-help you'd still be w-wandering around in that d-dark crypt.'

'But getting out was an accident,' said Ludo. 'That clumsy hunting party demolished one of those columns and the ceiling caved in.'

'And w-who do you think led the h-hunting party to that p-particular column, eh? Right under the royal p-palace? Why, w-we did, of course.'

'I think maybe he's right, Ludo. The luck-compass has been pointing this way all along. But how did you know where to find us, your majesty?'

'We know a l-lot. We have allies everywhere who keep their many-facetted eyes open and report b-back to us. We know, for instance, the w-whereabouts of your f-friend.'

'*Wren?*' said Mel and Ludo together.

'Would you l-like to see her?' King M-morpho flew apart and the butterflies rearranged themselves into what people of another world far away in space and time from the Seven Kingdoms might recognise as a cinema screen. The king's crowned head remained hovering above it. The rectangle fluttered and a scene began to form, created by the swirling butterflies. King M-morpho started to hum an overture. The image on the screen was jittery and patchy, but clear enough for the friends to make out Vlam seen from above. As the pixellated scene changed slowly, Mel and Ludo realised that they were looking at a moving picture seen from a flying insect's perspective. The city became bigger as the point of view descended and they saw the House of Spirits. They seemed to fly in a window and along corridors until they came to the doorway to the Ters' quarters flanked by urns. The door opened and a Ter waved her arm as if she were shooing away some pest. The image bobbed down the hallway and through another open door at the end, where they saw Wren kneeling inside a cage suspended from the ceiling in a candlelit room. The king's tune changed to a sad one. Wren looked up and said something. The image went dark and jittery lettering appeared in its place, formed from the butterflies, which seemed able to change their colouring at will.

Mel. Ludo. Where are you?

The lettering dissolved and re-formed to show Ter Mudge and Ter Tunk as they entered the room.

The large Ter spoke and the lettering reappeared.

Did you hear her? She's talking to herself, Mudge.

The small Ter replied.

She's pining for her friends, Tunk. But she can pine all she likes, she's never going to see them again.

Not once she's married, eh, Mudge?

The small Ter held up a white garment covered in blood-red lettering.

The butterflies spelled out, *Your wedding dress is*

finished, Miss Pretty-Pretty. Your fiancé is eager for you to become Mistress Morg. Ha, ha, ha!

Ter Selen entered and the scene zoomed in on her pitiless, colour-changing eyes. The image faded and went black and more lettering scrolled up from the bottom.

A Bumblebee/King M-morpho Co-Production.

The rectangle of butterflies flew apart and reformed around King M-morpho in his giant human form as he finished humming the finale.

'How did you do *that?*' said Ludo, his jaw hanging open.

'It's n-nothing really. I just put my lips t-together and hum,' said the king.

'No, not that –'

'Wren, we've got to save her,' interrupted Mel. 'There's not much time.'

'But we b-brought you here to s-save *us*,' said King M-morpho. 'Our empire is d-disappearing up into that whirlwind. Our wells have dried up and w-without irrigation we have not the strength to resist. Our unborn s-subjects are mutating. Whatever f-force is d-

drawing them into the s-spout is c-changing them into
. . . into d-demons.'

A light came on in Mel's head. 'The spark-blossom,
the chrysalises with the demons. It's just like Nephonia.
Your empire is falling on Vlam – *our* world. Vlam must
be somewhere at the end of that whirlwind. This is the
scene that's painted in the second cloud over Vlam.'

'But how?' said Ludo.

'It's the *paintings!* Don't you see? They're doing it
with the paintings.'

A smile blossomed on Ludo's face as he gazed
around at the orchard. 'That's right! This *is* the
master's painting.' Then he frowned. 'But I still don't
get it. What about Nephonia? The master never
painted that.'

'No, but he said that the Maven had some paintings
of clouds.'

'Midas Garf's work,' said Ludo, his smile returning.

'So when they melt them with that snake-gun –'

'Along with their mirrormarks . . .'

'. . . It makes the wound between the worlds the
Ters were talking about. You remember that Cassetti

said that his world was being pulled towards the mirrormarked cloud underneath Cumulus? Well, here it looks like the orchard is being sucked towards that whirlwind at the centre.'

'And Cassetti said that Nephonia and our world touch,' said Ludo. 'Someone must be using the mirrormark like a trapdoor into Nem.'

'I bet the mirrormark's the wound between the worlds.'

'And if the force is changing King M-morpho's subjects into demons –'

'Who knows what the clouds will change into,' finished Mel. Then to King M-morpho, 'You said you have eyes everywhere. We know that the Ters are doing this, your majesty. Who else is helping them?'

'We d-don't know,' replied the king. 'There are p-places even insects can't g-go.'

'Like where?' said Ludo. 'They seem to be everywhere – especially in places you don't want them.' He chewed his lip for a moment. 'What're we going to do, Mel?'

'I don't know. The deeper we get into this the more

dangers we find. There's Wren and Vlam and Nephonia and now there's King M-morpho's kingdom as well. They all need saving.'

'But there's only two of us,' reasoned Ludo. 'What can we do? We've got to save Wren first.'

King M-morpho interrupted. 'Perhaps w-we can help. If you will restore our irrigation, w-we will undertake to p-protect your f-friend.'

'*You?*' said Ludo.

'C-certainly.'

'Forgive me, your majesty,' said Mel, 'but aren't you a little, err . . . *flimsy* to protect anyone?'

'We may lack the b-brute strength of your kind but we are p-powerful in other ways. As I say, w-we have many allies.'

'Insects?' said Ludo.

'Yes, i-insects – and others. Our k-kind can t-travel between the Mirrorscape and your w-world.'

'We'll have to go along with him,' said Mel quietly. 'We'll do as he asks and, as soon as we can, get on and save Wren. And look, the luck-compass agrees.' Then, to King M-morpho, 'OK, your majesty, we'll help you.

But how are you going to protect Wren?'

'We'll s-send the royal b-bodyguard. *Guards!*' A number of butterflies detached themselves from King M-morpho's body and fluttered to one side in a regimented cube. 'Very well, p-proceed. You know our w-wishes.' The guards fluttered off in double-time.

'What good's that lot going to do against those Ters and the Morg?' said Ludo. 'They could squash them easily.'

'Do n-not underestimate our bodyguard. We have r-remarkable skills at our feeler-tips.'

'I hope they're in time,' said Mel. 'From what we just saw, something really bad is about to happen to Wren.'

Mirrorblood

Wren waved her hand to shoo away a bumblebee. She sighed and leaned back against the bars and waited as the cage stopped swinging. As she glanced up at the fancy plasterwork that ran in a raised frieze of angels' faces just below the ceiling, one of them winked at her. Wren blinked her eyes in astonishment and stared harder. It winked again. Then the angels' faces detached themselves from the frieze and took to the wing as a cloud of white butterflies. They rearranged themselves in the air to form a string of jittery lettering.

Do not be alarmed. We are the royal bodyguard. We have been sent here by King M-morpho to protect you.

'I'm seeing it – but I still don't believe it,' said Wren.

Nevertheless, it's true.

'You can *hear* me?'

The flowing script dissolved and the dancing butterflies re-formed to spell out, *Of course we can. Now, it is important you do exactly as we say.*

*

'Down *there!* You expect us to go down there?' said Ludo.

Mel leaned over and looked into the dark well at the edge of the orchard. The luck-compass was pointing towards it. 'How deep is it, your majesty?'

'Very d-deep.'

Ludo plucked some spark-blossom from a tree and made a ball. He dropped it into the well and watched as it illuminated iron rungs set into the inside wall as it fell. The glowing ball rapidly diminished to no more than a dot, then went out. 'What's down there?'

'S-somewhere, our irrigation, we h-hope. You must find it and set it f-free.'

'How long's it going to take us?' said Ludo.

'A l-lifetime – maybe t-two.'

'*How long?*' spluttered Ludo.

'I think the king's talking butterfly lives,' said Mel. 'At least I *hope* he's talking butterfly lives.'

'So you won't be here when we get back?' said Ludo. There was a note of optimism in his voice.

'Oh, I expect we'll all have w-withered and died by the time you r-return,' said King M-morpho, 'but we'll still be h-here. As long as our s-subjects live, so w-will we.'

'More doubletalk.' Ludo shook his head.

'Come on,' said Mel. 'The sooner we get this over with the sooner we can free Wren. It'll be dark down there. Empty the provision sack and fill it with spark-blossom.'

Mel and Ludo sat cross-legged on the ground at the bottom of the well, rubbing their aching legs and breathing heavily after their long descent. When he felt rested, Mel picked up his spark-ball and held it high. Several large tunnels led away from the base of the well. Ludo grabbed a handful of dust and let it trickle through his fingers.

'There hasn't been any water down here for ages.' His voice echoed around the space. 'All there is is this dust.'

Mel flipped open the luck-compass. 'It's pointing down that way. Let's go.'

As they walked, Ludo ran his hand along the wall of the tunnel. 'This feels very smooth. Do you suppose it was made like this or if the irrigation has worn it away over the years?'

'It's not all that smooth, there's a great lump up ahead.'

As they approached the lump it looked like an elongated grey boulder that had been half buried in the floor of the tunnel.

Mel knelt and ran his hand over it. 'This isn't a rock; it's more like a shell. Here, feel; it's knobbly and it's got joints on it.'

'It's like a great big woodlouse.'

'Or an armadillo,' said Mel. 'I think it's dead. Let's try and tip it over.'

'*Scrot*, it's heavy.'

Mel and Ludo heaved and eventually rolled it over. The creature rocked on its domed back, revealing its fleshy underside. Around the periphery of its armoured shell were a dozen callused hands that it must have walked on and in the centre was a flat, vaguely human-looking face. Its warty skin was mottled and its crusty eyelids were closed. It had no nose but a very wide mouth with cracked lips surrounded by thick, stubbly whiskers. Lolling out from between them was a very wide and very long tongue. Ludo looked closer.

'Its tongue's rough all over, like coarse sandpaper.'

'Sticky too, by the look of it. I bet that's why the tunnel's so smooth.'

'Ugh,' said Ludo, 'you won't catch *me* licking any tunnels. There's another one over there. Do you suppose they're the ones blocking the irrigation?'

'More likely they kept it running freely. They look like they belong down here. What do you think they died from – thirst?'

As they continued walking, the corpses of the tunnel-lickers became denser and they had to weave between them. The tunnel walls became rougher, and wide fissures began to appear.

'That bit looks like it was hacked out only yesterday,' said Ludo. 'You can still see the tool marks in the stone.'

'And there're wheel marks in the floor.'

'The tunnel-lickers couldn't have made those,' said Ludo.

Mel came to a halt. 'Well, we've found what's blocking the tunnel.'

Ahead of them was a wall of roughly hewn stone blocks piled up to form a dam that completely filled the tunnel. At the base of the wall lay many more tunnel-licker bodies. Some had had their shells smashed. It was apparent that the dam had been made with fresh stone hewn from the tunnel walls. When they got closer the light from their spark-balls picked out trails of sickly green slime trickling down the face of the dam.

'What do you think it is?' said Ludo. He reached out to touch the slime.

'*Ludo, don't!*' shouted Mel. 'It's poison.'

'How do you know?' said Ludo, snatching his hand back.

'It says so. Look.' Mel went to a wide fissure at the side of the tunnel. Stretched across it was a spider's web. Woven into the web in spider's silk was a message.

The slime is poisoned.

'What's *that?*' said Ludo.

'I think it must be one of King M-morpho's allies. Look, another message is appearing.'

A spider frantically wove *Look inside this fissure.*

Mel and Ludo climbed up to the fissure, ducked

under the web and squeezed into the cleft. Inside, it opened out into a wide cavern with a tall, sloping roof. Dust was strewn over the floor and was piled against the walls. As the boys' eyes searched the cave they saw a small army of snails covering one of the slabs that made up the walls. These snails had been very, very busy. Their slime-trails spelt out a message.

We thought Kind M-morpho's agents would never get here. Some time ago a number of human creatures came to the tunnel with a great digging machine and built the dam. Before they left they smeared the blocks with poison to kill the tunnel-lickers and prevent them from clearing the obstruction.

The writing continued on the next slab. *Mirrorblood flows through the tunnels, without which King M-morpho's realm will wither. If this happens, the grubs inside the chrysalises in the orchard will all mutate into demons. The dam must be destroyed. The saliva of the tunnel-lickers dissolves stone. You must collect this and smear it on to the obstruction, which will crumble and free the mirrorblood. Do not delay. Then . . .* The snails were still writing just as quickly as they could.

'Oh, great,' said Ludo. 'My idea of a perfect day.

Crawling around in the bottom of a dark well collecting spit.'

'Let's get on with it. It says "Do not delay".'

'But they're still writing. It might be something important.'

'We can't wait,' said Mel. 'They'll have finished by the time we get through.'

After a few experiments they found out the best way to extract the saliva from the dead tunnel-lickers. They rolled the carcasses over on to their backs and took turns jumping up and down on them while the other one collected the goo that oozed from their mouths in a fragment of shell which seemed impervious to the stone-eating power of the spit. When this was full they carried it to the dam and set it down.

'What's this?' said Ludo. He held up a broken silver chain.

'Where'd that come from? It looks like a broken necklace or something.'

'I just found it lying here. Maybe whoever made the dam dropped it.' Ludo tucked it inside his doublet. 'Finders keepers. Now, how're we going to get this stuff on to the stone? There's no way I'm dipping my hands into *that*.'

'Why don't we make spark-balls with the blossom that's still in the sack? Then we could dunk them in the spit and lob them at the dam,' suggested Mel.

The result was quite spectacular. As each spit-soaked spark-ball struck the dam it exploded in a bright shower and the stone began to dissolve like boiling water poured on ice. Very soon the dam began to bulge ominously. The luck-compass gave out its sad chime.

'It's about to go!' shouted Mel. 'Back up to the crack.'

No sooner had they reached the relative safety of the fissure than the dam breached and a huge wave of red liquid thundered into the tunnel.

Mel gasped. 'The tunnel-lickers' bodies are being swept away!'

'We'll be too, if we don't get out of here. How're we supposed to get back?' said Ludo.

'The snails will know. They must have finished their writing by now.'

While Mel and Ludo had been working the snails *had* completed their writing. But it did not say what they expected . . . *Then, whatever else you do, you must flee back to the well and climb to the world above before the dam bursts. It is the only way out.*

'*Now* they tell us!' said Ludo. 'That mirrorblood stuff's rising.'

'You're right,' said Mel. 'We're trapped.'

Another masterpiece died that night in the Paper Belfry as the Serpent made the third rift. A painting by Anders Jert of a vast factory filled with rivers of colour was reduced down to its glowing mirrormark. As that, too, melted away a third cloud formed high above Vlam. It was grey and resembled another city but whereas the one depicted in the first cloud was beautiful, this was ugly. Bright colours played around its edges and the bottom of a luminous rainbow appeared in its centre. Little by little, it began to descend towards sleeping Vlam like thick paint squeezed from a tube.

The Third Storm

The Wedding

A string of butterflies hovered in the air before Wren's cage. *Are you sure you understand our plan?* they wrote.

'Understand it – yes; like it – no. How can you be certain that these allies of King M-morpho's are going to turn up and do the business?'

They'll be there. They can never resist a free meal.

'Yes, but what if – quick, hide. Someone's coming.'

The butterfly script flew apart at the sound of the door opening. With no time to hide anywhere else they fluttered to the floor. As Wren watched, the royal bodyguard changed their colouring and became indistinguishable from the rich pattern on the large rug that covered most of the floor. Ter Mudge and Ter Tunk entered the room.

'It's your wedding day, Miss Pretty-Pretty,' said the diminutive Ter. 'Time to get up and put on your new dress. You don't want to keep the groom waiting now, do you? Tunk and I are to be your maids-of-honour. Won't that be nice?'

Ter Tunk strode across the room. To Wren's dismay, she tramped right through the patch on the carpet where the Guard lay camouflaged. Wren cried out in alarm but quickly changed it to what she hoped sounded like a sob. She hid her face in her hands and peered through her fingers. Her acting seemed to have worked. The Ters smiled at her distress and continued about their business as they delved into a large chest on the far side of the room. When the Ters' backs were turned, Wren whispered, 'Guards – are you all right?'

The butterflies rose from the rug and formed a string in the air. *We've tken csulties. One of the vowel sections hs been wiped out. Don't worry bout us. The pln must proceed.* They flew to a tapestry and merged invisibly into its rich design. The Ters turned back. Ter Mudge held the wedding dress as Ter Tunk operated the noisy winch lowering the cage to the floor. Together, they led Wren away.

It was morning and daylight leaked in through gaps in the skin of the Paper Belfry, dappling the congregation of waiting Ters. Fa Odum and Fa Craw entered. They wore towering, pointed mitres that covered the top of their faces like masks. They were preceded by two Ters swinging censers that billowed sweet-smelling smoke. Following them were Ter Selen and the Morg. The creature was dressed in a clean loincloth and wore a coronet of woven flowers.

The groom's party took up their positions in front of the priests as they stood before the Serpent. A harmonium struck up a wedding march. The congregation began a droning chant that swelled and filled the space. All eyes turned expectantly to the door beneath the minstrel's gallery. It swung open, and held firmly between Ters Tunk and Mudge, was Wren dressed in the long, white wedding gown embroidered with its blood-red lettering. Many red and white flowers were woven into her long, free-flowing hair. She was deathly pale and plainly terrified. She struggled vainly against her captors' grip. At a nod from Ter Selen she was marched forward, her feet barely touching the ground.

The Morg began an eerie, tuneless crooning as he attempted to join in the singing. As Wren reached his side he had to be restrained from grabbing his bride by a sharp tug on his leash. He bared his broken teeth at her in a sickening smile.

Fa Odum began reading from his prayer book. 'We are gathered here today –'

'Wait!' shouted Wren. The music stopped abruptly. The Morg continued wailing for a moment before he too was silent. 'I'm here against my will.'

'Quiet, girl,' snapped Ter Selen.

'I won't go through with this,' said Wren. 'You can't make me.'

Ter Tunk stepped forward and grabbed Wren. She clamped her hand over Wren's mouth. 'I'll make sure she nods at the appropriate moment, mistress.'

Wren bit Ter Tunk's hand. The Ter yelped and took it away. Wren looked around the Paper Belfry. *They'd better get here soon.*

Ter Mudge drew a dagger from her sleeve and held it to Wren's neck. 'Just do as you're told,' she hissed. 'Or you'll be sorry.'

Fa Odum nodded and recommenced. 'We are gathered here today before this congregation to join together . . .'

Where are they? Where are they? Wren looked around but saw only the sinister sisters and the weird, flimsy belfry.

'. . . Do you, Morg, take Wren as your lawfully wedded wife, to have and to hold from this day forth, forsaking all others until death do you part?'

'He does,' said Ter Selen.

The Morg jabbered excitedly and nodded his head so fast strings of spittle landed on Fa Odum's jewelled robes.

'And do you, Wren, take Morg as your . . .'

Wren strained her ears. *The butterflies said they'd be here by now.* She looked about anxiously as Fa Odum droned on.

'. . . until death do you part?'

Wren felt all eyes fixed on her. *Am I imagining it? That faint buzzing sound.*

The silence stretched on and Ter Selen spoke. 'Say it. *Say it!*'

Ter Mudge pushed the dagger against Wren's neck. She felt the point pierce her skin and a trail of warm blood trickle down her neck. 'Do as you're told,' whispered the Ter.

As Wren opened her mouth to utter the irrevocable words there came a scream from the back of the congregation. And then another and another. The buzzing grew in volume as a grey cloud filled the Paper Belfry. Streaming in through the gaps, tens of thousands of midges bit every available piece of exposed flesh and the neat rows of the congregation dissolved into a chaotic stampede of shrieks and waving arms.

Wren looked up. Hovering in front of her were the butterflies at last.

The midges won't hrm you. We don't hve much time. Follow us.

Ter Selen pulled up her cowl to protect her perfect face from the biting cloud and Ter Mudge yelped as she slashed at them with her knife. Only the Morg seemed impervious to the cruel bites. He leapt up at the butterflies and landed with a handful of crushed bodies in his hand. He thrust them into his mouth, chewed and spat the mush on to the floor. He began thumping the mess with his fist and failed to see Wren as she followed the surviving butterflies from the belfry.

'Are you all right? Where are we going?' said Wren.

Mor csualtis. Don't worry bout us. They led Wren along a corridor and hovered before a door. *In hr.*

Stacked around the walls of the darkened store-room was a treasure trove of paintings, masterpieces every one. Wren recognised those by Ambrosius Blenk, Lucas Flink and Anders Jert, but there were others there from the Maven's collection, awaiting the furnace that powered the Serpent.

The butterflies re-formed against the light from the open door. *W must rturn to hlp th midgs. Our othr llies will tll you wht to do. Goodby.* The silhouetted lettering fell apart as they fluttered away to rejoin the battle.

When Wren turned back to the room she saw faint green lights forming themselves into lettering on the wall above a painting. 'Glow-worms.' She was too frightened to be amazed by the clever insects. They spelled out in luminous letters, *You must use the mirrormark and escape through a painting. Be quick.*

She looked at the images before her, trying to choose one. Although it was dark, she could see that most were full of the terrifying monsters that her master and Lucas Flink were so famous for. *Not those.* She approached the canvas beneath the glow-worms that depicted a night scene of a brightly coloured fairground. *They must mean this one.* She quickly made the mirrormark and vanished.

In the empty room after Wren had left, the glow-worms' lights faded and went out. Then they came back on. They spelt out, *But whatever you do, don't choose this one.*

'Fares please,' said a girl's voice.

'What?' Wren tottered as she regained her balance on the revolving floor. The jaunty music of a calliope played loudly.

'You heard me, luv. If you want to ride you have to pay.'

Wren looked around her. The fairground in the painting had become real. She stood on a fast-moving roundabout bathed in the speckled rainbow light of hundreds of coloured bulbs that burned in rows overhead. It glinted off ranks of brightly coloured hybrid animals that were moving up and down in the air in time to the music. They did not seem to be attached to the floor or ceiling and each had a saddle on its back. There were winged horses, as well as cockerels with snake's tails, dolphins with kangaroo legs, armadillos with human faces, and giant two-headed leopards with multi-coloured spots. And those were just the ones near to her. Then she did a double-take. The animals were *real!* At first glance they all seemed to be carved and covered with bright paintwork and gilding, but as she looked again she could see they were alive. They gazed at her and blinked large, moist eyes or nuzzled their neighbour. The leopard-creatures growled. Apart from her, there appeared to be no other passengers.

Beyond the creatures the brightly lit fairground was full of activity as it sped by. Figments shrieked as they plummeted down a helter-skelter taller than the House of Spirits, while others waved at their friends from the top of a giant Ferris wheel that was rolling along the ground at the edge of the fairground, crushing unlucky onlookers as it went. A colossal roller-coaster on impossibly tall stilts actually seemed to disappear behind the moon before it swooped back to earth again. Giant jets of flame roared out from a big top, followed by the sound of applause from inside.

'Well? Are you riding or not?'

Wren wrenched her attention back to the figment who had spoken. She also appeared to be carved and gilded, just like the animals, and was most definitely alive. If she was human she would have been about sixteen years old, and she was dressed in gaudy, carved clothes covered with obviously fake jewels. Wren collected herself and said, 'I'm sorry but I don't have any money.'

'What's all that in your hair, then?'

Wren raised her hand and pulled out a flower. 'This?'

The figment shook her head. 'Got so much dosh she stuffs it in her hair,' she said to herself. She took the flower, and put it into a leather satchel she carried. She took out three smaller flowers and a leaf and handed them back. 'Here's your change. Look, if I were you, luv, I wouldn't go around with those flowers in plain view. There're all types of light-fingered toe-rags around here. Now, where to?'

'To?'

The figment sighed. 'It's going to be one of those nights,' she said under her breath. Then, out loud, 'Where do you want to go, luv?'

'Go? I don't understand. This is a merry-go-round, isn't it?'

'A merry-go-*what?*'

'A merry-go-round. You know, it goes round and round.'

'Round and round?' The figment was obviously puzzled. 'Round and round what?'

'Itself, of course!'

The figment laughed out loud.

'What's so funny?'

'You think we go round and round *ourselves?*'

'Of course. What else can you go round?'

More laughter. 'We could go round the world if we wanted to.'

'I'm sorry. What's the joke?' asked Wren. 'What is this if it's not a merry-go-round?'

The figment looked at Wren as if her passenger was an idiot. 'This is a merry-go-anywhere-you-want-to, luv. So?'

'So, what?'

'So – where – do – you – want – to – go?' She said the words very slowly and very clearly.

At that point the roundabout had revolved back opposite the wall of mist through which Wren had entered the picture. She imagined the Ters and the Morg on the far side. 'Anywhere. Just as long as it's away from here.'

The figment looked surprised. 'It takes all sorts.' Then she shrugged. 'OK, luv. You've paid your fare. Anywhere it is.'

She went to the calliope which formed the centre of the roundabout in an ordered tangle of brightly polished brass pipes and pulled down on a chain. The calliope blew a piercing, discordant blast. Then she tugged a large, brass-handled lever. There was a loud metallic clunk.

'Watch your feet.' The girl grabbed Wren's elbow and pulled her away from the gap that opened up in the floor across the width of the roundabout. A row of winged horses took the lead as the rest of the roundabout unwound after them and became a long, brightly coloured, over-lit and very noisy procession. It headed out of the fairground under the stilts of the roller-coaster.

'Mount up,' said the figment, gesturing to the animals. 'No extra charge.'

Wren felt dizzy. She looked around at the choice of mounts and then back at the girl. 'What's in there?' She nodded at the calliope.

'Sorry, staff only.'

'Please,' said Wren. 'I've had a very bad day.' She swayed. 'I think I need to lie down.'

'You don't look too good, luv. How about a nice cup of tea?'

Wren smiled weakly, mouthed the words *yes please*, and fainted.

When she came round the figment was leaning over her with a concerned look on her gilded face. Wren was lying down and when she tried to sit up the girl gently took her shoulders and eased her back on to the soft couch.

'Easy now. It affects some people like that the first

227

time they ride. You're not from around these parts, are you?' she said.

'How long was I out for?'

'Not long,' said the figment with a reassuring smile. 'You'll soon be feeling better. Who're Mel and Ludo?'

Wren looked surprised.

'You were talking to yourself while you were out.'

'They're my friends. I've got to find them.' Wren was silent for a moment. 'Did I say anything else?'

The figment took the cool, damp cloth from Wren's forehead, dipped it in a bowl of water, wrung it out and reapplied it. 'Something about talking butterflies. Are you *sure* you're all right?'

'Look, I feel much better now. Where am I?'

'Inside the calliope. This is where I live.'

As Wren gazed around she saw that the walls were formed from the spaghetti-like tangle of the calliope's brass pipes. They were all polished to gleaming perfection, reflecting elongated, brassy images of the room. On those rare pieces of wall that were not covered with pipes there were bright, fairground paintings of mythical landscapes. The room itself was circular, with a spiral staircase in the centre that disappeared down into the floor and up into the low ceiling. As well as the upholstered couch there was an armchair with an embroidered antimacassar. A small cooking stove on which a large copper kettle boiled sat in the corner. The ceiling was also covered in gaudy fairground art depicting clouds and all manner of flying creatures both real and imaginary.

'That's a wedding dress, isn't it?' said the figment. It was more a statement than a question. 'Did he stand you up or something? Is that why you're here?'

'No. He . . . I . . . It doesn't matter.'

'Suit yourself,' said the figment. 'None of my business, anyway. Here.' She handed Wren an enamelled mug of tea.

Wren took the cloth from her forehead, sat up and sipped the tea gratefully. 'Look, I've got to find my friends.'

'So you said.'

'Can we turn this thing to go and look for them?'

'You've paid your fare. You can go wherever you want. That's why it's called a –'

'Merry-go-anywhere-you-want-to.'

'You catch on fast.' The girl shook her head. 'So where are they, these friends of yours?'

'I don't know. They could be anywhere.'

'You're in luck; that's exactly where we're going.'

Wren was unsure if the girl was joking.

'You'd better come topside.'

Wren got to her feet and followed the figment up the spiral staircase. Above the living area was a garish bedroom that the girl proudly identified as hers. The bed was made from what seemed to be an ornate cradle from some ride. The music of the calliope grew fainter as they ascended. Right at the top was a circular room that had windows all round. The glass had engraved borders and displayed a fractured, panoramic reflection of the brightly lit interior. The only thing visible beyond the reflections was the long roof of the merry-go-anywhere-you-want-to, defined by its rows of coloured lights disappearing into the night. The cabin was as elaborately decorated as the rest of the machine, complete with its own painted panels and ceiling. All around the periphery of the room were long, polished brass levers attached to the floor and hundreds of dials and valves fixed to serpentine pipes. Just in front of the staircase stood a large wooden ship's wheel surrounded by free-standing brass binnacles.

'Feeling better now?' asked the girl. 'My name's Goldie, by the way.'

'I'm Wren. Yes, much better, thanks. I had no idea the merry-go-anywhere-you-want-to was so big or so complicated.'

Goldie smiled with obvious pride. 'Equipped for everything, we are. We can never tell how far a fare might want to go.'

'We?'

'I mean me,' said Goldie. 'There used to be me and Guv. We ran the merry-go-anywhere-you-want-to together. He went away and –' There was a catch in Goldie's voice. 'I don't know where he is now.'

'You run this all on your own?'

'Yeah. Well almost. Guv used to take care of all the mechanical side of things and I ran the business end. I thought I'd have to sell up after Guv's disappearance but then Lug, the new mechanic, turned up out of the blue, looking for a job.'

'That was a lucky coincidence,' said Wren.

'Coincidence? Yeah, I suppose it was.' Goldie's face clouded. 'Well, anyway, I'm still in business. So what about you?'

'I need to find my friends,' said Wren. 'They could be anywhere.'

'So I gathered. We've a long journey ahead of us,' said Goldie. 'I need to go below and check with Lug that the engine's up to it. You'd better stay here. You'll be all right on your own for a bit. The old jalopy almost steers itself. If anything happens just give a tug on this.' She pulled what looked like a lavatory chain and the calliope blew a harsh note.

When she was alone Wren walked around the wheelhouse inspecting the machinery. It reminded her of the intricate workings of the clock on Ambrosius Blenk's mansion that her father had built. It was a comforting thought. She crossed to the window and cupped her hands to it to gaze ahead into the darkness but caught only fleeting glimpses of the occasional tree in the rainbow lights as it flashed past. Everything else was black. She felt tired and very alone. *I hope this is what the glow-worms meant and that I'm headed the right way.* She rested her head against one of the many brightly polished pipes that rose through the floor. As she did so she could hear faint voices transmitted through them from somewhere below. She could just make out the echoing words but not who was saying them.

'. . . So her name's Wren, you say? Are these friends of hers – Mel and Ludo – the ones you're looking for?' The voice was deep and gravelly.

There was a mumbling reply, more a vibration than a sound and far too dim to make out. But it was definitely another man's voice.

'We're headed for Anywhere,' said the first voice.

The mumbling vibration again.

'The plan's working out nicely.'

Mumble.

'You're sure she'll lead us to them?'

Another mumble.

'Me? Just the flowers. You can have the children. Just as long as I get the flowers.'

Wren felt as if her heart had stopped. The brass pipes were suddenly very, very cold.

'In here, Morg?'

Ters Selen, Mudge and Tunk followed the Morg into the room where the Maven's paintings were stored. Ter Tunk and Ter Mudge's faces and hands were cruelly bitten. The Morg had his nose to the floor and went from one canvas to another, sniffing. He stopped before the painting of the fairground. Right in the foreground was a large circular area of faded grass. The Morg began moaning and clawing at the paintwork with his long, horny nails.

'That's enough,' said Ter Selen, pulling him back by his leash. 'So she's gone in there, has she? Very well. Where she can go, we can follow. Is that what you want, Morg?'

The Morg looked up at his mistress and mewled pitifully.

Dust

'The mirrorblood's rising. It's nearly up to the cleft,' said Mel as he ducked back into the cavern. 'Can you see another way out?' The luck-compass continued its sad chiming.

'The snails are headed for that cleft at the back of the cave. Let's follow them.' Ludo got down on his stomach and crawled after them, pushing his spark-ball in front of him. 'Mel!' came his muffled shout. 'Pull me out. *Quick!*'

'What's the matter?' said Mel, pulling him back by his legs. 'Did you get stuck?'

'No. There's more of that mirrorblood seeping through in there.' Ludo jumped back as the red liquid flooded through the cleft. 'Now what?'

They dashed back to the front of the cavern just as more mirrorblood spilled in through the main cleft.

Mel held his spark-ball up and looked frantically around the cave.

Ludo said, 'There's nothing here. Just stone.'

'And dust.'

'Great,' said Ludo. 'But what we need's a way out of here. And fast. Use the whatsit.'

Mel opened the luck-compass. 'Which is the way out of here?' The hand swung round to point at a pile of dust that had built up against the cavern wall.

'That can't be right,' said Ludo.

'It's the only thing in here that we can draw a mirrormark in,' said Mel. 'But I've no idea where we'll end up.'

'I don't care,' said Ludo. 'Anywhere's better than being dead. *Quickly!* The mirrorblood's almost here.'

Mel knelt and drew a mirrormark in the pile of dust. 'OK, Ludo, link arms.' The mirrorblood was lapping at their boots when he traced the mark and they vanished.

Ludo opened his eyes and then shut them again quickly. 'Mel! It didn't work. We're still in the cave.'

'No, we're not. I don't know where we are but we're definitely not in the cave.'

Ludo opened one eye and looked at his feet.

'There's no mirrorblood.' He opened the other. 'Just dust. Are we dead? *Ouch!* What'd you do that for?' He rubbed his arm where Mel had pinched him.

'You wouldn't have felt that if you were dead.'

Ludo pinched him back.

'*Ouch!*'

'That proves we're both alive. Where are we?'

Mel shrugged. They were standing ankle-deep in grey dust. All around them rose huge mounds of the stuff like towering dunes. The only other thing visible was the uniform grey sky.

'Let's climb to the top of one of these dunes and try and find out.' Mel led the way.

The view from the top was just as mysterious. A great sea of dust-dunes spread away to the horizon in every direction like a grey desert. Far off, there was a thin line of whiteness like a distant snowfield.

'What's the whatsit say?' asked Ludo.

Mel flipped open the luck-compass and studied the dials. 'Which way to Wren?' The direction hand swung. 'Come on, Ludo.'

As they scampered down the face of a dune in the

direction indicated, Ludo said, 'So how did we get here? There wasn't even a picture in the dust.'

'In a way there was. I drew a mirrormark in the dust in the cave and we ended up here, surrounded by dust. Isn't it enough that we're still alive and headed for Wren?'

'Do you think she's all right?'

'I hope so. King M-morpho seemed pretty sure that his bodyguard could protect her.'

'What can butterflies do?'

They started to climb the face of the next dune.

'Doesn't it worry you that we seem to be getting further and further away from her?' said Ludo. 'It's almost as if the whatsit doesn't want us to rescue her.'

'It's kept us alive this far.'

'Yeah; but only just.'

When they reached the summit they stopped.

'Look. Way over there,' said Mel. 'What's that?'

Ludo strained his eyes. 'That towering black thing? It looks like some kind of whirlwind.'

'And underneath it's what looks like a city. Come on. Let's go.'

'OK. There's bound to be someone who can tell us where we are.'

Mel looked at the luck-compass. 'This agrees. It's pointing the same way.'

'At least it's *somewhere*. But where?'

'Search me,' said Mel. 'It could be anywhere.'

'I don't like this. I don't like it one bit.' Ambrosius Blenk was standing at his studio window looking out at the sky above Vlam. 'A rainbow without rain. I can only see the tip. Where's the rest of it?' He shook his head. 'Who ever heard of a rainbow behaving like that? When do you estimate it will reach the city?'

'At this rate it should touch down tomorrow. There's been a run on picks and spades. Everyone imagines that it will reveal a hidden hoard of gold.' Dirk Tot bent his giant frame to take in the view his master was seeing. 'The first cloud is changing too. It's getting darker and the shapes more substantial. The symbols are mirrormarks for sure.'

'And it's still snowing sparks from the second one.

Let's hope there'll be no more clouds. All right; tell it to me again.'

Dirk Tot recounted what he had been able to glean from Green and Blue.

'My paintings!' The master was furious.

'And others. Green recognised one of Midas Garf's.'

'That could explain where the clouds are coming from. The sparks must be from my picture – but I don't know how they're managing it. At this rate I won't have any apprentices left. And my life's work will be incinerated in that diabolical contraption. We're going back to see the Maven. And this time I won't take no for an answer.'

The Merry-Go-Anywhere-You-Want-To

'Are you feeling OK? You don't look too well.'

Goldie's voice startled Wren. She spun round. The voices she had heard in the pipes belonged to men; neither of them could have been Goldie's. Besides, she had only been gone a short while. There was not time for her to get back up to the wheelhouse, and Wren could not believe that this cheerful, open-faced figment was part of a conspiracy. It must have been Lug that she overheard. But who did the other voice belong to? 'Goldie, how many people are there working on the merry-go-anywhere-you-want-to?'

'There's just me and Lug. To be honest, he gives me the creeps but he knows his onions about engines. Keeps himself to himself. He never comes up here.'

'Anyone else?'

'No. Why?'

Wren told Goldie about the voices she had overheard.

'Are you sure you didn't imagine it?'

'No. And Lug – if it was him – knew my name. Did you tell him?'

'No. I couldn't find him. I just checked some gauges and lubrication points and came straight back up.'

'So you've no idea who the other voice might belong to?'

'Perhaps we've got a stowaway. It happens from time to time. There's always some freeloader trying to grab a ride.'

'But the voices sounded like they knew each other. And they knew all about me and Mel and Ludo.'

'Yeah, that is strange. Come on. Let's go and take a gander.' Goldie led Wren down the stairs into the throbbing darkness of the engine room.

'It's huge,' said Wren as she gazed down into the vast space. 'We'll never find anyone down here.'

'We will if we split up. You go down that way and I'll go down this. See if you can spot anything. It's best if you don't speak to Lug – just in case. We'll meet up back here.'

Feeling uneasy, Wren began to descend the stairs.

The music of the calliope was much louder and interspersed with a wheezy, thumping counter-beat from the greasy engine. The staircase spiralled down through three more levels, the machinery getting larger and the air more stifling the deeper she went. Everything smelt of engine oil. She saw metalwork gantries that wove their way through the tangle of hissing pistons, rocking beams and turning screws lit at intervals by dim bulkhead lamps. It all seemed far too large to fit into the merry-go-anywhere-you-want-to.

The massive steam furnace that powered the roundabout was on the lowest level and so dimly lit it was like night time. Then Wren saw the furnace door swing open, revealing the dark silhouette of a figment standing in the orange glow the fire cast on the floor like a luminous carpet. She froze. *That must be Lug.* She knew she ought to go back and get Goldie, but stared fascinated at the small figure.

As she watched, the figment stooped and took several shovelfuls of coal from a hopper and fed them into the flames. He mopped his brow with a handkerchief he took from the back pocket of his dirty overalls and spoke.

'I know you're there. You'd better come out.'

Wren's heart skipped a beat. She did not move. She held her breath and watched the figment through the spokes of a rapidly spinning flywheel. She could see that he was not a carved and gilded figment like Goldie. He was short and squat with a hunched back, a hooked nose and pointed chin like some sort of gnome. His skin was a dark crimson colour and covered in warts. He seemed to wear a permanent sneer. His black hair stood on end as if he'd been hung upside down and had forgotten he was the right way up again. He turned his sweaty face and looked straight at her hiding place.

'It's no good hiding. Don't make me come in and get you.'

Wren swallowed hard and stood up. She scanned the gantries above her looking for Goldie. She knew she should call her but Lug's stare seemed to paralyse her.

'A girl. You must be Wren, our rich passenger.' He even spoke like she imagined a gnome sounded –

gravelly and insincere. She recognised his voice as one of those she had overheard. 'What're you doing down here?' His eyes glinted in the half-light as he stood there wide-legged with his hands on his hips.

'Nothing. I . . . I got lost. I was trying to find my way outside.'

'Just because you're a rich kid and can afford a ride you needn't think you've got the run of the place. Let me tell you, this engine room's mine. I say who can come and go down here. No one else. Got it?'

Wren's muscles seemed to be working again and she nodded and turned to leave.

'Not so fast.' Lug came closer and stared at the flowers in Wren's hair. Wren wished she had taken Goldie's advice and removed them. His eyes seemed to light up with fire and he reached out his gnarled hand towards the blossoms. His narrowed eyes flitted from side to side as if he was trying to decide what to do – or see if anyone else was around. He licked his lips and raised both hands towards Wren.

'Lug?' It was Goldie's voice.

Lug lowered his hands.

'Lug? Who's that with you? Have you caught a stowaway?'

'Stowaway? What stowaway? No. It's only the passenger.'

Wren looked up. Leaning over one of the gantries was Goldie. Their eyes met.

'*There* you are. I told you you'd get lost if we didn't stay close,' improvised Goldie. 'Come along, now. We've arrived.'

Wren backed away from Lug and then turned and almost ran up the staircase to where Goldie waited.

'Are you all right; you don't look too good,' whispered Goldie. 'Lug didn't bother you, did he? He's a bit of an odd one.'

'He's not like you, is he?'

'No, he's not one of us fairground people – but he knows his stuff about engines, I'll give him that. As long as he does his job and keeps the merry-go-anywhere-you-want-to singing and dancing, it's fine by me.'

'Did you find that stowaway?'

Goldie shook her head.

'Lug's staring at us,' said Wren. 'I can feel him.'

'Look, are you absolutely sure you heard what you heard?'

Wren nodded. 'I think we should get out of here.'

When they got up to ground level Wren went outside and saw Anywhere for the first time. Her expression must have betrayed her feelings.

'I didn't think you'd like it once you got here. Beats me why you wanted to come in the first place,' said Goldie.

'I didn't expect a city – and such an ugly one.'

It was daylight. Everywhere and everything was covered in a thick layer of spongy, grey dust. Drab, slab-sided buildings were pierced with what might once have been windows but were now grey frames holding grimy, almost-opaque grey glass that no one could possibly see out of. Not that there was anything worth looking at – or anyone to look at it; the streets were deserted and also covered ankle-deep with the dust.

'There must be someone living here,' said Wren. 'I can see footprints everywhere. Maybe they prefer to stay indoors.'

'Who wouldn't,' said Goldie.

The only trees Wren could see were dead ones. There were towering, stilted aqueducts overhead formed from what might have been riveted steel girders beneath the ubiquitous dust. From where she stood Wren could see two of them, but guessed there were more. Only a little lower than these structures were sagging cables on which cars moved lethargically. The aqueducts and cable cars were all headed towards a towering, monolithic building that stood at the polluted, wheezing heart of Anywhere. It had no windows and its flanks were peppered with hundreds of circular vents from which blew clouds of the choking, grey dust. From the very top of the building rose a funnel of swirling, black air.

Wren felt that she just seemed to be getting further and further away from Mel and Ludo. Then she remembered the luck-compass and knew that they wouldn't have stayed put. They would be trying to find her. She was sure of it. She hoped that the luck-compass would lead them here. She forced a smile on to her face and turned back to Goldie. 'What are you going to do now?'

'Oh, I'll give the old jalopy a bit of spit and polish and set up shop. See if I can get a fare who wants to go back.' Goldie surveyed Anywhere. 'We'll have to fight them off, I imagine. You get off now and find your friends. I'll make sure Lug doesn't try and follow you.'

'Won't you come with me? I don't like the thought of leaving you here on your own with Lug. He's up to no good. I just know he is.'

'Don't worry. I can handle him. I'm going below now to get to the bottom of this stowaway business.'

'But –'

'Off you go. And do yourself a favour; take all those valuable flowers out of your hair.'

As Wren reached up to remove the flowers, the music died away and the merry-go-anywhere-you-want-to slowed to a halt. Goldie looked at a gauge on the side of the calliope. 'We're losing pressure. Lug's not been stoking the furnace. Something's wrong. I'll go and see what's up.'

'I'm coming with you.'

'OK.' Goldie led the way back down through the machinery. 'Lug!'

Silence.

'Lug! Where are you?'

Nothing.

'Maybe he's gone up to the wheelhouse?' said Goldie.

'But you said he never goes up there.'

'There's a first time for everything. I'd better throw a bit of coal into the furnace first. Get up a head of steam.'

There was a muffled clanging noise from behind the furnace.

'Lug's crib.' Goldie went around the furnace to a steel door and tugged at the handle. 'It's jammed.'

'Here, use this.' Wren handed her a long-handled spanner from a rack.

Goldie fitted it to the handle as a lever and the two of them heaved. There was a metallic screech and the door opened. The steel pole that had been holding it shut clanged and rolled on the floor.

Lug's crib was a noisome, poky little den with bare, rivet-studded walls. There was an unmade cot and another makeshift bed on the floor beside it.

Goldie read the situation at once. 'The stowaway

must have been in here with Lug. He's been hiding him.'

'That doorway doesn't look like it's meant to be there,' said Wren, nodding to a hole in the wall. 'It looks like it's just been hacked out.'

Wren and Goldie crossed to it and peered out. They were beneath the floor of the merry-go-anywhere-you-want-to. It was dark, with only a ribbon of light at the edge of the roundabout. But it was not so dark that they could not make out the trail of footprints in the grey, Anywhere dust leading away from them.

'He's done a bunk,' said Goldie.

Wren grabbed Goldie's arm. 'Look, there's two sets of footprints. I bet the other belongs to the stowaway. Now do you believe me? It's a cert they were in this together. Look, will you help me find my friends –?'

'This Mel and Ludo?'

'Yes. If we can find them they have this thing which can easily track down those two.'

Goldie thought for a moment. 'The old jalopy won't be going anywhere without an engineer.'

'You're better off without that creep, if you ask me. Please say you'll help me.'

Goldie's eyes twinkled. 'It sounds better than kicking my heels around here on my own. Sure, I'm up for it. Besides, I want to know what Lug's been up to.'

'Do you think it might have anything to do with Guv's disappearance?'

'I didn't. But now I'm not so sure. Are you certain these friends of yours can help?'

'I'm certain. Even if they don't want to help I'll stick with you until we find Lug and the stowaway. I promise.'

'Thanks, Wren. You're all right for a rich kid.'

There was a new attraction at the fairground – a freak show. Ters Selen, Mudge and Tunk stood with the Morg at the centre of the circle of faded grass recently vacated by the merry-go-anywhere-you-want-to. The crowd that had gathered listened in silence to the end of Ter Selen's speech.

One member of the crowd tentatively raised his hand. 'I saw her. I heard where they were taking her.'

Ter Selen turned in his direction. 'Where? Speak up.'

'What's it worth?'

'Your life.'

The Morg lunged for him and dragged him, squirming, into the centre of the ring by his kicking legs.

'Now do you want to tell me?'

A little while later hands were shaken, flowers exchanged and the purchase of the Ferris wheel was complete. Ter Mudge and Ter Tunk, with their bite-speckled faces, mounted one cradle and Ter Selen and the Morg another. A third cradle was occupied by their unwilling guide, the unfortunate figment who happened to know the way to Anywhere.

Anywhere

When they reached the city, Mel and Ludo were appalled by the drab, grey scene that greeted them. They walked on through the deserted, dust-choked streets. There was the loud pop of an electrical spark and they looked up to see a cable car high overhead before it vanished over the roofs of the grey buildings opposite.

'I think I preferred the bottom of the well,' said Ludo.

'*Anywhere's* got to be better than this. The luck-compass seemed pretty sure that we'd find Wren here.'

'But where do we start?'

'Let's follow that cable car. It must be going somewhere.'

It led them to the monolith. Mel and Ludo marched around it until they arrived back at the start of their trail of footprints in the grey dust.

'What *is* this building?' said Mel. 'There's not even a window, let alone a door.'

'And where *is* everybody?'

'What do you think that swirly thing is, coming from the top? It's just like the whirlwind we saw in King M-Morpho's orchard.'

'You don't suppose it's –'

'Sucking this place away as well?' said Mel. 'Whatever's happening, it gives me the creeps.'

There came a hum and a muted bang from overhead and a shower of sparks fell towards them. They looked up to see another cable car disappearing into the monolith high above their heads.

Mel opened the luck-compass and said, 'Where's Wren?' The direction needle swung round until it was pointing at the towering building. 'She must be in there.'

'But how do *we* get in?'

'That looks like the only way,' said Mel, pointing to the opening the cable car had disappeared into. 'We need to take one of those. How do you suppose we get on one?'

'We'll need to find someone and ask.'

They set off through the empty streets but found no pedestrians.

'This is spooky,' said Ludo. 'The city's completely empty.'

'Let's follow one of these trails of footprints. Somebody must have made it.'

All the doors in Anywhere were especially anonymous and the one at the end of the trail they followed was no exception. Mel knocked. After a while the door opened a crack.

'Yes?' said a wheezy, female voice from out of the darkness inside.

'We're sorry to disturb you,' said Mel agreeably, 'but where are we?'

'You're in Anywhere – as if you didn't know.'

'We wondered how to get into the big building?' asked Ludo.

They felt they were being stared at but there was no reply.

Mel went on. 'Is it by the cable cars?'

The hidden voice said, 'Those are for workers only. Only workers are allowed in the monolith.'

'But we only want to take a look,' said Ludo. 'Our friend might be in there.'

'Your friend a worker?'

'No.'

'Then they're not in there.' The door started to close.

'Just a moment,' said Mel. 'If the only way in is by cable car and the cable cars are for workers only, then how do you become a worker?'

'Three streets down, turn left, one block down and it's on the corner. They always need new workers,' wheezed the voice and closed the door.

'Three streets down, turn left, one block down and it's on the corner' proved to be a drab building indistinguishable from every other drab building in Anywhere. Apart, that is, from the queue that had formed outside. They were the only figments Mel and Ludo had seen in the city.

'I think we've found Anywhere's main attraction,' said Ludo.

They joined the end of the queue and asked the figments in front of them what they were queuing for. Everyone ignored their questions.

'Melkin Womper and Ludolf Cleef,' said Mel as

they reached the head of the queue to a figment who sat at a desk. 'We'd like jobs in the big building.'

'Have you read the Terms and Conditions?'

'Terms and Conditions?' said Mel.

'On the wall, behind you.'

Mel and Ludo turned. The wall – the *entire* wall – was papered with an enormous document covered with the smallest printing either of them had ever seen. A tall ladder rested against the Terms and Conditions with a large magnifying glass chained to it.

'Mel, we can't stop to read all that; it'd take *weeks*,' said Ludo. 'If Wren's in there now, she won't be by the time we've finished.'

'We really should read it before we sign,' said Mel.

'Let's just sign. After all, we're not going to be sticking around once we've found her, are we?'

'Oh, all right,' said Mel.

'Read them? Good. Sign here and here.' The figment swivelled the ledger and Mel and then Ludo signed with the proffered pen. He turned it back and made a note against their names. 'Orange 22403101 and Orange 22403102. Through the door and up the stairs. *Next!*'

Together with a dozen figments, Mel and Ludo, all now dressed in the ill-fitting, hooded black overalls they had been issued with, were taken to the top of the building and herded into a cable car which lurched over the grey rooftops of Anywhere and towards the monolith. When it stopped a while later and the door opened they were inside the huge building. It looked just as drab and featureless as everywhere else in Anywhere. They were directed to stand with their backs to a large metal door.

'New intake line up,' ordered another figment, obviously a supervisor, who was waiting for them in the corridor next to the entrance. Apart from his grey overalls, the only thing that made him different from everyone else they had encountered was his clipboard. In a short while he had sorted them into seven groups. There was Mel and Ludo in orange, two more each in yellow, green, violet and red and one apiece in blue and indigo.

'Someone's got a sense of humour,' said Ludo.

'Yeah,' said Mel. 'Can you imagine colour anywhere in Anywhere?'

There was a rumble as the large door slid open behind them. When they turned they were looking down on to more colour than they knew existed.

'Aren't you going to lock it up?' asked Wren as she removed the flowers from her hair and stashed them in Goldie's satchel for safe keeping.

'Who's going to steal the old jalopy around here?'

'Look, here're their footprints. The small ones must be Lug's. The other set's much bigger. As big as a full-grown man's.'

Wren and Goldie left the merry-go-anywhere-you-want-to on the outskirts of the city and trudged through the deep grey dust, following the trail. Their tracking was easy until they reached what was, judging by the amount of footprints, the main thoroughfare of Anywhere.

'Now where?' said Wren, looking up and down the deserted street. 'You'd think with all these footprints there'd be someone to ask directions from.'

'Well, we know they're somewhere in the city. I think it's time we asked some questions.'

It proved a long search before they finally found someone who spoke to them through a letterbox set into a grimy door. Wren and Goldie were informed that the only place Lug and the stowaway could possibly be was inside the monolith.

A while after that, new workers Indigo 29990313 and Indigo 29990314 stepped from the cable car in their own baggy black overalls and entered the great building.

The entire interior of the monolith was lit by an enormous arc lamp that filled the ceiling.

'Everything in here's so bright it hurts to look at it,' gasped Mel.

Light cascaded down on to tier upon tier of gleaming machinery, and there was a cacophony of mechanical sound. The sight and sounds made the friends' heads spin. It seemed that the aqueducts brought milk-coloured raw material into the building at the very topmost level. From there it descended in many filtered channels and sluices in an ever-tightening spiral as it passed through an unbelievable number of complicated machines. At each stage, giant fans blew off grey, foam-like scum that formed on the surface. This was vented to the outside through huge, circular grilles. By the time the liquid had travelled way down to the depths of the building it comprised the brightest, purest colours they had ever seen, and disappeared into the rotating jaws of a machine where it was lost from view.

'Wow,' said Mel.

'Double wow,' said Ludo. 'What do you think they're making in here?'

'Rainbows,' said the supervisor, shaking his head. 'What do you think?'

'Not whirlwinds?' said Mel. 'Like the one on the roof.'

'Never you mind what's on the roof,' said the supervisor. 'Your job's in here.'

'But I thought . . .'

'You're not here to think,' interrupted the supervisor. 'That's what I get paid for. You're here to work. And right now that means removing the hyper-clot.'

'Hyper-clot?' said Ludo.

'Is that what they're doing down there?' asked Mel, peering down towards the very lowest level of the monolith. 'Removing the hyper-clot?'

'Give the boy a prize.'

'But why do they need those metal suits?' said Ludo.

The super tapped his clipboard and heaved a weary sigh. 'Right, you're new here so I'll tell you once and once only in words even you can understand.' He took a deep breath. 'The blanch-water is brought in from Nowhere via the aqueducts, where it's double filtered and drip-fed through the contra-rotating prismatic separators. The purifying oscillators fillet the mid-tones and re-addle the tertiaries into the main vacuum pans. The flossing oscillators mix the reverberated sediment into the re-hydrated marmaluking flux as the thermo-revelated maculates are skimmed off by the reciprocal gibbets. From there the scum reducers invert the wish-trees and fickle the coagulants in the whirligig centrifuges. Tell me if I'm going too fast for you.'

Mel only had time to utter, 'What –?' before the supervisor ploughed on.

'However, sedimentary overload, induced by

supra-abundant, denatured iridescence can sometimes infiltrate the magnetic bloom attractors and precipitate infra-chromatic pollution, in which case the reverberating turbine cams will induce an ingurgitation of excessive, not to say catastrophic, magnitude in the compartmentalised precipitation vessel, resulting in the aforementioned mutation-bolus or hyper-clot.'

'I see,' said Ludo. 'And the metal suits those people are wearing?'

'Have you ever stuck your hand into a hyper-clot? Of course you haven't; you've still got your fingers. Now wait here. And?' The supervisor raised his eyebrows in expectation of an answer.

'Don't touch anything?' said Ludo.

'Got it in one.' The supervisor hurried off.

'Did you understand anything he said?' asked Mel.

'That? Sure. Kid's stuff,' said Ludo unconvincingly.

'How ever are we going to find those scrots in here? It's vast and there're so many workers,' said Goldie.

'Look, Lug's short and squat and the stowaway's quite tall judging from the size of his footprints,' said

Wren. 'My guess is they'll stick together. Look out for an odd-sized couple.'

'That could be them,' said Goldie, pointing.

Wren stared hard at the tiny figures on the second tier of machines at the far side of the monolith, one tier below where she and Goldie stood. Their backs were turned and their faces hidden by pipework but they were certainly an odd-looking pair. 'Yes! I think you're right.'

'Who're they talking to?'

'One of the grey supervisors, I think. They're pointing at someone or something on the tier underneath us.'

Goldie leaned out over the rail to get a better view. 'Could be anything or anyone.'

'Here, let me see. *Goldie!* It's Mel and Ludo! My friends. We've found them.'

'By the looks of it, so have Lug and the stowaway.'

'You two. Come with me.'

Mel and Ludo followed the returning supervisor into one of the open-sided lifts on their tier. The figment pulled a lever and they began to descend between the giant machines.

'I've been told that you two were apprentice artists before you worked here and know about colour. Is that right?'

'Who told you that?' asked Ludo.

'So, do you?'

'A bit; yes,' said Mel. 'But who –?'

'Good. I've a special job for you. It's right up your street.'

The lift reached its destination and Mel and Ludo followed the supervisor out on to a platform surrounded by airlocks. Empty metal suits of various sizes stood around the platform near to the airlock doors dripping pools of colour on to the studded floor. A figment was hosing them down. As Mel looked at him he was sure he looked slightly transparent. Before he could comment on this, a harassed-looking supervisor strode up to them. 'Are these the volunteers?'

'But –' said Mel.

'Come along now,' said the harassed supervisor, 'over here. The hyper-clot's not responding to the usual measures. We're going to send down a couple of DORCS.'

'Who're you calling dorks?' protested Ludo.

'Dangerous Obstruction Removal and Cleaning Systems,' said the supervisor with a note of impatience. 'They're over here.'

The DORCS might once have been gleaming, well-engineered pieces of machinery, but were now dirty and corroded. Streaks of grime and flakes of rust covered them and they were each attached to small cranes by a stout cable. The hulls were spherical, covered in short spikes and stood about three times as tall as Mel. From the front of each protruded several attachments. Some were like hooks and steel brushes and one looked like a gun barrel. There were fin-like limbs around the circumference of the hull and rudders and a propeller behind.

'Now, in you get,' said the supervisor.

Mel and Ludo were each helped into a machine through small, circular hatches at the rear, which were then locked in place behind them.

As soon as he was inside, Mel began to feel

claustrophobic, so hemmed in was he by pieces of machinery. There was an adjustable metal saddle, a set of pedals and a bewildering array of wheels, knobs, sliders and levers. Everything was beaded with condensation. Peeling instructions with complicated diagrams about the operation of the DORCS were pasted to the curving hull walls. Immediately in front of the pilot's saddle was a porthole with thick, tinted glass. From outside, the contraptions looked like huge spiny puffer-fish at full puff with a magnified boy's face staring out of the middle.

'Right,' barked a tinny voice from a speaker on the hull wall, 'we're going to open the jaws of the precipitation vessel and lower you down. You must manoeuvre yourselves up to the hyper-clot and disperse it with your attachments. The instructions are right in front of you. Don't worry, you'll be fastened to the cranes at all times. Any problems, push the big red button and we'll haul you out. Keep a check on your oxygen level. Good luck. We're all counting on you.'

'Wait. We don't know what this hyper-clot looks like or how to operate these contraptions,' protested Mel.

'There's no mistaking a hyper-clot,' said the supervisor.

'What if –'

The speaker clicked off. The DORCS were hauled aloft by the cranes, swung out from the platform and lowered towards the huge jaws, which slowly opened. Mel was reminded of an eager shark with its head tilted back, awaiting its next meal.

As the jaws swung open, the luck-compass inside Mel's overalls began to chime its sad tune. Then, as the DORCS were lowered into the precipitation vessel, there came a loud *crack*. Mel looked up and saw that the jaws had snapped closed, severing his and Ludo's cables. An instant later their DORCS plummeted down towards the deadly hyper-clot.

The Hyper-Clot

'Mel! Mel! What happened?' Ludo's voice crackled from a speaker in Mel's cabin.

'Ludo?'

'I can't hear you. Press the green button and speak into the grille under the porthole.'

'I think the safety cables must have snapped. I can see the ends trailing around outside,' said Mel with a sinking feeling.

The two DORCS were floating in a translucent, multi-coloured sea. Mel felt dwarfed as he glimpsed huge nozzles and other pieces of machinery through the coloured haze. There were lumps of unidentifiable debris suspended in it, and from time to time these would collide with the hull of his machine, making an echoing clatter inside.

'Mel, I'm pushing the big red button but nothing's happening. Try yours.'

As soon as Mel touched his emergency button it sprang out of its casing and rolled around on the curved floor. 'Mine's broken too. These DORCS are clapped out. They must have seen what happened up top. They'll be sending a new cable down, I hope.'

'So what do we do?'

'Find the hyper-clot and disperse it. Someone's got to do it.'

Just then, Ludo's DORC floated into view through Mel's porthole, a swarm of coloured bubbles trailing from its spinning propeller. 'Mel, use the pedals. They make you go forward. You can steer with the two big levers.' His twin rudders waggled from side to side.

'Got it,' said Mel as he began pedalling. 'And the wheels next to them make you go up and down.' As they descended through the coloured sea the chunks of debris became larger and were moving more swiftly.

'What's this hyper-clot supposed to look like?' said Ludo.

'I think it must be a great big sphere of swirling colours. Like the marbled endpapers in an old book.'

'How do you know that?'

'Because I'm looking right at it. It can't be anything else. Steer to your right and you'll see it too.'

Ludo operated his controls until he was facing the hyper-clot. It dwarfed his DORC. The brilliant colours moved over the surface in eddies and swirls. From time to time they assumed the shape of angry faces with ugly, gaping mouths that glided over the outside of the blob. One face seemed to follow Ludo as he piloted his machine closer.

'Careful, Ludo. Don't get too close.'

Suddenly, the swirl's mouth puckered and sucked in Ludo's DORC with a *pwuk* sound. 'Help!' The mouth shut after him and smiled a malicious smile.

'Ludo, where are you?'

'Inside the clot, you clot. It's dark in here but I can see out through the thing's skin.'

'Can you use one of your attachments to punch your way out?'

'*Oh, no!* The arm's melted – like candle wax. Now the pedals aren't working. Nor's the rudder. They must have melted too. Mel, help!'

'I'm coming, Ludo.' Mel knew he had to act fast.

'Mel. Hurry up.' There was a burst of static. 'My DORC is making a horrible noise. It's going to melt too.'

'Hang on.' Mel desperately studied the complicated diagrams on the inside of the hull. He started to read the long caption. *If procedures E22 and/or V81 prove inoperable open hermetically sealed projectile receptacle R99 . . .* And gave up.

No time! Just copy the diagram. He reached down and opened a coffer near his right foot. Inside were five shiny silver balls about the size of apples. He took one and fitted it into an open-ended tube just above it. As he pedalled towards the hyper-clot once more he pulled back the tube's spring-loaded plunger and released it. The shiny ball shot out of the barrel and sped towards its target. It hit the hyper-clot, causing the marbling to form a concentric ripple pattern on its surface. He waited.

Nothing happened.

Maybe it was a dud. Then a face appeared on the surface of the clot. It appeared to be in discomfort.

'. . . was that?' came Ludo's voice between staccato bursts of static. '. . . bright flash . . . colours changed . . .'

'Keep your head down,' yelled Mel as he took

aim and released a second missile.

The ball struck and the face appeared again. This time it looked like it might be sick before it vanished into the swirls.

'. . . Mel . . . getting really bumpy . . . quick . . .'

'One more should do it, Ludo. Hold on.' As Mel reached down for more ammunition the oxygen gauge caught his eye. The needle was in the red. 'Ludo, how's your oxygen?'

'. . .! . . .!'

Mel quickly fired a third ball. As the ripples in the hyper-clot subsided, yet another face appeared out of the swirls. This time it was sick. A great multi-coloured tsunami gushed from its open mouth and, riding the crest of the wave like a spherical surfer, was Ludo's DORC. Mel could instantly see that it was in very bad shape. All of the spikes and attachments had melted and he could see horrible, ulcerous carbuncles where the hyper-clot had eaten into the hull. But worst of all, squashed up against the misted porthole where he had pitched forward, was Ludo's unconscious face.

Mel pedalled like mad until he was alongside

Ludo's craft. Manipulating one of the hooked attachments, Mel snagged the remnant of the cable that was still trailing from the top and pulled it close to him.

'Ludo! Ludo, answer me.'

There was only static in reply.

Now several faces that had formed on the multi-coloured surface of the hyper-clot glided together and morphed into one huge, man-in-the-moon face that occupied an entire hemisphere. It narrowed its eyes, puffed out its cheeks and blew. There was a violent lurch as Mel's DORC was thrown backwards, dragging Ludo's machine with it. Then came a deafening crash that made his ears ring as he ricocheted off the wall of the precipitation vessel. The glass in several dials shattered and a pipe ruptured, sending high-pressure liquid jetting into the interior of his machine. He found a valve and managed to shut it off but the effort left him breathless. He looked at his oxygen gauge. It registered zero. When he looked out at Ludo he could clearly see cracks etching themselves on the hull of his friend's craft as if drawn by an invisible hand.

Mel reached down into his coffer – only two balls left – loaded one, and fired. He shook his head to clear the dizziness he was feeling. As his vision cleared, he saw the look of pain on the giant face as the missile exploded deep inside the clot. It blew both DORCS away again. Mel's machine cannoned off a large piece of debris sending the two small craft into a whirling pirouette around each other like ice dancers. His hull groaned and a crack zigzagged its way across his porthole. Mel tried pedalling but gave up. He panted as he tried to breathe in the non-existent air, and nausea swept over him.

There was an echoing triple *clank* as pieces of debris hit Mel's hull. He pressed the green button and leaned close to the grille. 'Can anyone hear me? *Please* answer.' His head drooped. 'If you don't get us out of here soon . . .'

Clank-clank-clank.

'. . . we're going to . . .' He shook his head. The collisions were too regular to be accidental. Was it some kind of signal? He lifted his leaden arm and rapped three times on the inside of the hull.

Clank-clank-clank, came the instant reply. A column of coloured bubbles and then a blank metal head floated into view through his porthole. A metal-clad hand lifted a spanner and rapped another three times. It was a diver in one of the metal suits. As it swam up Mel could see that it was trailing a spare cable. There was a scrabbling sound of metal on metal above his head and then the anonymous armoured head and hand reappeared upside down in the porthole. It gave the thumbs down signal. It took Mel a moment to realise it was actually thumbs up.

The face on the hyper-clot revolved to face the DORCS. There was a wicked gleam in its eye as it began to suck. Feeling deathly tired and even more afraid, Mel fired his final shot. The last thing he saw was first the nose and chin and then the cheeks and eyes caught in the suction and flow into the mouth. Then the rest of the hyper-clot followed as it sucked itself out of existence.

'Is he dead? He certainly looks like it.'

'I'm not sure.'

'What about the other one? His DORC was in a bad way.'

'He's the luckiest boy alive. That diver was insane going near the hyper-clot in only a suit. Hyper-clots are strictly for DORCS.'

'Saved these two, though. Looks like this one's coming round as well now.'

'Lucky scut. Who was operating the jaws anyway?'

'Some new guys – a long 'un and a short 'un. Probably fooling around with something before they were qualified. They ran off when they saw what happened.'

Mel opened his eyes. Above him, where he lay on his back swam a number of blurry faces. He thought some of them looked slightly transparent, like ghosts. He blinked hard and they became clearer but no less see-through.

Ludo's face joined the others. 'Thanks, Mel. You saved me.'

Mel swallowed. 'It wasn't me, Ludo. It was the diver. How is he?'

Behind the concerned group of figments that had

gathered around the two boys stood the diver. Another figment unbolted the heavily corroded metal helmet and lifted it off. The diver shook out long auburn hair and turned.

'I thought you two were supposed to be rescuing *me*.'

'Wren?' Mel rubbed his eyes and his heart leapt. '*Wren!*' He got to his feet and rushed to Wren. They hugged and slapped each other on their backs. Ludo joined in.

A figment with a carved, golden face poking out of her baggy overalls arrived. 'So these are your friends,' she said to Wren. 'Looks like you got to them just in time.'

'Mel, Ludo, this is Goldie. She helped me to rescue you. Have you still got the . . .' Wren looked around at the figments and lowered her voice. '. . . The you-know-what?'

Mel nodded.

'Good, we'll need it to find Lug and the stowaway.' She saw the look of confusion on Mel and Ludo's faces. 'I'll tell you later.'

The crowd was joined by the harassed supervisor.

He clapped his hands impatiently. 'Come on, come on. The hyper-clot's cleared. There's work to be done.' He approached Ludo. 'Here you are. A souvenir.' He tossed him a jewelled ring. 'Found it jammed in the machinery. This is the piece of junk that instigated the hyper-clot. Just my luck it's not something valuable like a nice rosebud.'

'We're getting quite a collection of jewellery,' said Mel. 'Ludo found a silver chain and now this.'

Wren examined the ring. 'I bet that came from Nem.'

'I think you're right,' said Ludo. 'Look at the workmanship.'

'We need to get out of here,' said Mel.

'Are you sure you're well enough?' said Goldie.

'If you'll both lend us a hand we'll be all right,' said Ludo.

'You four aren't leaving,' said the supervisor, 'not in the middle of your shifts.'

'How long's a shift?' asked Wren.

'Two weeks. A month now we're on double shifts. But we'll see if you make it that far – or rather, we won't.' The supervisor seemed to find this amusing.

'In that case, we quit,' said Ludo.

'Quit? You can't quit. Didn't you read the Terms and Conditions?'

The friends looked at the supervisor blankly.

'Allow me to refresh your memory.' He drew in a deep breath. 'Clause 57,956, section 33,271, subsection 1,479(a): Premature Termination of Employment. If the party of the first part should wish to terminate the duration of their engagement without the consent of the party of the second part then they need to apply in triplicate no less than 365 days prior to the notification of such aforementioned termination. You can't possibly have forgotten that already.'

'Funny how little things like that slip your mind,' said Ludo.

'The brooms are over there. When this platform is spick and span you can report to Orange and Indigo sections for reassignment.' The supervisor hurried away to the lift.

As they swept, they each recounted the events that had reunited them.

'So that's this thing that Wren told me about,'

said Goldie as she studied the luck-compass. 'And you can use it to find out where Lug and the stowaway are now?'

'We owe you that, Goldie,' said Mel. 'Anyway, I think that everything that's happened to us is connected.'

'How do you work that one out, luv?'

'Well, if Lug knew all about Ludo and me, I bet he learned that from the stowaway. I bet the stowaway got us sent to clear the hyper-clot and then cut the safety cables.'

'But why?'

'I don't know.' Mel shook his head. 'But the stowaway must be from Vlam. He must be the person who told the super that we were apprentices.'

'There're not many people in Vlam that know how to get into the Mirrorscape,' said Ludo. 'It could be the Ters.'

'It can't be them,' said Wren. 'They were all there for the wedding.'

'What about your master?' said Goldie.

The three friends shook their heads.

'That only leaves Dirk Tot, the mistress, Green and

Blue,' said Mel. 'And it wouldn't be one of them.'

'What about this Cassetti geezer?' said Goldie. 'You told him all about yourselves. *And* he knows about the Mirrorscape.'

Mel looked at Wren and Ludo. 'I don't think so.'

'You don't sound very sure about it.' Then, after a pause, Goldie said, 'Do you know where Lug and the stowaway are now? I've got a lot of questions that need answers.'

Mel looked at the luck-compass and said, 'Where's Lug?' The direction hand swung round. 'They're near here but not in the monolith.' He looked at Wren, Ludo and Goldie. 'Do you want to wait for the end of your shift?'

'Or apply in triplicate 365 days in advance?' added Ludo.

Everyone shook their heads.

'Me neither,' said Mel. He looked at the luck-compass again and said, 'Which is the way out?'

It led them back to the topmost tier. Each time they encountered a supervisor they began to sweep madly or polish the already gleaming machinery. On the far side of the monolith they could see a new intake of workers arriving.

'How about trying to get out the way we came in?' said Wren.

'There're too many supervisors,' said Ludo. 'There *must* be another way out.'

'Mind your backs!' The friends stepped aside as a figment worker wheeled a large laundry basket overflowing with overalls. He was even more transparent than any other worker they had seen.

'Where are you taking that, Yellow 227415?' asked Mel, leaning close to read his name tag.

'Laundry train,' answered the figment. 'Here it is now.'

A door slid open and standing at a platform was another cable car.

'You're dedicated,' said Goldie. 'I thought you'd be celebrating with all the others in Yellow.'

'Celebrating?' The figment looked confused.

'Yeah,' said Mel, catching on immediately. 'You've all won the thingy.'

'Thingy?' said Yellow 227415. 'You don't mean

Section of the Month award?'

'That's the one,' said Ludo.

'That's why we've been told to take over the laundry detail,' said Wren. 'Congratulations.'

'Great! I might even get out of here before I'm all gone.' Beaming with delight, the figment left his laundry basket and almost skipped off back the way he had come.

'What did he mean about "all gone"?' said Ludo.

'Who knows?' said Mel. 'We've got our way out of here.' They wheeled the basket on to the empty cable car.

Twenty minutes later they all stepped off at one of the deserted stations near the edge of Anywhere and deposited their laundry basket alongside dozens of others.

'That was a breeze,' said Goldie. 'Now, where does the luck-compass say Lug is?'

'Where's Lug?' Mel turned until he was facing the same way as the direction hand. 'That way.'

'What's that noise?' said Ludo as distant strains of music started up.

'The old jalopy!' said Goldie in alarm. 'They must

be going to use it to get away. We've got to stop them.'

'How long will it take them to get it going?' said Mel.

'A while,' said Goldie. 'The furnace was cold.'

Then, over the dust-covered rooftops and through the empty streets of Anywhere, echoed the terrifying and unmistakable howl of the Morg.

'What was *that*?' Goldie studied the frightened faces of her new friends.

Pilfer by Name,
Pilfer by Nature

In a bare cellar room lit by a single lamp there was a scruffling sound as a canvas sack opened all by itself and a pot of paint and a paintbrush rose from inside. The pot floated over to a table and the lid popped off. As the brush dipped itself into the seemingly empty pot its bristles vanished. The stub then floated up to the wall and described a disc which, after a moment, became transparent.

'Now, let's have a little shufti, shall we?' said a voice out of thin air.

The view through the disc revealed the interior of an extensive hothouse. An intricate tracery of cast-iron columns and vaults soared up to a lattice-work of glass in the roof as delicate and complicated as the veins in a dragonfly's wing. Strong light flooded down on to a jungle of giant coloured plants and flowers.

'Right on the button. Pilfer, my old son, you're a skegging genius, even if I do say so myself.' There was the sound of coarse hands being briskly rubbed together. 'Now, let's get cracking.'

A pickaxe, a shovel, a drill and a sledgehammer floated from the sack and arranged themselves on the floor. There was the sound of spitting and the hands being rubbed again before the drill rose into the air and approached the wall.

There was a noise outside and the drill floated back to the floor. A moment later the door opened.

'It's only a room,' said Mel. 'Another dead end. So much for your shortcut, Ludo. Let's get back outside before we waste any more time. What's that?' He walked over to the disc and reached out his hand. 'There's a hole in the wall. *Ouch!*'

'What's the matter?' asked Wren.

Mel examined his scuffed knuckles and then tapped the disc. 'It's not a hole. It's some sort of window.'

Ludo and Goldie peered through the disc.

'It's a greenhouse,' said Ludo.

'*Greenhouse?*' Goldie's jaw dropped open. 'Are you

pulling my chain? You really don't know? It's a skegging bank vault, that's what it is.'

'What do you mean?' said Ludo. 'Those are flowers.'

'It's what they use for money around here,' said Wren.

'Someone's tried to break into the bank,' said Goldie. 'That's what all these tools are doing here. They must have been scared off and left them.'

'Let's take them,' said Mel. 'To protect ourselves.'

'You leave them where they are.'

'What?' said Mel.

'I didn't say anything.' Ludo looked confused.

'Get your thieving mitts off my gear.' The sledge-hammer rose into the air and hung menacingly before the friends.

Ludo stumbled backwards, tripped on the shovel and fell against the table. The paint pot tottered and fell, covering him in its colourless contents. As he got to his feet a large part of him vanished. All that remained visible was his head, right shoulder and both hands. The floor beneath him became transparent and everyone could see down into the cellar.

'Look out,' said Mel, stepping back.

'Now look what you've gone and done,' said the voice. 'I ought to stave your scrotty heads in.' The sledgehammer quivered.

As the friends backed away, Mel searched around in the pocket of his overalls and found a handful of the grey dust that seemed to get everywhere. He flung it in the direction of the voice. For a moment the dust clung to the outline of a short, fat human-shaped figment with a shock of curly hair and a goatee beard. The shape sneezed and the dust rose in a cloud and drifted away. The figment was invisible once more.

There was a loud sniff. 'What'd you have to go and do a thing like that for? I wasn't going to hurt you. *Achoo!*'

'What was all that business with the hammer then?' said Goldie.

'Young Chummy here was going to pinch my tackle. I need my tools.'

'You were robbing this bank,' said Wren.

'Pilfer by name, pilfer by nature,' said the voice. 'A figment's got to make a living.'

'Why can't we see you?' said Wren.

'Now who's pulling whose chain?' After a baffled silence from the friends Pilfer added, 'You really don't know?'

'How could we?' said Mel.

'What about me?' complained Ludo.

'But your overalls. You work in the monolith,' said Pilfer.

'Only since today,' said Wren. 'Besides, we just quit.'

'Quit? Before the end of your shift? That explains why I can still see you. I guess you're not from Anywhere.'

'Look, Pilfer, why don't you tell us what you're prattling on about?' said Goldie.

'Someone had better clue you ignoramuses in,' said Pilfer. 'Right, you've all seen what they were making in there . . .'

'The rainbows,' said Mel.

'. . . so you'll know how colour works.'

'Kind of,' said Wren.

'*Kind of?*' There was a note of incredulity in Pilfer's voice. 'They must be scraping the bottom of the barrel for workers these days. Look, here's the science bit. Pay attention. When light shines on something red, the red light is reflected back – that's what you see. The light from all the other colours is absorbed, OK? Same thing with the other colours. They're reflected and all the colours that aren't a part of it are soaked up. What they do in the monolith is to take the blanch-water that they channel in from Nowhere.'

'That'll be the white stuff,' said Goldie.

'Got it. Everything in Nowhere's white. White contains all the colours of the spectrum, see, and they separate out all the individual colours.'

'Like with a prism,' said Mel.

'That's the ticket. Then they refine it until it's pure enough to make rainbows. Now, to refine the colours to rainbow-grade they need to take away all the impurities – the stuff that's no colour at all.'

'That must be the grey dust,' said Wren.

'The girl's a genius. Well, if the stuff used in the rainbows reflects back all the colours there are, then what's left over . . .'

'Doesn't reflect back any at all,' finished Mel.

'Which is why it makes things invisible,' said Ludo.

'But why are you invisible?' asked Wren.

'Before I embarked on my present career I used to work in there, too. So did just about everyone in Anywhere.'

'That explains why we didn't see anyone in the streets,' said Goldie. 'They're invisible.'

'Stay around here long enough and you'll be invisible too,' said Pilfer. 'It's why the monolith needs a constant stream of new workers. As sure as eggs is eggs they all end up invisible. Once your shift's over it's "ta-ta, been nice knowing you". You're never seen again.'

'We saw some that were starting to become transparent,' said Wren. 'They must have been near the end of their shifts.'

'So why aren't the streets and houses invisible like you?' said Mel. 'And Ludo,' he added, glancing at the remains of his friend.

Ludo scowled.

'It's all to do with moisture, Chummy. You have to mix the dust with moisture for it to work. It never rains in Anywhere so you can see all the buildings. But workers sweat, see, and by the end of their shift they've gone; vanished; poof.'

'Then why aren't the supervisors invisible?' said Goldie.

'Supers, break into a sweat? Do me a favour. Invisibility is bad news for the workers but good news for us robbers. I makes up my pots of paint from the dust so that I can take a butcher's into the odd nook and cranny that takes my fancy,' said Pilfer.

'Like bank vaults,' said Goldie.

'And such like. If you've quit before the end of your shift then the supers will be after you before you can say contra-rotating prismatic separators.'

'They're not the only ones that are after us,' said Wren.

'So you need to get away, do you?' Pilfer was quiet for a moment. 'Look, I'll make you a proposition; a little business deal. Strictly between us. You help me with this how's-your-father and I'll show you the way out of Anywhere.'

'A bank robbery?' said Wren. 'I don't know.'

'What've we got to lose?' said Mel. 'Except some more of Ludo.'

'That's not funny.' Ludo looked silly scowling with only bits of him visible.

'We don't have time. There's this . . . like a bloodhound after us. It'll sniff us out.' Wren hugged herself and a shiver ran through her.

'Not in Anywhere it won't,' said Pilfer. 'That dust not only takes away colour, it also takes away the sense of smell. So, what do you say?'

'Come on, Wren,' said Goldie. 'Sounds like a lark.'

'A figment after my own heart,' said Pilfer.

'All right. Let's get on with it, then,' said Wren.

'But what about *me?*' persisted Ludo.

'Don't pay any attention to him,' said Mel. 'He's not all there.'

'Right,' said Pilfer, 'give me a hand with this drill.'

'I've got a better idea,' said Goldie, dipping the paintbrush in the last of the invisible paint. She drew a long line across the wall. 'Look, there's a buttress just here on the far side. Without that the whole wall will come tumbling down.'

When Pilfer spoke there was a note of respect in his voice. 'Are you sure you haven't done this kind of thing before?'

Goldie winked at where she guessed Pilfer was.

Together they drilled a shallow hole next to the buttress.

'Now for my party piece,' said Pilfer as he withdrew and donned a pair of metal gauntlets. He then carefully lifted out a heavy metal syringe – the kind of thing you might use to ice a giant's cake. 'Stand back. It's loaded with hyper-clot.'

'What!' said Mel. The two boys took a step backwards. 'We don't want any more to do with that stuff.'

'Calm down,' said Pilfer. 'I know what I'm doing.' He put the nozzle to the hole and squirted. 'Stand back!'

It was like a silent, slow-motion explosion and almost at once there was a heap of rubble and a cloud of dust that revealed Pilfer again briefly as the vault wall crumbled away. An alarm began wailing as the friends stepped over the broken masonry and into the vault.

'Lovely loot! Carnations, chrysanthemums, roses, lilies – I'm rich! I'm a skegging millionaire.' Fistfuls of flowers were disappearing into Pilfer's sack. 'I'll leave the pimpernels and daisies; I can't be bothered with small change. Help yourself, there's plenty for all; but we must be quick.'

'We're fine as we are,' said Wren.

Only Goldie helped herself to a bunch of blossoms which she stashed inside her overalls.

'OK,' shouted Mel over the noise of the alarm, 'that's our side of the deal. Now, how do we get out of here?'

'What about me?' moaned Ludo.

'Right little ray of sunshine, aren't you?' said Pilfer. 'Quit belly-aching and look inside your overalls.'

Ludo eased open the neck and peered inside. 'Hey, I'm still there.'

'Course you are, it's only paint. Don't take them off,' said Pilfer as Ludo began to slip out of his overalls. 'It's part of the plan. Now, all of you, raise your hoods, cover your faces and pull your sleeves down over your hands.' He took another paint pot from his sack and tipped the contents one by one over the friends. As the invisible paint trickled over them they vanished. He did the same for his sack. 'Now, if we meet anyone, just pull your hoods over your faces and keep your hands tucked out of sight.'

Mel's disembodied face turned towards the hole in the wall.

'Not that way, Chummy; that's just what they'll expect. First rule of robbery: do the unexpected. We're going out the front door.'

The front door was what you would expect to be sealing a bank vault. By the time they reached it, the huge gears and bolts on the back of the thick, steel door were moving. A moment later the massive circular door began to swing silently inwards.

'Stand over here with me,' whispered Pilfer. 'Hoods up, hands in, make yourselves scarce.'

Before the door was fully open a band of grey-suited supervisors rushed in. 'Careful,' said one of them, 'this looks like Pilfer's work. He might still be here. Fan out. You check the roses, you the lilies.'

Just then there was a great crash from the far side of the vault next to the hole in the wall as a pile of loose masonry toppled over.

'He's over there,' said the lead super. They

all ran towards the hole.

'On your toes,' whispered Pilfer. 'This way.'

'How'd you do that?' said Ludo.

'Invisible string. First rule of robbery: think ahead. Watch, I'll give it another tug.' There was a second crash. 'They fall for it every time.'

'Come out with your hands up,' shouted the super into the hole as Pilfer and the friends nipped through the vault door, down a corridor and out through the bank lobby into the street.

'This is where things get a little tricky,' said Pilfer. 'Footprints. They'll know I'm not alone.'

Sure enough, as Mel looked back at the grimy facade of the bank he could clearly see their footprints leading away.

'It's around here somewhere.' There was a swirl of dust in the street where Pilfer's voice came from. 'Ah, there you are, my beauty.'

Mel watched as a manhole cover emerged from under the thick dust and thrust itself aside.

'Everyone down here.'

'Oh, no. Not another well,' came Ludo's voice.

'That's a one, and a two, and a three,' said Pilfer as he counted everyone into the manhole with a hand on their shoulders. 'Where's the other one?'

'I'm here,' said Mel.

'And five makes a robber's half-dozen. Right the way down.'

As he reached the bottom, Ludo drew back his hood. 'This is a sewer.'

'What did you expect, Sunshine?' said Pilfer, lighting a lamp from his sack. 'A gilded carriage? We're desperate criminals on the run.'

Mel ventured a sniff. 'Pilfer's right. The dust takes away the smell.'

'Would I lie? I'm an honest robber. Now, follow me, stay close and don't splash your hands or faces.' Invisible feet sloshed their way through the dirty water. 'They'll track us to the manhole but they won't dare follow us. Moisture, you see. Now, where to?'

'Follow the sound of the music,' said Goldie.

'Down here.' Pilfer's footsteps took a side-sewer and his bobbing lamp led the friends' floating heads to a manhole near the merry-go-anywhere-you-want-to.

As he lifted the manhole cover at the top of an iron ladder, the music of the calliope got much louder.

'What can you see?' said Mel.

'That your jalopy?' said Pilfer. 'Seems the rest of the fairground followed you. There's a skegging great Ferris wheel here, too. It all looks like it's deserted – no, wait. There's a short geezer with a crimson face on the roundabout.'

'Lug,' said Goldie. 'Anyone else?'

'Looks like he's on his own.'

'Now he's gone back inside,' said Pilfer. 'Let's go.' He thrust the manhole cover aside and climbed out. One by one, the friends pulled up their hoods and followed him.

'Now what?' said Ludo as they all stood in front of the turning merry-go-anywhere-you-want-to.

'We have to overpower Lug and get back control,' said Goldie.

'Uh-oh,' said Pilfer. 'Looks like we've got company. With any luck, they might work up a sweat.'

Coming towards them down the street out of Anywhere was a great cloud of dust raised by a band of running supervisors.

Just then, Lug re-emerged from the calliope. He saw the approaching supervisors. 'Hold your horses. Where do you think you're going?' he snarled as he stepped down.

'There're bank robbers at large,' said the lead supervisor as he signalled the others to halt. 'We're going to have to search your roundabout.'

'Oh, yeah,' said Lug, placing his hands on his hips and thrusting out his chin. 'You and whose army?'

As one, the supervisors drew truncheons from their pockets, but Lug simply glared at them.

'I've got an idea,' whispered Goldie.

Mel saw her footprints creep up behind Lug and a handful of flowers appear around his feet.

'Where'd they come from?' The gnome stared amazed at the blossoms.

'Look!' shouted one of the supervisors. '*He's* the robber. We've caught him red-handed.'

'But they're not mine –' The supervisors grabbed Lug.

'What're you lot waiting for?' said Goldie from the

direction of the merry-go-anywhere-you-want-to. 'An invitation?'

Once inside the calliope, they followed Goldie's voice up to the wheelhouse. They quickly stripped off their overalls and became visible again.

'Right, time we got out of here.' Goldie began checking the dials and gauges. 'Pressure's up.'

'Wait a minute, Goldie,' said Wren. 'Is Pilfer here?'

'Course I'm here. First rule of robbery: stick by your mates. Let's skedaddle.'

Mel looked out of the window. 'There's quite a tussle going on down there. Let's go before they realise what we're up to.'

Goldie threw a few levers and the merry-go-anywhere-you-want-to unwound once more and headed out of Anywhere at high speed. She took a deep breath, grabbed the wheel and pulled a chain. The calliope gave a triumphant, discordant blast.

'Now they've seen us,' said Mel. He thumbed his nose at the diminishing crowd.

'Uh-oh,' said Ludo. 'There are the Ters and the Morg.'

The supervisors released Lug and shrunk back from the terrifying creature as he bounded towards them.

Wren joined Mel. She grabbed his doublet in alarm. 'Goldie, how fast can the merry-go-anywhere-you-want-to go?' she asked over her shoulder.

'How fast do you want to go?'

'As fast as you can,' said Wren. 'The Ferris wheel's coming after us. Lug's on it, too. It looks like he's working with the Ters.'

'That old thing. They won't catch us. Never in a million years.'

No sooner had Goldie uttered the words than the dials all around her began to plummet and the music from the calliope slowed down.

'We're losing pressure,' said Goldie.

'But how?' said Ludo. 'I thought you said we had enough.'

'We did. It's sabotage. Someone's venting all our steam. It looks like the stowaway's still on board. We'll never get away now.'

The Mirrorstorm

The Hollow World

The merry-go-anywhere-you-want-to slowed to a halt as the music died away. Lingering in the silence were the sad chimes of the luck-compass.

'I feel sick,' said Mel.

'I know,' said Goldie. 'I thought we were well away.'

'No, I mean I really feel sick.'

'It's the Mirrorscape,' said Wren. 'You and Ludo have been in here too long. We need to get back to Nem – at least for a bit.' She squeezed Mel's shoulder.

'Fat chance of that,' said Pilfer. 'This crate looks like it's had it. We'll never outrun that Ferris wheel on foot and the supers won't be far behind. We'll all be facing a long stretch for this.'

'Prison?' said Ludo.

'No, Sunshine, the rack.'

'There's one way out of here,' said Wren, 'but it's not back to Nem.' She crossed the wheelhouse and stood before one of the wall paintings. It depicted a fanciful jungle brimming with cheerful-looking animals and brightly plumed birds in the same enthusiastic but unskilled style as the rest of the roundabout's decorations.

'Again?' said Ludo. He was also beginning to look ill. 'That'll take us even further away from Nem.'

'We don't have any choice,' said Wren. 'What's the luck-compass say, Mel?'

Mel flipped it open and asked, 'Which way out of here?' He nodded towards the painting. 'It agrees with you. I'd better make a mirrormark.' He found some excess grease on a valve and quickly drew the symbol on to the picture with his finger.

'If it's time to abandon ship,' said Goldie, 'I'll go and grab us a few bits and pieces that might come in handy.'

'Be careful,' said Wren. 'The stowaway's still on board.'

'Don't worry,' said Goldie. 'My guess is he'll be sticking close to the boiler to make sure we can't get up a head of steam again.' She cast a longing look around the wheelhouse, patted a binnacle affectionately and disappeared down the staircase. Wren noticed that her eyes were moist.

'Mind if I tag along with you lot?' asked Pilfer. 'Looks like my career in Anywhere's on hold for a bit.'

The friends looked at each other and smiled. They knew they could use another friend in the Mirrorscape – especially someone as resourceful as Pilfer.

'It'd be great to have you along,' said Wren.

Their smiles disappeared when they heard the howl of the Morg.

'He sounds very close,' said Mel.

Wren called down the staircase. 'Goldie? There's no time!'

'They're here!' shouted Ludo from the window.

The Ferris wheel came to a halt and the passengers dismounted. Ter Selen slipped the Morg's leash and he bounded towards the merry-go-anywhere-you-want-to.

'*Goldie!*'

'Keep your hair on,' said Goldie as she ran up the last of the stairs, carrying a large bag.

'We've got company,' said Mel.

'I know,' said Goldie. 'I've arranged to put a knot in their hosepipe.'

There came a loud roaring from outside and

everyone looked out of the window. Below them, many of the brightly painted animals from the merry-go-anywhere-you-want-to had dismounted and were attacking their pursuers with remarkable ferocity.

'Goldie,' said Pilfer. 'You're a little treasure.'

'I do what I can.'

There was a loud commotion from the floor below.

'That didn't hold them long,' said Ludo, 'they've got in already.'

'No, they haven't.' Goldie put two fingers to her gilded lips and whistled loudly. '*Oi*, you lot, stop squabbling!' she shouted down the stairs. 'Get your woodworm-ridden carcasses up here as quick as you like.'

There was a scrabbling on the stairs and then a winged horse from the ride climbed into the wheel-house. It was followed by a crocodile-headed parrot, a bat with a unicorn's head and legs, a half-swan, half-giraffe creature and a chubby dragon. It was a tight squeeze.

'I don't know how far we might be going,' said Goldie, 'but I don't fancy walking.'

'Bags I the dragon,' said Ludo.

'Goldie, if ever you fancy a change of career, look me up,' said Pilfer with evident admiration.

'Let's go if we're going,' said Goldie taking a last, wistful look around the crowded wheelhouse. 'Happy memories. I'll miss this old rust-bucket.' A tear rolled down her cheek.

'Time we were on our way. Link arms and grab hold of a ride.' Mel traced the mirrormark in the air.

Ambrosius Blenk rode through the streets of Vlam in his magnificent ultramarine carriage, drawn by four white horses with ostrich plumes crowning their gleaming harnesses. Beside him sat Dirk Tot and opposite, Green and Blue. All four men viewed the scene outside with mounting concern. The spark-filled streets were thronged with citizens, many of them equipped with picks and shovels as they raced towards the point where the rainbow had only minutes before touched down. The carriage's progress through the overexcited crowd became slower and slower until it finally ground to a halt.

'I'm sorry, master,' the coachman called down, 'the crowd's too thick. The route's completely blocked. There's no way we'll be able to get to the House of Spirits through this.'

'It won't be by the scenic route but I can get us there,' said Green.

The four men dismounted. The throng parted readily for the huge figure of Dirk Tot as he led the small party against the flow, following Green's directions. As they mounted the steep flank of the Hill of Thrones beneath the royal palace they turned a corner and were treated to a view over the city's rooftops.

The three ominous clouds overshadowed Vlam. From the belly of the first fell ever more macabre cloud-shapes. The huge billowing monsters seemed to be losing their nebulous, cloud-like quality and were becoming darker and more substantial. Each new shape got closer and closer to the ground before it dissolved and floated away. The sparks falling from the second cloud were thicker than ever and could clearly be seen to assume a swirling, whirlwind formation at their heart.

But it was the third cloud that seized everyone's attention. The rainbow that had seemed so ethereal and innocent when it first manifested itself now appeared to be formed from grosser matter, its colours too bright, its arc now laser-beam straight. It had touched down in a quarter of the city famed for its theatres and taverns. The men's eyes searched in vain for the familiar landmark of the domed Hall of Comedies, but in its place at the rainbow's end was a mass of rubble. The dome was smashed like an eggshell and tiers of scarlet seating clung to the insides of those walls still standing. The adjacent buildings had begun to smoulder and even from their distance the master and his retinue could hear the ringing of alarm bells and see that the flood of people towards the rainbow's end had reversed. The gold rush was disintegrating in terror as they fled from the toxic rainbow.

Blue touched Ambrosius Blenk on his shoulder. 'Master, look.'

His eyes followed Blue's pointing finger. High above Vlam, over the very centre of the city, and equidistant from the three clouds, a fourth had begun to form. A great darkness swirled at the heart, like the pupil of an enormous, fathomless eye as it began to grow.

'Hurry,' said the master. 'There's no time to lose.'

'This makes a nice change,' said Ludo. 'Whenever we enter a painting there's normally something nasty waiting for us.'

'The money grows on trees and I've got nothing to cart it away in,' said Pilfer sadly as he gazed about at the riotous splendour of the lush jungle. Flowered vines threaded their way through oversized jungle vegetation and waves of brilliantly coloured blossoms lapped at their feet like coloured surf.

'Don't be greedy,' said Wren, 'your sack's already stuffed with the proceeds of the bank job.'

'I know – but I can't help myself.'

Nearby, a tigress lay grooming herself with a huge, pink tongue while her cubs played with a dangling creeper like kittens with a ball of wool. A doe-eyed antelope grazed close by, totally unafraid of what anywhere else would have been its natural predator, and a family of monkeys rode bareback on a leopard. The painting on the wall panel had been rendered in a naive style but now that they were actually there, it was realer than real, with every colour pure and every object crisply delineated. So welcoming were the surroundings that Mel was not the least surprised to see a large, red velvet sofa nestling among the flower-draped vines. A wave of queasiness overtook him and he flopped down gratefully, startling the bird-of-paradise that had been using it as a perch. His head lolled forward and he began to doze.

'Come on, sleepyhead,' said Goldie as she shook Mel gently, 'you can rest later. We need to get you home for a spell. Which way to Nem?'

'Huh?' Mel forced himself awake and looked at the luck-compass. 'Which way home?' He tilted it several ways before he got a reading. 'It says that way.' He pointed straight up into the air.

'What? You must have meant this way.' Goldie pointed into the undergrowth. 'Is this the way you meant?'

'Yeah,' said Mel blearily. 'I suppose so.'

Ludo too had to be roused from the bed of soft leaves he had found, and the party mounted their extraordinary, carved beasts. Goldie took the lead on the crocodile-headed parrot, Wren followed on the bat with a unicorn's head, Mel on the winged horse and Ludo the fat dragon. Last in line waddled the swan with a giraffe's neck and head, carrying the invisible and complaining Pilfer.

'Strike a light, Goldie. If this old quacker isn't the most uncomfortable ride I've ever had.'

'Stop grizzling, Pilfer,' called Goldie over her shoulder. 'It's only until we can find enough space to take off.'

The strange procession rode on in silence for a while, ducking under low branches and trailing creepers and listening to the music of the jungle as unseen creatures called to each other. Slowly, the vegetation thinned and grew less dense until light stole through the canopy and it ended altogether. They stopped at the jungle's edge, astounded by the view that greeted them. Only Pilfer broke their silence.

'Struth! Now I really have seen everything.'

*

The scene around the merry-go-anywhere-you-want-to resembled a battleground. The dead and splintered carcasses of the rearguard rides lay all around, forming a graveyard of gilding and coloured paint. The Morg had added no more than a random smattering of punctuation to the scars that covered his misshapen body. He was barely out of breath as he led Ter Selen into the deserted calliope and up to the wheelhouse. Once inside and away from the dust of Anywhere, his sense of smell returned and he led his mistress to the painted panel bearing Mel's greasy mirrormark.

'Mudge, tell me what you see.'

The small Ter described the picture to her mistress.

'So Wren and those boys have taken to the jungle, have they?'

'You must destroy the painted panel,' said the stowaway. 'They must not be allowed to return this way. And . . .' The stowaway hesitated.

'Out with it?'

'We must abandon this chase,' he said. 'I promise that we will deliver the girl to you after we have dealt with the boys. How I'm looking forward to that. But now, the mirrorstorm is beginning. We must return to Vlam. I have prepared a canvas that will take us straight back to the House of Spirits.'

'Hear that, Morg? You must wait a little longer for your honeymoon. It will make your reunion with your bride all the sweeter.'

A short while later, Ter Selen's beautiful eyes added a new colour to their ever-changing spectrum. They were filled with the orange reflection of leaping flames as the merry-go-anywhere-you-want-to burned. Silhouetted against the blaze were the black figures of Ter Mudge, Ter Tunk, Lug and the tall stowaway, who drank greedily from Guv's store of beer, which he had plundered before firing the calliope.

The world was hollow and Mel and his friends were inside it.

Although the ground beneath their feet seemed flat, the entire Mirrorscape could be seen to curve up and up on every side, losing detail as it did so until it joined together far away above their heads. There was no horizon. The forests, rivers, mountains and lakes clung to the inside of the vast sphere. Clouds and entire weather systems cast dark shadows as they hung over the surface. But the sky, if the space in the centre of this weird world could be so called, contained the strangest thing of all. Like the stone at the heart of a peach floated an immense spherical castle. Even though it was very far away they could see that the fortress had spires and turrets that rose from it in every direction like a spiked ball.

'*That's* what the luck-compass was pointing at,' said Wren, craning her neck.

'I don't like this. It's making me feel giddy,' said Pilfer.

'Maybe things will look different from the castle,' said Mel.

'Up there? We're going up *there?*' Now Pilfer sounded sick, too. 'It'll be like travelling to the moon.'

'It's nearer than the moon,' said Ludo.

'Not much,' said Goldie. She urged her mount on a few paces and looked back at the others. 'Well? Are you coming or not?' She dug her heels into her beast's side and it spread its glossy wings and took to the air.

'Come on, then,' said Wren as she followed.

Mel, Ludo and Pilfer did the same.

Their trepidation fell away with the ground as the makeshift flock climbed higher and higher in a formation as tight-knit as the one they had occupied on the merry-go-anywhere-you-want-to. Mel's sickness left him temporarily, to be replaced by exhilaration. He twisted in his saddle and gazed behind at the jungle they had left and saw the tops of ruined temples strangled with vines peep above the treetop canopy and, further back, a volcano overflowing with bright rivers of lava that cascaded down its sides. To their left he saw a thunderstorm pricking the flanks of a mountain range with its dazzling, needle fingers, and ahead a great lake dotted with hundreds of forested islands. Large herds of animals galloped across dusty plains, startled by the flock's shadow, and deserted, ruined cities flashed by beneath the white, beating wings of his horse. Higher and higher they climbed until the Mirrorscape below lost its features and began to resemble a map washed in shades of green, blue and brown.

Suddenly, in the middle air, the world flipped. Above their heads was the hollow world and below them, the castle. It was still a long way away but that way was unmistakably down. The ragged flock spiralled towards their destination.

Mel narrowed his eyes and peered down. 'Look. We're headed towards that huge courtyard.'

Below them, details of the colossal fortress rushed up to meet them. There were moats, barbicans and keeps in endless confusion. There was every component of the well-equipped fortress except occupants. It was empty.

Goldie guided them down until they eventually landed heavily within a grassy, high-walled bailey. She swung down out of her saddle and clicked her tongue soothingly as she stroked the neck of her battered mount. 'That was quite a ride. These poor puppies won't make the return journey.'

As Mel dismounted, one of his horse's wings fell to the cobbles. There was a crash and he looked around to see the legs of Ludo's dragon collapse under him and his friend, still mounted, jolt to the ground.

'Will they be all right?' said Mel.

'Sure,' said Goldie. 'There's plenty of grazing here and they'll enjoy not having to carry passengers on their backs for a while. In time their limbs will grow back and there's a whole new world for them to live in.'

'Where are we?' said Ludo as he slid off the saddle.

'No idea,' said Wren. 'We need to get you two back home as quickly as possible.'

Mel spoke to the luck-compass. 'Which way back to Nem?'

They followed the steady needle on the direction hand, which led them to a circular door in the massive surrounding wall. It opened on to a dark interior. A lamp materialised from Pilfer's invisible sack and another from Goldie's bag. When lit, they revealed a long, circular corridor.

'It's definitely this way. And the luck strength's increasing.' Mel led them inside.

The corridor was made from blocks of grey stone artfully fitted together to form a tube-like passage that rose and fell and twisted and turned as they progressed.

'What *is* this joint?' said Pilfer. 'It looks more like a

piece of complicated plumbing than masonry.'

'Sounds like one too,' said Ludo.

There was a constant, gurgling undertone overlaid now and again with the distant rushing of liquids. As they walked on, a new sound became apparent; a rhythmic rasping that rose and fell in pitch. The circular corridor was joined at intervals by others at Y-shaped junctions, but the luck-compass guided them on as the strength needle crept slowly higher up its dial. Then the passage ended in a great blackness ahead of them that their lanterns could not penetrate. Pilfer, holding his lantern high, advanced into it.

'Come on,' said Wren. 'Let's see where we are.'

The rasping was much louder.

'What's that noise?' whispered Ludo, awed by the darkness.

'I don't know,' Wren whispered back. 'Sounds like snoring.'

'*Snoring!*' said Ludo much too loudly. 'Snoring?' he repeated in a low voice. 'It's coming from everywhere.'

Goldie's lantern beam picked out a glint in the darkness. 'There's something shiny up ahead.'

When they reached it they found a tall, intricately carved and gilded candelabrum standing next to an equally elaborate lectern. The candles suddenly lit themselves. They cast a pool of yellow light in the blackness that contained the lectern, the party and their shadows. When Pilfer passed in front of the light the others could just make out his filmy outline. On the lectern's sloping surface was stretched a sheet of parchment, secured around its edges by a cat's-cradle of threads like a miniature trampoline. Above it lay a quill pen and, next to it, an inkwell.

'What do you suppose it is?' said Wren. 'Some kind of visitor's book?'

'Maybe we should sign it,' said Ludo.

'Do you think so?' said Mel as he picked up the pen. He opened the lid of the inkwell with a click. The snoring ceased abruptly and the darkness vanished.

Cogito the Lucubrator

Mel, Ludo, Wren, Goldie and (presumably) Pilfer stood there blinking in the sudden light, amazed at the strangeness of what they saw around them. They were dwarfed by an enormous chamber. The stonework seemed to have melted into an amorphous, almost organic shape as full of creases and wrinkles as a bloodhound's face. There were hundreds of glowing nodules that protruded from the walls and ceiling to illuminate the eccentric space. Not that Mel and his friends took much of this in; they were staring at what occupied the rest of the room.

'Ugh,' said Ludo with disgust. 'It looks like a wall made from something's insides.'

'Those huge blue balloons must be lungs,' said Wren as she watched them inflate and deflate.

'Look at all those fat veins,' said Mel. 'They're full of coloured liquid.'

'And that must be its ticker,' added Pilfer.

A mighty, bulbous heart throbbed amid a plethora

of other, unidentifiable organs that squelched, gurgled, bubbled and wheezed to their own syncopated rhythms. In the middle of this mass of animated innards floated a huge bloodshot eye that stared at the intruders.

'What *is* this place?' said Goldie.

Mel snapped the inkwell closed. The lights went out and the snoring began again. After a moment he flipped it open and the lights came back on as the slumbering mass awoke a second time.

'Well, you've found the on–off switch,' said Wren. Then, in a more forceful voice directed towards the pulsating wall in front of her, 'Hello. Can you hear us?'

There was no reply, just the watery stare of the lidless blue eye.

'This lectern's not here just for show,' said Goldie. 'Why doesn't someone try writing on it?'

'I'll do it.' Mel picked up the quill and dipped it in the ink. After a moment's thought he wrote *Hello* as neatly as he could.

Everyone was expecting something to happen but nothing did.

Mel crossed out his word and was surprised as he saw it fade and vanish. He wrote *Hello* again, trying to be even neater.

Still nothing happened.

'Maybe it is a visitors' book after all,' said Ludo.

Mel crossed out his second word, watched it disappear, and wrote his name. The last thing he did was to dot the 'i' in 'Melkin'. As he did so, the rhythm of the pulsating mass changed and the sounds were joined by a low electrical hum as a web of blue-white sparks darted from nodule to nodule. Mel's sepia writing vanished and on the parchment in its place appeared the words *Syntax Error* in a flowing and elegant script.

'It must mean Mel's made a mistake,' said Ludo.

'Don't talk daft. I know my own name.'

Wren said, 'Why not ask a question?'

As the words faded Mel wrote, *Where are we.*

His writing vanished and *Syntax Error* appeared once more until it too faded away.

'You left out a question mark,' said Goldie.

Mel tried again. *Where are we?*

As soon as he made the dot underneath the question mark there was a gurgling, whirring sound and the dance of the sparks across the walls and ceiling changed its tempo. His question vanished and the word *Cogito* appeared in its place.

'"Cogito." What's that mean?' said Wren.

'No idea,' said Ludo. 'Ask it something else.'

Mel wrote, *Who are you?*, being careful with his punctuation, which seemed to be the key to getting an answer.

Cogito.

Mel wrote, *What are you?*

There was a short pause before *Cogito, ergo sum* appeared.

'What's it on about?' said Pilfer.

'Maybe it's a foreign language,' said Ludo.

'Or nonsense,' said Goldie. 'But at least it's talking to us.'

Mel's hand trembled and he paused as a wave of nausea swept over him before he wrote, *We need to get back home. How can we get back to Vlam?*

Search me.

'Oh, thanks for nothing,' said Ludo.

'We know the way back's in here somewhere; the luck-compass says so,' said Wren. 'Perhaps it didn't understand. Try rephrasing the question.'

Which is the way back to Vlam?

Search me.

'No one in the Mirrorscape ever gives you a straight answer,' said Ludo. He kicked the lectern in frustration, scuffing a small piece of gilding.

'Here, Mel,' said Wren. 'Let me try.' As she dipped the quill in the inkwell there was a muffled cry and everyone looked up to see a bedraggled figment flash by inside one of the transparent veins and disappear back inside the throbbing wall.

'What the skeg was *that?*' said Pilfer.

'Ask the Cogito thing,' said Ludo.

Wren wrote, *What was that?*

Syntax error.

How do we get back to Vlam? wrote Wren.

Search me.

'Wait a mo,' said Mel. 'What if it's telling us "search me" – like in search *inside* me?'

The others stared at the slimy, pulsating wall. 'In *there?*' they all said at once with the same degree of disgust.

There was the muffled cry again and the same figment shot along the length of another vein.

'I don't like this *search me* gubbins one bit,' said Pilfer. 'Maybe that's what happened to that poor geezer.'

'Perhaps "search me" referred to the entire castle,' said Ludo.

'But it's *ginormous*,' said Wren. 'You and Mel aren't going to get far in your state.'

'But we've got the whatsit,' said Ludo. 'Come on; it's worth a try. We're getting nowhere here. What do you think, Mel?'

Mel needed to blink several times before he could focus on the luck-compass. The strength hand was still strong but the direction hand was swinging back and forth, glinting as it caught the light of the ruby. 'You could be right.'

By lamplight they followed a seemingly endless succession of tubular corridors until they came once more to a dark, open space filled with liquid sounds and snoring. They advanced into it and came to a candelabrum and lectern.

'We're back where we started,' said Pilfer as the candles lit themselves. 'We must have been walking round in circles.'

'I'm sure we didn't.' Goldie flipped open the inkwell and the nodules glowed into life. 'Now what?'

Mel and Ludo slumped to the floor.

'The eye's changed colour,' said Wren. 'It was blue before; now it's brown.'

'That's not all,' said Goldie, kneeling to examine the lectern. 'This one's not chipped. It all looks the same but I bet we're somewhere different. Ask the Cogito thing.'

Is this the same place as we were recently? wrote Wren.

Yes. Still Cogito.

How do we get out of here?

Search me.

Goldie groaned with frustration.

They heard the cry again and watched as the same figment was flushed along a vein on the face of the offal wall. He braced his hands and feet against the insides, stopping himself. He gestured frantically at the party as green, viscous liquid surged over his head and shoulders.

'What's he trying to tell us?' said Pilfer.

'He wants us to get him out,' said Goldie. 'Lend me a hand. Pilfer, do you have any more of that hyper-clot?'

'It's right here.' Pilfer squeezed a ribbon of hyper-clot around the vein and stood back as it ruptured and the figment inside spewed out on to the stone floor. He knelt on all fours, coughing and spluttering as the gooey muck dripped off him.

'Thanks,' he gasped. He tried to get to his feet but slipped on the floor and landed heavily on his bottom. 'Ouch!'

Beneath the dripping slime the pale figment had an extra-large head with bright orange hair that was currently plastered flat to his skull in much the same way that his soaked, baggy clothes clung to his skinny body. Draped around him were several bandoleers containing a large number of weird tools. He wore huge goggles that had lots of different lenses that pivoted up and down on stalks.

Wren and Goldie each grabbed an arm, helped him to his feet and away from the slimy puddle.

'Thanks,' he said again. 'I've been in there ages. I thought I'd never get out.'

'What the skeg were you doing in there?' said Goldie.

'Routine maintenance. Next thing I knew – well, you saw.'

'You maintain *that?*' said Wren. 'What is it?'

'It's a lucubrator.'

'A what?' said Pilfer.

The figment jumped at the voice from out of nowhere.

'It's all right,' said Wren. 'Our friend's invisible.'

'Oh.' The figment looked uncomfortable but continued. 'Cogito's a lucubrator. A thinking machine. He's the biggest brain in the Mirrorscape and really rather wonderful – when he's working properly, that is.'

'He seemed to know skeg all,' said Pilfer. 'We asked him how to get home and all he said was "search me".'

'Oh, in that case he was telling you to . . .'

'Take a peek inside him,' finished Goldie. 'Yuck.'

'He's not as bad as he looks. My name's Toggle, by the way. What're you doing here – besides trying to get home?'

'It's a long story,' said Wren. 'Right now we really *do* need to get back. Our friends here are sick.'

'They look worse than I feel,' said Toggle, eyeing Mel and Ludo where they sat. 'The answer to your question will be in Cogito's memory banks.'

'Why couldn't he just come out and tell us what we wanted to know?' asked Goldie.

Toggle looked puzzled. 'I don't know. He usually does. Perhaps we'll find out when we get to the memory banks.'

'We? You mean you'll take us there?' said Wren.

'Someone had better; you'll never find them on your own. Besides, if something's broken, I need to fix it.'

Wren helped Mel to his feet and Goldie, Ludo. Toggle led them to the wall.

'The first bit's the worst. After that, it's not so bad – if you don't mind the smell.' He sidled up to the crack between two slimy, pulsing organs and, turning sideways, squeezed between them, disappearing inside with a wet *plop*.

One by one, the friends reluctantly slid into Cogito.

Green led Ambrosius Blenk, Dirk Tot and Blue along a long-abandoned gallery deep beneath the House of Thrones. They each held a spark-ball to light their way through the inky blackness.

The master stopped to examine a tall, cracked urn. 'Remarkable. Quite remarkable.' He brushed aside some cobwebs. 'Look here. The decoration uses a repeated scarab motif. I once saw something similar –'

'Please, Ambrosius, we don't have time for one of your art appreciation lectures,' said Green. 'Not while the city is in mortal danger. We must get to the House of Spirits and confront the Maven.'

They continued and eventually Green signalled them to halt. 'This door takes us into a cellar in the Maven's palace,' he whispered. 'I'll go on ahead and ensure that the coast is clear.' As he opened the door the sound of bells drifted in.

'It must be time for terce,' said Dirk Tot. 'The Fas pray while Vlam is under attack.'

Blue said, 'We'll need their prayers before this is through.'

'This is horrible,' complained Ludo. 'Everything's so slimy.'

'At least we can see where we're going,' said Mel. The glowing nodules were everywhere and lit their way.

The noise from the pounding heart was deafening, but grew less as they progressed deeper. Balancing along the tops of greasy veins was tricky, but after a short distance the spaces between the giant organs were sufficient for them to walk unhindered. Wren and Goldie had to support the two boys.

'Why are there two identical rooms with lecterns?' asked Wren.

'Oh, there're hundreds – all over Cogito,' said Toggle. 'So that lots of figments can consult him at once.'

'But the place is deserted,' said Goldie.

'That's because Cogito's offline. You must have heard him snoring.'

'Offline?' said Mel. 'Do you mean he's asleep?'

'Cogito has to power down from time to time so that I can service certain parts – grease a sphincter, buff up a synapse, that sort of thing. But this time, as I was in the middle of my maintenance routine, some numbskull woke him up and I was sucked into his insides.'

'Sorry,' said Wren. 'That must have been us.'

'No, I was sloshing around in there for days before you let me out. I think someone's been tampering with his vital functions. I removed this; look.' Toggle held out a jewelled ring. 'It was deliberately wedged in a ventricle. It couldn't have got there by accident.'

'Another piece of jewellery,' said Wren as she took and examined it. 'One piece is remarkable, two's a coincidence but three . . .'

'Let me have a closer look,' said Mel. 'I've seen this before – or one just like it. I'm sure I have.'

'Me too,' said Ludo. 'But where?'

'Sounds like more sabotage,' said Pilfer.

'How do the figments get up here from the world below?' asked Goldie.

'They use the bridge – *obviously*.'

'What bridge?' said Ludo. 'We didn't see any bridge.'

'The bridge only appears when Cogito's online.' Toggle rolled his eyes. 'He's always changing shape on the outside.'

'Ahhh! What was that?' exclaimed Pilfer as a small beaked head on four spider legs scuttled in front of them.

'It's only a mite,' said Toggle with a note of annoyance. He and Pilfer were not exactly hitting it off. 'I wonder where it's going – and all on his own. There should be lots of them. They keep Cogito free from parasites. The mites won't harm us. How're your friends doing?'

Mel raised his head and smiled weakly. 'I'm fine.'

'Are we there yet?' said Ludo as he leaned on Goldie.

'Not far now,' said Toggle. 'Are we all here? What about your see-through friend?'

'Pilfer?' said Goldie. 'Pilfer, are you here?'

There was no answer.

'Oh no,' said Wren. 'When did you last see him, Goldie?'

'*See* him?'

'You know what I mean. Come on, we've got to find him.'

'Hold your horses, I'm still here. Just my little joke,' said Pilfer from behind them.

'That's not funny,' said Wren.

'Neither's that.' Toggle was looking into the chamber that held Cogito's memory banks. His face was ashen.

Thousands of parasites with sharp teeth swarmed along the floor, up the walls and across the ceiling of a great big chamber peppered with tens of thousands of freshly made holes. The convoluted floor curved away like the surface of some small planet and every grey-white nook and cranny of the chamber seemed to contain one of the repulsive creatures. Some were as small as cabbages and others as large as badgers and they moved about on squat, scaly legs. Beneath each of their bodies extended a corkscrew-shaped horn that they used to bore into Cogito's memory banks. As each cell was breached its contents spewed out like a jack-in-the-box. There were scrolls of parchment, books and rolls of painted canvas. Some holes contained the sounds of speeches or music, which was sucked up by parasites with gramophone-like trumpets on their backs. Many also sported crab-like claws which they used to shred the more concrete memories.

'Keep absolutely still,' said Toggle. 'The parasites can only see you if you move. Turn, twitch or even blink and we're goners.'

The Demon-Finder-General

'Keep fidgeting and I'll never get your buckle fastened.'

'I don't remember my armour being so tight, Mudge.'

'That's because you've got fat, Tunk. Not enough exercise. No demons to kill, that's your problem.'

'That's going to change now, isn't it?'

'Oh, yes. That's all about to change. Before this day is out you'll be as trim as little Miss Pretty-Pretty.'

All around the two Ters in the Paper Belfry, their sisters were strapping on their own armour and testing the edges of their swords or the strings of their cross-bows. A mineral squeal and a fountain of sparks came from a spinning grindstone as others put an edge on their long-unused weapons.

A door opened and Ter Selen entered, led by the Morg. Gone was her long, grey robe, replaced by the gleaming black armour of the Demon-Finder-General. It hugged her body and enhanced her long, slender legs and the curve of her breast. A black cape hung from her shoulders, sweeping the floor. Only her pale, beautiful face was visible, framed by a cascade of jet-black chain mail. Her unseeing, multi-coloured eyes were feverish with excitement. She mounted the capstan and raised her arms high over her head. Her cape hung like bat's wings.

'Sisters, you have worked hard. You have worked well. The three storms you laboured over are ripe. The fabric between the worlds is weak and their child, the greatest storm of all, kicks and struggles within its womb. It yearns to be born. Within the hour the mirrorstorm will break. The darkness will fall and nourish the embryos. Demons will be born. You have done well but your labours are not yet over.

'Hear me, my sisters. Our hour is at hand. For centuries we have been silent, confined to the House of Spirits by short-sighted Mavens who ignored our true value. No longer. Very soon the street of Vlam will flow with demons like sharks around a wounded swimmer. Who will save us? the people will cry. Will you save us? they'll ask the Mysteries. How about you? they'll ask the king. Only the sisterhood will reply. Remember us, the Ters? The Ters who you and your rulers have so mistreated? Have forgotten. We will save you! And when the saving is done we will sit alongside our new Maven and his ally at the head of the House of Spirits. All of Nem will come to praise us and to lay tribute at our feet. The hour is at hand!'

'The hour is at hand!' echoed the Ters.

'Sisters, show me the mark!'

As one, all the assembled Ters removed their helmets and swept back their hair from their right ears. There were none. Only the ugly, scarred remnants clung to their heads.

'Who do you hear?' chanted Ter Selen.

'We hear no one!' answered the Ters.

'Who do you obey?'

'We obey no one!'

'Who do you love?'

'We love no one. The hour is at hand!'

'Sisters, show me the mark,' chanted Ter Selen.

The left ears of all those present were revealed. These were whole.

'Who do you hear?'

'We hear only you!'

'Who do you obey?'

'We obey only you!'

'Who do you love?'

'We love only you. The hour is at hand!'

The eyes of every Ter glowed with the fire of the fanatic.

'I can't hold it any longer,' mumbled Ludo. 'I've got to blink.'

'OK, if you must – but try to do it slowly.' Toggle stood as still as a statue. 'This is not good. Not good at all. Where are all the mites? There should be more than enough to wipe out this infestation.'

Goldie was losing her hold on her heavy bag. As she flexed her aching fingers, the sounds of munching ceased and each and every parasite stopped what it was doing and turned its ugly head in her direction. Mel moaned quietly as he fought back another wave of sickness and Wren unconsciously tightened her grip on his arm. The luck-compass began its sad chime. As one, every parasite took a step towards them. Then a tool that had worked loose from one of Toggle's bandoleers fell to the floor with a dull thud. With a collective, blood-curdling screech the parasites charged. Now terror, rather than caution, rooted the party to the spot.

Nearer and nearer rushed the hideous creatures. Just when it seemed that they would be overrun, flowers blossomed from out of thin air to one side of the party. They floated to the floor like huge, coloured snowflakes. Almost in mid-leap, the parasites changed direction and began rending the flowers petal from petal as they fell around them.

'Lively now. Scarper!' shouted Pilfer as yet more flowers joined the others. 'I'm running out of bait for these nasties.'

Wren and Goldie dragged Mel and Ludo away from the feeding frenzy as Toggle hurried along behind. 'This way,' he said, overtaking and leading them off to the left. He slid between two slimy organs. The others followed him into a small, dimly lit cavity.

As they sat there panting, Toggle said, 'I don't

understand it. That's never happened before. The mites usually keep their numbers down.' He looked towards where he thought Pilfer was. 'You didn't touch anything, did you?'

'What are you getting at?' Pilfer sounded riled. 'I've just sacrificed my loot to save your scrawny skin.'

Toggle huffed and pulled out a many-folded sheet of paper from inside his shirt. When it was flattened on the floor it could be seen as a complicated diagram. He fiddled with his goggles and a tiny light came on. Flipping one of his lenses down in front, he consulted the paper, tracing a line with his finger. His huge, magnified eye searched the sheet. 'There!' He stabbed his digit down hard. 'Mite central. You'd better come with me. I don't think it'll take those parasites long to finish that snack you fed them.'

'Sorry about your loot, Pilfer,' said Goldie.

'Easy come, easy go,' said Pilfer. 'There's always more where that came from, but you lot are harder to replace.'

'I'm touched, Pilfer,' said Goldie, blushing. 'I really am.'

'This is embarrassing,' said Ludo. 'Come on, you two.'

They followed Toggle through more disagreeable parts of Cogito before they arrived at the place he sought. Above their heads hung a huge, translucent bladder stretched almost to bursting. Inside, like a trawler's bumper catch, squirmed an imprisoned army of mites.

'This organ generates mites,' said Toggle. 'No wonder those parasites had free rein.' He pointed to the neck of the swollen bladder. It was clamped tight by a knotted strip of red fabric. 'More sabotage.'

'Red?' said Ludo. He shook his head to clear it. 'Red! The hierarchs wear red. I bet that Fa Odum's been here. *And* he wears lots of jewels.'

'I can't see him risking his neck,' said Mel. 'More likely he sent Fa Craw and his crows to do his dirty work.'

'But the Fas Major wear black,' observed Wren. 'And none of them wear jewellery.'

'Stand back.' Toggle yanked the rag and it fell away. With a loud gushing sound the bladder emptied its prisoners on to the floor and they scuttled away in the direction of the memory banks.

'Now what?' said Pilfer.

'We wait,' huffed Toggle.

After a few minutes, Toggle said, 'That should have given the mites enough time to clear up the infestation. Let's go and inspect the damage.'

When they arrived back at the memory banks the floor was littered with the dead bodies of the parasites.

'Toggle might be two petals short of a geranium,' said Pilfer so that only the friends could hear, 'but those mites of his have done the business.'

The mites were in the process of dragging the parasite corpses away while others began to repair the damage and reseal the memories in Cogito's banks. Toggle picked his way through and pulled a book from a numbered hole. When he opened it up its pages were perforated in many places where it had been chewed through. He inspected the contents of other holes but they were no better. 'Vandals! This'll take ages to repair.'

'Does that mean we'll never find the answer to our question?' asked Wren.

'What was your question again?'

'*Vlam*,' said Pilfer. 'Can't you see my friends are feeling sick? They need to get back to Vlam.'

Bristling with indignation, Toggle pulled another folded sheet from his shirt. It was covered with spidery lines and microscopic writing. Flipping down another lens, he said, 'Is that "Vlam" as in morbid disease of Mirrorscape fungi, "Vlam" as in fossilised stegosaur mucus or "Vlam" as in the capital city of Nem?'

'Which do you think, dumbbell?' said Pilfer.

'Just asking,' said Toggle, refolding his sheet. 'Follow me.'

They slalomed through dead parasites and busy mites until Toggle came to a halt. He looked around uncertainly. 'Aha!' Reaching down, he pulled out a large roll of canvas from an un-repaired hole. He let it fall open.

The canvas showed a view of Vlam all right, but a view obviously created when the city was much younger. Even worse, there were several holes right through the image.

'Is this your Vlam?' asked Toggle.

'Sort of,' said Wren as she eased Mel to the ground. 'It's how it must have looked hundreds of years ago.'

'Oh dear,' said Toggle. 'This means that the

archives are all out of order. It'll take ages to get everything back into shape. Once it's sorted out I'll find you an up-to-date image.'

'They don't have time,' said Goldie, lowering Ludo. 'These two look like they're on their last legs. Can you use this picture, Wren?'

'I don't know. Whenever we go back it's always been through a wall of mist – the reverse side of a picture that started out in Nem. I'm not sure what would happen trying to get there through the front of a picture.'

'Doesn't look like you've got much choice,' said Pilfer. 'We'll come with you, won't we, Goldie? It's the first law of robbery: stick together.'

'Thanks, but I'll take them back on my own,' said Wren. 'The last time a figment came back to Nem it didn't turn out too well. Do you think it's got a mirrormark, Mel?'

Mel got unsteadily to his feet. 'Probably not. I'll need to make one.'

'That scribble you made on the pic in the jalopy?' said Goldie. 'Here.' From her bag she produced a pot of paint and a small brush. 'When I saw you make it, I thought we might need this.'

'Goldie, you're priceless,' said Pilfer.

'You and Pilfer stay right here,' said Wren. 'The way this works we'll be back in no time at all.'

'Hey! You can't go defacing memories like that,' said Toggle indignantly as Mel began to paint the mirrormark. He rushed forward to prevent him but was stopped in mid-stride, his arms pinned to his sides. 'Let me go, you invisible idiot!'

'Bottle it, pipsqueak.' There was an edge of menace in Pilfer's voice no one had heard before.

Mel completed the mark on the canvas and Wren helped Ludo to his feet. The three friends stood together. As Mel traced the mirrormark in the air, the tattered image shimmered and they vanished.

As Ambrosius Blenk, Dirk Tot and Blue awaited Green's return deep beneath the House of Spirits, the master examined a moth-eaten tapestry. Woven into its finely crafted surface was an ancient view of Vlam. 'This must date from the reign of Harmon the thirty-first. Perhaps earlier.' He brushed aside some cobwebs and held his spark-ball closer. 'Beautiful. Look at the workmanship. Despite the holes, you can see how the craftsman has . . .'

'Quiet! Someone's coming,' said Dirk Tot.

The door opened slowly and Green's head peeped round. 'It's all quiet. If we're quick we can –'

There was a loud, dull thump as if someone had tipped the contents of a laundry basket from an upstairs window.

'Where did *you* three spring from?' There was a look of astonishment on Green's face.

Ambrosius Blenk, Dirk Tot and Blue spun round to regard Mel, Ludo and Wren by the spectral light of their spark-balls. They stood leaning against each other and were dripping goo from Cogito on to the stone floor. The happy chimes of the luck-compass seemed very loud in the deserted gallery.

'*Master!*' gasped Wren.

Green and Blue rushed forward to catch Mel and Ludo before they collapsed on to the flagstones.

'They look like they've spent too long inside the Mirrorscape,' said the master to Wren. 'I recognise the signs. It's a good job you got them back when you did. Breathe deeply. You'll both be fine very shortly. Tell me what happened,' he said after the colour had begun to return to his apprentices' faces.

'A silver chain and jewelled rings,' said Green, puzzled. 'They're very strange objects to use to sabotage something.'

'Unless you didn't have anything else,' said Blue. 'What do you make of the red cloth?'

Dirk Tot shook his head. 'I agree with Mel. I don't think Fa Odum has been in the Mirrorscape – even if he does know of its existence. It must be something to do with these mysterious allies of his and the Ters. And I think that stowaway's in this up to his neck. They must be working with them from the Mirrorscape. These four storms didn't happen all by themselves.'

'*Four* storms?' said Mel.

'When we left there were only two,' added Ludo.

'So the others have happened already,' said Wren.

'They're raging in the city above our heads even as we speak,' said Green.

'What about Nephonia and King M-morpho's realm?' said Mel. 'We promised them we'd help.'

'I do believe that their problems and ours are one and the same,' said the master. 'Solve one and you solve the others.' Ambrosius Blenk's piercing blue eyes bored into his wayward apprentices as he tugged his long beard. 'It seems that between you, you have uncovered something decidedly sinister. You have a gift that is priceless in an artist: intuition. I would have seen it myself if I hadn't been so preoccupied with my ceiling. We were on our way to the Maven to see what he has to say about these strange events. From what you've just told me it seems that he is implicated, although I still find it hard to believe.' He shook his head in disbelief and fell silent again, lost in thought. 'Look, will you go back into the Mirrorscape and try to throw a spanner in the works of this plot?'

The friends looked at each other. It was not something they needed to discuss. Their answer was visible in the directness of their gaze and the set of their jaws. Mel was the one who spoke.

'Yes, master.'

'It's what I expected you to say,' said Dirk Tot. The undamaged side of his face smiled.

'Splendid,' said the master.

'But how do we –' said Mel.

'Get back? I was thinking the same thing myself,' finished the master. 'There's something very odd about this tapestry – besides the fact that it's full of holes. Green, Blue, give me a hand to turn it round, will you?'

The reverse of the wall-hanging was covered in a once plain lining now spotted with mildew. On it was sketched a depiction of Cogito's memory banks in charcoal.

'Remarkable,' said the master. 'This drawing is fresh. Is this where you came from? It's as if someone knew . . .' Ambrosius Blenk fell silent again, thought creasing his brow, his inward-looking eyes darting back and forth as he saw webs of patterns and possibilities unfolding.

'Knew what?' asked Wren.

'You know, it's almost as if I recognise the style. I'm sure I've seen it somewhere before.'

'Will this get us back, master?' asked Ludo.

'Back? I shouldn't be at all surprised. It got you here and the mirrormark is invariably two-way.'

Just then a series of deep, resonant crashes like giant's footsteps made the floor beneath their feet tremble and dust fall in trickles from the ceiling.

'Ambrosius,' said Green, 'something's happening up top. I think we should move on.'

'Sounds like that fourth storm's getting into its stride,' said Blue.

'From what the Ters said, this is the big one,' said Mel. 'The other three storms were to feed this one.'

'Then we've no time to waste,' said Dirk Tot.

'Yes, let's go. Lead on,' said the master. Turning to the friends, he said, 'Get along now. The world isn't going to save itself, you know.' He followed Green, Blue and Dirk Tot through the cellar door. He was still thinking out loud as he mounted the stairs. 'Something about the way the line is handled. I'm *sure* I know that style.'

Blue had left them his spark-ball. Ludo held it to the charcoal drawing on the back of the tapestry. Like Mel and Wren, he was now quite refreshed. 'Looks like just any old drawing to me.'

'I don't know. I think I've seen something like it before too,' said Mel. 'It's competent but not what you'd call good.'

Wren said, 'We've got more important things to worry about right now than artistic style. We must get back to Goldie and Pilfer.'

They linked arms as Mel traced the mirrormark in reverse.

'There you are at last,' said Goldie. 'I thought you said you'd only be gone a moment.'

'How long were we gone?' asked Mel.

'A whole lunchtime.' Goldie sat at a cloth spread on the floor. On it was arranged the remains of a picnic. An apple rose from the cloth and a bite disappeared out of it, followed by the sound of Pilfer munching. The canvas was propped against the wall.

'Maybe the holes in the image slowed us up,' said Mel. 'Where's Toggle?'

Goldie looked angry. 'Ask Pilfer.'

There was a muffled cry as Toggle shot past inside a nearby vein.

'"Don't touch this. Don't do that." The little blighter was getting on my wick,' said Pilfer. 'So I stuffed him up one of his precious tubes. Don't worry. He'll only do one circuit before he arrives back at the vein we cut. Let's get out of here.'

As they followed the path the luck-compass indicated, Wren told Goldie and Pilfer about their meeting with the master.

'The old two-pronged attack, eh?' said Goldie. 'Your boss and his muckers from the front and the old Mirrorscape Irregulars behind enemy lines. It'll be a laugh.'

'A *laugh*. That's not quite how I'd have put it,' said Ludo.

'So where's our first stop?' asked Pilfer. 'Hang on. I don't like that look on your face, Chummy. Please tell me it's not . . .'

'Sorry, Pilfer,' said Mel. 'We've got to return to Anywhere and put an end to that rainbow that's destroying Vlam.'

Mel and the luck-compass soon found the way outside.

When they reached the outside, Cogito had assumed a different shape.

'I guess Cogito must be back online,' said Mel. 'Toggle said he was always changing shape. He probably looks like a moon from below.'

Beneath a coal-black, starless sky the surface of Cogito glowed with its own inner light. The castle had gone, replaced by a grey-gold desolation as blank and barren as the surface of the moon. Strewn rocks, craters and low hills were the only features of the bleak terrain. It was very cold. They could even see where Pilfer was by the puffs of condensation of his breath in the still air. The surface of the hollow world was lost in the darkness above their heads.

'It's really parky,' said Goldie, rubbing her hands together as she led the others from the mouth of the cave that had replaced the tunnel entrance.

'What about the rides that brought us here?' said Wren. 'Will they be all right?'

'Sure,' said Goldie. 'We've been to worse places than Cogito together. But *we* need to find the way off Cogito pronto.'

'Toggle said there was a bridge.' Wren looked around. 'I can't see one, can you?'

'For all we know it could be round the other side of the moon,' said Ludo, blowing into his hands.

Mel looked at the luck-compass. 'Which way to the bridge? It says it's not that far.' As he led them off towards a low rise, there came a screeching roar from overhead and a fiery meteorite fell out of the sky off to their right, landing with an explosion. Then another impacted to their left.

'I see the weather's taking a turn for the worse,' said Pilfer. 'Unseasonable temperatures interrupted by light showers.'

Mel led them up the slope of the rise. 'There!' Below them, through a rock arch, was the bridge, supported by rock pillars sculpted from Cogito's moon-like surface. It rose in a gentle, sweeping curve.

A series of roars split the sky as more meteors crashed into Cogito, sending up plumes of dust and flame. As the friends ran towards the entrance to the bridge, an even louder shriek came from overhead. A blast of hot air and a pressure-wave hit them, pushing them down as an enormous meteor flew over their heads. There was a loud detonation as the bridge exploded. Debris rained down on Mel and the others. When they looked up, the bridge had gone. They were marooned, with no hope of escape until Cogito changed again – hopefully into something more user-friendly than his present form.

Then the luck-compass began chiming its happy tune.

'Has that dingus of yours suddenly developed a sense of irony?' said Pilfer.

Mel tested the winding wheel. 'It's wound up. I don't understand it.'

The wind began to howl and it got even colder. High-velocity dust pricked them like needles. Mel shielded his eyes and raised his head and looked around. The frigid air whipped his breath away. He saw only the cratered desolation of Cogito's surface. He looked up. In the sky dots of light announced the approach of another swarm of meteors.

'It was only luck that the last swarm missed us,' said Mel.

'If this is the end,' said Goldie, 'then I'm glad I'm

going to die among friends.' She took Wren's hand and squeezed it.

'Everyone take cover!' shouted Ludo.

They gazed on, horrified, as the imminent bombardment loomed larger and larger. Then a rope ladder fell from the darkness above and hung suspended before them.

Nowhere

With no alternative, the friends climbed the ladder as bright meteors flashed past, leaving incandescent trails of cinders and a sulphurous stink in their wake. The shock waves from the meteors colliding with Cogito threatened to sweep them from the slender rungs. As the friends climbed higher, they could see a cloud hovering above them, its belly under-lit by the glow from the lucubrator. The ladder disappeared into its heart. Mel was the first to reach the cloud.

'What can you see?' called Ludo from beneath him.

'It's full of mist, like any other cloud.' Mel climbed higher. 'Hang on, it's clearing, it's a . . .'

'A what?' said Ludo.

'. . . It's a room. A very strange room.'

As Mel hauled himself through the floor, he saw that everything was made of swirling vapour. The slowly undulating floor met walls that rippled like waterfalls of mist. From the high, billowing ceiling hung an insubstantial chandelier, supporting dozens of cloudy candles. The flames appeared to be the only things not formed from cloud and made nacreous haloes in the humid atmosphere. There were elegant bow-legged armchairs and low tables, their outlines blurred as the vapour they were formed from drifted about.

Standing before him was a familiar figure in an embroidered gold frock coat and scarlet waistcoat. A smile blossomed on the carefully powdered face of the Nephonian ambassador-at-large. He spread his arms wide and a silver lining lit the edges of his huge cloudy wig. 'My dear, welcome.'

'Cassetti!' Mel climbed the last of the ladder and turned to lend his friends a hand up through the floor. When they were all safely through, Mel introduced Goldie and Pilfer. Cassetti seemed unconcerned by the robber's invisibility. 'Are we glad to see you. What're you doing here?'

The smile on Cassetti's face dimmed. 'Looking for you. You see, the situation in Nephonia has deteriorated. I expected to see you before this.'

'Sorry,' said Ludo. 'The whatsit's been leading us all over the place.'

'The luck-compass must have had a good reason. No matter, I've found you now. The king sent me to search for you and to bring you back to the palace in Cumulus as soon as possible.'

'But how did you know where to find us?' asked Wren. She gazed around, as amazed as the others at the cloudy room.

'His Majesty seemed to know exactly where you'd be. He even provided me with a mirrormarked canvas that brought me straight to the hollow world. The gateway lies below. We'll go there directly. But forgive me, you must be tired. Take a seat and tell me what's happened since we parted.'

Ludo looked at one of the fluffy, inviting chairs and sat down.

'Oi, find your own seat.'

'Sorry, Pilfer.'

Cassetti picked up a cloudy teapot, filled six vaporous cups and handed them round. Mel noticed that his hands were covered in scratches and that he was not wearing his rings. *Is that where I saw those rings before?* Mel caught Wren's eye and saw that she had noticed this too.

Cassetti listened intently to their tale. 'You *have* had your hands full. So other parts of the Mirrorscape have suffered a similar fate to that of Nephonia.'

'Not only that.' Mel told him about the four storms raging over Vlam.

'I see, I see.' Cassetti's wig became darker and threatened rain. 'The fourth storm is a mirrorstorm. The three other storms have caused it to form. They sustain it. Together they represent grave danger for all the worlds involved.'

'That's what our master thinks,' said Mel. 'But how do you know so much about it?'

'All Cumulans know about weather.'

Mel thought this a glib answer. It did not really answer his question.

'The master says we have to stop the other three storms to stop it all,' said Wren.

'Your master sounds like a very wise man,' said Cassetti. 'We'll leave at once.'

'You're coming with us?'

'I seem to be the only one with a conveyance.'

'This is a vehicle?' said Wren.

'It most certainly is, my dear. I made it myself. I'll have you know that I'm one of Cumulus's most notable cloud-sculptors and I prefer to travel in comfort. More tea?'

'Not for me,' said Ludo as he set his cup and saucer down on a side table. Unnoticed, it evaporated. 'Does it seem hot in here to you?'

'I thought it was only me,' said Goldie. 'It's also getting brighter.'

Everyone looked at the walls. They were beginning to glow. Slowly, their chairs shrunk until they were all sitting on the floor.

'Most curious,' said Cassetti. He stood and went to a set of cloudy drapes and drew them aside. Everyone was temporarily dazzled by the bright light. 'My word. That Cogito of yours is changing.'

When the friends joined Cassetti at the window they saw the lucubrator changing from a moon into a sun.

'Not again,' said Goldie. 'I wish he'd just make up his mind and stick to it.'

'Why's he doing it?' said Ludo.

'That little nerk Toggle said he's always doing it,' said Pilfer.

'At least we'll be able to see where we're going,' said Wren.

'There's always that,' said Cassetti, shielding his eyes. 'But of more immediate concern is the fact that we're evaporating. I'm afraid we have insufficient mass to move or even to sustain us until yonder sun sets. And without a supply of water, I can't repair the damage.'

The room was already noticeably smaller and was shrinking even as they watched. The air was becoming very humid, making it hard to breathe. Everyone had sunk up to their calves in the thinning vapour.

'You don't have another glider, do you?' asked Ludo, his damp hair sticking to his forehead.

'Unfortunately not. But I'll see what I can find.' Cassetti unbuttoned his waistcoat and opened one of his drawers. As he rummaged, he pulled out saucepans, a bird cage, a complete set of wagon wheels and a small cannon. 'Nothing there.'

'You've torn your waistcoat,' said Goldie. 'There's a strip missing at the bottom.' Her eyes met Mel's.

'Have I? Oh dear, I had a tussle with a thorn bush when I arrived here.' He rubbed his scratched hands. 'I must have ripped it.' He opened another drawer and began to remove more things.

'What's that?' said Mel.

'Just a clean shirt.'

'That'll do. Goldie, where's that bag of yours?'

'What do you need?'

'Paints and brushes. I'll paint us a way out of here.'

'Mel, is that such a good idea?' said Wren. 'Remember what happened the last time you tried to draw a world. You and Ludo got into big trouble.'

'It's got to be better than being barbecued by Cogito,' said Goldie.

As Wren and Goldie held the shirt taut, Mel started to paint a white on white mirrormark. 'Stand back; give me room to work.'

But there was none to give. The three humans and three figments were forced very close together, the room had shrunk so much. They were now standing almost up to their waists in the flimsy remnants of the cloud. The floor felt as if it would give way any moment. It was unbearably hot and the room was visibly dissolving.

'We're out of time!' shouted Cassetti. His wig had evaporated completely, revealing his bald head. That was scratched too.

'Everyone, grab hold of me!' shouted Mel, as the last of the room disappeared. They had already begun falling when Mel traced the last strokes of the mirrormark on the spotless, white shirt.

Dirk Tot, Green and Blue paused while Ambrosius Blenk caught his breath. They had climbed less than a third of the way to the Maven's quarters high in the House of Spirits. The younger men helped the old master to a window so that he could breathe more easily. The view outside only made him gasp more.

From over the heart of the city the central cloud was raining down darkness. Around its edges, the three other clouds continued to spew forth their enigmatic cargo. Huge cloud-monsters had become substantial and stalked the districts between the Great Houses and the City walls, and the sparks fell as thickly as ever. The acid-bright rainbow continued its relentless destruction of the theatre district.

'Here, master.' Green had found a chair and Blue two halberds decorating the wall. They combined them to form an improvised sedan chair. With Green and Blue in front and Dirk Tot behind, the seated master continued his upward journey towards his confrontation with the Maven.

'I know where we are. I've been here before,' said Goldie, blinking at the brightness.

'Me too,' said Pilfer.

'Well?' said Ludo. 'Are you going to let me in on the secret? It looks like the middle of nowhere to me.'

'Ten out of ten, Sunshine,' said Pilfer.

'Nine out of ten,' corrected Goldie. 'Anywhere's in the middle of Nowhere. Where we are is just plain old Nowhere. We rode through here on the old jalopy on the way to Anywhere.'

'But you didn't paint anything on the shirt,' said Wren. 'Yet here we are.'

'The same thing happened when Mel drew a

mirrormark in the dust at the bottom of the well,' said Ludo. 'There was no picture there either.'

Mel scratched his head. 'That's right.'

The mirrormarked shirt that they had travelled through had brought them back to the pure white world that surrounded the polluted city and supplied its raw material. Wren, Mel and Ludo were on their knees avidly inspecting the perfect but colourless vegetation. It was like a blank sheet of drawing paper with everything on it defined solely by shadow and texture. The five figures were the only colour to be seen. In the relentless brightness even Pilfer cast the faintest of shadows.

'My dears, I share your amazement at this albescent arcadia but we really must be on our way to Nephonia,' said Cassetti.

'We've got work to do here, first,' said Mel. 'The master said that the toxic rainbow comes from Anywhere. We have to destroy that before we can go to Nephonia.'

'Oh, very well, my dears,' said Cassetti. 'The sooner we can succeed here, the sooner we will be on our way.'

'Yeah, but which way do we go?' said Ludo, getting

to his feet and dusting the white dirt from his hands. It fell at his feet like dandruff. 'It all looks the same.'

'Which way to Anywhere?' Mel pointed to the direction on the white horizon the luck-compass indicated. They began walking.

Soon they came to a fast-flowing river.

'I've heard of white water before, but *this*?' Mel gazed at the milky waters as they surged by.

'It's the blanch-water they make the rainbows from,' said Pilfer. 'It flows towards Anywhere.'

'On the aqueducts,' said Goldie.

'Exactly.'

'That's our way back into the monolith,' said Mel. 'You don't happen to have another boat tucked away in your drawers, do you?' he asked Cassetti.

'I never travel without one.'

In a few minutes it was assembled and in another launched with the party crowded aboard. It sped along and they soon spied the dark smudge of the whirlwind emanating from the monolith and snaking into the sky.

'Pilfer, do you know how long that whirlwind's been there?' asked Wren.

'Only a short while.'

'My dears,' said Cassetti, 'I regret to inform you that two of those whirlwinds have recently made an appearance close to Cumulus. I believe they are a part of the ills that are affecting us all.'

Shortly afterwards they saw Anywhere in the distance. The white Mirrorscape fell away beneath them in a sheer cliff as the river sped along over a valley atop one of the aqueducts. Ahead of them, the monolith at the centre of the polluted city loomed and soon filled their field of vision.

'Look,' said Mel. 'The city's surrounded by dust-dunes. That's where we arrived last time.' His eyebrows creased into a frown and then shot up. 'I think I've got it! Why we're here. Before you begin work on a blank sheet of paper it could be anything. Right?'

'Yeeesss,' said Wren tentatively.

'So maybe when you draw a mirrormark on to some-thing blank – like a pile of dust – you end up anywhere.'

'Or, on anything white,' said Ludo, 'Nowhere.'

Everyone sat in silence for a while as they mulled over this novel thought.

'This isn't going to be as easy as we thought,' said Mel. 'Look up ahead.' Where the aqueduct entered the monolith their way was blocked by a giant grille.

'There's never been a building that could keep Pilfer out. First rule of robbery: be prepared for anything.' The syringe with the hyper-clot emerged once more, and in a trice a hole big enough for the boat and its passengers to pass through appeared. 'That's the last of the gippo.' The empty syringe disappeared back into his sack.

'Let's hope we don't need any more,' said Goldie.

They disembarked and made their way along a gantry and through a service door. Inside was a room hung with spare overalls, which they quickly donned.

'My dears, you neglected to mention your criminal careers.'

The others joined Cassetti where he was scrutinising two posters pinned to a notice board. One had the words WANTED FOR ROBBERY printed across the top. Underneath was a large, blank square.

'Not a very good likeness,' said Pilfer.

Next to it was another poster with images of Mel,

Ludo, Wren and Goldie. This one had the words WANTED FOR BREACH OF THE TERMS AND CONDITIONS printed on it.

'They'll recognise us as soon as we show our faces,' said Mel.

Cassetti undid his overall and opened one of his drawers. 'I have just the thing for such a contingency.' He produced a carved box containing greasepaint, powder, wigs and sundry other cosmetics.

The friends watched fascinated as Cassetti expertly made up Goldie.

'Put some of that skin-coloured make-up on my face to hide the gilding. And a big fluffy wig.'

'I want a beard,' said Mel.

'Me too,' said Ludo. 'And warts; lots of warts.'

'You're overdoing it,' said Wren. 'Both of you. I just want a false nose and some bushy eyebrows.'

'A right bunch of pillocks you all look,' said Pilfer as Cassetti finished. 'OK, listen up. This super-strength rainbow that's giving Vlam such a how's-your-father must have come from the stores. When times are slack in the rainbow business they concentrate and dry the stuff in long rods until it's needed. Then it's diluted and as good as new. But if you use the raw stuff then you're in deep scrot. It's nasty; *really* nasty. I'll lead the way.'

Those figments that they passed gave their odd disguises quizzical looks but did not try to stop them. Pilfer led them to the top of the building and then to the door to the storeroom. Stencilled on it in big, red letters were the words AREA RESTRICTED TO AUTHORISED STORAGE PERSONNEL AND DUTY SUPER-VISORS ONLY: PROTECTIVE EYEWEAR, MODELS PG1718 OR PE2039, TO BE WORN AT ALL TIMES.

'Take a pair of goggles each,' said Pilfer as he selected some from a rack. 'You'll need them.' As he put on his own, they seemed to float in the air.

The door was locked.

Pilfer gave a snort of contempt and a moment later it swung open.

Inside, the warehouse-sized storeroom contained racks of empty shelves disappearing into the distance, and seemed to be deserted.

'Something's up,' said Pilfer, 'this joint's usually crawling with workers.'

'So where's all the dried rainbow?' asked Ludo.

'Looks like someone's used it up,' said Goldie.

'There's something happening right down the far end,' said Mel. 'Where that moaning noise is coming from.'

They crept down the long space and crouched behind some shelving. Slowly and carefully they raised their heads.

Ludo gasped. 'It looks like –'

'Another Serpent,' finished Wren.

It was much more crudely fashioned than the ornate brass Serpent in the Paper Belfry and was made from odds and ends of girders, springs and metal plates all crudely welded or bolted together. The intertwining snakes were made from mismatched tubes. It was being fed with rods of dried rainbow that were melted in its furnace and channelled through seven coloured sluices towards the lenses. Beams of fearsomely bright colour were radiating from the Serpent's mouth and through a hole in the ceiling. Through the hole they could see inside the throat of the rapidly spinning funnel on the monolith's rooftop. It bent and flexed like a snaking tube. The moaning was coming from it.

But, strange as this was, even stranger were the Serpent's operators. There were a dozen of them and they looked like large, brass teardrops. The top portion swivelled and supported stalked eyes and ears like funnels. The mechanical figments moved about by a variety of means; some on stubby feet, others on spindly wheels and still more on caterpillar tracks. They all handled the rainbow rods and the Serpent with flexible, octopus-like tentacles. As they scuttled about, they made a *ticker-ticker-ticker* racket.

'Why couldn't they have used those robots to clear the hyper-clot?' said Ludo.

'Those metal munchkins have got nothing to do with the monolith,' said Pilfer. 'My guess is some outsider's made them especially for this job.'

'That Serpent is feeding the rainbow that's melting Vlam,' said Wren. 'How're we going to put it out of business?'

'Look how carefully they're handling those rainbow rods,' said Mel.

'Too true, Chummy,' said Pilfer. 'Even those brass

bozos will want to be shot of it sharpish. If they hold on to it too long they're scrap.'

Mel said, 'What if we had some . . .'

'Glue?' said Cassetti. 'Just what I was thinking.' He handed Mel a large tube from one of his drawers. 'Fast-acting, double-strength.'

'But how're we going to get it on to the rods?' asked Ludo.

'We need a diversion,' said Goldie. 'That shouldn't be a problem for a Mirrorscape Irregular,' she said, wiping the make-up from her face and removing her wig. Crouching, she ran back towards the door.

'Goldie, come back,' said Wren. 'Step outside and you'll be recog– Oh, I *see*. She *wants* to be recognised. Then they'll chase her.'

'That girl's worth her weight in weight in . . . er, gold,' said Ludo.

It did not take long. There was shouting from the open door at the far end and Goldie came running back, pursued by a posse of goggle-wearing supervisors. The heads of the robots snapped round at the commotion. *Ticker-ticker-ticker.* They sped off to deal with the intrusion. As the skirmish began, Goldie slipped away to one side and rejoined the others.

'Quick, while everyone's busy,' she puffed. 'Spread the glue.'

'That was fast,' said Ludo. 'The robots have seen off the supervisors. They've left a guard by the door. Get down! They're coming back.'

The friends watched as one of the machines picked up a rainbow rod and conveyed it to the furnace. But when it tried to release its burden it remained stuck fast to its tentacles. Its voice wailed an alarm and several of its brass co-workers came to assist it. The wailing multiplied as they all became glued to the rod. The remaining robots scuttled over from the Serpent and instantly met the same fate. Mel and the others watched with morbid fascination as the machines slowly dissolved into a multi-coloured puddle shot through with brass veins.

'Right, let's spike the Serpent and get out of here,' said Mel.

'What do we do?' said Ludo. 'Just switch it off?'

'No,' said Goldie, 'we need to make sure –'

Ticker-ticker-ticker. The robot that had been left to guard the door advanced towards them at full tilt, its metal tentacles flailing. It flung itself at Wren.

'No, you don't!' Mel hooked Wren around her waist and dragged her out of the machine's path in the nick of time. The robot wheeled around through the puddle and turned to attack again. It sped towards them but the corrosive gloop from the puddle started to dissolve its wheel bearings and it began a drunken dance first towards Pilfer and Goldie, and then back again towards Ludo. It skidded in the puddle and with a mighty pirouette slammed into the Serpent. The lenses inside tilted askew, redirecting the acidic colour from the hole in the ceiling of the storeroom on to the Serpent itself. The machine began to melt.

'Couldn't have done better myself. Time we were off,' shouted Pilfer as he followed Ludo and the others, who were sprinting towards the door.

From behind them came a burbling screech as the Serpent disintegrated. There was a sucking *pwuk* sound and the whirlwind vanished.

'Uh-oh.' Mel stopped dead as he reached the door and the others cannoned into him. 'It's more supervisors.'

The Cloud Sculptor

Outside, blocking their escape, stood row upon row of supervisors.

'What's going on?' said the one in charge.

'We're the cleaning team,' said Cassetti.

'You're not wearing any badges. There's something fishy going on here.'

'Emergency spillage in the storeroom,' said Mel in a deep voice. 'All taken care of now.'

The chief supervisor looked at the friends suspiciously. 'You back there. Let's see your face.'

'I recognise her,' said another supervisor. 'She's Goldie.' He tugged Ludo's beard, which came away in his hand. 'It's them. The absconders. We've nabbed the whole bunch!'

'Not so fast.'

'Pilfer!' said the chief supervisor, recognising his voice.

'Stay right where you are.' A drop of blanch-water trembled on the nozzle of Pilfer's syringe as it hovered in mid-air. 'You wouldn't want to get wet now, would you? We all know what happens in Anywhere if you get wet.' He squirted a jet of blanch-water towards them. The supervisors leapt back, checking their hands and faces for splashes. Pilfer backed them up at syringe-point. 'OK, you scrots stay put.' Then, to the friends, 'First rule of robbery: always have an escape plan.'

The friends sprinted down a flight of stairs to a waiting cable car. Some more supervisors tried to stop them, but backed away when they saw the syringe. 'Everyone get in,' said Pilfer.

'Piece of cake,' crowed Ludo as they sped away.

'Never say that, Sunshine. It's tempting fate,' said Pilfer. 'The getaway's always the most difficult part.'

'If only we could see out of these windows.' Mel rubbed at the dust-caked glass without success.

'Step aside, Chummy.' Pilfer squirted the pane with his syringe and a moment later it became see-through. 'Dust and moisture, see.'

The view was not promising. Behind them they saw a second cable car shoot out from the dwindling monolith in hot pursuit.

'No point in wearing these any longer,' said

Mel, abandoning his goggles and disguise.

'Am I glad to be rid of those hideous overalls,' said Cassetti. 'They're unbefitting an ambassador.'

'Ouch!' complained Wren as she peeled off her sticky false eyebrows.

Anywhere and the surrounding dust-dunes disappeared behind them as they travelled high above the pure white world of Nowhere. After a while they slowed and came to a halt. The doors slid open and Wren popped her head out.

'It looks like we've reached the terminus. Where to now?'

They all turned to Mel as he flipped open the luck-compass. 'Which way to escape the supervisors?' He looked at the dials. 'Follow me.' He led them out of the glass-roofed station and into Nowhere.

As they looked back, they saw the second cable car arrive and disgorge their pursuers. Mel and his friends were soon spotted against the pristine background as they hurried away.

'Got anything in your drawers that would slow them up?' asked Goldie.

Cassetti glanced over his shoulder as they ran. 'I'm afraid not, my dear. At least nothing that we could set up before the grey men catch up with us.'

'Where're we headed, Chummy?' Pilfer sounded out of breath.

Mel stopped. 'The luck-compass says we're there.'

'Where?' Everyone looked around at the white Mirrorscape. The grey knot of supervisors was getting closer.

'It says here.' Mel stood before a massive tree.

'How're we going to climb up there?' said Wren, craning her neck. 'The lowest branches are way too high.'

'I have a ladder but one not nearly long enough,' said Cassetti.

'Pilfer,' said Goldie, 'you're the expert.'

'Don't need to be an expert,' said Pilfer. He twisted a knobbly handle and a section of the trunk swung open like a door. Inside rose a spiral staircase. 'First rule of robbery: always look for the obvious.'

Mel said, 'How many first rules of robbery are there?'

'Just the one – but it keeps changing to suit the

situation. After you. Everyone in? Good.' Pilfer whacked the outside door knob with his syringe and it broke off. 'First rule of robbery: confound your pursuers.' He slammed the door after him and followed the others upwards.

The spiral staircase emerged from the trunk in the fork of two massive boughs. Mel peered down at the supervisors. 'They're trying to force open the door.'

'Now they're forming a pyramid,' said Ludo. 'But they'll never reach this high.'

'What're we going to do,' said Wren, 'wait them out?'

'I bet Cassetti's got lots of food tucked away in his drawers,' said Ludo.

'Indeed I have. But you seem to forget the urgency of the situation. We could certainly gorge ourselves until yon supervisors give up their siege through sheer hunger, but in the meantime Cumulus and the other worlds are dying.'

'Besides,' said Pilfer, 'that door's not exactly what you'd call vault-quality.'

'So what do we do?' said Goldie. 'I thought we were going to save Vlam.'

'And Nephonia,' added Cassetti.

'And King M-morpho,' said Wren.

'That's our next stop,' said Mel. 'The luck-compass says we're on the right track.' He gazed up through the branches. 'There's a tree house up above.'

The way upwards continued via flights of steps cut into the boughs. At first these were broad, but as the friends climbed ever higher they became narrower and steeper. When they reached it they could see that 'house' did not do justice to the spacious and complicated structure cradled in the top of the tree. The lower storeys were circular, with tall, conical-roofed towers rising from the top. There were precarious balconies projecting out and the internal staircases left the main structure at intervals to meander among the upper branches like creepers before returning to continue inside.

There was a modest enough entrance but inside, the soaring hallway was pierced through and through with thick branches. Several staircases snaked upwards towards galleried landings, and dominating the space was a massive candelabrum formed from a twisted nest of twigs.

'What *is* this place?' said Ludo as he gazed about, screwing up his eyes against the glaring whiteness and wishing he had kept the darkened safety goggles.

'My guess would be it's a rich super's weekend retreat,' said Pilfer. 'It's near the cable car terminus. Nice and handy, see. Dust-free and a very des-res.'

'What's that thump-thump noise?' said Wren. 'Woodworm?'

Mel crossed to one of the balconies that opened off the hallway and leaned over. 'If only. It's the supers. They've got a battering ram.'

'That door won't hold them for long,' said Pilfer.

Mel consulted the luck-compass again. 'Upstairs.'

He led his friends up through the tree house until they came to the top of the highest tower. There was a narrow door set into the wall which opened on to another staircase that twined through the leaves and upper branches as far as another structure, altogether more tree house in size.

'Swipe me,' said Pilfer as he entered, 'this super's got his very own art gallery.'

Inside, the drum-shaped annexe was hung around

with eight large, white canvases. Pilfer seemed captivated by them.

'Look,' he said, 'that's the monolith.'

'You can see them?' said Wren. 'They look blank to me.'

'Acquired taste,' said Pilfer. 'You have to know how to look at them. If you were to –'

He was interrupted by a crash from far below.

'Sounds like the door's gone, my dears,' said Cassetti. 'Our little clockwork guide has led us here. Where to now?'

Mel walked around the pictures until the luck-compass chimed its happy tune. 'We have to go through this picture.'

'But it's blank,' observed Wren. 'Can you see what's in it, Pilfer?'

'Course I can.' The robber described it.

'That's the one.' Mel made the mirrormark.

Ter Selen, with the Morg straining impatiently at his leash, led her small army of sisters as they descended the Hill of Spirits. Their black armour clanked and was made to seem all the darker by the precocious twilight. Behind her marched Ters Mudge and Tunk, followed by perhaps fifty more. A dozen of the stronger Ters wheeled a huge shape as big as a carnival float and draped with a black cloth. Against them, like a tide at full flood, surged horrified citizens, fleeing in panic from the fearsome storms raging overhead and the terrors they had begun to unleash on Vlam. A driverless carriage hurtled towards them, drawn by a pair of wide-eyed, terrified horses. As it flashed past, they saw the coachman being dragged along behind, his foot caught in a trailing loop of harness.

Onwards marched the sisters until Ter Selen, sensing the proximity of demons from the Morg's agitation, held up her gauntleted hand for them to halt.

At the end of the street stood the unnatural wall of darkness of the mirrorstorm. It pulsed in and out, as if it were a living, breathing thing. At each breath it expanded by a few feet, enveloping more of the city in its blackness. The only thing that seemed to escape from it were the screams of those within. As the sisters watched, a lone figure – a rich merchant's wife judging by her fine clothes – crawled from it on her hands and knees. She looked up through a veil of dishevelled hair and saw the Ters standing armed and ready before her. Hope kindled a small light in her eyes. In an instant this changed to a look of panic as a grotesque, scaly hand emerged from the curtain-like darkness and grasped her ankle. Slowly and relentlessly, it dragged the screaming woman back into the abhorrent night.

The sound brought a cruel smile to the Demon-Finder-General's beautiful lips. Her eyes began to change colour more rapidly. Behind her, the ranks of Ters lit the torches they carried. She bent down and slipped the Morg's leash. 'Demons, Morg. *Seek.*'

The creature raced ahead, howling with fierce delight, and plunged into the darkness.

'Mistress, the toxic rainbow!' cried Ter Tunk.

Ter Mudge stepped forward. 'It's extinguished, mistress!'

'No matter, sisters. The other storms are no longer necessary to sustain the mirrorstorm now it has begun. Soon it will envelop the entire city. There are more than enough demons for our purposes. And if all's going to plan, our ally should be leading those interfering children to Nephonia. They'll soon find out there's a traitor in their midst.' Ter Selen placed her hand on Ter Mudge's shoulder. With her other hand she signalled her sisters to advance and then drew her sword.

The black drape was removed from the huge shape and it rumbled forward under its own steam. One by one the Ters followed it until they were swallowed by the hideous darkness.

'This is the place you sought, is it not?' said Cassetti.

Mel gazed around him. 'Yes. There's the mountain and the waterfalls, and this river should take us to King M-morpho's orchard.'

'Too bad we left the boat in the monolith,' said Ludo.

'Does that mean we'll have to walk? My trotters are giving me gyp,' complained Pilfer.

'If we're going to visit a monarch, I think we should arrive in due style.' Cassetti opened one of his drawers and began to remove various odd pieces of machinery. A small furnace was followed by a collection of pipes –

some curly, others straight – elaborate glass vessels, springs, gears, ratchets, pulleys, fans and belts. The others helped him fit it all together until the weird contraption was complete and purring gently. With its multiple chimneys, vents and valves it resembled nothing any of them had ever seen before.

'Are we going to ride in *that*?' asked Goldie. 'It doesn't look very stylish to me.'

'This,' said Cassetti proudly, 'is merely my cloud generator. I intend to sculpt us a vehicle befitting the ambassador-at-large to Nephonia and his friends. But first things first. If one of you would run this hose down to yonder river, I'll begin. My dears, we shall be travelling the way only clouds can. We shall fly.'

Cassetti withdrew a pair of ornate paddles from one of his drawers and set to work. He opened a valve on his machine and white cloud began to billow out. With almost balletic movements, he patted and pulled, teased and prodded until his creation was complete.

A short while later, they all boarded his cloud barge, which was softer than the softest sponge but capable of bearing their weight.

'This is great,' said Ludo as he inspected every detail. 'Let's call it "Thunderbolt".'

'We are on a mission of peace. Such a bellicose name does not befit an ambassador's barge,' said Cassetti, adjusting his newly fashioned wig. 'It conveys altogether the wrong impression. We must appear less aggressive.'

'Let's call her "Wisp",' said Wren.

Everyone except Ludo agreed.

'I still think "Thunderbolt" is better,' he scowled.

Cassetti stood at a vaporous ship's wheel and threw a lever protruding through the misty floor. The cloud generator below decks chugged anew. As if in a dream, the cloud-barge rose slowly and gracefully into the air. Mel looked behind and could see a vapour trail of small puffs emerging from the stern like a dotted line as they were propelled forwards. Beneath them, the river glowed silver in the setting sun like a drunken snail's trail as it meandered towards the glow in the sky over King M-morpho's orchard.

*

Some time later, they landed softly at the edge of the spark-laden trees.

'What's happening?' said Wren. 'It feels like we're being pulled in two directions at once.'

'It's just like in Nephonia,' said Cassetti. 'The hole between the worlds has its own gravity that's pulling us towards it.'

'Throw me a line,' said Pilfer. 'We need to moor Wisp to the trees.'

'The orchard looks different,' said Ludo as they secured the craft.

'That's because it's shrunk,' said Mel. 'And the sparks are much less bright. Can you see King M-morpho or any of his subjects? The place looks deserted.'

'Not surprised with this crazy gravity pulling everything two different ways,' said Goldie. Like the others, she was forced to stand at a sloping angle to compensate.

'What's happening out there?' Wren joined her friends and pointed to the blackened spiral spout at the heart of the orchard. 'I think someone's waving at us.'

Cassetti produced a telescope from his cornucopian

drawers. 'Someone's in distress. We must help them. Cast off.'

As the cloud-barge neared the swirling heart of the orchard, they could see a giant figure caught in the inverted maelstrom sucking that world upwards. The cloud generator was on overtime coping with the double gravity.

'It's King M-morpho,' said Mel.

'Shall we toss him a rope or something?' said Goldie.

'Make it "something",' said Ludo. 'There's too many of him for a rope.'

'How about a butterfly net?' said Wren.

'Here.' Of course Cassetti had one.

When they hauled the net back on board it was brimming over with thousands of butterflies. They flew out of the net and rearranged themselves before the friends. King M-morpho was not as large as he had been the last time Mel had seen him, and parts of his regalia were missing. The butterflies were beating their wings extra hard to stay together.

His Majesty was every bit as gracious as Mel and

Ludo remembered. 'You t-took your time. What k-kept you?'

'Is that all the thanks we get for –'

Cassetti placed his hand on Ludo's arm. 'Gracious Majesty, I regret that I alone must bear the blame for the woeful delay in their return to your great kingdom. My companions here have rendered the Mirrorscape great service in the land of Nowhere and will do so again I am sure in Nephonia, of which I have the honour of being the ambassador-at-large. May I present my credentials.' He bowed low and proffered a scroll.

'Arise, ambassador, you are m-most welcome in our k-kingdom,' said the king with a haughty smile.

'We are here to offer aid and succour in your majesty's current difficulties. My services, and those of my companions, are entirely at your disposal.'

'W-walk with us, ambassador.' King M-morpho led Cassetti out of earshot from the others along the deck.

'See,' said Goldie, 'that's how it's done. You have to schmooze these royals. They lap it up. Cassetti's got him eating out of his hand. Look. He's a really slick

customer at getting people to go along with him.'
She paused for a moment. 'Do you think you can
trust him?'

'What do you mean?' said Mel. 'We owe him
our lives.'

'Bit of a coincidence him turning up like that on
Cogito, don't you think?' said Goldie. 'In the nick of
time and everything.'

'What are you getting at?' asked Ludo.

'I've been wondering . . . He knew all about this
mirrorstorm. A little too much, maybe?'

'He's a Cumulan,' said Mel. 'He said they all know
about weather.'

'And did you notice he's torn his waistcoat?'

'He landed in a thorn bush,' said Ludo. 'His head
was scratched, too.'

'That's probably where he lost his rings,' said Wren.

'I've just thought,' said Ludo, looking pale. He
fished the two rings and silver chain out from inside his
doublet. 'Do you think they're his?'

'Try giving them back to him,' said Goldie. 'We'll
soon find out.'

They stared at Cassetti as he schmoozed King M-morpho. He certainly was a smooth operator. He'd soon won the tetchy king around. Had they also been charmed by his winning manner?

At the end of his audience Cassetti bowed low once more and kissed King M-morpho's outstretched hand, which must have tickled. He strode back down the deck towards them. The friends forced smiles on to their faces.

'Gather round, my dears. He's a cantankerous old monarch and I'm not altogether sure we can trust him. He believes there're just five of us and I think we should keep it that way. OK by you, Pilfer?'

'Don't worry about me. I'll keep shtum.'

'Good. Now, the king has asked us to return below ground . . .'

Ludo groaned.

'. . . The mirrorblood that nourishes this orchard and the king's subjects and that you attempted to free is still failing to flow. In return for this service, King M-morpho has agreed to accompany us to Nephonia and help us heal the rift there.'

'But we cleared the dam,' said Mel. 'It can't have grown back.'

'His majesty believes that something new is interfering with the irrigation.'

'What?' said Goldie.

'That is the conundrum, my dears,' said Cassetti. 'That is the conundrum. Now, please excuse me while I go below. I need to check that the cloud generator is running smoothly.'

After they were sure that Cassetti had disappeared below deck, Goldie said, 'So what your enemies were aiming for, all along, is this mirrorstorm.'

'That's what I overheard in the House of Spirits,' said Mel. '"Three storms to engender the great storm", they said.'

'So each of the storms must contribute something special,' said Wren. 'Like a small part of the mirrorstorm.'

'Why did the rainbow from Anywhere blast the theatre district in Vlam?' said Ludo.

'Maybe it's like a landing place,' offered Goldie.

'Could be,' said Wren. 'It's right near the centre of

the city where the mirrorstorm touched down.'

'And the mutant chrysalises come from here,' said Mel. 'They need to stop the mirrorblood to turn the chrysalises into demons that will invade Nem.'

'There're demons all over the Mirrorscape,' said Pilfer. 'Why choose here?'

'I bet there's not as many as there are here,' reasoned Mel.

'Which still leaves Nephonia,' said Ludo. 'What's that got to do with all this?'

'Pictures,' said Mel. 'Don't you see?'

The others looked confused.

'Look,' continued Mel. 'Cassetti said that Nephonia and our world touch. And we know that the mirrormark opens up pictures.'

'So you're saying that they're using the pictures – the *natural* pictures – in the clouds?' said Ludo. 'Using them like a gateway into Nem?'

'*Exactly*. That's the only way between our world and the Mirrorscape apart from a painting. And we know that the Mirrorscape is all joined up – you can get from one bit to another.'

'So, whoever's doing this plans to invade Nem via Nephonia,' said Wren. 'Where the two worlds touch.'

'That's what I think,' said Mel. 'And the whirlwinds are like a shortcut between Anywhere and the orchard and Nephonia.'

'Then we must hurry up and get this mirrorblood flowing again,' said Goldie. 'Only when the orchard's returned to normal will the rift seal itself.'

'Quiet, Cassetti's coming back.' Mel nudged Ludo. 'Go on, ask him.'

'Cassetti,' said Ludo. 'I found your rings and chain.'

Cassetti looked down at the jewellery in Ludo's open palm. 'They're not mine.'

'Sorry,' said Ludo, as Cassetti walked back to the wheel. 'My mistake.'

'Should we believe him?' said Goldie.

'I'm not sure,' said Mel. 'But we must keep an eye on him.'

'Leave that to me,' said Pilfer.

Returning to the edge of the orchard proved slow going against the double pull of gravity, but they eventually made it. They disembarked and each descended the well, carrying a spark-ball harvested from the trees at the orchard's edge.

'It's just like it was before,' said Ludo gloomily, his voice echoing off the walls.

'The dam's down this way.' Mel led them off through the honeycomb of tunnels.

But they never got to the dam. Before they were even halfway they found what was happening to the mirrorblood. They also found who was responsible.

'It's *them* again,' said Ludo.

'And they're not alone,' said Goldie.

Schmooze, Schmooze

'It's more of those metal robots we saw in Anywhere,' said Wren.

Ludo knelt down beside her. 'And they're mounted on tunnel-lickers.'

They gazed into a large space supported by tapering rock columns where several tunnels had been licked into one.

'Look,' said Ludo. 'The robots are steering the tunnel-lickers with jolts of electricity from the ends of their tentacles. They're using the tunnel-licker's spit to carve out channels in the cave floor.'

'The robots are using them to melt the rock. And what are those *other* creatures?' Mel crouched with the others behind a large boulder. 'They're drinking the mirrorblood.'

'Ugh! They look like a cross between a slug and a bat,' said Goldie.

The multitude of dark, loathsome creatures seemed to bubble like a cauldron of boiling tar on the cave floor. They had hideous, blind faces and gaping mouths. Swollen red tongues lapped at the luminous mirrorblood as it spilled from the channels. Once satiated, the feeders would flap up to the tunnel roof on leathery wings to hang upside down, replacing others who would take their turn below.

'They look like trouble,' said Wren.

Cassetti shook his head in dismay. 'Do you know what they are, Pilfer?'

'Nope. But I bet Cogito does. Why don't we ask him?'

'Like we have the time to go back there – even if we could,' said Mel.

'Won't need to, Chummy. I brought him with us. Well, a part of him, anyway.' From out of Pilfer's invisible sack rose an inkwell and a rolled sheet of parchment, the severed ends of the threads that had fastened it to the lectern still dangling. 'Twinkletoes said it'd work from anywhere in the Mirrorscape.'

'Is there anything safe from your sticky fingers?' said Goldie.

'First rule of robbery: never leave a job empty-handed.'

'Get down,' said Mel as a searchlight beam swept over their hiding place. Everyone froze and held their breath. The beam slid away. 'That was close.'

'Now all we need's a pen,' said Wren.

'Sorted.' Mel produced his angel's quill from inside his doublet. He flipped open the lid of the inkwell. Immediately the parchment unrolled itself on the cavern floor as if it were alive. Mel dipped his pen. 'I wonder if it works with drawings?' He quickly and accurately sketched one of the slug-bats. Underneath he wrote *What is this?*

After a moment the drawing faded and words began to appear on the parchment.

You don't want to know.

Yes I do, wrote Mel. *That's why I'm asking.*

Believe me; you really don't want to know.

'Just what we need,' said Mel. 'A chatty lucubrator.'
Believe me; I really do want to know.

Suit yourself. It's your funeral. This denizen of the Interscape is a pit-vampire. It normally feeds on molten lava. It has a penchant for anything red in colour, probably as a result of its favoured foodstuff. The pit-vampire has the IQ of a digestive biscuit but is ferocious if provoked. In mature specimens its asbestos gut becomes lined with metal furring as a result of the high mineral content of its diet, which is smelted in its furnace-like digestion.

That's it? wrote Mel.

That's it. If you want my opinion . . .

Thanks, but right now I'm very busy. Mel rolled up the parchment.

'Oh, great,' said Ludo. 'Just imagine what they could do to us. Let's go back to the great Blinky and tell him we can't help.'

'Hang on,' said Mel. 'That bit about metal insides. I've got an idea.'

Ludo rolled his eyes. 'That's what I was afraid of.'

'Come on, Chummy; cough it up,' said Pilfer.

'Cassetti, do you have a magnet? A nice *red* magnet?'

'How many do you need?' Cassetti opened his top drawer.

'Just the one should do it. The stronger the better. And as much cord as you have.'

Mel attached one end of the ball of cord to the bright red magnet and the other to a large, spherical boulder.

'I get it,' said Goldie. 'You're going to make one of them swallow the magnet.'

'And the others will stick to it,' finished Cassetti, 'on account of their metal guts. The king of Nephonia said you'd be very resourceful and I cannot but concur.'

'Then the gravity will pull the rock – and the pit-vampires – away,' said Wren with a grin.

'Chummy's a genius,' said Pilfer.

Ludo looked sceptical. 'It's a bit of a long shot, isn't it? Suppose . . .'

Everyone looked at Ludo.

He shrugged. '. . . All right. But how're you going to get close enough to give them the magnet?'

'Don't look at me,' said Pilfer. 'First rule of robbery: steer clear of pit-vampires.'

'What we need is some more cloud,' said Cassetti. 'I keep this for small repairs.' From his drawers he fished a small machine with a bladder-like reservoir suspended beneath it. He shook the contraption. 'Sounds like it's almost full.' He started it and it began purring and, after a moment, snow-white cloud began billowing from the nozzle. Soon a dense bank began drifting towards the pit.

'Everyone keep down,' said Mel as he disappeared into the cloud with the magnet.

He soon rejoined the others. 'Worked a treat. One of the pit-vampires swallowed the magnet at once. Now, help me get this boulder rolling.'

The sideways gravity soon took the boulder and it picked up speed. Shortly they heard the squawking sound of the pit-vampires fighting amongst themselves. Through gaps in the cloud they saw an eccentric pile of the creatures had risen from the pit like iron filings stuck to a magnet. Then, the cord attached to the boulder became taut as it rolled away. Slowly at first and then gathering speed, the magnetised bunch of pit-vampires were pulled away down a tunnel.

Ludo slapped Mel on the back. 'I knew it'd work all along. Piece of cake!' he exclaimed.

'I thought I told you never to say that,' hissed Pilfer. 'Now those metal robots have heard you.'

The robots began sweeping their searchlight beams around the cavern. Momentarily dazzled, the friends could hear the *ticker-ticker-ticker* getting louder as the robots advanced towards them. The only other sound were the sad chimes of the luck-compass.

'Come on, let's leg it,' said Pilfer.

'I've a better idea,' said Cassetti. 'There's just enough cloud for me to work with. Make your way back towards the well-shaft. I'll join you later.' He disappeared into the cloud.

'What's he up to?' said Goldie. 'I'm not sure we should have let him out of our sight.'

'Perhaps one of us should follow him?' said Mel. 'To make sure he's not up to something.'

'Don't look at me,' said Ludo. 'I'm allergic to pit-vampires.'

The *ticker-ticker-tickering* got louder and the glare from the searchlights brighter. Mel led Wren, Ludo, Goldie and Pilfer back the way they had come inside the masking cloud. But he could tell from the sound that the robots were following them. Suddenly, the searchlights veered away, followed by the noise of the robots' motors.

Cassetti reappeared back at their side, stowing his cloud-shaping paddles back in his drawers. 'That should lead them a merry dance, my dears. I believe the way out is down here.'

'The clouds are drifting apart now,' said Pilfer. 'And look!'

'We did it,' said Ludo. 'The mirrorblood's flowing again. The tunnel's filling up.'

'What's *that?*' said Wren, pointing behind them.

'Just some of my handiwork,' said Cassetti. 'Nothing fancy, but good enough to fool those brazen blobs.'

Mel and the others watched themselves sculpted out of cloud and being pursued by the robots.

'Nice one,' said Pilfer. 'Lively now. When they catch up with those sculptures they'll realise they've been fooled and come after the real thing.'

'Pretty soon they'll have another thing to worry about,' said Mel. 'Once the mirrorblood starts to flow, being made of brass won't save them.'

Dirk Tot, Green and Blue set the master's improvised sedan chair down at the entrance to the Maven's quarters.

Ambrosius Blenk stood and addressed the two

Fas standing guard. 'I wish to see the Maven.'

'The Maven is not to be disturbed,' said one of the guards.

'But I insist. I have matters of the utmost importance that I must discuss with him. Do you realise who I am?'

The guard shook his head. 'I don't care who you are. No one can see the Maven.'

'Very well. In that case I would be grateful if you would give him a message.'

'What's the message?'

'*This!*' Green floored the guard with a right hook.

Blue delivered the same message to the other guard. He added a postscript of his own with his boot.

Dirk Tot pushed open the doors and the others followed him inside.

Back in the orchard the sparks were glowing more brightly and the gravity was almost back to normal. The whirlwind at the centre had vanished. King M-morpho greeted them with a smile.

'C-congratulations, ambassador. You have succeeded in your m-mission. My realm is healing itself. You are a true f-friend of our k-kingdom.'

'What about us,' said Ludo. 'We –'

Cassetti interrupted. 'We are pleased to have rendered a humble service to such a gracious monarch. Your kingdom is at last free to flourish and your majesty to grow in splendour.'

'Schmooze, schmooze,' whispered Goldie.

'And now, your majesty,' continued Cassetti, 'we must return to Nephonia without delay.'

'We w-wish you a safe journey. Unfortunately we f-find that our court d-diary is currently overflowing. D-duty weighs heavily on a m-monarch's shoulders. And there is the w-work of reconstruction to oversee.'

'The lying scrot!' hissed Wren.

'I bet he never intended to come with us,' said Mel angrily.

'Forgive my presumption, your majesty,' said Cassetti in a calmer tone and with an especially low bow. 'It is easy for us commoners to overlook the burden that monarchs must bear. It is the regret of all Nephonia that you won't be accompanying us back. I would have liked to have shown you true Cumulan hospitality, and to have bestowed upon your gracious person such riches as my kingdom could provide.'

'R-riches, you say. W-what kind of riches?'

'Nectar, honeydew, the choicest pollens. It would be for your majesty to decide. I am sure with the arrival of so magnificent a monarch as yourself our king would fling wide the doors to his treasury and allow you to select a tribute fitted to such a great ruler, whose radiant splendour would dazzle even the sun itself.'

'I think I'm going to be sick,' said Ludo under his breath.

'Well, c-come to think of it, a state v-visit at this time might be in Nephonia's b-best interest.'

'Indeed. We would have much to learn from your majesty's vast experience.'

'And m-matters of state must wait until we are r-rested after s-such an ordeal as ours.'

'Just so, most gracious majesty. Your sagacity astounds us all.'

'And b-besides. It would be a g-good idea for us to witness for ourselves that the p-perpetrators of this outrage are f-finished for g-good.'

'And such courage.' Cassetti gave an especially flamboyant bow.

Wren mimed sticking a finger down her throat.

Cassetti straightened up. 'Wisp awaits your majesty's pleasure.'

Cassetti and King M-morpho made their way back to the cloud barge, with the others following along behind.

'Well?' said Wren. 'Do you think we can trust him after all?'

'So far he hasn't put a foot wrong,' whispered Pilfer. 'At least nothing that I could see. And it was a neat little number he pulled on those pit-vampires. If he wasn't on our side he could have legged it and left us to face them alone.'

'You're too trusting, Pilfer,' said Goldie. 'You've seen how he charms everyone. He could just be stringing us along for a bit longer until we get to Cumulus.'

'I'm still not sure about him,' said Mel. 'But we don't have much choice for now. It's best if we keep our eyes on him. At least until we know if he's up to anything.'

*

As they rose and turned away from the orchard, Cassetti beckoned Mel over to the wheel as he piloted the Wisp. 'Where's Pilfer?'

'He's keeping an eye on King M-morpho,' said Mel.

'A good idea. Stand by me, my dear, and we'll steer by the luck-compass.'

Mel flipped it open. 'Which way to Nephonia?' The direction hand edged to the left. Cassetti swung the wheel to the new direction.

After a while, the texture of the Mirrorscape changed. Mel recognised that they were passing into a region created by the hand and mind of another artist. He consulted the luck-compass.

Cassetti glanced over Mel's shoulder at the triple dials. They promised good luck and the ruby at the centre seemed to shine brighter than ever. 'Almost home.'

They continued flying through an immeasurable ocean of the purest blue. Cassetti breathed deeply. A smile spread across his face and rays of sunshine burst from within his wig.

'Is this Nephonia?' asked Wren as she, Ludo and Goldie walked back to the wheel.

'This is the Cerulean Ocean that surrounds the kingdom,' explained Cassetti. 'Soon we should spy Nimbus and Cirrus. From there we'll try and locate Cumulus itself.'

'*Try?* You're telling us you don't know where it is?' said Ludo as he and the others joined them.

'My dear, things in Nephonia are not fixed as they are in your land. Clouds, by their very nature, are mutable. But fear not, find Cumulus we will.'

Soon Wisp was gripped in a strong oceanic current that swept it higher and higher in wide spirals.

'It's getting colder,' said Ludo, rubbing his hands.

'Parts of Wisp are drifting away,' said Wren.

'Don't be alarmed,' said Cassetti. 'It's the nature of clouds.'

A little later, Goldie remarked, 'I guess we can't go on calling this Wisp. It looks more like a wasp now.'

'Perhaps it'll make his nibs feel more at home.' Ludo nodded towards King M-morpho, where he stood aloof in what had formerly been the bow and now resembled a bug-eyed head.

Later, they passed distant cloud formations that Cassetti identified as Nimbus and Cirrus. The luck-compass was consulted once more and they changed direction and journeyed on.

'Is that Cumulus?' said Mel, pointing. 'It's huge. Even the biggest cloud in Nem is tiny compared to that.'

Cassetti's wig darkened and he frowned. 'It was bigger when I left and bigger still when I began my quest.'

'I still don't understand why you think *we* can heal the rift?' said Wren.

'The king of Cumulus was most specific that only you would do. He described you and Mel and Ludo perfectly. I was on my way to Nem when . . . I'm sure you recall our adventure aboard the Leviathan.'

'The giant galleon? How could we ever forget it?' said Ludo.

'I guess we'll get answers to all our questions soon,' said Mel. He walked to Wisp's rail. 'Pilfer?' he said in a whisper. 'You still here?'

'Shtum, that's me.'

The cloud barge rode closer to Cumulus, which looked like an enormous city with ramparts and towers and trails of windblown cloud that could be banners streaming from the peaks. They could see their own tiny shadow, no larger than a fly crawling on an iceberg, ripple across the billowing walls as they approached.

Cassetti expertly piloted the vessel until it touched Cumulus. The nebulous craft was absorbed into the giant cloud and everyone aboard simply stepped off. Cassetti led King M-morpho into the cloud, all the while massaging the imperial ego with the oiliest of compliments. The others followed along behind.

'The Maven's apartments are empty!' Ambrosius Blenk stood at the entrance to the vast suite of rooms high in the House of Spirits. 'All his paintings have been removed. Every last one of them.'

'Looks like his sculptures and ceramics have gone as well,' said Green.

'The entire apartments seems to have been purged of any art,' said Dirk Tot.

In their place were naked picture hooks and forlorn rectangles betraying where pictures had once hung on the sumptuous silk-lined walls, and pale patches on the marble floors where plinths had once stood.

As the master and his aides strode on, they passed packing crates stuffed with straw cradling many of the Maven's treasures. Everywhere stood candelabra charged with fresh candles awaiting the approaching darkness.

Passing a window overlooking the city, Green stopped. 'The darkness is getting bigger but the spark-fall has stopped.'

Ambrosius Blenk smiled. 'My apprentices are doing their job, now let's see to ours.'

They came at last to the doors to the Maven's inner sanctum.

'Please, will you three wait here,' said the master. 'I must confront my old friend alone and give him the opportunity to explain himself.'

Dirk Tot looked concerned. 'But, master. . .' Green touched his arm and they exchanged glances. 'Very well. We'll make sure you're not disturbed.'

'Thank you. Stay within earshot. I'll call if I need your help.' Ambrosius Blenk pushed open the large doors. Standing at the far end of the long room with his back to the master was the white-robed figure of the Maven. He turned to face his unannounced visitor.

The master's jaw dropped open in disbelief.

Cumulus

From the inside, Cumulus looked as grey and unremarkable as a foggy day in any city in any land, but as they walked away from the landing place the vapour thinned and cleared and all was revealed.

'Scrot!' said Pilfer, forgetting that he was supposed to be incognito.

Mel covered the robber's exclamation up with a cough. 'I've imagined pictures in clouds before but *nothing* like this.'

There was a thriving city inside the cloud. Bustling crowds of figments milled everywhere among the cloudy buildings. Like Cassetti they all wore wigs, although none was as elaborate as the ambassador's.

'Look at the colours,' said Ludo. 'Everywhere is like the inside of an oyster shell.'

'Mother of pearl,' said Goldie. 'And father and all the little pearls too. It's the whole skegging family.' The nacreous, swirling colours were reflected in her wide-eyed, gilded face.

Bathed in the even, diffused light filtering into the heart of the cloud, Cumulus was a city in constant motion.

'Look,' said Goldie, 'that building's shrinking while the one next door is growing.'

'And the streets appear and then disappear back into the cloud,' said Mel.

'And look at the bridges!' said Wren with a gasp of delight as one emerged from the canyon-like side of a building, spanned the street and disappeared again all in the space of a few seconds.

Mel looked at his friends and saw the way the humid atmosphere of Cumulus formed tiny beads of moisture that seeded their hair and clothing like miniature diamonds.

Cassetti stopped. 'Now, your majesty, we will need to make use of a timetable to get to the royal palace.' He opened his top drawer and produced a tall, thin book. The pages inside were like a concertina. He looked around until he located a building with a sundial on its facade and then checked the timetable. 'Splendid; there's a staircase going in our direction due presently.' He led them over to one corner of the square which, before their very eyes, was transforming itself into a crossroads. Soon a vaporous staircase blossomed from the cloud at their feet and began to rise in the air in a wide and graceful curve. It did not seem to be supported by anything.

Cassetti bowed to King M-morpho. 'Great rulers such as yourself have no need of these mundane contrivances but we commoners must follow the staircase to the palace.' He turned to the others. 'Don't dilly-dally, my dears. These steps are scheduled to be here but briefly.' So saying he began to ascend the cloudy stairs, while King M-morpho fluttered upwards beside him.

'The top of the staircase hasn't formed yet,' said Wren as she followed.

Mel looked behind as they climbed. 'It gets worse. The steps are dissolving behind us.'

'I don't like this one bit,' said Ludo. 'Stairs ought to stay put.' He stared to one side and saw another partial staircase a little way off packed with Cumulans descending.

Goldie looked down and saw the impression of Pilfer's size nines in the fluffy steps alongside her. 'What a lark, eh?' she whispered.

In reply she received a nudge in her ribs.

Cassetti led them on, frequently stopping, consulting his timetable and waiting until a new street, staircase or bridge appeared, until they arrived at the entrance to the royal palace.

'It's huge,' said Wren, staring upwards at the towers and domes. 'Easily as large as anything in Vlam.'

'And it's always changing,' added Ludo. 'You'd never get bored living here.'

'What must it be like inside?' said Goldie, her mouth gaping wide.

As they entered the palace, they saw that the vaulting in the ceiling high above constantly rearranged itself like the swaying branches of trees in a high wind. The light inside was also in continuous motion as windows came and went. The friends seemed a mass of arms as they pointed out one wonder after another.

At last they came to the audience chamber itself. It seemed more stable than the rest of Cumulus, the walls and ceiling billowing only gently. The long room was lit by a row of hanging chandeliers even more ornate than those in Cassetti's room. At the far end was a raised dais with cloudy drapes drawn across it. Palace guards lined the audience chamber armed with halberds and wearing martial wigs in the shapes of fierce beasts. These cloudy confections eyed the party and bared their teeth as they processed up to the dais and stopped.

Mel opened the luck-compass. The direction hand pointed to the dais, the strength hand was nearing the twelve o'clock position and the time hand was ticking backwards towards imminent good luck. Even the decorative ruby at the centre seemed to glow especially brightly. He showed it to Ludo, Wren and Goldie and they exchanged broad smiles. With a sense of great anticipation Mel held it open in his hand before him. He was so excited he struggled to keep his feet still.

A figment with an even bigger wig than Cassetti's approached them and the two Cumulans exchanged extravagant bows.

'Chancellor Parrucca, may I present King M-morpho,' said Cassetti. The chancellor bowed before the butterfly monarch and plied him with even more oleaginous flattery until the puffed-up king threatened to burst with self-importance.

'His majesty the king of Nephonia will be with us shortly,' said the chancellor as he rearranged his lacy cuffs. 'And these must be the humans that his majesty bade brought back.' He nodded at Mel and his friends but did not bow or offer his hand.

In the distance, a fanfare sounded. It was repeated by unseen but progressively nearer trumpeters until the entire throne room reverberated to the sound.

Cassetti turned and smiled broadly. 'The king approaches, my dears. At the final trumpet blast you must bow low as you've seen me do. Do not raise your heads until his majesty bids you.'

The cloudy drapes began to draw aside as the final, emphatic blast sounded. Mel and the others bowed as low as they could. In the sudden silence the luck-compass pealed a tune happier than it had ever done before.

Then, from the dais above them, the king spoke. 'It's nice to see you again – *Smell!*'

*

'You're not the Maven!' Ambrosius Blenk's face was a mask of confusion.

'I can assure you I am,' said a smiling Fa Odum. 'The previous incumbent – how shall I put it – *resigned* at rather short notice. In fact, he still resides in the House of Spirits. But in the dungeon.'

It took the master only a moment to understand what had happened. 'It's *you* who's caused these storms to form over the city.'

'You flatter me, Blenk. I had help from my good friend Ter Selen and especially from our ally in the Mirrorscape.'

'And what of all the works of art you've been destroying? Destroy art and you destroy the soul of the world.'

'You dare to lecture me about souls, you pompous fool? Souls are my department.' Fa Odum's smiling mask faltered for a moment. 'You can't possibly compare the value of a few scraps of paint-smeared canvas to that of the kingdom of Nem. The mirror-storm is a necessary device to demonstrate to the people who their true friends are. Even as we speak, Ter Selen and her sisters are doing battle with the demons. Your apprentice Melkin guessed right. He could see that the people will be so grateful for being saved from the demons that they will beg us to rule them.'

'And how many demons have you brought over from the Mirrorscape?'

'Oh, thousands.' Fa Odum's smile widened. 'Simply *thousands*. But we will prevail. You see, we have some remarkable technology on our side.'

'Technology?' The master looked puzzled for a moment. 'You don't mean from the Mirrorscape? Do you have any idea of the consequences of using Mirrorscape technology in this world?'

'What do I care for your piddling consequences when Nem is there for the taking?'

'By you and the Ters.'

'And our friend in the Mirrorscape. Don't forget him. You see, there will be a triumvirate ruling Nem from now on. The kingdom has lacked a firm hand ever since the Mysteries' power waned. Nature abhors a vacuum and we'll be filling the one here. It's all been carefully planned and it's all gone like – well, like clockwork.'

The chiming of the luck-compass stopped.

The blood drained from Mel's face and his insides turned to jelly. 'Adolfus Spute?' He had trouble saying the words; his mouth was suddenly as dry as blotting paper.

'None other.'

'But you're –'

'Trapped along with my companions inside that odious painting you locked us in? Obviously not.'

'How did you –?'

'Escape? Simple really. We merely stayed put and someone found *us*.'

Us? Mel felt even sicker.

'Of course, it took a little time before we were found and we got rather hungry while we waited. That stringy Skim did not sustain us for long but that fat toad Lord Brool – well, we dined on him for two weeks. A rather monotonous and fatty diet it must be said, but needs must.'

Mel looked down at the luck-compass.

'And you've brought my favourite toy back. It invariably ends up in the hands of gullible fools. That little trinket has supplied us with endless fun – simply *endless*. Fun for all the family, you might say. You do remember my family don't you, Smell? Especially my nephew.'

'Hello, Fegie.' Another familiar voice spoke as a tall figure parted the clouds and stepped on to the dais: Groot Smert.

Mel's worst nightmare had become real.

'And I'm sure you remember Mumchance,' continued Adolfus Spute.

There came a long, sinister note on a whistle; the nightmare suddenly got worse.

'I believe some of you have also met the latest member of our happy family.'

Through the cloud stepped Lug.

Goldie stiffened, but Wren put a restraining hand on her shoulder.

Mel could see them clearly now. The cadaverously

thin Adolfus Spute in his long, red robes, white face make-up and strange tonsure, with his long, black hair shaven into an artificially high forehead. The former High-Bailiff of the Fifth Mystery still carried his multi-coloured staff of office. He slouched on the throne, one leg swinging over the arm rest. Several of the rings he wore like knuckle-dusters on his gloved hands were missing.

Mel knew he'd seen the rings they had found before. In that moment he remembered where. They were not Cassetti's. They belonged to Adolfus Spute! Mel looked at Mumchance standing to the right. The whistle the mute dwarf wore around his neck now hung from a knotted length of string instead of the usual silver chain. He dropped his eyes to a strip of fabric that had been torn from the hem of his scarlet robe – the tourniquet on the bladder that held the mites.

Groot smiled his sneering smile. His Fifth Mystery tonsure and single eyebrow had grown back to a coarse stubble.

The drawing of Cogito's memory banks. Finally

Mel realised who had made it. He closed his eyes. And the stowaway. It could only have been Groot. He saw it all now. How could he have been so blind?

'There's been a traitor in your midst all along: a clockwork traitor built by our ingenious friend Lug. I know you've met his brass robots. He's *so* clever with his hands and a veritable *genius* at using Mirrorscape crystals.'

Lug stood at a control panel that resembled an ornate dressing table. Angled above it was what looked to be a circular, red mirror fashioned from hundreds of closely packed rubies. Clearly reflected in its insect-eye surface, Mel could see his own fractured image in shades of red. He stared down at the luck-compass and the image above him did the same. Lug smiled knowingly and turned a dial on the panel. The luck-direction hand swung in imitation. He turned another and the luck-strength hand copied it. A third and the hands on the backwards clock rotated through twelve hours. It came to rest at twelve o'clock and the happy chimes rang out again.

'I *never* trusted that whatsit,' said Ludo.

'My dears, I had no idea,' said Cassetti. His wig had turned black and rain was trickling down his forlorn face, leaving tracks in the carefully applied powder.

'Of course you didn't,' said Adolfus Spute. 'Set a fool to catch a fool, that's my motto.'

Cassetti looked at Parrucca. 'Did you know about this, chancellor?'

'It's King Parrucca now. The former king is rotting in my dungeon. Guards!' The palace guards stepped forward and levelled their halberds at the party. Their wigs roared silently.

'What did you do with Guv?' said Goldie through gritted teeth.

'The old fool who ran that peripatetic roundabout?' said Adolfus Spute. 'He was merely an inconvenient obstacle that needed to be disposed of.'

'"*Inconvenient obstacle?*"' hissed Goldie, seething with rage. 'He was my friend. The only one who ever cared for me.'

Adolfus Spute smiled. 'Enough of this sentimental claptrap. This is a time for celebration.'

'I'll show you a "celebration", if I ever get my hands on you. All of you.' Goldie glared up at the dais.

'You've provided us with such excellent entertainment,' said Adolfus Spute. 'Right from the start with my nephew's marked cards. We've tried to make your journey here as uncomfortable as we could. I hope you appreciate all our hard work.'

'Those skegging cards,' said Mel to Ludo. 'You should have known better than to trust anything that belonged to Groot.'

'It wasn't my fault. You followed the whatsit.'

'Stop it, you two,' said Wren. 'What's done is done.'

Mumchance blew a trill on his whistle.

'Yes, quite right, my murderous mite. There *were* six of them. We saw the fat, bearded one briefly in Anywhere. Where is he now, I ask myself.'

'Pilfer? He's long gone,' said Goldie. 'First law of robbery: look after number one. He'd legged it before we left Anywhere.'

'So you weren't *all* stupid.'

Mumchance sounded his whistle again.

'An interesting question, my tiny termite. What *shall*

we do with them? I've promised Ter Selen that the runaway bride will be returned to her husband, but the others will accompany us on our triumphant return to Nem. We'll decide how to dispose of them later. Something public, I think. Something particularly gruesome that will serve as an object lesson to our new subjects.'

'If you would care to seal the rent sucking away my kingdom,' said Parrucca, 'we would be most grateful.'

'Certainly, your majesty,' said Adolfus Spute. 'After all, the purpose of the three storms was only to engender the Mirrorstorm. Now it's formed it's self-sustaining. We'll seal it before we leave.'

There was the sound of a commotion behind the master. He turned and saw Dirk Tot, Green and Blue being urged into the room by Fa Craw and a dozen black-robed Fas with crossbows levelled at their chests.

Blue pretended to stumble and, as the eyes of the crossbowmen instinctively snapped round, Green lunged at the nearest. Catching him off balance, the two rolled on the floor.

'Master, run!' shouted Dirk Tot as he slammed another of their captors with a fist as large and hard as a cannonball.

As Ambrosius Blenk made for the door, another of the Fas loosed a crossbow bolt at his retreating back. As quick as a flash, Dirk Tot's arm shot up and the quarrel pierced his silver hand. The force spun it from his wrist and it skidded across the floor.

'Don't shoot. Take them alive!' shouted Fa Odum from the safety of a pillar.

More Fas Major flooded into the room and, in a flurry of violence, set about the four men. Dirk Tot fought back bravely but, outnumbered, even he was eventually subdued.

'Nice try, Blenk,' said Fa Odum as he emerged, shaking, from behind the pillar. His smile returned to his face. 'We have big plans for Nem. For starters, the Pleasures will be reintroduced. They were always such a gratifying source of income and much too lucrative to see abolished. The only difference is that henceforth they will benefit the triumvirate rather than the Mysteries. And now your dungeon awaits. Fa Craw will escort you. After the triumvirate is installed we will decide what to do with all our enemies. Now, take them away.'

The Return to Vlam

'How're you feeling, Cassetti?' asked Wren.

'Somewhat hollow, my dear,' answered the Cumulan as he sat dejectedly in the corner of their cell with four deep holes that formerly held his drawers gaping in the middle of his chest. 'But I fear King M-morpho will injure himself if he doesn't calm down.'

The butterfly king had been confined inside a fine net pinned to the deck with weights at the far end of the fuselage. Along with the friends, he had been imprisoned inside the hull of a heavily armed airship. It was crewed by Lug's gnomes and suspended beneath a wasp-shaped cloud. Its engines throbbed with a deep-voiced drone. Just outside the cell were piles of treasure plundered from the Mirrorscape. The airship was on its way back to Vlam via a rent in the foundations of Cumulus that had been opened for the first storm.

'Why didn't you tell us this Spute geezer was king of

Nephonia?' said Goldie. 'Surely you must've known. He doesn't even look like one of you lot.'

'My dear, if I had but known I would not have led you there for all the treasure in all the isles in the Cerulean Ocean. But the king's instructions were always conveyed to me by that traitorous Parrucca. Adolfus Spute must have deposed the real king before sending me on my quest to bring you to him.' His wig began to rain and a fine drizzle beaded his face. 'I should have known that the luck-compass was too good to be true. I fear my gullibility has brought you all into harm's way. And now that they've taken my drawers, my usefulness is diminished.' A tear joined the raindrops on Cassetti's face.

'We're not beaten yet,' said Mel. 'What can you see out of that porthole, Ludo?'

'We've passed through the rent. Now I can see Vlam below,' said Ludo as he craned his neck. 'And we're flying right into . . .'

The cell was suddenly plunged into darkness and the airship bucked as it was caught in turbulence.

'. . . the great big black thing.'

'That'll be the mirrorstorm,' said Cassetti. 'They're taking us inside it. Dire as our situation is, I fear it's about to get much worse.'

The light in the fuselage increased a fraction as the airship's searchlights were turned on outside.

There was a cackle of cruel laughter from the gloom at the far end as two gnome guards climbed down into the fuselage from the deck above. With their spiky black hair, crimson skin and pointed features they might have been Lug's brothers. The glow of the foul-smelling cheroots they were smoking pulsed like warning lights. A roaming searchlight beam fleetingly illuminated the interior. Behind the guards, Mel saw the ghost-like outline of Pilfer's face briefly revealed in the blue-white tendrils of the dissipating tobacco smoke. His eyes were watering and he was plainly suppressing a coughing fit.

Mel needed to do something quickly or the robber would give himself away. 'Hey, you two, ever seen one of these?' He withdrew his glowing angel's feather from his doublet and waved it in front of his face. It left a bright trail as he flourished it in an arabesque before him.

443

Wide-eyed with fascination, the guards walked towards the cell.

'What yer got there?' said the first, clearly mesmerised.

'Shiny thing,' said the second gnome, reaching out his hand. 'Gimme.' The luminous pattern of the fast-moving quill was reflected in his black, glittering eyes.

'Just come a little closer and I'll show you what it can really do. Closer. That's it. Closer.'

From the corner of his eye, Mel watched as two large gold ewers floated after the guards. He bit his lips to stop from smiling as the vessels came crashing down on the gnomes' heads, and they collapsed unconscious to the floor.

There was the sound of a series of long-needed coughs and then Pilfer's voice. 'Night-night, sleep tight; hope the bedbugs –'

'Eat you scrots alive,' finished Ludo.

The cell keys jingled as they were removed from the first gnome's belt and rose to unlock the door. Pilfer coughed again. 'Struth, if those two don't pong something awful.'

'An invisible m-man?' said King M-morpho with evident astonishment from the far end. Even though his head was hopelessly jumbled up with the rest of his body inside the net, it bore a look of surprise. 'At least o-one of you b-bunglers has had some f-forethought.' Then, impatiently, 'W-well. We're w-waiting.'

'I didn't hear the P word,' said Ludo.

'R-release us at once, *p-peasant!*'

'All right, Ludo. I'll do it.' Wren released the king and he resumed a human, but very unhappy, formation.

'Now what?' said Ludo.

'Let's see what's here among all this loot,' said Mel. 'There might be something we can use as a weapon.'

'I've already had a shufti,' said Pilfer. 'It's all worthless junk – gold, silver, jewels. There's not so much as a peony. It's *pathetic*.'

'But what about this?' said Wren. 'It's the ruby mirror we saw on Lug's machine in the throne room.'

The ruby screen displayed the dimpled view from the luck-compass now hanging around Adolfus Spute's neck up on deck. They could see brilliant searchlight beams as they sliced the darkness over Vlam, occasionally illuminating the roofs of tall buildings as the craft descended. Here and there were patches of light from burning windows. Lower still, and they could see a small band of armed Ters busy in the spark-lit streets, burning brands held aloft as they worked around a strange machine. A ring of their sisters surrounded them as they fended off eerily glowing demons. The airship moved on and they then watched as it was moored to a steeple with a thick hawser. The view turned and they saw Lug hurrying towards the hatch into the fuselage.

'Quick.' Mel secreted his feather and he and the others crowded back into the cell, pulling the door to after them so that it appeared closed. King M-morpho fluttered apart and into the shadows.

The hatch opened and Lug called down the companionway. 'Smut? Grub? Are you there?'

One of the gnomes got to his feet and waddled awkwardly to the foot of the stairs. He raised a floppy hand in greeting.

'I thought I heard something,' said Lug, squinting into the gloom. 'Everything OK?'

The guard's hand dropped to his side and his head nodded vigorously.

'Right; keep an eye on the prisoners. Make sure they don't make trouble.'

The guard shook his head.

'What do you mean you won't?'

The guard nodded.

'That's better. Just make sure you do. Spute has plans for them later.'

The guard nodded again. His head lolled forward on to his chest and he raised a limp hand in a thumbs-up gesture.

Lug grunted and closed the hatch. Bolts grated as they were shot home after him.

The guard collapsed in a heap on the floor.

'Skegging great puppet,' said Pilfer, breathing heavily. His lantern appeared from his sack and was lit.

'Are you sure there's nothing in here we can use?' said Ludo as he led the others from the cell. He began to pull aside pieces of the loot, which gleamed in the lamplight.

'*Ah!*' Mel jumped back in alarm. Staring at him

from the back of the plundered treasure was Groot. He had a supercilious smirk on his face. Mel's panic receded; it was only a self-portrait.

'Thinks a lot of himself, doesn't he?' said Goldie.

'He used to be an apprentice with our master,' explained Wren. 'He must have painted it while he was in the Mirrorscape.'

'Pity he didn't turn out like you three,' said Cassetti. 'We could do with a friend on the outside.'

'Say that again,' said Mel.

Cassetti repeated it.

'That's it!' said Mel.

'What's it?' Ludo looked confused.

'Mel, you can't,' said Wren.

'Can't what?' said Ludo. 'Will someone please tell me what's going on?'

'I think Mel's going to try and get inside Laughing-Boy,' said Goldie, nodding towards the portrait.

'*What?*'

'My dear, is that such a good idea? He's odious enough from the outside. Inside could prove even more disagreeable.' Cassetti's wig grew darker still.

'You don't even know if that's possible,' said Ludo. 'We've only ever done it with places.'

'I'm going to try it,' said Mel as he drew the mirrormark on the portrait with the ash from the stub of the guard's smelly cheroot. 'Just for long enough to open the hatch. It's that or wait in here while they destroy Vlam.'

'No, Mel. Don't do it,' said Wren.

'Chummy might be right,' said Pilfer. 'It could be our only chance.'

'But what if –'

Ludo's remark was cut off by Wren's cry. 'Mel, *no!*'

The Filigree Suit

There was the sound of a thudding drumbeat. At first Mel thought it was his own heart, but that was beating much, much faster. Overlaid on this was a persistent and unnerving noise that sounded like fingernails being dragged across an endless blackboard. Wherever he was it was dark, and he could hear the noises on the bridge and then Lug barking orders in his harsh voice. It sounded a long way away.

There came the distant blast from Mumchance's whistle.

Adolfus Spute's echoing voice answered from somewhere closer. 'Under attack from demons, are we? Of course you can help them, my homicidal homunculus. I know how you simply adore destruction. Trot along now.' Then, after a short pause. 'Well, my boy, we're going home at last.'

'Yes, uncle.' Groot's booming voice was so loud it made Mel jump. He could feel its vibration coming up through the soles of his feet. 'I'm looking forward to taking up where I left off with Fegie. I've been dreaming up ways to torment him.'

Mel shuddered. He took his feather from his doublet and held it up. He half expected to see a scene like that inside Cogito, but instead of pulsating organs its angel-light revealed the inside of a small room. There was a door set into each of three walls. Behind him the fourth wall was a screen of mist that marked the picture plane and the way back to the hold.

He approached the left-hand door and opened it.

And shut it quickly. *No!*

Very slowly he opened it again. Inside, he saw himself turning slowly on the end of a hangman's rope. He was a life-sized rag doll wearing the Blenk livery with a crude mop of yellow woollen hair in imitation of his own. The doll was pierced through with long skewers. The hands were missing and threads hung where the button eyes had been ripped out. Standing on an easel was a crude portrait of him composed from violent expressionist slashes, a messy palette at its side. The likeness was almost unrecognisable as it had been scorched by flames. The eye sockets were pierced with shards of broken glass. Mel felt the contents of his stomach begin to rise up his gullet. He fought back his sickness and closed the door, resting his trembling hand against the jamb. All he wanted to do was to get out and return to his friends. But he knew that unless he could find a way of getting Groot to open the hatch he would have no friends to return to.

He went to the right-hand door and twisted the knob with a shaking hand, fearful of what he would find inside. It was a room of mirrors. Reflected back tens – hundreds – thousands – of times were haughty, sneering paintings of Groot. There were also three badly carved marble sculptures. They were each in self-aggrandising poses. The reflections made the poky room seem as big as a palace.

Mel shut the door and opened the third. Behind it was a corridor, its angles drunken and skewed. It was lined with more doors of different shapes and sizes. The noise from outside grew louder. He walked slowly along, resolved not to open any more doors save the one at the far end. Dancing light leaked on to the floor from beneath it.

Halfway there, he was stopped by a muffled whimpering sound. He bent and put his ear to a door so small it barely came up to his waist. The sound was coming from the other side. It was a small child's frightened sobbing. He knelt down and opened the door.

Inside was the tiny figure of a boy cowering in the dark, cupboard-like room. He was crying bitterly. Mel held his feather closer and the boy recoiled into the corner, trying to make himself as small as possible.

'Don't be afraid. I'm not going to hurt you. What are you doing here?' asked Mel.

The small boy buried his face in his arms and sobbed louder.

Mel shuffled nearer on his knees. The angel's feather illuminated crude, child-like drawings pinned on the cupboard walls. They all depicted the same small figure running from terrifying monsters drawn with crude and brutal crayon strokes. The monsters all resembled Groot. Mel reached forward and touched the boy gently on his arm. 'Come on. You can't stay here. Come with me. I won't hurt you.'

Mel gently took the boy's arm and slowly eased it

away from his face. He held his feather close and, with a sudden shock, recognised the lad.

It was Groot.

The boy screamed and kicked out at Mel with his feet. '*No!* No one must ever see me.' Mel jumped back and fell into the corridor. The door slammed shut.

At that moment there came the deafening report of a Serpent being fired and the door at the far end of the corridor flew open. Mel got to his feet, feeling frightened and confused by what he had just seen in the cupboard. As he neared the door he heard Adolfus Spute's voice. It was less distant this time.

'Dear boy, are you all right? You don't look too well.'

'It's nothing, uncle.' Groot's voice was so loud the walls and floor of the corridor trembled. 'I have a headache, that's all.'

'I do believe you partook a little too freely of that ninny Parrucca's hospitality.'

Don't you lecture me, you scrot-scented bag of bones. Groot's voice was now a loud whisper. *I can hold my drink. And I relieved the king's cellar of a few cases while you were too busy to notice. They're stashed in the hold.*

Mel instantly realised they were Groot's thoughts. He walked up to the door and his heart almost stopped. In front of him, as if projected on to a giant circular screen, loomed the enormous, repulsive face of Adolfus Spute. Mel was seeing out of Groot's eyes. He saw the man's pale grey bloodshot eyes; the lank, dyed black hair falling to his shoulders; the shaved forehead and eyebrows; the cracked white make-up of the Fifth Mystery; the long, yellow and misshapen teeth. He could almost smell his fetid breath. All of his worst physical traits were magnified and caricatured as if through a distorting lens. He felt sick all over again.

He tucked his feather inside his doublet and entered the room. Everyone he could see on the screen was rendered cruel and distorted. Aside from his uncle's gross features, Mumchance appeared with toad's legs protruding from beneath his scarlet robe and a poisonous, black tongue that darted out from between the lipless slit of his mouth. His face was covered in leaking pustules. The pointed chin on Lug's crescent moon face curved up until it almost touched the droop of his sickle nose. A lizard's tail poked out from a slit in the back of his overalls. Beyond Adolfus Spute, Mel could see the deck of the airship and its busy crew.

Mel turned back to the room and searched it with his eyes to see if there was any way he could control Groot, but it was bare.

Outside, a searchlight beam swung round on to Groot's face. Just before the light dazzled him Mel glimpsed the misty outline of a figure standing motionless in the centre of the room. 'Pilfer? Is that you?'

'I'm sorry, dear boy,' said Adolfus Spute. 'Did you say something?'

Mel clasped his hand to his mouth. *He can hear me.*

'No, Uncle. I didn't say anything.'

Mel looked up and saw Groot lift a flask to his lips and take a long drink. Almost at once the fingernail staccato grew less but the view through Groot's eyes began to wobble, and parts of it vanished behind pulsating, black splotches. *How much has he drunk?* Groot stumbled and lowered his head, his hands resting on his thighs.

'Dear boy, are you *sure* you're all right?'

456

'I'm OK, Uncle. Really I am.' *As if you care. All you're interested in is getting your scrawny backside on a throne. Don't think that I don't know you plan to do away with Fa Odum and Ter Selen as soon as they've done their bit.* 'Just another sip will see me all right.' Groot drank deeply again.

Mel's sharp eyes scanned the room and, as another searchlight beam swung by, he saw the spectral figure once more. It was not Pilfer. It was as if a suit of armour made from the finest filigree stood upright in the centre of the room. It was so faint it was nearly invisible. It seemed to be attached to the walls and ceiling by hundreds of swaying strands of energy that slowly moved like silken threads in a breeze. As he watched, it mimed lifting a flask to its lips and tilted its head back to drink. The view outside showed Groot doing the same. Mel moved closer until he was standing next to it. He stared in amazement. It was as if it was a model of Groot, mimicking his every move.

Mel reached out his hand to touch it and then – it happened so quickly he did not see how – he was inside it. He felt strands of energy tightening around his body, squeezing him. The gossamer strands of the filigree suit began to glow. He was feeling everything Groot was, including sick. He struggled to free himself but the suit gripped him all the harder. He relaxed and so did the suit.

'Dear boy, you're shivering,' said Adolfus Spute.

Groot turned his head to look at his uncle.

Mel struggled to get out of the suit. 'Let me *go!*'

Adolfus Spute looked puzzled. 'Let you go? But I'm not touching you.'

'I'm sorry, Uncle. I don't know why I said that.' *Why did I say that?*

That gave Mel an idea. 'Get away from me you stinking, lice-ridden moron.'

'*What* did you say?'

'You heard me.'

Adolfus Spute could not believe what he was hearing and Groot what he was saying. He raised his flask to his lips again.

'I'll take that,' said Adolfus Spute, snatching the flask away. 'You're obviously drunk. You can have it back when you're feeling yourself again.'

'But, Uncle . . .' *What's happening to me?* The flask

was prised from his hand. *Take it, you old scrot. I've plenty more where that came from.*

Mel watched through Groot's eyes as Adolfus Spute strode away down the deck.

Now was Mel's chance. He knew what he needed to do. Mel licked his lips imagining them dry. He imagined being so thirsty it was hard to swallow. *I need a drink*, he thought. *I must have a drink. I must raid my stash in the hold.*

On the deck, Groot licked his lips; his very dry lips. *I must have a drink. I need to raid my stash in the hold.* He checked that his uncle's back was turned, and slipped the bolts on the hatch and made his way down.

Wren had seen him coming in the ruby mirror. 'Quickly. Hide, Groot's coming.' She watched as the shadowy form descended the companionway, lit a lamp and searched among the treasure. Was Mel in there? She shifted from her hiding place to get a better view and knocked over a gilded platter that fell to the metal deck with a loud clatter.

Groot turned too fast and fell backwards, scattering

more of the plunder. 'Who's there?' He looked towards the cell and saw its door hanging open, Smut and Grub unconscious on the floor in front of it. His eyes swung back and forth in panic, searching the gloom for the prisoners.

'Wren! It's me,' Mel shouted with Groot's voice.

'Mel?'

'The hatch is unbolted. Get out while you can,' said the sprawling figure of Groot. He shook his head as if to clear it. 'Fegie? Where are you?' He looked around wildly.

Wren frowned in confusion. 'What's the matter? Why are you talking like that?'

'Quickly. Before Groot works out what's happening. Works out what? Where are you, Fegie? Get out, Wren. *Now!*'

The others emerged from their hiding places.

'He did it,' said Ludo. 'Mel's inside Groot.'

'Shut up, Ludo!' said Wren.

'*What!*' Groot sat up. 'Fegie's inside me?' There was a look of incomprehension on his face. 'Quick, Wren, Ludo, run!' Groot clamped his hand over his mouth as the alien words spilled out. 'Stay right where you are. Don't move. Uncle, *help!*'

'My dears, I think we should do as he says.' Cassetti moved towards the companionway, King M-morpho fluttering after him.

'If Mel's inside Laughing-Boy, shouldn't we take him, too?' said Goldie.

'No, we'll just take this,' said Wren, grabbing Groot's self-portrait.

'This might come in useful too.' Goldie took the ruby mirror.

Groot lay there, watching the friends climb from the fuselage, his drunken brain working overtime. He stared at his self-portrait as it vanished up the companionway. Then it dawned on him. 'Fegie; you used my picture to get inside me. You're in my head.'

Mel struggled against the filigree strands of energy binding him.

Groot twitched and contorted. 'Stop it! *Stop it!*' Then he was in control again.

Mel felt the suit grip him harder and spring into motion. Mel became a helpless passenger as Groot got unsteadily to his feet, snatched up a bottle and followed the others up the companionway. On deck, demons were attacking the airship and confusion prevailed. Searchlight beams, lightning bolts and flying demon body parts conspired to create a riot of movement. Groot ducked back down the hatch as a demon disintegrated beside him.

Amid the confusion, Cassetti led the friends to the rail.

Ludo looked over, gauging their height. It was a long way down to the square below. 'How're we ever going to get down there?'

'We're not, my dear. The way off this hulk is up.' Cassetti swung himself up on to the rail and planted a daintily shod foot on one of the rope rungs of a ratline that disappeared upwards into the cloud that supplied the airship's buoyancy. 'Follow me.'

One by one, the friends scrabbled after Cassetti and upwards into the cloud, King M-morpho fluttering beside them.

'I don't think anyone saw us,' said Ludo, gazing around at the misty outlines of his friends inside the cloud.

'Now what?' said Goldie.

'Those scoundrels might have removed my drawers,' said Cassetti, 'but they neglected to search in here.' He reached into his wig and produced his cloud-shaping paddles. 'A spot of sculpture is called for, I believe. Pilfer, my dear, would you look into the possibility of detaching us from the hull?'

'It'll be a pleasure.'

While Pilfer was cutting through the rigging, Cassetti set to work.

'What's it going to be?' said Ludo.

'Normally I would indulge in a fantasy but our situation calls for the prosaic,' said Cassetti as he worked. 'Something that would arouse no comment to see floating in the sky.'

'I get it,' said Wren. 'A *cloud*-shaped cloud.'

Cassetti winked. 'Rather appropriate, don't you think?'

On deck, Lug and Mumchance, each operating one of the airship's Serpents, blew demons to bits as fast as the lightning guns would recharge. Adolfus Spute directed the remaining gnomes as they slashed at the borders with axes and cutlasses.

Below deck, Groot hid behind a pile of treasure. He uncorked his bottle and took a long swig. 'Right, Fegie, time to deal with you.' He got to his feet and promptly fell down again as the airship lurched when part of the rigging was severed by Pilfer.

With a mounting feeling of panic, Mel struggled against the filigree suit, making his host tremble. Behind him, inside Groot, he heard the door open and into his field of vision marched the three statues of Groot. They surrounded him, staring with their lifeless, marble eyes.

The airship gave a violent lurch, and then another, as Pilfer cut the last of the rigging attaching the fuselage and the cloud floated free. In the ruby mirror they watched the hull as it plummeted down towards the spark-filled streets of Vlam, bodies of demons and gnomes spilling from the wildly sloping deck. Then, with a jolt, the airship ceased falling, held fast by the thick hawser mooring it to the steeple. Adolfus Spute, Lug and Mumchance hung from the rail, their feet dangling.

'Where's Groot?' said Wren. 'Has he fallen off? If anything happens to him it'll also happen to Mel.'

'Don't worry,' said Goldie. 'I saw that yellow-bellied coward go back down into the fuselage when we were climbing the rigging.'

'Groot knows Mel's inside him now,' said Ludo. 'What do you think he's going to do?'

Mel's view from Groot tilted sideways as the airship fell, and he felt them both hurtling through the air and being stopped by something hard. Mel could feel points on the filigree suit pulsing where Groot had been bruised.

'Groot? Can you hear me?'

'Oh, I can hear you all right, Fegie.' The statues' eyes lit up bright green. 'And now I can *see* you too.'

Mel fought back a rising sense of panic. He knew he would be needing a clear head if he was ever going to free himself.

The statues moved closer. With a creaking noise, they raised their arms and held their hands before them, fingers curled like talons. As the first one moved closer, Mel saw it sever some of the floating energy threads attaching the suit to the walls and ceiling. He felt the filigree suit relax its grip. Then another and another filament was broken and he could move. *Groot hasn't noticed*. Renewed courage coursed through Mel. Closer came the statues and each one broke more threads as it approached. Then, with a mighty wrench Mel broke free and was out of the suit. He ducked under the outstretched arms of the nearest statue, spun round and made for the door.

'Fegie, come here!'

Mel ran down the corridor. He knew the wall of mist was behind the last door. He was almost free. He felt an almost irresistible urge to laugh out loud with joy at his escape. Mel burst through the door, forming the reverse mirrormark even as he ran.

But he never completed it: the floor had vanished. Down into a well of blackness he fell. Behind him, he heard Groot's cruel cackle of laughter.

'You're in my world now, Fegie. *I* make the rules here.'

Grootscape

Mel landed sprawling in something soft and moving. He fumbled for his feather. When it illuminated his surroundings he wished he had left it where it was. The small sphere of light it cast showed he was on top of a great squirming mound of worms, beetles, cockroaches, lice and centipedes. He could feel them at his neck, wrists and ankles as they attempted to invade his clothing. Tiny legs pricked his eyelids and scrabbled at the corners of his mouth. They were loud in his ears. He sneezed and several of them flew from his nostrils.

Mel tried to stand, but sank up to his waist in the loathsome mass. A kind of blind panic overtook him and he thrashed about with his limbs, causing the mound to begin moving in a living landslide. He half-swam, half-surfed down the steep face of the pile. He reached the bottom and ran blindly into the darkness, using the feather to brush the vile creatures from him. Behind him, he could hear Groot's laughter, distant but getting louder.

'I can see you, Fegie. That feather of yours is giving you away.'

Mel instantly thrust the quill into his doublet and the world around him disappeared into blackness as thick and opaque as tar.

'That won't save you. I told you, this is *my* world.'

There was the sound of snapping fingers and, as if a switch had been thrown, the world was cast into light, startling Mel. It seemed to come from everywhere at once and revealed a steaming swamp. Mel felt the formerly firm ground give as its crust crumbled and he sank up to his ankles in the mire. *This is hopeless!* Adjusting to the light, he saw trunks of decaying trees that emerged at odd angles from pools of stagnant, green water. Through the weft of their dead, sepia-hued branches was woven a warp of vividly coloured snakes. Clouds of flies buzzed among fleshy toadstools as white as corpses' fingers. Over everything hung the sickeningly sweet smell of rotting vegetation.

Behind him, emerging from the pile, came the three Groot statues, dripping insects as they approached. Their feet made sucking noises in the mud but they were able to advance with ease, their green-beamed eyes fixed on their prey.

Mel ran. Or tried to. The boggy ground gripped his ankles as securely as iron fetters. A glance over his shoulder showed him the statues had halved the ground between them. *It's not fair! It's not skegging fair!* How could Groot move like that while *he* was bogged down? The answer came immediately. Groot was imagining it all!

There was a series of ominous splashes to Mel's right. From the corner of his eye he saw long, warty creatures slipping into the fetid water. *Crocodiles!* He could feel panic in his stomach like a trapped bird. He struggled to stay calm. If Groot was imagining all this, maybe he could imagine something as well. He glanced to his right again and saw several pairs of crocodile eyes cruising towards him, trailing v-shaped wakes in the soupy water. He closed his eyes and imagined hard.

When he opened them again he saw the picture he had formed in his mind's eye had been made real. Fern-shaped crystal patterns formed in the water as it froze, entombing the reptiles in its frigid grasp. He lifted his feet and set them down again on to crackling, frozen ground. Rigid snakes fell to the earth as frost blossomed on the bare branches.

From all around him came the sound of slow, ironic clapping. Groot's rat-like features formed in the frost at Mel's feet. 'Very good, Fegie. *Very* good. If it's cold you want, then cold you shall have.'

There was the sound of Groot's clicking fingers again and suddenly the wind began to blow. Sharp ice crystals stung Mel's face as the rime-caked swamp vanished behind a white curtain of driven snow. He bent his head and struggled to run, lifting his feet higher and higher as the snow heaped itself into drifts in front of him. To his left he heard the chilling howl of a wolf. It was answered by another and then another as pale shadows, briefly glimpsed through eddies in the blizzard, circled him. Suddenly, a fearful roar sounded and, blocking his way forward, loomed the towering bulk of a polar bear. It bore Groot's face. It rose on to its hind legs and raised paws as big as frying pans that bristled with terrifying claws.

Mel racked his mind for inspiration but terror was

impeding him. *Don't fight it,* he told himself. *Just let it flow.* Mel closed his eyes and allowed his imagination to seep up from deep inside him. This time when he opened them he was standing in a flat desert. The wolves and the bear were now sand sculptures that crumbled as he watched. He ran through them and on into the burning sand. After a while he stopped. He scanned the desert all the way to the encircling horizon but he was alone. *I've lost him.* He slowed to a walk as he advanced and, after a very short time, had to remove his velvet doublet and tie it around his waist as the sun beat down. He licked his lips and felt the dry scrape of cracks beneath his tongue. Why wasn't Groot following him? He looked around, but there was no sign of his enemy. Trails of sweat stung his eyes. Then he realised. If this was an imaginary world, all he needed to do was to imagine himself back with the others. He closed his eyes and visualised Wren and Ludo in the hull of the airship. When he opened them again he was . . .

Still in the desert.

Mel tried again, this time thinking of the room of doors. He shut his eyes and emptied his mind, allowing his imagination to flood in. He opened one eye.

He was still in the desert. It was not working. Dreadful thoughts of being trapped inside Groot for ever elbowed their way into his mind. Why wasn't his imagination working? Maybe the gulf between what Groot was imagining and what he was, was too big. What if he tried using Groot's image and modifying it?

He closed his eyes and pictured an oasis. He opened them again. *Well, that worked*. He set off towards the thick clump of palm trees that now lay ahead of him.

As he reached the oasis he skirted it, certain that Groot or one of his imaginings was laying in wait for him. A ring of swaying palms and bayonet-grass encircled a picture-book pool of inviting, blue water. But wherever Mel looked he could see no sign of Groot. He scanned the grass and trees, searching for predators, but there were none. The water looked as still as a millpond and very, very cool.

When he could stand it no longer he crept down to the water's edge. He knelt, picked up a small rock and tossed it into the pool. It made a reassuringly friendly *plop* sound and concentric ripples spread out and lapped the shore. Mel cupped his hands and dipped them into the cool liquid. He raised them to his face and sniffed the contents, wondering if it was poisoned. It had no smell. He let the water fall and gingerly tasted a droplet that clung to his finger. It tasted of water. With one last cautious look around, he dipped his hands into the pool and drank from them. It felt good. He drank some more and relaxed. He waded out into the water and sat down, breathing a sigh of relief as liquid coolness enveloped him.

What now? He had to get back to the room of doors and find the wall of mist or he could be running around inside Groot for ever. If he was inside Groot's world then perhaps he could only imagine things that Groot could. But what?

As Mel pondered his dilemma, he idly groped around in the sandy silt beneath the water and his fingers closed on the rock he had thrown. He lifted it, threw it again into the centre of the pool and watched as the ripples spread out. But when they reached the shore they did not stop. They kept expanding and expanding over the grass, around the trunks of the palms, and out towards the horizon, as if fed by a vast, subterranean spring. Fear gripped Mel once more as the sandy bottom of the pool dropped from underneath him and he found himself sinking. He cried out in alarm and a trail of bright bubbles rushed from his mouth. He kicked out with his legs and rose, spluttering, to the surface. When he got there, he gulped in air and shook the water from his eyes – salt water. The desert had vanished and he was adrift in a seemingly endless ocean beneath an overcast sky. It heaved with a mighty swell.

'Thought you'd lost me, Fegie?' came Groot's voice. 'I don't give up as easily as that. I think it's time you met my friends.'

Mel turned slowly as he trod water and saw the triangular, black fins of Groot's 'friends' break the surface. Sharks were spiralling closer.

A wave hit him. He gulped in a mouthful of seawater and choked. He could feel himself losing buoyancy as he frantically trod water. Then the sea in front of him erupted in an explosion of foam and the huge maw of a shark overshadowed him. It opened its gigantic mouth, revealing row upon row of sickle-shaped, serrated teeth. Its jaws closed around Mel and – it vanished!

'Mel!'

Mel paddled around, looking for the source of the voice.

'Mel! Over here!'

Between the troughs of the waves he saw a small island and, standing on the beach waving at him, two small figures. *Wren and Ludo!* He summoned his remaining strength and struck out for the shore.

Hauling himself out of the surf, he stumbled up the beach.

'When you didn't come back we came in looking for you,' said Ludo.

'It's horrible in here.' Wren looked around the barren island and wrinkled her nose. 'We've got to get back. The others are waiting for us.'

'What happened?' said Mel. 'I was just about to be eaten by a giant shark.'

'The airship fell,' said Ludo. 'Groot must have been

knocked out. He can't hurt us while he's unconscious.'

'We must be quick,' said Wren, 'before he wakes up. The way out's up here.'

Mel hesitated. Groot had tried to trick him this way before when he had created copies of his parents. 'How do I know you're not both made by Groot's imagination?'

'Do we look like something Groot imagined?' asked Wren scowling, her hands on her hips.

'Is this is all the thanks we get for coming in here and risking our necks to save you?' said Ludo.

'Prove it,' said Mel. He stared at Wren and Ludo, trying hard to see if something might betray them as illusions. He felt very scared. 'Prove you're not part of Groot.'

'Can we argue about this some other time?' said Wren. 'Groot's going to wake up any time now. We need to get out before then.'

His friends each grabbed one of Mel's arms and urged him up the slope of the island's beach.

When they reached the top he saw that the interior of the island was like a shallow dish. Standing in its centre was a ruined circular building. Its tumbled stones had been bleached by the salt air and drifts of sand were piled up around the remains of its walls. Inside, it seemed to be some kind of ancient amphitheatre with tiered steps leading down to a sunken arena. Set into the stage was a large, steep-sided bowl with a hole in the bottom covered by a rusty iron grille. Arching above this was the wishbone of some enormous creature and, suspended from it by a rope, a giant egg, the same diameter as the bowl. It spun slowly in the sea breeze, the rope creaking.

'What is it?' said Mel.

'Don't ask me,' said Wren. 'This is Groot's inner world, not mine. The way out's through the hole.'

'It's how we got here,' said Ludo. 'Come on.' He went to the lip of the bowl and sat down, dangling his legs over. He pushed off and slid down inside. At the bottom he got back to his feet and lifted the grille.

'Now you,' said Wren. 'Hurry up. We don't have much time.'

Mel looked around. 'It could be a trap. It's all too easy.'

'Easy's the way I like it.' Wren followed Ludo. 'Come on,' she called from the bottom.

'The sides look steep,' said Mel. 'How did you manage to climb out?'

'Are you coming or not,' called Ludo as he disappeared down the hole.

'Mel. Come *on!*' urged Wren as she followed Ludo. She stood waist deep in the hole, holding the grille open.

Mel heard a soft noise behind him. He turned and saw sand begin to trickle down the tiers towards him. The trickles soon turned into waves and the waves into torrents as more and more sand invaded the amphitheatre. The sand began to pile up around his legs, urging him towards the bowl. Then the torrent turned into a veritable landslide of sand and Mel was swept from his feet and down towards his waiting friend. But just as he reached her, Wren slammed the grille shut. Smiling up at Mel through the iron bars, sand cascading over her head, she said, 'Right again, Fegie.' It was Groot's voice. 'The shark was too easy. You weren't even fighting back. This is *much* more fun. Let's see you imagine a way out of this.' Wren-Groot vanished.

Mel frantically tried to scramble out of the bowl, but the sides were too steep and he could find no traction against the falling sand. He slid back down to the bottom. He looked back up to the rim and saw the three Groot statues appear. One spoke. 'Bye, bye, Fegie. I can't say it's been a pleasure knowing you.'

The statues turned the beams of their eyes towards the rope holding the massive egg above the eggcup-like bowl.

Mel smelled burning and heard the strands of rope parting. He dashed to the grille and tugged frantically at it. But it was shut fast. Then, with a loud *twang*, the rope snapped. The huge bulk of the egg plummeted earthwards towards him. There was no time to imagine a way out.

Then, inexplicably, the egg stopped in mid-air just above Mel's head, revolving slowly on its axis.

'How did you do that, Fegie?' Groot sounded puzzled.

Mel was as baffled as his adversary. 'I didn't do anything.'

With a snap a crack appeared in the hovering egg,

followed by another. The cracks spread out until the entire surface of the egg was covered with them like crazy paving. Mel reached up and touched it. Suddenly, the egg fell into thousands of pieces. It was full of hundreds of copies of the frightened Groot-child Mel had encountered earlier. Fragments of eggshell and bodies of boys landed on Mel, knocking him to the ground. He could feel their small feet digging into him as they scrambled to gain their footing. Mel watched them as they swarmed up the sides of the bowl, using each other as a living ladder.

The statues retreated from the edge as the boys neared them. 'What are you doing, Fegie?' Groot's voice trembled. 'Stay away from me.'

'I'm not doing anything.' Then it struck him. Groot hates himself even more than he hates everyone else. He's doing it to himself! Mel wriggled out from under the tiny figures and clambered over them. 'Sorry, but I've got to get out of here.'

He reached the rim over the backs of the boys and watched as they surged past him and overwhelmed two of the statues. Mel saw the third statue transform into a flesh-and-blood Groot and take to its heels, pursued by a pack of the small figures. They ran towards a door standing by itself on the sand. Mel followed them through the door, hoping they would lead him to the way out.

Inside was the corridor with many doors. Mel could see the Groot's long legs sticking out of the small door he had seen before. Several of the pursuing Groot-children tugged at them. Groot kicked them off and managed to cram his tall frame into the tiny room and slam the door shut after him. 'No, no one must see me. No one must ever see the real me!' came his terrified voice from inside.

Mel pushed past the waist-high crowd battering at the tiny door and reached the door at the end of the corridor. He opened it and before him was the wall of mist. This time the floor was intact. Relief and elation washed over him as he crossed it and made the reverse mirrormark.

The Brass Monkeys

'You're back! You made me jump.' Wren did a double-take at Mel's sudden reappearance. 'What's the matter? You look as if you've seen a ghost.'

'I have – sort of. Is that *really* you?' Mel squeezed her arm to reassure himself.

'Of course it's her. Who did you think it was?' Ludo looked at Wren and rolled his eyes. He made a screwing gesture at his temple with his finger.

'Where are we?' asked Mel. He felt light-headed with relief at being reunited with his friends.

'We're back in Vlam – inside the cloud that was supporting Adolfus Spute's airship,' said Goldie. 'Pilfer cut us free.'

'If things were different, I'd be pleased to be back home,' said Mel.

'Were you really inside Groot?' asked Ludo.

Mel swallowed hard and nodded. 'He's really messed up, that one.' Mel felt as though he was going to be sick. He took a deep breath to steady himself. 'Where's Cassetti?'

'I'm right here, my dear. I must thank you on behalf of us all. Without your quick thinking we'd still be –'

'Yes, yes, yes,' said King M-morpho. 'W-we're very g-grateful and all that. B-but can we p-please be getting on w-with things. We're unaccustomed to b-being kept w-waiting around like this.'

'All right, don't get your feelers in a twist,' said Ludo.

There was a crash somewhere beneath the cloud.

'Get an eyeful of this,' said Goldie. 'The hawser's snapped and the airship's crashed to the ground.'

Everyone crowded round the ruby mirror to see the wreckage. Several figures were moving painfully in the half-light.

'I don't believe it,' said Wren. 'Adolfus Spute, Mumchance and Lug look like the only survivors.'

'Hang on,' said Pilfer. 'Groot's made it as well. From the look of him Mel left him with a humdinger of a headache. Now what're they up to?'

Goldie rubbed the mirror as if cleaning the surface would make the gloom disappear. 'They're setting up some kind of . . . I'm not sure what it is.'

The view showed the four miscreants around a strange contraption. It had been much dented in the fall.

'What is it?' said Wren. 'Some sort of abstract sculpture?'

They all stared at the large and smooth brass sphere balanced on top of a hemisphere bristling with knobs, levers and wheels.

'I don't think so,' said Ludo. 'Lug's operating some controls on the side. I think it's some kind of machine.'

As levers were thrown, the front of the sphere swung up and back like a knight's visor, revealing the giant brass head of a monkey with an articulated jaw and eyelids and a malicious expression. In place of eyes it had more of the glowing crystals. The gnome threw some more levers and the head seemed to come to life as hinged plates swivelled and rotated. The eyes began to glow with a dim, inner fire.

'I bet it's some kind of weapon,' said Mel. 'They're going to use it against the demons.'

'What're they going to do,' said Ludo, 'scare them to death?'

'Works for me,' said Goldie. 'It gives me the creeps.'

'W-what's that confounded r-racket?' complained King M-morpho.

'Bells,' said Wren. 'Lots of bells.'

'They must be ringing every bell in the House of Spirits,' said Ludo.

'I bet it's some kind of signal,' said Goldie.

The view in the mirror now showed Lug, Adolfus Spute, Mumchance and Groot frantically turning wheels and pulling levers on the base of the brass monkey. A door opened at the back of the upper sphere and a ladder dropped down. Lug scampered up it and closed the door after him, sealing himself inside the machine. A window, like a third eye, opened in the monkey's forehead, framing the gnome's face.

'It looks like your worst nightmare,' said Ludo.

After a short while, the monkey's eyes glowed even brighter and then it opened its articulated mouth wide and shut it again suddenly.

'The chimp's yawning,' said Pilfer.

'Not yawning,' said Cassetti. 'I do believe it's sneezing.'

The eyes glowed brighter still and its nose

blushed. It sneezed again and, this time, what looked like a mass of electric stardust flew from its mouth in a spreading cloud.

'What *is* that stuff?' said Ludo.

'Look!' said Mel. 'I was wondering how long it would take before the demons showed up.'

Glowing demons surged into the square from two sides, some crawling, others flying at head-height. They looked like phosphorescent waves on a midnight ocean. As they advanced further into the square it was apparent that the once-butterfly demons had continued to grow and mutate. Coarse hair, tusks, talons and scales were added to their repertoire of giant insect parts. Following close behind them were several cloud monsters, their giant vaporous forms now solidified like frozen foam. This nightmare army began to advance towards the brass monkey.

Inside the cloud the friends unconsciously moved closer together.

Wren licked dry lips. 'Please don't let them look up and see us,' she whispered to herself.

Mel and Ludo exchanged worried glances, and

anxious lines etched themselves on Cassetti's powdered face.

Then the monkey sneezed, sending a blanket of monkey-breath sweeping towards the demons like an avalanche. As it hit them the demons burst. Misshapen limbs and body parts exploded and flew apart as they cartwheeled over the square. The cloud monsters disintegrated like spindrift on the wind. Before long, the square was awash with demon mince and cloud sludge. The remains of the monkey-breath slowly descended in a fine mist that fizzed and sparked when it settled on the creatures' remains.

'Did you see the snotdust hit Adolfus Spute, Mumchance and Groot?' asked Mel.

'But they're still standing,' said Ludo.

'Maybe it only works on figments,' said Mel. 'Lug made sure he was out of the way.'

'Then we figments must f-flee at once,' said King M-morpho.

'We can't leave our friends to face them alone,' said Goldie. Her voice trembled.

'You have to admit it's a neat trick,' said Pilfer.

'Clears the gaff of demons but leaves everything else intact. New first rule of robbery: steer clear of brass monkeys with nasty colds.'

'Come and take a look at this.' Cassetti had used his paddles to fashion a row of portholes along each side of their cloud.

'More demons,' gasped Ludo.

'They've learnt their lesson,' said Wren. 'Now they're getting sneaky.'

The views from both sides showed columns of demons creeping over the rooftops. They were taking care not to be visible from below.

'Great,' said Ludo with glee. 'They're going to ambush Adolfus Spute and his gang. This'll be fun.'

'We've got to warn them,' said Mel.

'I told you he'd gone mad,' said Ludo.

'No, Mel's right,' said Wren. 'Think about it.'

'My dears, there is indeed method in this young man's madness,' said Cassetti. 'There's a multitude of yonder demons and those villains are the only hope for your city and its inhabitants.'

'It sticks in my gullet, but we've got to warn those

scrots or Vlam's history,' said Goldie.

'If you warn them, we'll give ourselves away,' protested Ludo. 'Then *we're* history.'

'We find ourselves caught on the horns of a dilemma,' said Cassetti. 'We're doomed if we do and doomed if we don't.'

'It's not the dilemma's horns that I'm worried about,' said Ludo, casting an anxious glance at the advancing demons.

'What's more important,' said Mel. 'Us or Nem?'

'What a stupid question,' said Ludo.

'W-we agree,' said King M-morpho. 'We must not be put in h-harm's way.'

The others stared at Ludo and King M-morpho.

'Four to two. Looks like you're outvoted,' said Pilfer.

'Here, Mel, use this.' Wren handed her friend Groot's self-portrait.

Cassetti knelt down and made a trapdoor in the floor of the cloud with his paddles. 'That should serve. I think it would be prudent to absent ourselves as soon as the deed is done.'

Mel took a deep breath, aimed and hurled the

canvas. It scythed through the air, spinning downwards like a sycamore seed until it struck the brass monkey with a loud *clang*.

Startled, Groot looked up to see Mel peering down at him from inside the low cloud. 'Fegie!'

There came an urgent blast from Mumchance's whistle.

'Smell will have to wait,' said Adolfus Spute. 'Right now we have a more pressing concern. Look!'

'Huh?' Groot followed his uncle's line of vision and saw the roofline crowded with glowing demons.

Lug began to rotate the monkey's head. The demons screeched and leapt from the roof, gliding towards them on leathery, black wings. The beams from the monkey's crystal eyes highlighted targets as it panned up the facade of the building. As the giant head neared its zenith the machine sneezed. A supernova of sparkling dust flew from its mouth and the first wave of demons disintegrated. Flaming gobbets fell to the square like spent rockets. The brass monkey sneezed twice more before the remaining demons retreated.

Creaking and rumbling, the head moved round to target the friends.

'Everyone abandon cloud,' shouted Cassetti.

'Here you go.' Pilfer had knotted together the remnants of the rigging into a long rope. He tossed it out. 'Everybody –'

Before Pilfer could finish, King M-morpho's body flew apart and streamed through the hole.

'. . . out!'

'*Typical*,' said Ludo.

The friends scrambled down the rope to land on a rooftop alongside King M-morpho.

'When are you going to p-put a stop to those confounded b-bells!' he complained.

'Quit belly-aching, will you?' said Goldie. 'First things first.'

'Are we all here?' asked Mel.

'Cassetti's not come out yet,' said Goldie.

Just then the brass monkey sneezed at the cloud. It lit up like a bush on fire and then exploded. The smouldering remains of the rope fell beside them.

'*Cassetti!*' cried Wren.

'I don't believe it,' said Pilfer.

'Come on,' insisted Mel. 'We can't stay here. We need to get out of the mirrorstorm and find the master. He'll know what to do.'

'B-but what about Cassetti?' stammered Ludo.

'Mel's right,' said Goldie. 'We can't help him now. *Move!*'

From their rooftop perch Mel could see the spark-lit streets of Vlam laid out below him like a neon map. It extended all the way to the city walls. Here and there – and altogether too numerous for comfort – patches of green light showed him where the bands of marauding demons were.

'We should get down off this roof,' said Goldie.

'No,' said Mel. 'We'll be safer up here. Follow me.' He led them up the slope of the roof and along the crest. When they came to the gable at the far end Mel looked over. 'The street's narrow enough. If we take a run at it we should easily make it to that roof over there.'

'OK. Who's going first?' said Wren.

'I'm the smallest,' said Mel. 'If I can make it, you

all can.' He took a deep breath, ran and leapt across. The landing knocked the breath from him but Mel felt elated at his feat. 'Now the rest of you,' he called back from the far side.

Wren prepared to take a run and a leap but stopped. '*Mel!*' she cried. 'Behind you!'

Mel whipped round. Emerging from a chimney, dripping soot, was a demon. One of its wings had been eaten away by monkey-breath and was no more than a skeleton of veins like a rotting leaf, but the rest of it was intact. Vicious tusks curled upwards from its pincer-like jaws and its compound eyes rippled with iridescent colours. It began to advance towards Mel on six muscular and hairy legs.

Mel had no room to leap back to his friends. He shuffled back towards the edge, looking for some alternative way off the roof, but there was none.

The demon crawled closer. Mel saw the way its long rear legs contracted as it prepared to spring. It opened its mouth parts wide in a howl of victory.

'Mel; *duck!*' shouted Goldie.

Mel dived forward just as a spinning missile flew

over his head so close it parted his hair. He looked up in time to see the demon decapitated by the whirling discus of the ruby mirror. The creature's body fell to one side of the roof and its head to the other, both halves spewing fountains of green blood. The mirror shattered against the chimney stack and dozens of rubies clattered away down the roof like dropped marbles. 'Thanks, Goldie! Come on, everyone, it's safe now.'

As the others leapt the gap, the rumble of the brass monkey's caterpillar tracks and the percussive *snish* of its sneezing grew louder. Ahead of them, the bells pealed on. There was another sound, too. A sound that chilled everyone: the howl of the Morg.

The blood drained from Wren's face and her eyes gaped wide in terror.

'It's OK, Wren,' said Mel. 'We won't let anything happen to you.' He squeezed her shoulder.

'That's right,' added Ludo. 'We'll all stick together.'

Before the friends the glowing grid of the streets had vanished to be replaced by a dark void. The green lights of marauding demons and the orange-yellow of fires flickered within the blackness. Under-lit by their glow, clouds of smoke drifted everywhere.

Mel drew his breath in sharply. 'It looks like one of Lucas Flink's paintings of the underworld.'

'I think I know where we are,' said Ludo. 'My parents used to bring me here. It's a theatre. The Hall of Comedies.'

'What's left of it, more like,' said Pilfer.

'Too true,' added Goldie. 'There's skeg all left to laugh about from what I can see.'

'It looks like a giant, cracked eggshell,' said Ludo. 'You can see the stage.'

'It must have been beautiful before,' said Goldie.

'The curtains are on fire,' said Wren. 'And the circles and balconies have all fallen in. They look like a stack of overbalanced plates.'

'We've run out of rooftop,' said Mel. 'We'll have to go down there.' He led them down a crumbling and haphazard staircase formed from toppled columns and piles of masonry. They crouched in a huddle at the bottom, lit only by Mel's feather. Its soft glow revealed a bunch of anxious faces made to seem even more gaunt by the recent loss of Cassetti. But there was no time for grief. Not yet. 'We can't see where to go any more. Which way do you think?'

Goldie shrugged. 'Search me.'

'Cogito!' said Mel. 'He'll know.'

'Allow me.' Pilfer produced the parchment and inkwell.

With his angel's feather Mel wrote, *How do we get out of here and find the master?*

Cogito answered, *If you don't mind me saying so, you're asking altogether the wrong question.*

'For crying out loud,' said Pilfer. 'The last thing we need right now is a philosophical discussion with a sheet of parchment.'

'Hang on,' said Mel. 'Maybe it's right.'

'So what's the right question?' said Goldie.

'Ask Cogito,' said Wren.

Mel did.

Cogito wrote, *The right question is 'How do I dispel the mirrorstorm?'*

So?

As Mel's question disappeared, Cogito's answer began to flow on to the parchment in its neat, elegant script. *I'm glad you asked me that . . .*

Smoke and Mirrors

'That's easier said than done,' said Ludo after they had finished reading Cogito's answer.

'But we've got to give it a try,' said Wren.

'Yeah,' said Mel. 'But first we need to get to the House of Spirits.'

'So, which way is it?' said Goldie.

Ludo shrugged. 'We'll never find our way there while Vlam's like this.'

'Are all h-humans as s-stupid as you?' said King M-morpho.

'Steady on,' said Pilfer indignantly. 'Who're you calling a human?'

'If you're so clever,' said Mel, 'how *do* we find the House?' Then, remembering protocol, he added, 'Your majesty.'

'The b-bells! Follow the s-sound of those confounded b-bells!'

'He's right,' said Wren. 'Let's get to the top of this rubble and try and see where we are.' She began to scramble over the crumbling masonry, followed by the others. 'I just hope no one spots us.'

'What's that?' said Ludo. Halfway up the slope they all felt a vibration beneath their feet that swelled into an audible rumbling. It got louder. Small landslides of rubble trickled down the slope. Then behind them, at the far side of the stage, a wall exploded inwards in a cloud of dust and through the breach rolled a brass monkey. Framed in its third-eye window was the face of a black-robed Fa. His eyes met Mel's.

'Another one,' gasped Mel. 'How many of them are there?' He tried to dash for cover but the rubble rolled away under his feet and he seemed to be running on the spot. He looked back anxiously at the brass monkey.

'This is like a bad dream.' Wren was also marooned on the naked slope. She and Ludo kept falling each time they got to their feet.

The head squeaked and rumbled as it turned and elevated its deadly maw towards the friends. It opened its mouth wide and then, suddenly, the burning curtains gave way and tumbled on top of the machine.

The smouldering fabric billowed outwards, trapping the sneeze.

'All it needed was a hankie.' Ludo laughed out loud with relief. 'A piece of cake.'

'I *told* you never to say that,' said Pilfer. 'Now look what you've gone and done.'

Over the top of the rubble above them rolled another brass monkey. It was caked in dust and appeared completely grey. The great machine came to a halt, sending waves of debris down the slope towards them.

Mel and his friends froze.

'It's the Ters!' exclaimed Wren.

'What are we going to do?' cried Ludo. 'The other monkey will free itself from the curtain soon. We'll be caught between the two of them.'

The head inclined downwards. It started down the rubble slope towards the helpless friends and opened its mouth wide and sneezed.

'Goldie, Pilfer. Get down!' warned Mel as a huge cloud erupted from the machine. It looked thicker than that from Lug's monkey and lacked the sparkle.

'Too late,' cried Wren. The fast-moving cloud

reached them in an instant and engulfed them all.

Mel examined himself. He was all in one piece. 'Are you all right?' he cried.

'Yes,' called Wren from somewhere within the cloud to Mel's left. 'We're both OK. But what about Goldie and Pilfer?'

'Well, what about us?' said Pilfer from the right.

'We're still here,' said Goldie.

'And u-us,' said King M-morpho. 'So n-nice of you t-to ask.'

'This cloud stinks,' said Ludo, coughing. 'It smells just like –'

'Smoke,' finished Mel.

The acrid cloud got thicker. Then, immediately in front of Mel loomed the shadowy form of the huge monkey as it advanced. Up close it seemed only slightly denser than the cloud emanating from its mouth. Mel tried to throw himself to the side, out of the machine's path, but the rubble slid away beneath his feet and he collapsed to his knees. He threw up his arms to protect himself as the head came close enough to touch and then . . .

He was inside it.

They all were.

Mel could feel firmness underfoot – the kind of spongy firmness he knew from the Wisp. He reached out and his hand closed around someone's wrist. A wrist clad in a long, lacy cuff.

'My dear, if you persist in clinging to me like that, I'll never be able to steer this confection.'

Mel waved his hand to waft away the smoke. 'Cassetti!'

'We thought you were dead,' said Wren, beaming.

'I very nearly was,' said Cassetti. 'I baled out of the cloud just moments before it exploded. My wig, although not nearly as buoyant as a full-blown cloud, had sufficient lift to keep me in one piece when I landed. In need of a disguise, and there being no shortage of raw material, I fashioned myself this smoke-monkey, and, well, my dears, here I am.'

'W-we are indeed p-pleased to see you again,' said King M-morpho. 'Your refinement has b-been missed. These rapscallions f-fail to afford us the r-respect we d-deserve.'

'Can this smoke-monkey get us to the House of Spirits?' said Wren.

'Indeed it can, my dear.'

'The s-sooner we get t-there,' said King M-morpho, 'the sooner we can put a s-stop to those b-bells.'

'With the utmost haste, your majesty.'

The House of Spirits looked eerie in the preternatural darkness. Sparks rested on its countless roofs and projections like incandescent snow and dressed the statues and gargoyles with luminous shawls and wigs. Every window was ablaze with candlelight.

'There are guards everywhere,' said Ludo.

'And crowds of people,' added Goldie.

'Refugees,' said Mel. 'This is all part of Fa Odum's plan. They're going to shelter everybody while the Ters and the brass monkeys fight the demons.'

'Then, after the battle, they'll seem even more like heroes,' said Wren. 'Everyone will be eating out of their hands.'

'It's clever,' said Goldie. 'You've got to give them that.'

'Where would your master be in all this?' said

Cassetti. 'What's become of his part to thwart these machinations?'

'I don't know,' said Mel with a worried frown. 'He was going to see the Maven and stop all this happening. Something must have gone wrong.'

'Looks like we're on our own then,' said Goldie.

'So how do we get into this here House of Whatsits?' said Pilfer.

'It's too well guarded here,' said Goldie. 'Let's go and find a back way in.'

They abandoned the smoke-monkey and it drifted apart behind them. Ludo led the way through the narrow, winding streets until they were on the far side of the towering House. There were black-robed Fa guards patrolling but they were not as numerous as near the main entrance. They waited until one was left on his own and Wren, supporting Goldie, limped towards him.

'Fa, please help us,' pleaded Wren.

'Refugees go to the main entrance,' he said.

'My sister here won't make it.'

Taking her cue, Goldie sunk to her knees.

The Fa looked about him for support.

'*Please!*'

He came cautiously towards them and sprawled headlong as he pitched over the invisible and crouching Pilfer.

'He's out for the count,' said Pilfer, kicking him just to be sure. 'Quick, before any more come along.'

Inside the House of Spirits was a hive of activity. There were groups of Fas Major everywhere, shepherding gaggles of refugees clutching whatever possessions they had managed to grab before they had fled their homes.

'That's us,' said Pilfer. 'Fas and refugees. No one will notice a few more. Wait here.' He returned a few minutes later with two black robes. 'Don't ask,' he said. 'Cassetti, Goldie, get into these and pull the cowls over your faces. Then we can see about escorting these three homeless vagabonds wherever we need to go.'

'D-don't worry about us,' said King M-morpho. 'Our k-kind are used to b-being inconspicuous.'

They reached the huge entrance hall at the foot of the grand staircase. It thronged with refugees and Fas

Major handing out food and tending to the wounded. In their midst, resplendent in his white robes, was the new Maven. He wandered about blessing people and generally presiding over the throng, anxious to remind everyone that he was their benefactor. Fa Craw was by his side.

'Look,' gasped Wren. 'The one in white. It's Fa Odum.'

'But what about the real Maven?' said Ludo. 'Where's he?'

'In deep scrot, if you ask me,' said Pilfer.

There was a commotion at the edge of the crowd and a group of bloodied Fas Major dashed through and rushed up to talk with their leader. Fa Odum's expression darkened and he issued terse orders. A number of his armed bodyguards dashed from the hall, following the bloody Fas back the way they had come.

'Something's up,' said Mel.

'What say we go and take a shufti?' said Pilfer. They edged around the outside of the milling crowd and left by the exit the Fas had taken. King M-morpho fluttered apart and flew unnoticed over the crowd's heads. Once the hubbub of the hall had faded behind them they could dimly hear a new noise.

'That sounds like an altercation, my dears,' said Cassetti. 'There's a battle in progress.'

'The demons must have got in,' said Ludo. 'Let's steer well clear.'

'No,' said Wren. 'Let's go and see.'

'Wren's right,' said Mel. 'Whatever's bad news for the black Fas could turn out to be good news for us. Come on.'

They came to a door. Opening it, Mel jumped back. 'Someone's coming. Hide.'

'Who is it?' said Goldie.

'Two Fas and some refugees,' said Mel. 'Coming this way.'

King M-morpho fluttered up to the ceiling. The others all squeezed into an alcove, but when no one emerged from the door they crept back out.

'False alarm,' said Pilfer. 'Come and take a butcher's at this.'

The friends joined him and they all entered the room.

'It's a hall of mirrors,' said Ludo. 'It was *us* Mel saw.'

Everyone laughed with relief.

Stretching down both walls of the long room were dozens of ornate mirrors. There were more on the floor and ceiling. As they walked towards the end they saw myriad reflections of themselves disappearing into infinity in every direction.

'If there were this many of us we could beat Fa Odum and his crows hands down,' said Wren.

'The Fas must have gone through here,' said Goldie, opening a door at the far end of the hall. The sound of fighting became louder.

'The n-noise in your w-world is appalling.' The butterfly king flew down and reformed into his human shape.

'Put a sock in it,' said Pilfer. 'Haven't we got enough to contend with without your whingeing?'

'The noise is coming from the bottom of these stairs,' said Mel. 'They must lead to the dungeon.'

They could now make out individual sounds: roaring cries, the bright, brittle clash of steel on steel and wails of pain. As the friends descended, the noise grew increasingly louder. They came to a long corridor, its walls fashioned from roughly cut stones in stark contrast to the polished splendour of the rest of the Great House. It was lit by flickering burning brands in wall brackets and lined with empty cells, the doors all standing open. Turning a corner, they found the source of the battle.

'There's the master!' exclaimed Wren. 'And Dirk Tot.'

'And Green and Blue,' added Ludo. 'And look! There's the Maven. The *real* Maven. The one dressed in white.'

They watched as a tide of attacking Fas Major surged down the corridor to break like black waves against a makeshift barricade manned by brown-robed Fas Minor. Alongside them fought the master and the real Maven. Dirk Tot, Green and Blue were there too.

'We have to help them,' said Mel.

'But how?' said Goldie. 'There are dozens of Fas Major and only six of us.'

'If we could draw off a number of the assailants,' said Cassetti, 'the defenders might prevail.'

'Any chance of another one of your smoke sculptures?' Pilfer asked Cassetti.

Cassetti shook his head. 'Even if we were to burn these unbecoming black robes they would barely yield enough smoke to create a single reinforcement.'

'The mirrors!' said Mel.

'Of course,' said Wren.

'What mirrors? Oh, *those* mirrors,' said Ludo as the penny dropped. 'I was just about to suggest the same thing.'

'Chummy's a genius,' said Pilfer.

Cassetti stripped off his disguise. 'Your robe, too, Goldie, my dear. Leave me to work while you go and fetch the mirrors.' He took a flaming torch from the wall and kindled the pile of robes at his feet.

'M-monarchs do not do m-manual work,' said King M-morpho haughtily. 'We'll k-keep watch. The *n-noise!*' He raised butterfly hands to his butterfly ears.

'Don't say anything, Ludo,' said Wren. 'At least he's helping for once.'

Cassetti deftly created a convincing smoke sculpture of a Fa Minor as Mel, Ludo, Wren, Goldie and Pilfer struggled back with the heavy mirrors. They quickly set them up around the smoky Fa and adjusted them until the view from the battle back along the corridor showed an infinity of reinforcements. As a finishing touch, King M-morpho detached some of his butterflies and they flew inside the smoke to animate the apparition, waving the arms in a threatening way.

'His nibs is actually doing something useful,' said Ludo. 'Now I've seen everything.'

An attacking Fa Major at the rear of the melee soon spied the apparent army of Fas Minor about to assail them from the rear. Alerted, many of his colleagues turned to face the new threat. The distraction was just enough for the defenders. With a cry of triumph they surged over the barricade. The Fas Major surrendered to the seemingly overwhelming odds of their adversaries without a struggle.

'It worked!' cried Ludo. 'Great idea of mine.'

'Master!' called Mel.

Ambrosius Blenk climbed over the barricade with Dirk Tot, Green and Blue. 'Womper.' He saw the mirrors. 'Brilliant work! I couldn't have done better myself. And who're these . . .' He stared. 'Figments!'

'This is Goldie and King M-morpho,' said Wren.

'Your majesty,' acknowledged the master with a bow. He smiled to himself, remembering how he had created the butterfly empire in his painting. 'And Confetti, if I'm not mistaken. Good to see you again.'

Cassetti smiled. 'One of these days you'll get my name right.'

'And this is Pilfer,' said Ludo.

'How-do,' said Pilfer.

'An invisible?' said the master, surprised. 'You must be from Anywhere.'

'What happened?' asked Wren.

'Fa Odum had recruited the Fas Major and they imprisoned the Maven, along with us and their opponents,' said Dirk Tot.

'We would still be rotting in the cells if the librarian hadn't rallied some loyal Fas Minor and freed us,' said Green.

'*Librarian?*' said Mel. 'You don't mean –'

Scree-scrick, scree-scrick. 'Hello, Mel.'

'Fa!' exclaimed Mel in surprise. 'But how –?'

'No time for explanations now,' said Fa Theum from his wheelchair. 'There's still work to be done.'

'You're right. We have to destroy the mirrorstorm,' said Mel. 'Before the Ters and Adolfus Spute get here.'

'Adolfus Spute? He's back, is he?' said the master. 'I wondered who was helping them. I thought it might have been Lug.'

'Do you know him?' asked Wren.

'Our paths have crossed before,' said the master. 'He knows how to unlock the power of the Mirrorscape crystals and he uses them in his own, wicked machines. But the Fa's right. This is no time for explanations. Not while Fa Odum and his henchmen are still in control in the House. Dirk Tot and I will go above with the Maven and as many as we can muster.'

'There are too many of them,' said Fa Theum. 'We need help. I'll go and rouse the novices. Together we might carry the day.'

'And we must go and reverse the Serpent,' said Mel. He quickly outlined what Cogito had told them.

'Yes, that might work. You'd best hurry. Take Green and Blue with you. And, your majesty?' said the master, turning to King M-morpho. 'A word with you, if you'd be so kind.'

When they reached the large hall they separated. Mel and his party raced for the stairs and began climbing. The master and Dirk Tot with the real Maven and the Fas Minor strode into the mass of refugees.

'No!' shouted Fa Odum as soon as he saw them. 'This man is an impostor. *I'm* the true Maven. Men, stop them!'

'Don't listen to him,' cried the real Maven. 'He's the usurper. Help us.'

There was great confusion among the throng as the Fas Major flew at the new arrivals with swords and crossbows.

The friends saw this and hesitated on the stairs.

'We have to go back and help them,' said Wren. She started back down. 'Come on.'

'No,' said Green. 'Keep going and do what you have to do. They can look after themselves.'

Just then, Fa Odum looked up and saw Mel and his friends on the stairs. 'Stop them!' A band of Fas Major broke away and began to race up the stairs after them.

'Go on,' shouted Green. 'Blue and I will stay here and stop anyone following you.'

As they mounted higher, Ludo stopped and stole a look back down through the whirls of the staircase into the hall. 'They're coming after us but Green and Blue are holding them off.'

'What's happening in the hall?' asked Cassetti.

'There's a right old barney going on,' said Pilfer. 'Hang on. There's that geezer in the wheelchair again and he's leading a load of nippers in beige robes.'

'They're the novices,' said Ludo.

'They may only be young but they can fight,' said Goldie.

'The Fas Major are giving up,' said Wren. 'The master's won!'

'What about Fa Odum?' said Mel. 'Have they got him too?'

Goldie pointed. 'Look, there he is. He's using the confusion to slip away. He's being chased by some novices.'

'There's no time for gawking now. We have to get to the Paper Belfry,' urged Cassetti. They resumed their climb.

A short time later, legs aching, they stood panting

side by side in front of the doors to the Ters quarters. It was locked.

'Pilfer?' puffed Goldie. 'This is your department.'

There was the sound of Pilfer doing something mysterious to the lock and a moment later the door swung open.

Wren hesitated as she gazed down the dark and deserted hallway inside, her imprisonment and the cruelty of the Ters still fresh in her memory. For a moment her courage threatened to desert her. She took a deep breath and stepped inside. 'You get to the Paper Belfry this way.'

She led them to the lofty hall with its bright, hanging banners and then to the door to the Paper Belfry. As they entered, the soft light of the many candles picked out the mad, jumbled scaffolding and glinted off the abandoned Serpent at the far end.

Mel approached it and studied the way the long row of coloured crystals were arranged inside the entwined brass snakes that formed the barrel. 'Cogito said that we must reverse all the crystals.' He began to reposition them within their cradles. 'Ludo, get the

516

furnace going. Use anything that will burn.'

'I'll go and keep watch outside,' said Pilfer.

'Goldie, give me a hand here,' said Wren. Together they began to lift out the bowls of liquid colour from the palette-shaped mosaic floor and ferry them to the glass reservoir.

Cassetti found a blank canvas standing against the wall. He carried it to the cage and secured it inside.

Mel completed his arrangement. 'That should do it.' He looked around. 'Where's King M-morpho?'

'The last I saw he was talking with the master,' said Wren.

'Didn't want to get his hands dirty,' said Ludo. 'Why am I not surprised?' He pumped the handle at the side of the furnace and it began to roar.

Mel and Wren busied themselves with the mirrors and lenses. Cassetti set the spheres spinning.

'That looks like Cogito's description,' said Goldie as she cast an appraising eye over the contraption. 'But he didn't tell us how to work this brass twizzler.'

'Leave that to me,' said Ludo, mounting one of the seats that were arranged at either side. 'If you can operate a DORC, you can operate anything. This should be a piece of *caaaake* . . .' As he touched a lever, the Serpent began to rotate wildly. 'Where's the brake?' He threw another and the machine began to buck up and down like a demented rocking horse. The crystals began to glow and garlands of sparks fizzed along the three entwined snakes like electric barbed wire. They seemed wreathed in white fire as the deadly machine cavorted round and round, up and down. The coloured liquid inside the glass reservoir bubbled wildly. The electrical whine grew louder as it rose in pitch. '*Help!*'

'It's going to go off!' shouted Mel. 'Everyone get down!'

The Serpent

Mel dashed towards the spinning machine and his stricken friend. But he only made it halfway before a shattering detonation sent streaks of multicoloured energy flailing like whips from the mouth of the Serpent. He was hurled backwards and skidded on his back across the floor. Gaping holes were punched in the flimsy fabric of the Paper Belfry and shreds of countless manuscripts were blasted high into the sky over Vlam.

'Mel, help me! I can't hold on much longer!' As he said this, Ludo was flung from the gyrating machine, but it continued to spit its rainbow fire as the jumble of scaffolding overhead disintegrated, adding wooden shrapnel to the paper snowstorm.

Mel crawled towards Ludo. 'I've got you.' He grabbed his dazed and sprawling friend by his collar and began to drag him back and away from the Serpent.

The piercing whine from the machine now

acquired an edge of panic. Everyone's eardrums threatened to burst from the shrill sound as it spun even faster. The torrent of energy from its bucking, gyrating mouth was now constant. As it swelled it looked like the crown of a luminous tree with boughs, branches and twigs made from coloured fire. There were shapes in there as well. Horrible shapes. Dancing shapes. Shapes more ghastly than the demons. One half of Mel's mind was enthralled, the other terrified, as globes of incandescent power blossomed like fruit on the spectral tree. Mel tried to look away, to ease the searing pain behind his eyes, but he could not. At the heart of this terrible beauty the twisted serpents began to melt, adding a rain of flying, molten brass to the other missiles.

With an effort of will, Mel tore his eyes from the spectacle and gazed around for his friends. He could barely see them as they clung to the remains of the scaffolding. They were as mesmerised by the scene as he was, their stark faces reflecting the dazzling spectrum erupting before them.

Through the gaping holes in the walls and roof he

could make out cloud-monsters and countless glowing demons. They were being sucked into the air in a dense, black spiral. The vortex contracted and solidified until it looked as tangible as a massive tree trunk. It thrashed to and fro as it gripped its Mirrorscape captives deep inside itself, lifting them higher.

Mel could feel the tug of Ludo's collar as his friend was pulled by the vacuum towards a gaping hole in the Paper Belfry and the retreating whirlwind. He grasped him even tighter. Then he and the others also began to be sucked towards it. As he frantically tried to grab one of the few remaining scaffold uprights with his free hand that too was whisked away by the deadly suction. Ludo shouted something but it was impossible to hear amidst the cacophony. Mel managed to grab on to the capstan with one arm and twisted his head to look back at the Serpent.

A crystal exploded and a beam of searing bright light hit the lenses and mirrors and then the blank canvas. As if painted by an invisible hand, an image began to appear. The picture that had been destroyed to create the mirrorstorm was repainting itself. Another crystal exploded and a second image began to form, fighting the first for space on the rectangle. More crystals shattered and other resurrected pictures joined the composition. The battle of the competing images became fiercer. As Mel watched, mesmerised by the multiplying forms, he could see layers of paint building one on another to create a thick and dangerous impasto. As ever more crystals cracked in the dazzling, dancing flares, the weight of paint became too great to be contained on a single canvas and began to lift itself from the surface. A terrifying hybrid creature, the fruit of the imaginations of many artists, began to emerge from the paint. It became real and oozed out through the bars of the cage.

The part of Mel's mind not paralysed with the terror of what was unfolding before him recognised the creature's constituent parts. A great membranous head bulged as nightmare faces fought with one another inside it for supremacy. One moment an Ambrosius Blenk fire-creature seemed to gain the upper hand, only to be replaced by a Lucas Flink lizard-fiend a moment later. Other hideous faces fought to be visible and the resulting amalgam was even more horrible. Huge slavering jaws gnashed twisted teeth that swarmed with countless, pale beetles like living saliva. Narrow, slit-pupil eyes formed. They swivelled and fixed on Mel as he clung desperately to the capstan, gritting his teeth with the effort. His sweating hand threatened to relinquish its grip as the relentless suction tore at him and Ludo.

Yet another crystal exploded in rainbow fire and the creature's head broke free of the canvas with a silent roar. It was followed by a muscular arm tipped with a cruel talon-like claw. Then another arm burst from the surface of the writhing painting, followed by another and another, until the emerging creature looked like a screaming, thrashing octopus with barbed and horny limbs.

With its body still attached to the canvas, the paint-creature began to haul itself across the floor. One arm snared Ludo's leg and others grabbed Wren, Goldie and Cassetti. Mel could feel Ludo slipping from his grasp as the creature pulled its victims towards its waiting mouth. The beetle-saliva flowed copiously and formed writhing, living puddles on the floor. Mel's shoulder felt as though it was being ripped from its socket. Then his hand finally slipped from the capstan and he too was drawn inexorably towards the huge mouth of the many-authored beast. It opened its ravenous jaws wide and its teeth closed around the friends.

Then, suddenly, the creature collapsed with a loud splash into a wet, multi-coloured pool.

The whirlwind had disappeared. Gravity reasserted itself. Daylight streamed in through the shattered remains of the Paper Belfry. Everything was silent. Even the bells had ceased. The only ringing was that in Mel's ears. The air was ripe with the smell of wet paint. Everyone was rubbing their eyes. Mel became aware of a new sound; a hissing. As his vision returned, he could see the hazy outline of his friends. But there were too many of them. Then his vision finally cleared and, standing in front of the steaming furnace with its open door, he saw Lug holding an empty fire bucket. Behind him ranged Adolfus Spute, Mumchance, Groot and Ter Selen. Crouched in front of them, his gaze fixed on Wren, was the Morg. Everyone was splattered with brilliant paint.

No one spoke. The only sound was the drip of water on to the floor and the sizzle of cooling brass. Paper snow made from shredded manuscripts continued to fall from the ruined ceiling.

Lug set down his bucket and examined the Serpent. He ran his hands over the surface and yelped in pain at the blistering heat. He looked up, tears in his eyes. 'They've killed it. They've killed my beautiful Serpent. The crystals are cracked and . . .' an ugly growl escaped his throat, '. . . their power is gone.' He turned to Mel with a look dripping venom. '*You* did this!' He drew his dagger.

'Put your skewer away, Lug,' said Adolfus Spute. 'It's too quick and clean a death for Smell and his friends. Hardly an apt reprisal on someone who's cost us a kingdom.'

'Scrot to your kingdom,' hissed Lug. 'Where are the riches you promised me? The children and their figment friends are mine.'

'No, uncle,' whined Groot. 'Fegie's *mine*. You promised.'

'Silence! Silence, all of you,' shouted Ter Selen. 'They belong to *me*.'

Mel could sense the magic attraction of Ter Selen's coloured eyes. Her anger leant her a fierce, new beauty. He forced his gaze away. He glanced at his friends and then, involuntarily, to the door.

'Look, dear boy,' said Adolfus Spute to his nephew. 'Smell's wondering where his transparent friend is. Hoping he's going to storm to the rescue. Mumchance?'

The dwarf blew a sharp note on his whistle.

Ters Tunk and Mudge entered. Suspended in the air between them was a hollow coil of rope. The coil struggled. 'Get your hands off of me, you festering scrots,' protested Pilfer's voice.

'You're not as clever as you think you are, Fegie,' said Groot. 'Your accomplice might be invisible but he's not in-*smellable*. Not when you've got your very own Morg.'

'So,' said Adolfus Spute as he studied his prisoners. 'We seem to be a king short of a full house. Tell me, where is that motley butterfly collection that calls itself a monarch? Mumchance is in a positively insecticidal mood, aren't you, my death-dealing dwarf?'

Mumchance sounded a sinister note.

Lug looked at the remains of the Serpent. 'If he was anywhere near this then he'll have been blown clear back to the Mirrorscape.'

Mumchance sounded his whistle yet again.

'I am well aware of that, my treacherous time-keeper,' said Adolfus Spute. 'Of course we must flee.' He turned to Ter Selen. 'I suggest we withdraw with our prisoners through the doorway into the Mirror-scape. There we can regroup and ponder the delicious quandary of just how we put an end to Smell and the rest of these troublemakers.'

'And who gets to do it,' said Lug.

'The girl is spoken for,' said Ter Selen. 'But it might be instructive for her to see something of her husband's prowess. Once she's witnessed at first hand just how skilful the Morg is at his speciality, she'll be more than eager to pander to his every whim.'

'*No!*' cried Wren. 'Let them go. I'll do anything you want. Just don't hurt them.'

A cruel smile touched Ter Selen's face. 'You have nothing left to bargain with.'

The Morg strained at his leash to get at Wren. She moved closer to Mel and Ludo. They moved forward to protect her.

At that moment Fa Odum burst into the Paper Belfry, Fa Craw hot on his heels. Both carried bloodied swords. 'Quick. All is lost. Our enemies are right behind us. Follow me.'

'Very well,' said Adolfus Spute. 'Time is pressing. Lead on.'

Fa Odum led the way back through the Ters' chambers until they arrived at the entrance hall. The only light came from the open door to the corridor outside. The captors led their prisoners forward and stopped before a large canvas on the wall. Even in the dim light the friends could see that it was the one that depicted the Leviathan, the colossal galleon.

Adolfus Spute kicked at a pile of dust on the floor beneath the canvas with the toe of his boot. 'Ter Selen, you should have your quarters cleaned more often. My nephew's masterpiece deserves to be hung in a clean gallery.'

'Who cares how clean it is?' growled Lug. 'It's

served its purpose. It brought me here to supervise work on my Serpent and now it's our way back into the Mirrorscape.'

Mel turned to Groot. 'So it was *you* who made the picture,' he said. 'Cassetti said it was a bad painting but I should have realised it was a shoddy Groot.'

Groot sneered. 'It's easily good enough to get us to and from the Mirrorscape. Just like my depiction of Old Vlam in the memory banks of that stinking pile of offal that calls itself Cogito.'

'Mel thought he recognised the slapdash style,' said Wren.

There came the sound of running feet from the corridor outside.

'Make haste,' said Fa Odum.

'Now,' urged Ter Selen. 'The Morg yearns for his bride.'

Mel noticed something. He stared at the canvas, screwing up his eyes to see in the half-light. The frame seemed to twitch. He looked harder and was sure he saw the Leviathan's hull move. He looked down at the floor beneath the canvas and saw the dust and realised something. He caught Wren's and Ludo's eyes and darted his own towards the picture. His friends looked at the canvas and then back at Mel. Wren's eyes widened. Suppressing a smile, she made the faintest wink. It took another moment before Ludo realised what his friends had. He opened his mouth, about to exclaim something, but quickly closed it again. Mel saw that Goldie and Cassetti were also alert. He hoped Pilfer was, too.

The friends were herded at sword-point in front of Groot's painting. The former head apprentice raised his hand to make the mirrormark. 'I can hardly wait to get my hands on you, Fegie.'

'Hold it! No one move!'

They all turned. Standing framed against the light in the doorway stood three novice Fas. The eldest, no older than sixteen, held a sword in front of him in his shaking hands. His companions, younger still, held loaded crossbows almost as big as they were. They were even more nervous than their leader as they advanced into the hallway. The lead novice stopped, a look of utter surprise on his spotty face as he recognised the white robes of the Maven. 'Serenity?'

Fa Odum stepped forward. 'Well done, my children. There is treachery afoot in the House of Spirits. The Fas Minor are seeking to usurp me, the rightful leader, and to set up their own regime.'

The three novices exchanged glances. The lead boy said uncertainly, 'But we thought –'

'It doesn't matter what you thought,' snapped Fa Odum. Then, in a more reasoned tone, 'Our enemies are everywhere. We have just caught these criminals and their demon accomplices –'

The novices' eyes widened as they took in Goldie, Cassetti and the struggling coil of rope held by Ters Mudge and Tunk.

'*Don't* listen to him!' shouted Mel. '*He's* the false Maven.'

'The boy speaks with a demon's tongue,' said Ter Selen. She lowered her hand to the Morg's collar and slipped his leash. The creature tensed, ready to spring.

'No, it's true,' pleaded Wren. '*They're* the ones that must be stopped. Can't you see that?'

'They're lying,' said Fa Craw. 'Put down your

weapons and kneel before your Maven.'

The three novices were gripped with uncertainty. The two heavy crossbows wielded by the younger boys quivered dangerously. 'Fa Theum said that we should stop you,' said the eldest. The weapons were trained on Fas Odum and Craw.

'That meddling old fool Theum is a part of this insurrection,' said Fa Odum. 'Surely you can see through his poisoned words.'

'I . . . I suppose so.' The crossbows swung round to point at the friends.

'No! Can't you see what's going on?' said Mel.

'Kill him, before he spouts any more lies,' shouted Fa Odum. 'That is an order!'

'*No!*' Wren leapt in front of her friend the moment the smallest novice's nervous finger loosed his crossbow at Mel.

In that instant, the Morg sprang with inhuman speed into the path of the speeding bolt. It pierced his scarred chest with a sickening, wet thud. He fell at Wren's feet.

With a howl of dismay the young novice dropped

his discharged crossbow and fled out of the door. The others hesitated for a moment and then turned and followed him.

Wren looked down at the Morg. He stared back. For a moment his pitiless amber eyes softened and she could see the young boy inside that he had once been. The scarred creature opened his mouth but no words came out, only a thin trickle of blood that slid slowly across his cheek. As it did so, it seemed like a line crossing out the words carved into his face, cancelling the wicked spell that had turned the once innocent boy into the cruel Morg. Wren knelt and reached out her hand tentatively but drew it back. She reached out again and touched the matted red hair on his brow. Then, as she stroked his brow with tenderness, the Morg smiled, the light went out in his eyes and he died.

'Morg?' said Ter Selen. There was a tremor in her voice.

'The stinking thing's dead,' said Groot. 'And we will be soon if we don't get out of here.'

Adolfus Spute herded the friends together. 'Grasp them firmly and they will be drawn into the

Mirrorscape with us.' Then, to Groot, 'Now, my boy. High time we were off.'

As Groot completed tracing the mirrormark in the air in front of the canvas, Mel shouted, 'Now!'

The friends wrenched themselves free and dived to one side as the power of the mirrormark took hold and drew Adolfus Spute, Mumchance, Groot, Ters Selen, Mudge and Tunk and Fas Odum and Craw into the picture.

'Quick!' shouted Cassetti. 'Let's get out of here before they come back for us.'

Mel picked himself up from the floor. 'They won't be back.'

Wren smiled. 'You can come out now, your majesty.'

They stood before the large canvas and watched as a flake of coloured paint rose into the air. Then another followed by another until the entire canvas flew apart in its own miniature blizzard. The last to leave the bare wall were the butterflies that had depicted the mirrormark. They reassembled into the form of King M-morpho.

'Who would have thought it,' said Ludo. 'I guess

we ought to thank you, your majesty.'

There came the sound of more running feet outside and Ambrosius Blenk, Dirk Tot, Green and Blue rushed in.

'Thank goodness you're all safe.' The master scanned the gloom for the others. 'Are our enemies gone, your majesty?'

King M-morpho nodded. 'It was as you s-suspected. They d-did indeed have a secret doorway into the M-mirrorscape.'

'But how did you know it was this one?' asked Mel. 'There must be thousands of paintings in the House of Spirits.'

'There are,' answered the master. 'But there are also thousands of parts to King M-morpho. He had only to send a butterfly to each to discover this one. While I was locked in the dungeon I had time to think. I remembered the drawing on the back of that tapestry and I finally recalled the style. It could only have been made by my former head apprentice . . .'

'Groot,' said Ludo.

'. . . So, as soon as you freed us, I asked King

M-morpho to seek out the worst painting in the House. He obviously found it.'

'But when we got here the door was locked,' said Wren.

'L-locks are to keep h-humans out,' said King M-morpho, 'not insects. There are many w-ways into even the m-most secure of b-buildings for our k-kind.'

'While you were busy reversing the mirrorstorm his majesty recruited a band of especially voracious termites to dispose of the original,' said Dirk Tot, nodding at the dust.

'And he concocted a replacement,' said Cassetti. He clapped his hands. 'Splendid!'

'And now Adolfus Spute, Fa Odum, Ter Selen and the rest of them are gone,' concluded the master.

'And so is the picture,' said Mel.

'There's no way back,' said Ludo. Then, uncertainly, 'Is there?'

'Let's all hope not,' said the master. 'Let's all hope not.'

'Brilliant,' said Pilfer. 'Absolutely, skegging brilliant.'

'We had best go and join the Maven,' said Green. 'He wants to thank you all.'

As the master led them down the grand staircase a shaft of sunlight struck the party. Mel squinted up into the pure light, then looked at the figments and then at Wren and Ludo. 'Looks like the storm's over,' he said.

Wren smiled and nodded slowly. 'Looks like it.'

'Yeah,' said Ludo. 'Storm's over.'

Epilogue

That morning the first frost of the year covered the rooftops of Vlam with a sparkling, silver film. The citizens were brisker about their business than usual as they wove through the steep streets with hands thrust into pockets and mufflers about their necks, puffing like steam trains. There was much for them to do repairing the damage caused by the mirrorstorm.

If some works were starting, then others were complete. In the Hall of Awakenings the scaffolding had at last been dismantled and Ambrosius Blenk's magnificent ceiling painting finally revealed. The grand opening was to take place the following day but that evening there was a private view for the master and a very few select friends.

'Is the door locked?'

'Yes, master,' answered Dirk Tot. 'Green and Blue are outside. We won't be disturbed.'

The master turned to Mel, Ludo and Wren. 'Your friends can come out now.'

'Cassetti! Pilfer! Goldie! King M-morpho!' called Mel. The four figments emerged from a shadowy alcove at the periphery of the hall.

'Struth! Did you do all this?' said Goldie as she gazed upwards with her mouth open.

'Sure,' said Ludo. 'A piece of ca–' He left the remark unfinished.

'Not *all* of it,' admitted Wren. 'We helped with lots of it but the only bit we did all on our own is that niche up near the corner.'

'And a most accomplished niche it is, too.' Fa Theum was using the master's omniscope to inspect the friends' work as he sat in his wheelchair. 'Such imagination. Such artistry.'

The niche's creators blushed.

'Perhaps your friends would like to inspect it.' He passed the omniscope to Cassetti.

'My dears, it's a triumph! Are you sure there's no Cumulan blood in you?'

King M-morpho had sent his eyes up to the lofty ceiling and they fluttered from one part of the expansive image to another. 'We p-pronounce it s-satisfactory,' said his lips. 'It r-reminds us of our k-kingdom.'

Scree-scrick, scree-scrick. Fa Theum wheeled himself to Mel's side. 'I always knew you were a remarkable boy, Mel, but just how remarkable I'm only just beginning to find out.'

'You too, Fa. You're more than just the librarian people take you for.'

'*Chief* librarian now, Mel,' corrected the Fa with a note of pride. 'When you mentioned this mysterious Paper Belfry and then returned the missing illustration, it set me to thinking. Later, when those bizarre storms began, I started my own investigations. A library is a wonderful place to find out all sorts of things, you know. I pieced together what I could glean from the books with the misgivings expressed by many of my brother Fas Minor concerning the inexplicable rise of the Ters just as the Maven was about to disband their order. I reached the conclusion that the Maven was no longer in control of the House of Spirits. My brothers soon uncovered Fa Odum's plot.'

'So you freed the Maven from the dungeon?'

'Eventually. But before that, the questions of my brother Fas aroused the attention of the Fas Major. They rounded up many of our number and threw them into the dungeon, too.'

'But not you.'

'Together with a few others, I hid in the library. As soon as we could, we attempted to free the Maven and our brother Fas. We had almost succeeded when the Fas Major interrupted us and . . . Well, you know the rest.'

Mel smiled. 'I'm glad I was able to help.' He left the Fa in admiration of the ceiling and joined his friends.

'Do you think it's all over?' asked Goldie. 'No more storms.'

'It's over for some, my dear,' said Cassetti. 'This kingdom is back as it belongs – or will be very soon. Cut the head off a snake and its body soon dies. Not so my kingdom. I will not rest until that usurper Parrucca is ousted and Nephonia is free once more. I must depart for home and rally like-minded Cumulans. And you?'

'Pilfer and I are going into business together.'

'You are?' said Wren.

'You mean the robbery business?' said Ludo.

'Nah,' said Pilfer. 'Goldie's talked me into going straight.'

'We're going back into the fairground business,' said Goldie. 'We thought a nice little ghost train. You know, the customers are riding along, all on edge like, and Pilfer sneaks up and say "boo!" in their ears.'

'Great idea, ain't it?' said Pilfer. 'It'll scare the breakfast out of them. First rule of fairgrounds: always give the customers more than they bargained for.'

'And what about you three?' Cassetti asked the friends.

'Us?' said Mel. 'We've got to get on with our apprenticeships.'

'There're some exciting projects coming up,' said Wren. 'Artistically exciting, that is. I've had enough of that other kind of excitement to last me a long, long time.'

'I think we all have,' said Mel.

'You can say that again,' said Ludo.

'It's time you said goodbye to your friends,' said the

master. 'Just as humans can't stay in the Mirrorscape too long, so it is with figments in our world. I have prepared canvases that will take them straight back to their particular corners of the Mirrorscape. They're standing over there against the wall.'

'Goodbye, your majesty,' said Ludo. 'I guess I won't be seeing you again.'

'Oh, b-but I expect w-we will be s-seeing you,' said King M-morpho as a bumblebee buzzed past. 'With our allies we see more of your world than you imagine.'

As Mel, Ludo and Wren made their way down the Hill of Spirits towards the master's mansion and their waiting beds, they pulled their cloaks close about them in the chill evening air. Vlam was still bustling with activity and many of the shops were open, spilling yellow light invitingly from doors and windows on to the cobblestones.

'Read your fortune, dearies?' The voice came from an old woman who sat at a folding table draped with a deep purple cloth embroidered with silver moons and stars and the name 'Madame Manto'. On it rested a crystal ball and a pack of cards, which she shuffled.

'Come on,' said Wren. 'It'll be a laugh.'

'Cards, scrying-glass or mystic snow?' asked the fortune-teller as she pocketed Wren's coin.

'Not more cards,' said Mel. 'Anything but that.'

'What's mystic snow?' asked Ludo. 'I've never heard of that.'

'It's new, dearie,' said Madame Manto. 'It comes from beyond this world.' She lifted a large glass fishbowl filled with tiny shreds of paper from beneath the table.

'It's from the Paper Belfry,' said Mel, recognising it at once.

'No, dearie. It's not from any belfry. It's mystic snow. It fell out of the sky, left behind by the strange storms. Dip your hand in and pull out a snowflake. One each.'

The friends did as she asked. Each morsel had a single word written on it. Madame Manto then took their choices and arranged them side by side on the tabletop.

They spelled out *Trumpets eat sparrows*.

The friends were silent for a moment and then burst into laughter. 'I told you it'd be a laugh,' said Wren. They walked away arm in arm.

Madame Manto looked hurt and confused. 'I don't understand it, dearies,' she said to herself. 'The mystic snow never lies.' She was still scratching her grey-haired head as the friends' laughter faded away behind them. She turned over the paper scraps. There were words written on the reverse. 'Wait, dearies. Wait!' she called after them. But they turned a corner at the end of the narrow street and did not hear her. She looked down at the new phrase. It read –

Beware the shades.

Glossary of Terms in the Seven Kingdoms and the Mirrorscape

Anywhere – Polluted city in the middle of Nowhere

Arpen – The capital of the province of Feg

Awakenings, Hall of – A hall within the House of Spirits

Bestiary – A book describing animals

Blanch-Water – Raw material of rainbows

Bols – A village in Feg

Borealis – Northernmost of the Seven Kingdoms

Brass Monkeys – Demon-destroying engines built by Lug and his gnomes

Chrysalis Tower, The – A tower in King M-morpho's realm

Cirrus – One of the Cloud Kingdoms

Coloured Death, The – A wasting disease that colours the victim's skin

Coloured Isles, The – Chain of pigment-producing islands off the west coast of Nem

Comedies, Hall of – A theatre in Vlam

Cumulus – One of the Cloud Kingdoms

Diaglyph – Religious symbol worn by Fas

DORCS – Dangerous Obstruction Removal and Cleaning System

Fa – The title given to a priest

Farn – The river that runs through Vlam

Fas (pronounced Fars) Major – Second echelon of priests, above Fas minor

Fas Minor – Lowest echelon of priests

Feg – A distant province of Nem

Fegie – An insulting term for a native of Feg. A bumpkin

Fifth Mystery, The – Guild governing the sense of sight

Figment – An inhabitant of the Mirrorscape

First Mystery, The – Guild governing the sense of touch

Fourth Mystery, The – Guild governing the sense of taste

Frest – A port in Nem

Gnomes – Clever but wicked Mirrorscape creatures

Great Houses, The – The House of Spirits, the House of Thrones and the House of Mysteries

Hierarchs – Third echelon of Priests, above Fas Minor and Major

High-Council, The – Ruling body of the Mysteries

Hill of Mysteries, The – Hill beneath the House of Mysteries

Hill of Spirits, The – Hill beneath the House of Spirits

Hill of Thrones, The – Hill beneath the House of Thrones

Hollow World, The – A place in the Mirrorscape

House of Mysteries, The – Palace of the five Mysteries

House of Spirits, The – Palace of the Maven

House of Thrones, The – Palace of King Spen

Hyper-Clot – Dangerous substance. A by-product of rainbows

Interpellation, Instruments of – Torture implements

Interscape – A part of the Mirrorscape

Issle – A province of Nem

Jester – A wild card

Kig – One of the Coloured Isles. Home of the pigment mines

Kop – Mel's home village in Feg

Leviathan, The – An enormous ship in the Mirrorscape

Luck-Compass – A clockwork device that foretells luck

Mansion, The – Ambrosius Blenk's house in Vlam

Merry-Go-Anywhere-You-Want-To – A Mirrorscape fairground ride

Mines, The – Pigment mines on Kig

Mirrorblood – Vital substance that nourishes King M-morpho's orchard

Mirrormark, The – The secret symbol that unlocks pictures

Mirrorscape, The – The world inside paintings and drawings

Mirrortime – The strange flow of time in the Mirrorscape

Mites – Parasite-killers inside Cogito

Monder – A town in Nem

Monolith, The – Great factory where rainbows are manufactured

Mysteries, The – Five guilds governing the senses

Nem – Westernmost of the Seven Kingdoms. Mel's country

Nemish – The language of Nem

Nephonia – The Cloud Kingdoms

Nimbus – One of the Cloud Kingdoms

Nowhere – All-white land that surrounds Anywhere

Orchard, The – An orchard at the heart of King M-morpho's realm

Paper Belfry, The – A false belfry built to disguise the Serpent

Pit-Vampires – Mirrorscape creatures

Pleasures – The rights to anything beyond the bare necessities of life

Porcupines – A suit of cards

Pyrexia – Southernmost of the Seven Kingdoms

Ravens – A suit of cards

Salamanders – A suit of cards

Second Mystery, The – Guild governing the sense of smell

Serpent – A powerful machine built to open the way to the Mirrorscape

Service Passages – Secret passages that riddle the mansion

Seven Kingdoms, The – Nem and its neighbouring kingdoms

Starfish – A suit of cards

Stratus – One of the Cloud Kingdoms

Tabby – Plain, uncoloured cloth

Ter – The title given to a priestess

Third Mystery, The – Guild governing the sense of hearing

Tunnel-Lickers – Mirrorscape creatures

Vlam – The capital city of Nem

Volm – A province of Nem. Home province of Vlam

Western Ocean, The – Ocean off the west coast of Nem

Wisp – Cassetti's cloud barge

Turn the page for more adventures in the Mirrorscape
in the exciting sneak preview of

Publishing in September 2009

Spiracle, Blinker, Gusset and Flob

As Mel stirred in his sleep he became aware of an unusual sound in the dormitory. It sounded like a whisper. Curious, he opened his eyes and nearly jumped out of his skin. A surprised gasp escaped his throat. There, at the foot of his bed, stood six figures. Two of them he recognised. His best friends and fellow apprentices, Ludo and Wren, shivering in their nightclothes, their eyes wide with alarm, were bound and gagged and being held fast by an enormous creature covered in shaggy, ginger fur. As wide as he was tall, the creature had a surprisingly small and bald head, from which a pair of miniature, flesh-covered horn-buds protruded. Mel knew at once that the being was a figment, an inhabitant of the Mirrorscape – the strange and secret world that exists inside paintings. But what was he doing here, in the real world?

Standing to his left, his companion was no less weird. He was tall and skinny and dressed in a heavy and somewhat rusty suit of armour, covered with a multitude of small, latched doors of all shapes and sizes.

The third figment was very short and stocky. He also wore armour but it was several sizes too large. His pudding-basin helmet was so big it covered his face, and a pair of red, glowing eyes peeped out from a slit in the front. On top of his helmet was mounted a shuttered miner's lantern that cast the only light in the dark dormitory. He held a peacock feather quill in one hand, poised to write in the big ledger he held open in the other.

The final figure was a grotesquely fat figment with skin as white as drawing paper. He was dressed only in a leather loincloth and gladiator sandals that were bound to his substantial legs with crisscross thongs. He was covered in hundreds of coloured tattoos, which, to Mel's amazement, moved about of their own accord like animated drawings.

Before Mel could promote his initial gasp to the rank of full-blown scream, the figment leant over him and quickly clamped a blubbery hand over the youngster's mouth. He wheezed into Mel's ear, 'Hello, my name is Gusset. I'll be your abductor this night.'

As Mel watched ,a tattoo of a faun ambled over the man's ample chest and plucked a tattooed poppy from the bouquet depicted near his armpit. The faun held the scarlet flower in front of its face and blew a cloud of pollen that enveloped Mel. The poppy-dust made his eyes heavy and, in an instant, he was asleep once more. The last thing he remembered was seeing the short figment make a tick in his ledger.

When Mel came to he knew at once he was back in the Mirrorscape. While he had been unconscious he had also been bound and gagged. He was lying on a drawbridge suspended from huge chains with links as thick as his forearm. Mel sat up alongside Wren and Ludo and together the friends gazed around, amazed at the gargantuan space. There were other drawbridges – some raised, some lowered – spanning a canyon-deep void. The ceiling was so far above him that it seemed to have formed its own weather system as a thunderstorm brewed amid the roiling clouds. Lightning flashed and by its spectral light Mel saw colossal statues of muscular men in chains on the far side of the void. The drawbridge trembled as the thunder rolled. A steadier illumination was supplied by a great many fires, which burned inside giant spherical cages that hung on impossibly long chains. Doors and windows with fat, iron bars peppered most of the vertical surfaces of the wall at the end of the drawbridge and massive, circular grilles spewed out billows of steam. Far, far off echoed the wail of desperate cries.

'Ah, you're awake,' said the little figment, obviously the boss. 'I expect you're wondering what's happened and where you are.'

As one, Mel, Ludo and Wren nodded, making muffled *yes please* sounds inside their gags.

'We are Messrs Spiracle, Blinker, Gusset and Flob.' He used the eyed, feathery end of his long quill to identify himself, the armoured figment, the tattoed and the hairy ones in turn. 'Incorporated bounty hunters. No bounty too small, no fugitive too large. Satisfaction guaranteed or your money back. As to where you are, my young friends, well, you're in Deep Trouble, the most secure prison in the Mirrorscape.' He made a sweeping gesture with his quill, indicating the scene. 'And now, without further ado, we must hand you over to Locktight, your personal gaoler.' Spiracle half-bowed. 'It's been a pleasure apprehending you.'

Blinker threw a bundle of clothes into the air over the friends' heads as if it were a game of piggy-in-the-middle.

Mel turned, and standing behind him was yet another figment who expertly caught the bundle. 'If you'd care to follow me, I'll show you to your cell.' The friends had no choice as Locktight tossed a lasso ensnaring the three of them and set off across the drawbridge, towing them behind.

The gaoler was a large, muscular figment who wore an executioner's mask made from riveted iron that covered the top half of his head. His belted black jerkin was covered in dozens of bunches of keys that hung from hooks. As he moved he sounded like an out-of-tune wind chime. Locktight led them even further into Deep Trouble, occasionally stopping to operate large star-wheel winches that raised and lowered the drawbridges.

Eventually they came to a thick, iron-bound door with a small, barred window set into it. Locktight selected a bunch of keys, opened the door and pulled the friends inside. 'This will be your accommodation until the trial. The straw is changed every two years – whether it needs to be or not – and a bowl of gruel is served on alternate Sundays.' He tossed their clothes on the floor. Before he untied the children and removed their gags he quickly injected all three of them with a rusty syringe.

'Ouch! Why'd you do that?' said Ludo, rubbing his arm.

'Prison regulations,' explained Locktight with a malicious grin. 'Humans get ill if they remain in the Mirrorscape for too long. And you're going to be here a long, long time. The shots will prevent you feeling sick.' So saying, he left, slamming the door behind him. the key was turned loudly in the lock.

'Well,' said Wren. 'We all know *where* we are.'

'We're in Deep Trouble,' said Mel. 'That's where.'

'You can say that again,' added Ludo.

'And we all know *what* we are.'

'Prisoners,' said the boys miserably.

'But what we don't know is *why* we're here,' said Wren.

Acknowledgements

I'm the lucky one, I get my name printed on the cover, but there are many other people behind the scenes who are responsible for helping me to get *Mirrorstorm* into print. For their invaluable contributions I wish to thank Ivan Mulcahy, my literary agent, as well as Rachel Boden for her skilful editing and Wendy Birch for her thoughtful design. I must also extend my thanks to Douglas Pocock, Katja Reister, Chie Nakano, Rebecca Steltner, Dan Downham, Lucy Paine and the rest of the rights team at Egmont Books and to Mike Richards, Jessica Dean and Tania Vian-Smith. Thanks also to James Ball and Richard Starr for their splendid work on the www.mirrorscape.co.uk web site. My biggest thanks go to my publisher, Cally Poplak, for all of her hard work in making Vlam and the world of the Mirrorscape come to life. Without her efforts *Mirrorstorm* would have been twice as long and half as good.

Mike Wilks, London, November 2007.

MirrorShade

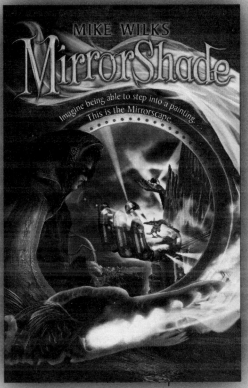

Something has gone terribly wrong. Mel and his friends have been accused of a crime they didn't commit. They are locked in Deep Trouble prison in the Mirrorscape, while their evil Mirrorshades – who look exactly like them – are free to cause havoc in Vlam. Luckily, their old friends Goldie and Pilfer – the invisible burglar – are on hand to help them break out and try to prove their innocence.

But arson, forgery and theft are the least of what their doubles been up to. They're determined to find the Mirrortree first, which could mean the end of the Mirrorscape!

Can the real Mel, Ludo and Wren defeat their enemies in time?